THE HOUSE
─── OF ───
LASSENBERRY 1970H

THE HOUSE OF LASSENBERRY 1970H

DANIEL WEBB

ARCHWAY
PUBLISHING

Interior Graphics/Art Credit: Clark Stoeckley

This is a work of fiction. All of the characters, names, incidents, organizations, and dialogue in this novel are either the products of the author's imagination or are used fictitiously.

Archway Publishing books may be ordered through booksellers or by contacting:

Archway Publishing
1663 Liberty Drive
Bloomington, IN 47403
www.archwaypublishing.com
1 (888) 242-5904

ISBN: 978-1-4808-4735-4 (sc)
ISBN: 978-1-4808-4736-1 (e)

Library of Congress Control Number: 2017907663

Print information available on the last page.

Archway Publishing rev. date: 05/23/2017

THE HOUSE OF LASSENBERRY 1970h is the continuation of the Lassenberry family fighting for independence in the criminal world from the Mafia and the National Agreement. This ongoing battle takes the Lassenberry clan over international waters.

Daniel WEBB is the author of the first installment, The House of Lassenberry. All reviews were positive, Daniel's unique style of detailed description of characters kept readers intrigued from page 1, to page 318.

—— CHAPTER 17. HIDE-N- SEEK ——

Pacing the floor of his new residence at castle Lassenberry, Edward the 2nd stopped when he heard a knock on the office door. "Come in!" he shouted. Entering the office was a tall NA agent of African American descent. "Still no sign of him sir." the agent said. In a fit of rage, Edward the 2nd kicked his desk. "2 days, and you ass holes can't find him? I'm tired of this hide-n- seek bullshit!" he shouted. "We have no video of his whereabouts sir. He must've hid within the catacombs." The agent said. Edward the 2nd wiped the sweat from his shaved head. "If you must, take down walls. Do it! Now, get the fuck out!" Edward the 2nd said. "With all due respect sir, that wouldn't be practical." The agent said in a calm voice. Edward the 2nd stared at the agent with fury in his eyes. "Just get the fuck out, and let me think!" Edward the 2nd shouted. The agent left the office.

Elsewhere, at the Okeechobee, Florida home of Stanley Harrison hart, known to those as sleeves, Brandon stood on the patio looking out at the lake as he listened to his grandfather speak. "These are intense times we're living in! Really intense!" said sleeves. "How so, grandpa?" Brandon asked. "I've just received a call from the new boss of the organization this morning." Sleeves said. "New boss?" Brandon asked with a shocked expression on his face. Sleeves chuckled. "Yes! Krayton Lassenberry, who calls himself Edward the 2nd!" sleeves chuckled. "What happened to Sir Marcus?" Brandon asked. "From what this Edward the 2nd is telling me, he stepped down. But, if this kid is anything like his uncle, Sir Marcus is dead." Sleeves said. Brandon shook his head. "I have to call terry to see how she's taking this!" Brandon said. Sleeves put his hand on Brandon's shoulder. "You can deal with that later! I told you to fly down here so we can discuss your future in the organization!" sleeves said. "Grandpa! I'm making good money selling merchandise for the Lassenberry people, especially with the Boeman cars! Why would I want to let that go?" Brandon asked. Sleeves squeezed Brandon's shoulder. "I want to see to it that you move up in the Lassenberry echelon." Sleeves said. "How?" Brandon asked. Sleeves cleared his throat. "Tony Kerouac's body was found yesterday in a land fill out in Staten Island. It looks like someone wanted to pin it on the Italians, but from what I know about the streets, this was an inside job." Sleeves said. "I thought you retired from the life grandpa!" Brandon said. Sleeves had a scowl on his face. "Percy is gone! Spade, gone! Jabbo, gone! Even the great Benny Lassenberry is no longer around! I'm the last of the original group! Retired or not, I still have respect from these people! That's why this kid called me. He may not have said it, but I think he's going to need my counseling. I'm going to pay a visit to this Edward the 2nd in a few days.

Later that evening, Edward the 2nd decided to take a stroll through the halls of castle Lassenberry. Closely being followed by 2 NA agents riding in a golf cart, he walked the halls of the west wing, Edward the 2nd became agitated. He turned around towards the agents. The golf cart came to a halt. "What the fuck? Can I just be alone with my thoughts for one second without you fuckers breathing down my back?" Edward the 2nd shouted. The 2 agents glanced at each other. "Of course, sir. Enjoy the rest of your evening sir." The agent behind the steering wheel said. "Thank you!" Edward the 2nd shouted. The agent made a quick U-turn back towards the office. Edward the 2nd shook his head and continued his stroll down the long corridor.

After 5 minutes into his journey inside the castle walls, Edward the 2nd entered the south wing. He was making his way down the corridor until he noticed the fabulous floral designs on the walls. He also noticed that this part of the castle had to be uninhabited for some time. There were dust bunnies where the floor and walls met. He rubbed his fingertips across the small ledge just below the floral designs. His fingertips were so caked up with dust, that he had to slap his hands together a few times to make his hands dust free. "Damn!" He said, as he looked down at the filthy red carpet covering the floor of the wing. As he ventured further down the corridor, the stench of urine flooded his nostrils. Edward the 2nd pinched his nostrils shut. He noticed that there was a small piece of white paper on the floor. He picked the paper up. It was rolled up tight like a marijuana joint, about 2 inches long. He unraveled the paper which had numbers written on it. It didn't take Edward the 2nd long to figure out it was a combination lock number. He looked behind him to see if any of the agents had followed. The corridor was clear. He also noticed that the combination wasn't written in pen, pencil nor crayon. He figured out that it was dried blood due to the smeared numbers. He folded a crease into the paper and stuffed it in the front pocket of his uniform he wore since his meager coronation. Edward the 2nd turned around and trotted back down the corridor, heading back to the west wing.

Moments later he arrived at the door of his office where the 2 agents were standing guard dressed in their black suits and wearing their signature dark shades. "listen! I don't want anybody coming in my office for the next 2 hours! Y'all understand?" Edward the 2nd said. "Yes sir." the 2 agents said simultaneously. Edward the 2nd entered the office. To be on the safe side, he locked the door. He walked around the office in a panic looking for the lock to this combination number in his hand. "Fuck! Fuck! Fuck! There's gotta be a safe in this bitch, somewhere!" he whispered to himself.

After 15 minutes of frantically searching for a safe in the office, Edward the 2nd was about to give up on his search. He stopped in his tracks before unlocking the door to leave, when he turned to the oil painting of a vase located on the opposite side of the office from his desk. He then ran over to the painting and felt around the edges behind the wooden frame. He lifts the painting off the supporting hooks. The art work had a considerable amount of weight to it, causing Edward the 2nd to struggle to gently place the painting on the floor. He had a smile from ear-to-ear when laying eyes on the safe. He then took out the paper with the combination and began spinning the dial. The last number was smeared, but Edward the 2nd knew that it had to be a double digit. After a few minutes had passed, he figured out that the number was 13. "Yeah boy!" he shouted with joy. He then pulled the metal handle down to unveil the contents of the safe. To his disappointment, there was no sight of cash within the safe, just a thick black binder. He took the binder out of the safe. "What the fuck is this shit?" he whispered to himself. He took the binder to his desk. He opened it. The binder had to be at least 4 to 5 inches thick, full of information. Edward the 2nd flipped through the pages, he was amazed at all the accumulated entries. The binder had information dating back to the mid-1940's. Edward the 2nd found misspellings throughout the binder, but was able make out its contents. "Jabbo! This gotta be Jabbo's writing!" he whispered to himself. Edward the 2nd continued flipping further back into the binder. There were names of public officials from the local level, all the way to congress in Washington DC on the payroll. There were names of corporate big shots who ran fortune 500 companies, who had illegal dealings with the Lassenberry organization. Edward the 2nd slammed his hand on the desk. "I can't believe this shit!" he chuckled. He couldn't believe his eyes when he read that some of these important characters were married with children, but at the same time had sexual escapades with prostitutes of the homosexual and transgender persuasion.

Suddenly his mobile phone rang. He pulled it out to see who was calling him. It was hakim. "Yeah, what's up?" Edward the 2nd asked. "What the fuck, man? 3 of my street bosses were just found decapitated in Westside park! You ordered that shit?" hakim asked. "What?" Edward the 2nd shouted. "You heard me! Did you order the hit?" hakim shouted. "Nigga! You must be crazy! If I did do that shit, the last thing I would do was to admit it over the fucking phone!" Edward the 2nd said. "Now all my runners in that area spooked! Niggas hiding out, not making money!" hakim shouted. Edward the 2nd took a deep breath. "Yo ass the expert in that shit! Do some detective work or something! just keep pushing that product! Bills gotta be paid!" Edward the 2nd shouted. Hakim turned off his phone. "I guess I told his ass!" Edward the 2nd chuckled. He continued to skim through the binder.

It was around 10pm when hakim made the call to Edward the 2nd. He and Chewie, one of his top aides were sitting in the back room of his night club BIG SHOTS. "What the boss say to you?" Chewie asked. "Boss? I'm the fucking boss around here! Fuck him!" hakim scoffed. Chewie shrugged his shoulders. "You got it." Chewie said in a soft voice. There was a knock on the door. Chewie stood from his seat. He pulled out his pistol from his holster. He went to the door. "I thought you locked the fucking front entrance! Damn! Am I the only one that's on point around here?" hakim shouted. "Who is it?" Chewie shouted through the door. "It's me! Gunz!" the voice said. Chewie looked at hakim. Hakim gave Chewie a nod to open the door. Chewie opened the door. Gunz entered the room wearing a black leather trench coat. "Damn, it's cold as a bitch out there!" Gunz shouted. "Never mind that shit! What's the word on the streets?" hakim asked. "Ain't no word! Niggas scared! From South orange ave., to 15th ave., ain't nobody on the streets!" 2 Gunz said. "Fuck that! That whole area generates

50 grand a day! I ain't losing that shit to no fucking head hunters! Fuck that shit! We gotta get them niggas back on them corners!" hakim shouted.

A day after the mock coronation of Sir Edward the 2nd, cousins Butch and Dubbs were sitting at a bar, both dressed in jeans and leather jackets on the Upper East side of Manhattan. Butch had paid the manager of the bar a generous amount of cash to shut the bar down so he and his cousin could have absolute privacy. Obviously, the bartender was allowed to stay. It was around mid-night. Butch was sipping on a mixed drink, while Dubbs was on his third shot of whiskey, chasing each shot with a gulp of beer. While his head was wobbling from his consumption of alcohol, he turned to his older cousin, noticing Butch had a worried expression on his face. "What the fuck is wrong with you?" Dubbs asked. Butch didn't turn towards his cousin. He just stared at the mirror behind the bar. "Somethings telling me that they should've killed that boy from the beginning." Butch said. "What the fuck you are talking about?" Dubbs asked. Butch looked down at the other end of the bar to see if the bartender was listening. Butch stared at his cousin. Butch looked agitated. "I'm talking about hakim!" butch whispered. "Oh!" Dubbs said. Butch took a sip of his beer. "But, it ain't our fight." Butch said. "Maybe it is." Dubbs said as he shrugged his shoulders.

It was going on day 4, and no sign of Sir Marcus. Edward the 2nd was sitting in his office thoroughly reading the Lassenberry organization events that occurred over the years. He sighed just looking at the thickness of the B.O.I, but continued reading. Suddenly there was a knock on the door. The knocking startled Edward the 2nd. "What the fuck?" he whispered. He quickly hid the B.O.I in one of the drawers of his desk. "Come in!" he shouted. The door opened. Entering the office was an NA agent of Asian descent. "Sir. Your cousin Kimberly is at the gate. Should I let her through?" the agent asked. "Who?' Edward the 2nd asked. "Kimberly Lassenberry. The wife of your cousin Sir Marcus, sir." The agent said. "Oh, yeah! Yeah! Bring her here!" Edward the 2nd ordered. "Right away, sir." The agent said. The agent left the office, shutting the door behind him. Quickly, Edward the 2nd took the Book of Information from the desk. He ran over to the other side of the office and took the painting down from the wall, exposing the safe. He then placed the B.O.I back inside the safe.

Edward the 2nd had changed out of his uniform a day before. He wore a pair of jeans, a button up shirt and a pair of expensive sneakers. After putting away the B.O.I, he grabbed one of the encyclopedias from the book shelf. He then went over to his chair and kicked his feet up on the desk. He opened the book to a random page.

5 minutes later, there was a knock on the door. "Come in!" Edward the 2nd shouted. The door opened. The agent entered the office, followed by Kimberly. Edward the 2nd closed the book, putting it on the desk. He stood from his seat. He had an ear to ear smile on his face. "Hey cuz! Long time, no see!" he shouted. Edward the 2nd gave the agent a nod to leave the office. The agent backed out of the office, closing the door. Edward the 2nd went over and gave Kimberly a firm hug. She barely returned the gesture by patting him on the back with one hand. Her smile looked disingenuous. "Damn cousin! You fine as hell!" Edward the 2nd chuckled as he gently held Kimberly's hands. Kimberly pulled her hands away. "Where's my husband? I called his phone for days, and no one answered! I called his parents, and No one has a clue of his whereabouts! It's driving me crazy! By the way! Why are you in his office,

sitting at his desk?" Kimberly asked. Edward the 2nd cleared his throat. "It's complicated!" he said. Kimberly looked nervous. Her hands started trembling as she covered her mouth. "Come over to the couch cousin!" he said. Edward the 2nd gently tried to lure Kimberly over to the couch. She pulled away. "I'd rather stand! Now answer my question! What happened to my husband?" she shouted. Outside the office doors, the agent standing guard could hear Kimberly's voice. "Calm down cuz!" Edward the 2nd whispered. he gently grabbed her forearms. Kimberly pulled away once more. "No! No! tell me! Where is my husband? As his wife, I order you to tell me Krayton!" she shouted. Edward the 2nd shook his head, expressing a sinister grin. Edward the 2nd then loses is grin. "Here's the deal cousin. I'm running things now. Your husband, my cousin, was sent on hiatus, by me. He was suffering from a nervous breakdown." He said. "Where is he?" Kimberly asked. "I had to keep him isolated from the world for a while. Can't have him ruling the roost half baked! There is just too much at stake!" Edward the 2nd claimed. "So, you're telling me I can't see my husband?" Kimberly asked. Edward the 2nd sighed. "Listen beautiful. I got everything under control. Your husband is safe and kinda sound." Edward the 2nd chuckled. Kimberly didn't deem his words to be funny. Kimberly put her hands up in a surrendering gesture. "I don't want to hear anymore! Just tell him I went back to the island!" Kimberly said. Before Kimberly could open the door, Edward the 2nd grabbed her by the hand. "Hey! Hey! Take it easy cousin! He told me, when you show up, to keep you close! He said you could be a great asset to me until he returned!" he said. Kimberly smelled bullshit. She just rolled her eyes. "Damn, you look sexy as hell when you do that with your eyes!' Edward the 2nd chuckled. "I have to go home to my son!" Kimberly said in disgust. Edward the 2nd shut the door as soon as she opened it. "Okay! Okay! For real. I need your help." He said. "Help for what?" Kimberly asked. "Help me run this organization! Duh!" he chuckled. "Where's Tony?" Kimberly shouted. Edward the 2nd couldn't look Kimberly in the eye. He turned towards his desk. "Man! That motherfucker told me I ain't got what it takes to be my uncle!" Edward the 2nd said. Edward the 2nd turned around, facing Kimberly. "Your husband turned everything over to me though! I got the paperwork to prove it! I had to let tony go after saying that shit! He's dead to me now!" Edward the 2nd said. "What am I supposed to do to help? I know nothing about this business!" Kimberly said. Edward the 2nd walked over to Kimberly. He stood about an inch or 2 shorter than her. He put his hand on her shoulder. "Come on beautiful! I heard through the grapevine you speak about a thousand languages!" he said. "Kimbundu, Portuguese, Swahili, Chokwe and some Spanish to be exact." Kimberly said. "Some Spanish?" he asked. "Only because of my friend Carmen!" she chuckled. Edward removed his hand from her shoulder. He smiled at her. She smiled at him. The black phone on the desk rang. They both just stared at the phone for a few seconds before Edward the 2nd went over to answer. "Hello?" Edward the 2nd asked. "Hello, Edward the 2nd?" the voice asked. "Yeah? Who's this?" Edward the 2nd asked. "Hey kid! It's sleeves! We're still on for tonight? I'm bringing my grandson with me!" sleeves said. "Yeah! Sure, sure!" Edward the 2nd said. "See you around 10 kid." Sleeves said before hanging up. Edward the 2nd hung up on his end as well. Kimberly folded her arms. "May I ask who was that on the phone. This is my home still." Kimberly said. Edward the 2nd just shook his head smiling. He was enamored by her beauty.

Kimberly wore a long-pleated skirt down to her ankles, covered by her suede trench coat.

Even though she had a nice tight body, just like her husband, Edward the 2nd was under the spell of her beautiful flawless face. "Damn woman! You're a fine ass red bone! You should've been mine!" he said. "Focus Krayton! Who was that on the phone?" she shouted. "Oh. By the way. Everyone, including you, must address me as Edward the 2nd." He said. Kimberly just stared at Edward the 2nd for a few seconds. Suddenly, she burst out laughing. The new head of the Lassenberry organization didn't find it funny. He had a scary blank look on his face. Kimberly realized that he was serious. She tried to cut her laughter short. "I'm sorry! I'm truly sorry cousin!" she chuckled. Edward the 2nd looked at his wrist watch, which was encrusted with diamonds. "I got guests coming over tonight. Check it out. This what's going to happen. You and your son can stay here if you want, but you have to move your things out of this wing." Edward the 2nd said. Kimberly put her hands on her hips. "Why the hell should I move my belongings out of the west wing?" she said with a sassy attitude. "From now on, this wing and the south wing will be off limits to everybody but me! I'll have the agents move all your stuff to the east wing!" Edward the 2nd said. "The east wing? The east wing? Really?" Kimberly shouted. "Don't worry. My uncle didn't die there. You don't have to worry about ghosts." Edward the 2nd chuckled. Kimberly, with her hands-on hips stepped in closer to Edward the 2nd, standing 5 inches away from his face. "Are you sure about that?" she asked. Edward the 2nd leaned in to her and took a long whiff of her perfume. "Woman! You smell good as you look!" he said with a big smile on his face. Kimberly sighed with disgust before waving Edward the 2nd off to leave the office. When Kimberly opened the door, standing in her path was the Asian NA agent. "Is everything ok, sir?" the agent asked Edward the 2nd. "Yeah! Mrs. Lassenberry was just about to give praises to the house before leaving." Edward the 2nd said. "What?" Kimberly shouted. "Before you leave the presence of the head of this house, you must yell out Long live the house of Lassenberry. Long live the Edward the 2nd." He said. "You are crazy! I've never done it for my husband! So, I'm not doing it for you!" Kimberly shouted. The agent refused to let Kimberly pass until the words were uttered. "It's a new day, beautiful!" Edward the 2nd said. Kimberly looked frustrated. She took a deep breath while looking at the agent, who obviously wouldn't let her pass until the words were spoken. Kimberly's eyes teared up. She turned to Edward the 2nd. "Long live the house of Lassenberry! Long live Edward the 2nd!" she shouted. "Now, you can leave." Edward the 2nd said in a calm voice. The agent had let her pass. Kimberly stormed out of the office. "Make sure she makes it back to the island safe!" Edward the 2nd ordered the agent. "Of course, sir." The agent said. "Oh yeah! Tell the chef to have dinner for 3 set up by 8 tonight, and get one of the other agents to have my uniform and boots laid out for me to wear tonight too." Edward the 2nd said. "Yes sir." The agent said before closing the door.

That evening, Edward the 2nd was in his office bathroom standing in front of a body length mirror. Unlike his cousin, Sir Marcus, he didn't have an assistant to tend to his every need. He was pissed that the appearance of his uniform wasn't up to par. The red sash that crossed over his chest had wrinkles. His jack boots had small scuff marks around the edges. When making his complaints to the NA agent in charge, Edward the 2nd was told that their sole purpose at castle Lassenberry was to guard him with their lives. Not to perform menial tasks. Edward the 2nd exited the bathroom with a disgruntle look on his face. There was a knock on the door.

"Come in!" he said. The Asian agent entered the room. "What the fuck is it now?" Edward the 2nd sighed. "Your 10 0'clock dinner engagement is here sir." The agent said. "My what?" Edward the 2nd shouted. "Mr. Stanley Hart and guest have arrived for dinner sir." The agent said. Edward the 2nd looked at his watch. "Damn! It's only 9:30!" he said. "Shall I give the order to have them pass through the gate sir?" the agent asked. "Yeah! Let them wait in the guest area! Keep them company while you're there! I'll be there in a few! Now go!" Edward the 2nd shouted. "Yes sir." The agent said before leaving the office. "Useless mother fucker!" Edward the 2nd whispered as he kneeled on one knee. He took some saliva from his mouth to try his best to spit shine the scuff off his jack boots. Edward the 2nd left the office. Standing outside his office were 2 NA agents standing at parade rest. As soon they see Edward the 2nd, they both stand at attention. Edward the 2nd noticed one of the customized golf carts parked next to them. He looked down the corridor in both directions. He walked towards the golf cart and jumped in. the agents became alarmed. "Sir! We can assist you if need be!" the black burly agent said. "Stay here and make sure no one enters the office while I'm gone! Understand?" Edward the 2nd shouted. "Yes sir!" both agents shouted simultaneously. Edward the 2nd sped off down the corridor as the 2 agents go back to standing at parade rest.

While on his way to the east wing, Edward the 2nd made an instinctive detour towards the south wing. The closer he came to his destination, more of a foul stench filled his nostrils. He parked the golf cart out of sight just in case an agent showed up. The smell grew much stronger since the last time he visited that area of the castle. His gut instinct served him well. What he saw were 2 pieces of paper rolled up this time. He quickly picked them off the floor. He stuffed the 2 pieces of paper within his left jack boot. He noticed a small slit in the stone wall. He put his eye up to the slit in the wall to see what was on the other side. It was pitch black. Edward the 2nd jumped back quickly when he realized the horrible smell of urine was coming directly from the slit in the wall. He then jumped back into the golf cart and took off towards the east wing.

"I know this is a huge place, but Jesus Christ! How long does it take this kid to get over here?" sleeves whispered to his grandson. Sleeves and his grandson Brandon were just frisked for weapons prior to entering the castle grounds. 4 NA agents accompanied them while waiting for Edward the 2nd. At the same time, Brandon checked his wrist watch, as Edward the 2nd came zooming around corner in the golf cart. Everyone stepped to the side when the golf cart came to a screeching halt. "Sorry y'all! Ain't used to driving one of these things!" He said. Sleeves turned to his grandson and rolled his eyes. Edward the 2nd hopped out of the golf cart. He went over to shake sleeves' hand. "Long time, no see kid. I'm glad we have the time to somewhat of a sit down. This handsome young fella here is my grandson Brandon." Sleeves said. "Pleased to meet you." Brandon said as the 2 men shook hands. "So, let's get right to it!" Edward the 2nd said. He turned to one of the agents. "Is everything prepared?" he asked the agent. "I've just received word from the kitchen that your evening meal is ready sir." The agent said. Edward the 2nd smiled and rubbed his hands together. "Shit! Let's get our grub on then!" he chuckled. Edward the 2nd hopped in the passenger's seat of the golf cart, while Brandon sat behind him. Sleeves was assisted by one of the agent into the cart due to his frail ageing body. One of the agents hopped in the driver's seat. "To the dining hall agent! Oh, yeah! Take that other cart back to my office!" Edward the 2nd said to one of the other agents. "Right away sir." Said one of the agents. The golf cart with sleeves and company sped off towards the north wing.

Less than 5 minutes later, they arrived at the huge double doors to the north wing. Standing at the doors were 2 NA agents, one Caucasian, the other a African American. The agent driving the golf cart jumped out to assist sleeves out of his seat. The 2 agents standing guard at the doors opened them simultaneously.

The dining hall was arranged this night differently from any other day. There was a different dining table, much different from the 25-foot-long solid oak table that was usually there. This table was made of solid oak, but the size of a card table. Standing in the back ground was the dining butler. He was dressed in the appropriate attire. He was of African American descent, about in his mid-60's. His name was Clarence Whittle, who was hired by Kimberly before her marriage to Sir Marcus

All 3 men came to the dining table. An agent assisted Edward the 2nd to his seat. Another agent assisted sleeves in his chair. The agent then took sleeves' walking cane, leaning it up against the wall. Clarence excused himself to the kitchen. Sleeves noticed that the silverware was expensive from the weight of the butter knife in his hand. Sleeves held the butter knife up to the light of the chandelier. He noticed a smudge on the tip of the knife. "Ever thought about hiring a silver butler kid?" he asked Edward the 2nd in a smug matter. Edward the 2nd looked bewildered. "What the fuck is that?" he asked. "Oh, forget it." Sleeves said as he wiped the butter knife with his linen napkin.

As Clarence served appetizers, the main course and dessert, an agent stood next to Edward the 2nd sampling each dish before Edward the 2nd commenced to eating for security reasons.

"So, kid, how's business these days?" Sleeves asked. "All due respect sleeves! I don't like talking business while I'm eating!" Edward the 2nd said with a mouth full of food. Sleeves nodded his head. "fine by me kid! I'd rather discuss it over a snort and a nice cigar!" Sleeves said. Edward the 2nd looked shocked. "I got cigars for you in my office when we get there, but I don't keep blow or weed on the premises, man!" Edward the 2nd said. Sleeves sighed as he looked at his grandson Brandon, who covered his mouth with his napkin to keep from laughing. "A snort means a quick shot of liquor kid." Sleeves said. Edward the 2nd stopped chewing his food. "Oh! That's what you meant? Damn! My fault, old man!" he chuckled. Sleeves and Brandon laugh as well.

It was 11:35pm, when the 3 men arrived at the office in the west wing. Sleeves and Brandon were seated at the desk of Edward the 2nd, while he grabbed a bottle of Scotch and 3 shot glasses from the bar. He then pulled out a box of cigars from the lower drawer of his desk. Sleeves took a cigar. He offered Brandon one. Brandon declined. "Come on man! These are the best of the best!" Edward the 2nd said with a smile on his face. Brandon looked towards his grandfather, then looked at Edward the 2nd. "I would take one, but I don't want to get ashes on my 8-thousand-dollar suit!" Brandon chuckled. Edward the 2nd smiled. "All right player! Go ahead with Yo bad self!" Edward the 2nd chuckled. He filled the 3 shot glasses. Each man took a glass. "Excuse me if I don't stand kid. My legs feel older than me. But, I would like to make a toast." Sleeves said. Brandon and Edward the 2nd stood, raising their glasses in the air.

"Long live the house of Lassenberry! Long live Edward the 2nd!" Sleeves shouted. Brandon looked confused. He had never heard these words before. He gulped his drink down anyway. "Now. We can talk business." Edward the 2nd said as he sat in his seat. Sleeves lit his cigar. He shook out the flame of the wooden match. Sleeves cleared his throat. "Now kid. I've come here to advocate my grandson's position on the legitimate side of the Lassenberry organization. In saying that, I think he's deserving of a greater position." Sleeves said. "By the way, man! Congrats on the engagement to my cousin!" Edward the 2nd said as he shook Brandon's hand. Edward flicked the ashes from his cigar into the ceramic ashtray on his desk. He brushed the excess ash off his uniform. Brandon raised an eyebrow. "From what I 've read in my records, you, Allen Sunn and Kent Mooney got y'all shit together far as bringing in the cash! Why would you want to let something like that go?" Edward the 2nd asked. Sleeves took a puff from his cigar. "We know you need a right-hand man. The truth is, I'm too old to watch your back kid. Brandon here, was educated by one of best schools in the country. He's sharp, vibrant and a hard worker!" Sleeves said. "What do you know about the streets, man?" Edward the 2nd asked. "Oh! He knows a lot!" Sleeves said. "No disrespect, but I rather here it from Brandon." Edward the 2nd said. "Well, I know what the streets want. From the time, I took over the sale of merchandise, to the present, sales in Boeman cars have increased by 63% throughout the north east. And may I point out especially in the urban areas! Steigalhoff beer sales have risen since I told the dive bars owned by your family to put a slice of orange in every bottle, and in every beer mug to kill that god-awful taste!" Brandon chuckled. "You got me there. Me personally, I wouldn't even bathe in that shit. Don't let what I just said leave this room. Understand?" Edward the 2nd ordered. "Got it." Brandon said. "This is what you can do. Get your people to advertise showing that slice of orange sticking out of every bottle, can, whatever, to every liquor store in Jersey. I bet you that shit will catch on throughout the rest of the country in no time. Maybe the whole damn world! If the Mexican brewers say to put lemon wedges in their shit, we can do the same thing." Edward the 2nd said. "Sounds good to me!" Brandon said.

Edward the 2nd poured himself and his 2 guests another shot of scotch. "I want you to go home and pack yo shit. Within the next 2 days, I want you to move your things here." Edward the 2nd said. "So, that means I'm your right-hand man?" Brandon asked. "Not officially." Edward the 2nd said. He pressed the silent alarm button on the side of his desk to alert the agents out in the hall. seconds later the burly black agent entered the office. What can I do for you sir?" the agent asked as he had his hand on his gun holster. "I want Brandon hart put on the register as a permanent resident here." Edward the 2nd ordered. "As you wish sir." The agent said. Sleeves patted his grandson on the back as the agent left the office.

"My records also show that my uncle and cousin were paying yo ass 1.5 million a year. If you can prove to me you're the man for the job, we'll see about increasing that. Sounds good?" Edward the 2nd said. "Sounds good to me sir!" Brandon said. Edward the 2nd stood from his seat with his drink in hand "Stand up, man." Edward the 2nd ordered. Brandon stood as well. "Once you take on this new life, ain't no going back. I want you to swear your loyalty, and your life to me and this to organization! Right here! Right, now!" Edward the 2nd said with a serious look on his face. Brandon looked down at his grandfather. Sleeves gave his grandson a nudge on the side of his leg. "Go on young man! Trust me! You won't be sorry!" Sleeves said. Brandon looked at Edward the 2nd. "I do." He said in a faint voice. The 2 men tapped shot glasses before gupling their drinks. "That should be it for tonight. Go get some rest. In the morning, you start looking for someone to take yo place selling those cars and washing machines!" Edward the 2nd chuckled. The 2 young men shook hands. Sleeves struggled out of his seat after gulping down his drink. "Trust me kid. He won't let you down." Sleeves said to Edward the 2nd. Edward the 2nd pressed the silent alarm once again. This time, a different agent entered the office. "Escort these gentlemen to their car." Edward the 2nd ordered. "Thank you for this opportunity!" Sleeves said as he and Edward the 2nd shook hands. "Like my grandfather said. I won't let you down." Brandon said to Edward the 2nd. "Glad to hear it." Edward the 2nd said. Sleeves stood at attention. "Long live the house of Lassenberry! Long live Edward the 2nd!" he shouted. They both look at Brandon. Brandon stood at attention. "Long live the house of Lassenberry! Long live Edward the 2nd!" Brandon shouted. The agent held the door open as sleeves and Brandon exit the room. Sleeves stopped in his tracks at the doorway. "You sure you can handle all of this kid?" sleeves asked while looking around the office. "Good night old man." Edward the 2nd said.

Once everyone had left, Edward the 2nd exhaled. He fell back into his chair. He sat there in a daze. About a minute later, he snapped out of his trance. "Damn! I really gotta focus!" he said to himself. He reached into his jack boot and pulled out the 2 pieces of paper. He unrolled one of papers. Just like the piece of paper he read just days ago, this one was also written in blood. The paper said for Edward the 2nd to meet the writer of the note at an area on the out skirts of the castle grounds. Edward the 2nd then unrolled the second piece of paper. He looked bewildered after reading the note which was also written in blood. Edward the 2nd quickly struck a match and burned both notes. He tossed the burning papers into the ashtray. He watched as the papers disintegrate into embers. Instinctively as an extra precaution, he scooped the ashes with his hands and ran to the bathroom in his office. Edward the 2nd then flushed the ashes down the toilet. Standing at the bathroom sink, he washed his hands. He looked in the mirror. "You can do this! Prove them all wrong!" he whispered to himself.

It was around 3 in the morning. Edward the 2nd was sitting at his desk. After 4 more shots of scotch, he still found it hard to sleep. He stared at the ashtray on his desk. He popped tall from his seat, leaving the office. Edward the 2nd walked up the spiral stone staircase. He then entered the bedroom of his cousin Sir Marcus.

Edward the 2nd slowly strolled around the bedroom, observing his surroundings. He walked over to the dresser and opened one of the drawers. Out of all the drawers in this dresser, this one was not stuffed with clothing, but a snub nose revolver. Edward the 2nd held the weapon in his hand. He then concealed it in the waist band of his uniform pants. "Ok! You can do this shit!" he whispered to himself.

Moments later, Edward the 2nd pulled up to the castle gates alone riding in one of the golf carts. 2 agents were guarding the gate. "I can't sleep. I need to go for a walk." Edward the 2nd said. "I can assign a small detail for your protection sir." One agent said. "It's fucking 4 in the morning! Protect me from what? The birds chirping?" Edward the 2nd shouted. "Sir. We are assigned to guard you with our lives." The agent said in a calm voice. "Damn! Let me breathe for a minute! I got my mobile phone on me! If I ain't back exactly within an hour, send a detail out to come find me! Understand?" Edward the 2nd said. "As you wish sir." The agent said. The agent gave the signal to open the gate from the control room. Edward the 2nd watched as the gate made of thick iron bars automatically slid open. Edward the 2nd crossed the over the mote on to the main land. A search light was beaming down on Edward the 2nd as he walked further away from the castle's perimeter.

About 15 minutes had passed. It was dark and silent while Edward the 2nd walked down the road. The only sound he heard was his jack boots hitting the pavement. He looked at his wrist watch. I got about 45 minutes before the sun comes up and these clowns come looking for my ass!" he whispered to himself.

About 2 miles away from the castle grounds, Edward the 2nd stood at the edge of a grassy hill, looking out at the view of a couple of mansions in the distance. He slowly took out the hand gun in his uniform pants. "Ok! I'm here! It's safe to come out!" he shouted. Edward the 2nd looked around in the darkness. Suddenly a shadowy figure appeared in front of him with one hand in the air. "Hey cousin." The person said. "What's up cousin." Edward the 2nd said.

It was Edward the 2nd's predecessor, his cousin Sir Marcus. He stood there in his tattered and soiled Uniform. He stood there holding up his uniform pants around his waist because of the considerable amount of weight he had lost. Edward the 2nd had to pinch his nostrils for a moment because his cousin smelled like a sewer.

"Good thing there's a drainage system in that damn dungeon big enough for me to fit through!" Sir Marcus chuckled. He stopped chuckling when he saw that his younger cousin didn't show any expression at all. "We got approximately 25 minutes' cousin, before they come looking for my ass." Edward the 2nd said. Sir Marcus looked down at the ground in shame. "I guess I dropped the ball big time!" Sir Marcus said as he looked up at his cousin. "I guess you did." Edward the 2nd said. "Listen Krayton. If it means anything, I just want to say I'm sorry I put you in this position." Sir Marcus said. "It's Edward the 2nd." He said. "What's that, you say?" Sir Marcus asked. "Everyone's ordered to address me as Edward the 2nd. Butch, Dubbs, Mookie, even Hakim, if you can believe that shit!" he chuckled. There was a moment of silence between the cousins. "Is Kimberly and my boy safe?" Sir Marcus asked. "Your boy is fine. Kimberly is fine! Real fine!" Edward the 2nd said with a sinister smile. "Is tony gone?" Sir Marcus asked. Edward the 2nd nodded his head. Sir Marcus started balling like a child, but quickly regained his composure. "I'm starving!" Sir Marcus said. "Give me a couple of hours. I'll put a basket of food with some fresh clothes behind one of the dumpsters at the train station." Edward the 2nd said. Edward the 2nd tossed the hand gun to Sir Marcus. "I don't think I can protect you if they find you. If you run into an agent or hakim and the fellas, shoot to kill! I'll send someone we both can trust" Edward the 2nd said. "Thanks cousin!" Sir Marcus said. "Shit! It's your gun!" Edward the 2nd said. "Trust me! I'm going to make this right!" Sir Marcus said. "You best get out of here, and head over to the train station!" Edward the 2nd said. "I guess we're running out of time." Sir Marcus said. He put the gun away in his uniform pants. Sir Marcus stood at attention. "Long live the house of Lassenberry!" he said as his eyes teared up. Sir Marcus turned and walked away. "Hey, cuz!" Edward the 2nd shouted. Sir Marcus turned to face his cousin. "On one of those pieces of paper said Project Lassenberia! What's that?" Edward the 2nd." Shouted. "The info should be in the B.O.I!" Sir Marcus shouted.

CHAPTER 18. NOT OUR FIGHT

Elsewhere, hakim was sitting in the back room of his night club BIG SHOTS, counting the take for the evening 2 Gunz had brought before him an hour earlier. Chewie was standing by the door with a sub machine gun in hand. Gunz was lying on the sofa looking at the spread in a porn magazine. "Let' see, 250 thousand in this pile, and 220 thousand in this pile. All we have to do is wait for Mackie to bring in his cut, and we're good until December." Hakim said. "Man! I wish we could go straight to the source to get our refill instead of going through that punk ass Krayton!" 2Gunz said. "Don't let him hear you call him that!" hakim chuckled. Gunz placed the magazine down. "I don't care how stupid the name Krayton sounds! Shit! That's his name, ain't it?" Gunz said. "All right! Don't say I didn't warn yo ass!" hakim said shaking his head. "I can't believe this year is almost over! We're going into 2002! Time is flying like a motherfucker, Shit!" Chewie said. "Yeah. I can see you got more gray hair." Hakim chuckled. Chewie didn't say a word. He gave hakim the finger when he wasn't looking.

Suddenly, there was a knock on the door. "Who is it?" Chewie shouted. "It's me!" The voice shouted. Chewie recognized the voice and opened the door. Mackie entered the room carrying a suitcase. Hakim rubbed his hands together. "All right! What you got for me?" hakim asked. Mackie placed the suitcase on the floor next to hakim. Hakim noticed an unpleasant look on Mackie's face. "What's wrong with you?" hakim asked. "It's Irvington, man! Once they got the word about what happened at Westside park, niggas stop working them corners!" Mackie said. "So, you're telling me, not only Newark's west ward running scared, Irvington is shaking in their boots too?" hakim asked. "Yeah! That's what I'm telling ya!" Mackie said. Hakim became enraged. He stood from his chair. "See! This is the bullshit! So, you're telling me this suitcase is lite now?" hakim asked. "I ain't 100 percent, but I think we're 300 thousand short!" Mackie said. "Get the fuck outta of here!" Hakim shouted. "Why you think I came in here with one suitcase instead of two?" Mackie asked. "Besides that, everything is cool?" Hakim asked. "I still got Bloomfield, Belleville, Montclair. I thought I would tell you about Irvington before I made the collection from them." Mackie said. "You ain't never heard of calling from a mobile phone?" Hakim shouted. "I thought it would be better to bring you the suitcase and tell you face to face before I finished my collection!" Mackie said. "Man, get back out there, and get the rest of my money. I'm serious." Hakim said in a calm voice. Mackie nodded his head. Chewie opened the door for Mackie. Just before he left the room, he stopped and turned towards Hakim. "Oh. One more thing. I got word these Vauxhall niggas shooting one of those gangster rap videos in Weequahic park." Mackie said. "That's Mookie's crew, ain't it?" Hakim asked. "Nah! I heard they ain't nobody! A bunch of wannabe's!" Mackie said. "You know what? Get some body over there and shut that shit down! I'm tired of these fake as young bucks getting on TV pretending to do what we do! Fuck that! Gunz! Help me put all this cash in the safe! Mackie! Go get the rest of my money! The rest of us gonna pay a visit to Weequahic park!" hakim said.

Back at Lassenberry castle, Edward the 2nd had retrieved the Book of Information from the safe. He impatiently flipped through all the pages of the B.O.I, looking for an entry pertaining to Project Lassenberia. "Where the fuck is it?" he whispered as he grits his teeth. He then pulled out his mobile phone. The phone on the other end rang 3 times before someone picked up. "Hey kid! I just landed! Everything ok out there?" Sleeves asked. "Yeah! Yeah! I forgot to get Brandon's phone number!" Edward the 2nd said. "Just give me a sec. I have so many darn numbers, I can hardly remember them off hand!" Sleeves chuckled. Sleeves ran through the address book on his mobile phone, when he came across his grandson's number. "Here we go! It's 973-555-0001. Got it?" Sleeves said. "Thanks, old man!" Edward the 2nd said before he clicked off his phone.

Edward the 2nd gave his new assistant a call. Brandon, who was lying in bed with his fiancé Terry Lassenberry, answered his mobile phone on the end table. He sat up from the bed, rubbing his hand through his curly afro. "Hello?" Brandon asked. "It's your boss! I need you to get back out here! Pronto!" Edward the 2nd said. "Sir Edward?" Brandon asked. "Nigga! Don't ever say my name over the phone again! just get out here!" Edward the 2nd shouted. "I'm on my way!" Brandon sighed. Brandon clicked off his mobile phone. Terry turned over in bed, facing Brandon. "Who was that baby?" she asked. "I gotta go! Your cousin wants me at castle Lassenberry. Pronto!" Brandon chuckled. Terry sat up, clicking on the lamp. "You just got here!" Terry whispered frantically. "Things have changed sweetie! I have my orders!" Brandon said. Brandon stood up. He headed over to the bedroom closet to get dressed. "We'll see about that!" Terry said. She picked up her mobile phone from her side of the bed. "What are you doing?" Brandon asked. "I'm calling my brother! He'll handle this!" Terry said. Brandon quickly jumped on the bed and grabbed the mobile phone from Terry. "What the hell is wrong with you?" Terry shouted. "Baby! Listen to me! Things have changed! Changed big time! I can't explain it to you now, but the last thing you need to do is to get your brother involved! Trust me baby! Please!" he begged Terry. Brandon placed her mobile phone down on the bed and gave Terry a long sultry kiss. Terry fell under his spell. "Okay. Just be careful out there." She said. Brandon continued to get dressed. Moments later, Brandon grabbed his coat. He kissed Terry on the forehead. "I should be home by lunch time. Love you." Brandon said before leaving the bedroom. Terry sat there in bed for a few minutes. She grabbed her mobile phone. She contemplated whether she should call her brother or not. She pressed the speed dial to her brother's number. *"The number you have dialed, is no longer in service. The number you have dialed, is no longer in service."* The recording said. Terry sighed with a troubled look on her face.

About a half hour later, hakim and his crew arrive in Weequahic park where the gangster rap video was being shot. Chewie parked the Boeman SUV out of sight. Hakim, Gunz and Chewie checked their weapons for a second time before exiting the vehicle. "I was thinking. Maybe it ain't a smart move for anybody to see you." Chewie said to hakim. "What?" hakim shouted. "I'm just saying. All me and Gunz gotta do, is go over there in these ski masks and shake these mother fuckers up." Chewie said. Hakim looked over at the film crew. He scowled at the sight of these rappers throwing money in the air like they were in a strip club. There was a big industrial fan blowing the money in every direction. "Fuck that! Let's go!" Hakim shouted. Hakim and his crew stepped out of the vehicle. Chewie and 2 Gunz had donned their ski masks. Hakim didn't care. He wanted the cast and crew of the rap video to see his face. Gunz and Chewie were strapped with sub machine guns, while hakim pulled out a Glock from his waist band. As he came closer to the crowd, hakim started breathing heavily. He could hear his own heartbeat. He reminisced on all the murders he had committed, especially slamming the weight on the head of tiny back at FCI.

Once the crew reached the crowd, hakim grabbed the clapperboard from a young white guy who was the clapper loader. "Hey! What gives?" the white guy shouted. "Shut the fuck up!" Chewie shouted before smacking the young man to the ground. The cast just stood silent as 2 Gunz pointed his weapon at them. "Any of y'all make a move, I'm spraying motherfuckers!" Gunz shouted. Chewie pointed his weapon at the crew behind the cameras.

"Listen up! Ain't nobody making no fucking bullshit videos without my say so!" Hakim shouted. A young man, who happened to be a light skinned black guy with corn rolls in his hair, approached Hakim. "What the hell man? We're in the middle of a shoot! You just can't barge in like this!" the man shouted. "Who the fuck you supposed to be?" Hakim shouted. "I'm Drew Cool! The director of this video!" he said. Hakim had a smirk on his face. He noticed the boojie mannerisms of the director, which he saw as a sign of weakness. "Well, Mr. Drew Cool, I'm Hakim! I run this city! In fact, I run all of Essex County! I don't appreciate you coming out here doing business without my permission!" Hakim shouted. "I work for Big Bad Records, and I have a permit from the city of Newark to make this video, sir!" Drew Cool shouted. "Oh Really?" Hakim said in a high-pitched voice. "Who the fuck is the star of this show?" Hakim asked. It was still silent amongst the crowd. "You heard the man! Who the fuck is rapping out here? Step up!" Chewie shouted at the crowd. Reluctantly one figure stepped out from the crowd.

It was a young dark skinned burly looking kid looking about in his early 20's, late teens. He was loaded with gold chains around his neck, with gold rings on each finger. The top row of his teeth was filled with gold caps. "It's me, man!" he said in a low meek voice. Hakim approached the rapper. "What's your name son? What they call you?" hakim asked. "MC Gutter!" The rapper said as he trembled in fear. Hakim noticed that he was wearing the latest fashion in designer clothes and sneakers. Hakim stared him up and down. Hakim looked at the ground and noticed one of hundred dollar bills. He picked it up. "What the fuck nigga? This shit ain't even real!" hakim shouted. Hakim turned towards the cast and crew waiving the fake c note in the air. "Y'all shooting a rap video about being gangster, about living the good life, and y'all throwing fucking fake shit in the air! What the fuck is the world coming to?" hakim shouted to the crowd. Everyone was still silent. "You ever do a bid in prison? You ever had to put a body down?" Hakim asked the young rapper. The young rapper shook his head while trembling like a leaf. "Well, I did both!" Hakim shouted. Hakim then pointed his Glock at the lighting equipment, then fired it. He shot out the lights. Everyone ducked as the sparks from the lights flew in all directions. The female actors in the video screamed in terror. "Now, you go back to Big Bad Records and tell your masters if they wanna misrepresent my territory with this fantasy shit, they best see my people first and get permission! Understand?" Hakim shouted. "Drew Cool nodded his head in fear. "Let's go!" Hakim ordered Gunz and Chewie. As hakim and his crew walked away, hakim turned towards the young rap star. "Gold is played out kid! If you really wanna represent the hood, get some ice around your neck and fingers!" Hakim shouted. Hakim walked away with a big grin on his face.

A few hours later, Brandon arrived back at castle Lassenberry. His eyes were blood shot red. He sat at the opposite side of his new boss's desk continuously yawning before Edward the 2nd started speaking.

"Hate to drag you back here, but you gonna have to realize this is a 24-hour gig." Edward the 2nd said. "I understand." Brandon said as he rubbed his eyes, yawning. "First thing I want yo ass to do, is take that big ass picnic basket on the couch over there and place it behind one of the dumpsters at the train station here in town! Remember! What I'm about say to you! Whoever you see down at the train station, I don't want you speaking to that person! Don't ever mention to anyone but me if you run into this person while dropping off the picnic basket. If the name of that person you might run into at the train station gets out to the public, even yo grandfather won't be able to save you from a violent, torturous death! Understand, my man?" Edward the 2nd whispered. Brandon looked terrified. "Did you hear what I said man?" Edward the 2nd shouted. "Yes! Yes! I understand!" Brandon said nervously. "Now, if you think someone is following you, I put something in the basket that you can use to destroy the evidence! Now go and hurry up back!" Edward the 2nd whispered. Brandon stood from his seat. "Long live the house of Lassenberry! Long live Edward the 2nd!" he shouted before grabbing the picnic basket and leaving the office.

It was November 12th, 2001. It was a week later from the time hakim had paid a visit to a rap video being filmed in Weequahic park. Hakim was being chauffeured around the streets of his territory by Gunz in a 2002 Boeman sedan. Belleville, Essex Fells, North Caldwell, Newark and all the other municipalities of Essex County were under the microscope of the narcotics king pin. "They need to shovel these streets! I don't wanna be out here stuck in no damn snow!" hakim said. "You ready to head home now?" Gunz asked. "Yeah! Might as well.

Gunz made a left at the light. Gunz immediately slammed on the brakes. "What the fuck nigga?" hakim shouted. Hakim looked ahead and realized why Gunz made the sudden stop. There was limo blocking the street. Standing in front of the limo were 2 white guys wearing overcoats and fedoras. Gunz reached under the seat for his Glock as one of the men approached the vehicle. Hakim sat there in shock, not saying a word. The man came to the window. Gunz rolled down the window and quickly stuck his gun in the face of the man. "No need for that!

No need for that! Follow us! It's important business we must discuss!" the man said with a thick Italian accent. The man took baby steps back to the limo, hoping not to fall on the slippery street. "What you wanna do?" Gunz asked Hakim. Hakim didn't say a word. He was silently trying to regain his composure. "Yo, Hak! What you wanna do?" Gunz asked again. "All right! Go! Just be ready to blast these fuckers in the face if shit go bad!" hakim ordered.

2 Gunz followed the limo over the Verrazano Bridge towards Staten Island. "You sure you don't wanna turn back around?" Gunz asked. "Nah. I wanna see what this shit is about." Hakim said. Hakim pulled out his mobile phone. After 2 rings, someone picked up. "What up boss?" the voice said. "Get Mackie. I want y'all to get strapped and come out to Staten Island. Some shit might go down." Hakim said. "It's gonna take a while. I'm laid up with this bitch out in New Brunswick." Chewie said as he heads towards the window. He peeked through the blinds of the woman's apartment and saw that his Boeman truck was almost submerged in snow. "Shit!" he shouted. "What's wrong?" Hakim asked. "Man. I'm snowed in!" Chewie said. "Well, dig yo self out, and get yo ass out here nigga!" hakim shouted. Hakim clicked off his mobile phone. Hakim made another call to Mackie. After 4 rings, Mackie picked up. "It's me! Where you at?" Hakim asked. "I thought I told you I was down here in Atlanta visiting my kids! What's wrong?" Mackie asked. "Nothing. Fuck it!" Hakim said. He clicked off his phone. "Shit!" Hakim shouted. "Give Butch a call!" Gunz said. "Fuck butch! That nigga been ignoring my ass since we left the castle!" hakim said. "I guess we're on our own then!" Gunz said. Hakim pulled out his Glock from inside his coat. He checked to see if it was fully loaded.

After an hour of following the limo to Staten island in the snow, Gunz and Hakim arrive at an abandoned linoleum factory on the West Shore. "I ain't never been out here before!" hakim said. "For years, this place was known for getting rid of bodies. I know. Your pops had us drop off a few a long time ago." Gunz confessed. "Oh, now you tell me this shit?" hakim asked in a fit of rage. "Yeah. This place brings back a lot of memories." Gunz said. "Yo Gunz! Do me a favor, man. Don't ever call that nigga my father again." hakim said in a calm voice. Gunz looked back at Hakim through the rear-view mirror. "All right." Gunz sighed.

One of the men jumped out of the limo. He gave Gunz and Hakim the signal to stay put in their vehicle. He walked over to the dock and banged on the huge metal garage door. A few seconds later, the door rises. The limo drove into the factory. The man gives Gunz the signal to follow the limo. "What we gonna do now?" Gunz asked. "We're here now! Let's do this!' hakim said. Gunz drove pass the entrance, inside the factory.

Standing in the middle of the factory floor was a short elderly white man in a suit and tie. The limo stopped about 5 feet in front of the old man. The driver exited the limo. 2 more men get out of the back of the limo. "Dillo a Don Domenico lui è qui!" the driver shouted to the old man. The old man nodded his head and walked towards the office in the facility. As soon as Gunz entered the factory, the huge garage door was lowered. "It's game time." Hakim said. "This ain't no game!" Gunz said before exiting the vehicle. He opened the door for Hakim. One of the men from the limo approached Gunz. "Have to frisk you." The man said. Gunz raised his arms. He was frisked from his ankles to his wrists. The man said the same to hakim. Hakim raised his arms as well. "Sono pulito!" the man said to his associates. "Follow us sir." The man said to Hakim. As Gunz was about to follow Hakim, he is stopped by one of the Italian gentlemen. "What the fuck?" Gunz shouted. "You stay here!" the man who just frisked him said. "It's cool." Hakim said to Gunz. Hakim followed 2 of the men to the back office. Hakim looked around the place and noticed that it hadn't been in operation for years. "Y'all own this place?" hakim asked the 2 men. Neither man acknowledged him. They just continued to walk on either side of Hakim.

Inside the office, hakim saw an elderly man sitting at a desk. Standing by his side was the elderly man in the suit that raised the garage door. "Puoi lasciare noi." The man in the suit ordered. The 2 men who escorted Hakim to the office leave. "Mr. Bates. May I introduce you to Don Fernando Domenico." The man in the suit said. Don Domenico held out his hand in a friendly gesture. Reluctantly, Hakim shook hands with the Don. "Can we offer you something to drink Mr. Bates?" the man in the suit asked. "Nah, man! Just tell me why I'm here?" Hakim said as he stared at Don Domenico. "È essere schietto con lui! Se lui non è d'accordo con I nostri termini, prendere il suo veicolo e dare il segnale di prendersi cura del suo autista!" Don Domenico ordered. The man in the suit nodded.

"The Don isn't fluent in your language. So, I'll tell you why you're here." The suit man said. Hakim looked at the Don and scoffed. The man in the suit walked over to a tall file cabinet over in the corner of the office. He grabbed a metal pale from behind the cabinet. He then placed the pale on the desk. He reached in the pale and pulled out a decapitated human head. "What the fuck?" hakim shouted as he backed up against the door. "You recognize this head?" the suit man asked him. Hakim stepped in a little closer to get a better look. "Oh shit! That's Gino! I ain't seen his ass since I was a kid!" Hakim said. "This piece of shit was in a position he shouldn't have been in! He was a member of our organization, but he's wasn't one of us!" the suit man said. "Hey! Did y'all cut off the heads of 3 of my people in Westside Park a while back?" Hakim shouted. Don Domenico and the suit man look at each other shrugging their shoulders. "We have no idea of what you're talking about! This is the only decapitated head that was ordered by us young man!" the suit man said. "What the fuck is going on?" hakim asked with a bewildered look. "Pay attention! The Lassenberry organization has been working for us for many years until this piece of shit took over! Because of him, we've lost our connection in South America! Obviously, you're still doing business with our South American associates! We want back in!" the suit man said. "Man! This shit you asking, is way over my head! I just leave my cash, and take my product!" Hakim said. "Well tell us, who's in charge now? We know it's not Benny Lassenberry, or your homo father Eddie!" the suit man chuckled. "Like I said man, all I do is drop off the cash and take the product!" Hakim said. "To whom and where do you make the transaction with?" the suit man asked. "Yo man! You in way over your head!" hakim chuckled. "Oh, you think this is funny Mr. bates?" the suit man asked. "I'm just saying, the game and the players have changed! That's all!" Hakim said. "Wait here Mr. Bates!" the suit man said in a calm voice. Hakim watched as the suit man left the office. He turned back to see that Don Domenico was pointing a pistol at him. The Don just started laughing.

Less than 20 seconds later, the suit man returned. "Digli Accetterò 40 millioni di cassa entro domani a mezzanotte! Digli saremo di nuovo qui a 2 settimane per parlare di modalità di pagamento!" Don Domenico ordered. "What now?" hakim asked. "You will pay the Don 40 million by tomorrow, midnight!" the suit man said. "40 million? Nigga! I ain't got that kind of money!" Hakim shouted in a high-pitched voice. "You pay 40 million to us tomorrow. Come back here 2 weeks from now, and we'll set you up with a payment plan!" the suit man said. "Man, y'all crazy!" Hakim said. The suit man took the pistol from the Don. The Don started chuckling. "Let's go kid!" the suit man said as he opened the doors and shoved Hakim out.

When Hakim left the office with the suit man right behind him, he noticed the 3 men that lead him and Gunz there were standing in front of his vehicle. The man standing in the middle was wiping blood off his switch blade with a handkerchief. The men stepped to the side to reveal one of Hakim's worse fears. The fear of standing alone, facing the enemy. "Man! Y'all ain't have to do this shit! It ain't even have to go down like this! You ain't have to do that to him, man!" hakim shouted in a wining voice. Lying on the hood of Hakim's vehicle spread eagle, was the man who he'd knew all his life.

Leon Thompson a.k.a 2 Gunz. The man who served and protected Eddie Lassenberry for many years had met his demise with a switch blade. "We're keeping the body, the car and everything in it, even your weapons! Now walk your black ass back to the ferry!" the suit man said. The garage door opened. The blistering cold air rushed into the facility. Hakim closed the collar to his coat. "Don't worry Mr. bates. We'll give him a proper burial. Now go!" The suit man chuckled. Hakim's eyes teared up as he gazed upon Gunz for the last time. He slowly exited the facility. He then turned around to watch the garage door being lowered down.

About a half hour later, Hakim continued to stumble through the snow, on his way to the Staten Island Ferry. Just before he was about to cross the street, a black van pulled up. The side door slid open. Hakim startled, stepped back with his hands in the air as 2 figures jumped out fully suited up in military body armor. The 2 figures were each wielding sub-machine guns. Hakim couldn't identify them because their faces were covered with black ski masks. There a white male who stuck his head out of the passengers' window. The man was a NA agent. "Get in Mr. Bates. We're taking you home. Lord Lassenberry sent us to look after you." The agent said. "Where the fuck y'all been? My man just got his throat slit! Why y'all ain't come bum rush the place?" Hakim shouted. "Our orders were to survey your whereabouts, not to engage in combat. As of now, it's not our fight." The agent said. Hakim just shook his head. He hopped into the back of the van. The 2 battle ready agents hopped in the van after him. The van sped off, heading towards the Verrazano Bridge.

— CHAPTER 19. RIGHT HAND WOMAN —

It was November 15th around noon. Edward the 2nd had summoned Kimberly to his office at castle Lassenberry. She entered his office wearing a long black dress covering her arms. She was still in mourning of the disappearance of her husband Sir Marcus.

"Come have a seat beautiful! Damn! You look better every time I lay eyes on you!" Edward the 2nd said. Kimberly sat down across from Edward the 2nd at his desk. "Lord Lassenberry! I like the way that sounds!" he said. Edward the 2nd smiled as he leans back in his chair, interlocking his fingers behind his head. "Glad to see you've excepted the way things are. Now I gotta convince the elders in the family to do the same." He said. Edward the 2nd pulled out a sealed envelope from the top drawer of his desk. He slid it across the desk towards Kimberly. "What's this?" she asked. Edward the 2nd pointed to his ear several times. He then twirls his index finger in the air to indicate that they were under audio surveillance. Kimberly caught on quick. She just nodded her head and stuffed the envelope inside her bra. "Why aren't you in a relationship by now?" she asked. "I'm waiting for you beautiful to change your mind!" he said. Kimberly responded by holding up her ring finger, showing off her wedding ring. "Ok! I get it!" Edward the 2nd chuckled. "I want to introduce you to a friend of mine. She seems like she would be your type." Kimberly said. Edward the 2nd sighed. "Look at me! Look around you! I can't be hooked up with some average chick! I got noble blood running through my veins!" he said. "She comes from a very affluent family. She's not average. Trust me." Kimberly said. Edward the 2nd thought for a moment while tapping his fingers on the desk. "What's today?" Edward the 2nd asked. "It's Thursday!" Kimberly sighed. "What's her name?" he asked. "Viola Carr." Kimberly said. "All right. Set us up for a date this Saturday then." He said. "I'll have to see if she's not busy that day!" Kimberly sighed. "Ok! Just let me know when can we hook up! Now go take care of that thing for me." Edward the 2nd said. Kimberly smiled from ear to ear. She stood from her seat. "Long live the house of Lassenberry! Long live Edward the 2nd!" she said in a sweet voice.

Right after Kimberly left the office, the black phone on the desk rang. Edward the 2nd slowly picked up the phone. He puts the receiver to his ear. "Hello." He said. "1224t! Quiero hablar con 1224t!" the female voice shouted. "What? Who the fuck is this?" Edward the 2nd shouted. "1224t! 1224t!" the woman shouted. "I don't understand what the hell you're saying!" Edward the 2nd shouted. He immediately hung up the phone. Suddenly, there was a knock on the door. "Who that?" Edward the 2nd shouted. "It's Brandon! I'm coming in!" he shouted. Brandon entered the office.

He was wearing dress pants, shoes, and a t-shirt. "Who was the pretty lady I passed in the corridor?" Brandon asked. "Don't worry about that right now!" Edward the 2nd said. "Well, anyway, you have to restock the kitchen. You call these agents robots, but they still have to eat." Brandon said. Edward the 2nd just sat there staring at the black phone. "What's wrong?" Brandon asked while eating a sandwich. "Man, some Spanish chick was on the black phone screaming at me! She said something about 1224t or something!"" Edward the 2nd explained. At that moment, the black phone rang again. Edward the 2nd just sat there, staring at the phone. Hesitant at first, Brandon finally picked up the phone after 6 rings. "Hello!" Brandon shouted. "Quiero hablar con 1224t!" the woman shouted. "¡Espere! Si está hablando en código, toque el teléfono 3 veces!" Brandon shouted. The woman tapped the phone 3 times. "What the fuck? Everybody knows how to speak a different language but me?" Edward the 2nd shouted. Brandon ignored his boss and continued to converse with woman on the phone. "¿Quién es encargadode, su envío llegará esta noche a medianoche en el área designated! No llegue tarde!" the woman said. "Estamos bajo un nuevo régimen ahora! ¿Dónde está la zona designada?" Brandon asked. "What did she say, man?" Edward the 2nd asked. Brandon put his index finger over his own lips to signal Edward the 2nd to be quiet. "Encuentra 1224t. Él sabra qué hacer." The woman said. She then hung up the phone. "What's going on, man?" Edward the 2nd asked. "Who is 1224t? she said he'll know what to do!" Brandon said after hanging up the phone. Edward the 2nd looked around the office while taping his fingers on the desk. "What now?" Brandon asked. Edward the 2nd snapped his fingers. "Oh shit! I got it!" he shouted. Edward the 2nd made a dash to the safe behind the picture on the wall. "Listen! What I'm about to show you, only you and I know where this is! Understand?" Edward the 2nd whispered to Brandon. Brandon put his hands up in a surrendering gesture. "Ok! I understand!" he said. Edward the 2nd opened the safe to unveil the B.O.I. The only source he and Brandon had to solve this enigma. Edward the 2nd took the B.O.I out of the safe. He placed it on the desk. He quickly skimmed through the pages. "Here! You look through it! Find anything that has to do with 1224t!" Edward the 2nd whispered.

Elsewhere, hakim and his henchmen, Chewie and Mackie held their defenses at BIG SHOTS. Chewie and Mackie were both wielding machine guns while standing outside the back room. Hakim was in the back room sleeping on the couch with a pistol lying on his chest. On the card table was a briefcase. Suddenly, there was a knock on the door. Mackie burst in unannounced. Hakim jumped up from his slumber. His pistol fell on the floor. "Man! What the fuck? Can't you knock first?" Hakim shouted. "I did." Mackie said. "What you want?" Hakim asked. "Man. This is crazy! It's been a few days now! They ain't show up yet to collect!" Mackie said. "I got 12 million in that briefcase over there! We stay put until they show up! I'll negotiate the rest of the cash!" Hakim said. "If they ain't here by now, they ain't coming at all!" Mackie said. Hakim was sitting on the couch wearing nothing but a pair of jeans and socks. He hadn't showered or shaved in a few days. "They killed Gunz, man! Believe me! They're coming!" Hakim said. "Call Lassenberry, kid! We can't take out the mob on our own!" Mackie said. Within that moment, Chewie entered the room. "They're here y'all!" he said. Hakim sighed. "Toss me my shirt off the back of the chair!" Hakim ordered Mackie. "What you want me to do?" Chewie asked. "Fuck, man! Offer them a drink or something! Shit! I don't know!" Hakim said as he put on his sneakers. Chewie just stood there shaking his head in disappointment of his young boss's defeated attitude. Mackie turned to Chewie. "Go man. Just do it." Mackie said in a calm voice. Chewie left the room, closing the door behind him. Mackie tossed hakim his button up shirt, having it land on his shoulder.

Out on the dance floor of the club stood the suit man and 3 of his henchmen, all wearing wool trench coats and fedoras. The suit man looked small in stature compared to the 3 brutes. Chewie walked behind the bar and laid his weapon on the bar counter. He put his dreadlocks in a ponytail with a rubber band he grabbed from his front pocket. Can I make you cool cats a drink?" he asked the crew. "Fuck the drinks! Where's Hakim? Where's the money?" the suit man asked. "Straight ahead. In the back room." Chewie sighed. "È 2, resta qui e tenere d'occhio questo cazzo ventosa." The suit man said to his men. 2 of the suit man's men stood on the opposite side of the bar, keeping a close watch on Chewie. One of the henchmen grabbed Chewie's machine gun just to feel safe. "Y'all don't trust a nigga! I get it!" Chewie chuckled.

The suit man and his remaining henchman walked towards the back room at a fast pace. The henchman pushed open the door, allowing the suit man to pass through first. The suit man stood in the doorway. He saw Hakim standing behind the card table with his hand on the briefcase. Mackie was standing next to him twirling one of his dreads with one hand and holding his machine gun with his other hand.

"Damn, man! What took y'all so long? I thought y'all changed y'all minds!" Hakim said with a smile on his face. The suit man looked dead serious. "Is that my money in that briefcase?" he asked hakim. Hakim cleared his throat. "Let me explain before I answer that!" Hakim said nervously. The suit man reached inside of his coat and pulled out a pistol. He pointed it at Mackie's head. "Yo! Hold on man!" Hakim shouted. The suit man squeezed the trigger. The gun goes off. Hakim flinched as Mackie's body fell to the floor like a wooden board. "What the Fuck man? Fuck!" Hakim shouted as he stomped his feet on the floor.

Chewie was startled from the sound of the gun shot. One of the henchman pointed the machine gun at Chewie. Chewie raised his hands in the air. "Ok! I ain't making no moves!" Chewie said.

In the back room, Hakim looked down at his jeans, which were stained with urine. "Oh fuck!" hakim shouted. "Questo ragazzo ha una vescica debole!" the suit man said to the henchman. Hakim became more embarrassed when the henchman chuckled at his incident. "Fuck y'all!" Hakim cried. "Now, what is you wanted to tell me?" the suit man asked. Hakim took a few seconds to compose himself. "I swear to you! All the cash I have is in this briefcase! 12 million! After this, I'm broke than a motherfucker! I swear!" Hakim cried. The suit man turned to his henchman. He then turned to hakim. "What about your next shipment?" the suit man asked. "That's just it, man! I can't afford a next shipment! Y'all taking everything I got!" Hakim cried. The suit man sighed. "Follow me." He said to hakim in a calm voice. Hakim slowly followed the suit man out of the room. The henchman grabbed the briefcase and followed Hakim. They walked pass Chewie and the other 2 henchmen. "Everything cool Hakim?" Chewie shouted. Hakim didn't say a word when walking by. Hakim, the suit man, and the henchman stepped outside. Parked in front of the club was a black limo. They all walk up to the limo. The rear window rolled down. Sitting in the back was Don Domenico. "Che cos'è?" the Don asked. "Ha detto che tutto ciò che deve il suo nome è di 12 milioni in questa valigetta." The suit man said. The henchman handed the Don the briefcase. "E la sua prossima spedizione?" the Don asked. "Ha detto che non può. Tutto il denaro che ha è nella valigetta." The suit man explained. The Don looked at Hakim with fury in his eyes. He looked Hakim up and down. The Don burst out laughing. The suit man and Hakim look at each other. "Un uomo che piscia nei pantaloni come un bambino deve essere dicendo la verità!" the Don chuckled. "Allora, cosa facciamo con lui?" the suit man asked. "Digi Torno la prima settimana di dicemdre per il resto. Poi, si può iniziare pagamento regolari a gennaio. Andiamo!" the Don Chuckled. The henchman went back inside the club to fetch the other henchmen. The suit man placed his arm around Hakim. "This is your lucky day! The Don is giving you until the first of December to get the rest of the money! After that, comes regular payments starting in January! If you don't have the money by December, you will witness the execution of your other friend in there!" the suit man said. He gave Hakim a tap on the face. All 3 henchmen exit the club. One of them opened the limo door for the suit man. He hopped in the limo. The henchmen followed. The limo crushed the chunks of snow as it sped off down the street. Hakim just stood there shaking with rage. He looked down the street, then slowly walked back in the club.

Hakim walked to back to the game room. He saw Chewie kneeling over Mackie's body. Chewie looked up towards Hakim. "This shit is way above our heads! It's time to call Lassenberry!" Chewie said. Hakim nodded his head. "Give him a call!" Hakim said.

Back at Lassenberry castle, Edward the 2nd and Brandon find the information they were looking for to receive the next shipment of cocaine. "I'll take a few agents with me to Port Elizabeth and make the transaction." Brandon said. "No. You stay here. I'll call Butch. More than likely he can vouch for me being a Lassenberry. Suddenly, Edward the 2nd felt his mobile phone vibrating in his front pocket. He takes it out to check the number. "This fucking hakim is a fucking pain in my fucking neck!" Edward the 2nd shouted. He answered the phone anyway.

3 days later, on the 18th of November, Kimberly arrived back from her mission. She and Edward the 2nd took a stroll outside of the castle grounds. The air was frigid. Edward the 2nd was willing to face the cold rather than being spied on inside the castle walls.

"Glad to see you made it back in one beautiful piece cousin. So, tell me what's going on in the land of Lassenberia?" Edward the 2nd asked. "I'm glad to see you've realized we're cousins, cousin!" Kimberly said. "First, that's a nice big chunk of land!" Kimberly said. "1,213 square miles, my notes said. About the size of Rhode Island." Edward the 2nd said. "The thing that upset me was that your family didn't take the time to oversee the condition of this huge piece of land! The entire eastern side of the Island is a total dump site! Literally, a total dump site!" Kimberly shouted. "Shhhh! Keep yo voice down! Who knows who's listening out here!" Edward the 2nd whispered. "For miles and miles, I saw nothing but toxic and organic waste stacked as high as 50 feet." Kimberly said in a melancholier tone. "Wait a minute! You can't put this on my entire family! This was a top-secret project started by my uncle over a decade ago! From what I've read, my uncle wanted to build a new home for us! But, the lack of funds brought that shit to an end!" Edward the 2nd said. "I was so disgusted that I couldn't tour the entire island! What we need to do is go to the United Nations or the International criminal court system! From the people, I've spoken with, the dumping is coming from Mozambique! I wouldn't put it pass Madagascar either!" Kimberly said. "Hold on now, woman! I know what you're saying, but I got my hands full as it is! One of my generals got problems with the damn mafia!" Edward the 2nd explained. "At least go out there and see for yourself!" Kimberly said. "Listen. It's Sunday. You did a lot for me these past few days, and I appreciate that. You need to go relax and spend time with your son." Edward the 2nd said. "There's no getting any rest with a one-year-old!" Kimberly said. Edward the 2nd scoffed at Kimberly. "Please! You probably got a hundred nannies!" he chuckled. "All right! You got me!" Kimberly chuckled.

Kimberly and Edward the 2nd hug before parting ways. "I have a question. Who was that young man I passed in the corridor a few days ago?" Kimberly asked. "Oh! You know Sleeves Hart, right?" Edward the 2nd said. "Of course! He's legendary! Not like my father, but he's up there!" Kimberly chuckled. "Yes! Jabbo was a hard act to follow!" Edward the 2nd chuckled. "So, who was he?" Kimberly asked. "That was his grandson Brandon." Edward the 2nd said. "Does he work for you?" Kimberly asked. "Possibly! But don't worry. You're still my right-hand woman." Edward the 2nd chuckled. "Please! I'm not worried!" Kimberley scoffed. "let's end this meeting beautiful! It's colder than a mother fucker out here!" Edward the 2nd shouted. The two hug once more. "Damn you feel good!" Edward the 2nd chuckled. Kimberly pushed him away. "You're sick!" Kimberly chuckled. "Nah! I'm just horny." Edward the 2nd chuckled. "Anyway! Long live the house of Lassenberry! Long live Edward the 2nd!" Kimberly sighed. She leaves Edward the 2nd, walking towards the main gate where her chauffeured driven car was waiting.

— CHAPTER 20. TALKING WALLS —

oments later, Edward the 2nd returned to his office. He took off his leather jacket and tossed it on the sofa. He went over and sat at his desk and opened the top left drawer. He pulled out a note pad and ink pen. He thought for a moment, then pressed the buzzer on the side of the desk. The buzzer sent an electronic signal to the NA agents standing out in the corridor. Within seconds, a Caucasian agent entered the office with his hand on his holster. "Is everything all right sir?" the agent asked. The agent wore the regulation black suit and tie with dark shades. "You guys need a new look." Edward the 2nd mumbled. "What was that sir?" the agent asked. "Nothing! From now on, starting today, I'm gonna need 3 hours of me time!" Edward the 2nd said. "Me time sir? I don't understand." The agent said. "Listen, man. I ain't use to people crowding me. I ain't my uncle or cousin. That means for 3 hours a day don't follow me. Don't contact me over the intercom. Don't ask me where I'm going! Understand?" Edward the 2nd ordered. "Sorry sir, but I have to get approval of that order from my superiors." The agent said. Edward the 2nd stood from his chair. "I'm yo mother fucking superior! Understand?" Edward the 2nd shouted. The agent responded with no emotion. "Very well. As you wish sir." The agent said. "My 3 hours start right…about…now! Now get the fuck out!" Edward the 2nd shouted as he stared at his wrist watch. "Yes sir." The agent said. The agent left the office. Edward the 2nd sat back in his chair. He started writing on the note pad.

After a few minutes of writing, scribbling out words, and then more writing, Edward the 2nd placed the ink pen and note pad back in the drawer after he tore off the 2 top pieces of paper. He was afraid someone would find the note pad and try to read the ident on the second sheet of paper. He folded the paper numerous times in a tight little square. He then stuffed both pieces of paper in his front pants pocket before leaving the office. Outside the office stood 2 agents at their posts. Edward the 2nd glanced at his watch. "Remember! 3 hours." Edward the 2nd said. "Yes sir." Both agents said simultaneously. Edward the 2nd went for a walk towards the south wing. About 5 minutes later, he picked up the combined smell of urine and disinfected cleaner. "Getting close." He whispered to himself. A few yards into walking down the south wing, Edward the 2nd stood before a crack in the wall. The crack had a one inch slit that led to the other side, he put his nose to slit and smelled the cleanser. Edward the 2nd looked down both ends of the corridor. He took the folded piece of paper out of his pocket. He then squeezed the paper through the slit until it fell through the other side. "Mission accomplished. Hopefully." He whispered to himself. Another 6 minutes had passed when Edward the 2nd could see the 2 agents standing in front of his office. He then approached the 2 agents. "Now, drive me to the front gate." Edward the 2nd ordered. One of the agents jump in the drivers' seat of the golf cart, the same time Edward the 2nd jumped in the passenger seat. The golf cart took off down the west wing corridor towards the main entrance.

After an hour of walking the streets, peeping around corners, making sure he wasn't being followed, Edward the 2nd ended up at an urban runoff system located on the Jersey side of the Delaware River. He sat on a hill covered with rocks, watching the water flow downstream. Edward the 2nd sat there rocking back-n-forth to keep warm.

About an hour later, he could see a familiar face approaching. It was his older cousin Sir Marcus standing a few yards away from him shivering and soaking wet. "I've been waiting out here a while for you cuz! I'm risking a lot being out here!" Edward the 2nd said as he yawned. "I've traveled out here in the freezing cold through this filthy water just to meet with you! I probably have an incurable disease buy now!" Sir Marcus shouted. Edward the 2nd had a smirk on his face. "You know what, you're right big cuz. I shouldn't have said that. My fault." Edward the 2nd said. Sir Marcus walked over and sat next to his cousin. "I hope you don't think I'm putting my arms around you to keep yo ass warm!" Edward the 2nd chuckled. "Screw you." Sir Marcus said. "Don't worry! I'll send Brandon out here with some dry clothes and boots for you." Edward the 2nd said. "Tell him to make it quick before I die of hyperthermia! I'm running low on food! I also need coffee! Lots of coffee!" Sir Marcus complained. "I thought it was kind of warm behind the walls!" Edward the 2nd said. Sir Marcus turned towards his cousin. "Am I behind the walls now? No! I'm out here with you shivering my ass off!" he shouted. Edward the 2nd just nodded his head. "Now, what's the report?" Sir Marcus asked. "On what?" Edward the 2nd asked. "On everything! The dive bars! The 5 generals! Terrance! My wife and son! Everything! By-the-way! Did you give the family their envelopes yet?" Sir Marcus asked. Edward the 2nd smacked himself on the forehead. "Shit! I forgot about that! Damn!" he said. "You can't forget things like that cousin! The family, our fathers are like spoiled children! If you forget the envelopes, family or not, they will turn on you! Trust me! I know!" Sir Marcus said. "You're right cuz!" Edward the 2nd said. "You should've vouched for Tony! You should've kept him alive! He would've had your back so things could run better!" Sir Marcus said. "What was I supposed to do? Hakim said he would bring me to the other generals and they would all agree to make me boss because you lost your nerve!" Edward the 2nd said. "I thought it was my duty as a Lassenberry to keep this thing going! I didn't know Hakim hated Tony like that!" Edward the 2nd explained. "So, Hakim is your right-hand man now?" Sir Marcus asked. "Hell no, man! That nigga called crying to me about how the mafia fucking with him" Edward the 2nd said. "It's Brandon then?" Sir Marcus asked. "Kinda, sort of." Edward the 2nd said. "What's that supposed to mean?" Sir Marcus asked. Edward the 2nd looked around in all directions. He took a deep breath. "It's, it's Kimberly." Edward the 2nd sighed. Sir Marcus jumped to his feet. "No, you didn't! Oh, no you didn't!" Sir Marcus shouted as he looked down at his cousin. Edward the 2nd stood up. I had to! I needed someone to go to

Lassenberia! We gotta whole fucking island between South Africa and Madagascar, that ain't been tended to for over a decade!" Edward the 2nd said. Sir Marcus grabbed his cousin by the collar. "I swear to god, man! If my wife gets hurt in all of this! It's gonna be me and you, to the death!" Sir Marcus shouted. Edward the 2nd yanked his cousin's hands from his collar. "Man, listen! Because of her, I know that they've been over there turning our property into a dump site! I'm trying to figure out a way to get out there without letting that psycho Terrance from knowing!" Edward the 2nd said. Sir Marcus paced back-n-forth with his hands on his hips. He then turned to his cousin. "Does the family know about this?" Sir Marcus asked. "Man, everything happened so fast! The family don't even know I'm officially running things! I gotta get yo pops, my pops and uncle Danny together as soon as possible!" Edward the 2nd said. Sir Marcus grabbed his cousin's shoulders. "This is what you do! Don't tell the family about Lassenberia! Try to figure out a way to get out there underneath Terrance's radar! Second thing! Go give Hakim the help he needs to get those wise guys off his back! Essex County is the most lucrative territory we have! We lose that to the mob; we'll slowly lose everything! Last thing! When you call that meeting with the family, make sure you bring those envelopes with you! That's the only way they'll take you serious!" Sir Marcus said. Edward the 2nd shook his head. "I'm confused about this shit! I thought I was head of this organization!" Edward the 2nd said. "Let's be honest with each other cousin. You summoned me because you're in over your head." Sir Marcus said. Edward the 2nd didn't say a word. There was a few seconds of silence as Edward the 2nd stared off into the open landscape. "Are you ok?" Sir Marcus asked. Edward the 2nd nodded his head. "Are we ok?" Sir Marcus asked as he extended his hand in a friendly gesture. Edward the 2nd gave his older cousin a firm handshake. Sir Marcus smiled as he gave his cousin a hug. Edward stepped back. "You better get back to the castle! Yo ass colder than a snow cone!" Edward the 2nd chuckled. Sir Marcus just smiled. "Oh! Before we part, remember, we have 18 dive bars and 30 bed-n-breakfast spots all in Butch's territory. Excluding the legit cash, that's a half a million a month of dirty cash coming out each of those spots, and it all belongs to us! I'm not saying Butch is suspect, but dirty money doesn't come with a receipt. So, stay on top of that." Sir Marcus said. Edward the 2nd nodded his head. Sir Marcus stood at attention as he faced his cousin. "Long live the house of Lassenberry. Long live Edward the 2nd." He said. Sir Marcus remained at attention waiting for a reply. "Same to you cuz." Edward the 2nd said before walking away. Sir Marcus realized that his younger cousin loathed the idea of returning words of respect. He just let it go and walked off.

November 20th, 2001. Edward the 2nd was in his office, sitting at his desk. He was on his mobile phone with one of his generals.

"Yo Bex, Man! You there?" Edward the 2nd asked. "Yeah, Yeah! I'm here!" Bex said. "Man, I've been trying to get in touch with you for the past few days now! What's all that noise in the back ground?" Edward the 2nd asked. We gotta a card game going on!" Bex shouted. "Card game? Nigga! I got 50 kilos out here waiting for yo ass, and you down there playing cards with them hill Billie's! Man, you better get up here and make this transaction!" Edward the 2nd shouted. "Yeah, man I'll be up tomorrow!" Bex said. "Man, you're gonna bring yo high yella ass up here tonight, and get this product!" Edward the 2nd shouted. "Ok! Ok! Me and my people will be at the spot around 10 tonight! Damn! Y'all can't be leaning up against the wall! The paint ain't dry yet!" Bex shouted. "Remember, man! It's 20 thousand a brick!" Edward the 2nd said. "Hey! I thought it was 17!" Bex shouted. "It was nigga, until you let this shit sit around for a couple of days! Mookie, Hakim, Dubbs and Butch got they're product the same day it came in!" Edward the 2nd shouted. "Damn! My fucking hand hurts! Yo! Get me another beer, man!" Bex shouted to someone in the back ground. "Yo Bex! You heard me, Man?" Edward the 2nd shouted. "Yeah! I heard you, man! 20 grand!" Bex said. "Don't make me come looking for you!" Edward the 2nd said. Edward the 2nd clicked off his mobile phone. He then started giggling like a child. "That's right! I run shit!" Edward the 2nd said to himself.

Edward the 2nd just kicked up his feet to enjoy his power for a few moments, until there was a knock on the door. "What the fuck? Come in!" he shouted. An agent of African American descent entered the office. "What the fuck is it?" Edward the 2nd asked. "Mr. Haggerty just arrived at the main gate, my lord." The agent said. Edward the 2nd's feet dropped to the floor. He stood from his seat. "How the fuck he's gonna come here without notifying me first?" Edward the 2nd shouted. There was no response from the agent. "Why the fuck am I asking you anyway? Just go tell him I'll be here waiting! Now go!" Edward the 2nd ordered. "Yes, my lord." The agent said before leaving the office. Edward the 2nd nervously walked around the office making sure that nothing was out of place. He was most concerned with the painting on the wall. He walked over to it to make sure it was leveled, not tilted so it would grab Terrance's attention. If Terrence realized there was a safe hidden behind the painting, it would spell trouble for Edward the 2nd and the Lassenberry organization. The B.O.I was the only thing that gave Edward the 2nd leverage.

It was about an hour later, as Edward the 2nd was waiting impatiently for Terrance to come to the office. He paced back-n-forth, staring at his wrist watch for the seventh time. Suddenly, there was a knock at the door. Edward the 2nd took a deep breath. "Come in!" he shouted. The door slowly opened. In came the African American agent, followed by 2 agents donning black military body armor from head-to-toe. Their faces were covered with black ski masks. They were armed with high tech machine guns. "May I present Mr. Terrance Haggerty, my lord." The agent said. The 2 armed agents stepped to the side against the wall. Terrance gaily entered the room with his fingers interlocked behind his back. He was wearing a dark blue silk suit with a pink bow tie.

Terrance looked around the office with a big grin on his face. He rubbed his 2 fingers across the top of the desk, checking for dust. Edward the 2nd put on a big smile as well. "Terrance, my man! What took you so long? Should've told me in advance that you were coming! I could've prepared some food or entertainment for you!" Edward the 2nd said. Terrance stood face-to-face with Edward the 2nd. "There's no way in hell you could've prepared for the kind of entertainment I desire." Terrance chuckled. "Have a seat, man! Please!" Edward the 2nd said. Terrance walked over to the chair on the opposite side of the desk. The agent pulled out the chair for Terrance. "You can go now!" Edward the 2nd said to the agent. The agent looked to Terrance. "You all may leave us now." Terrance ordered all 3 agents. Edward the 2nd looked agitated seeing that his order was overwritten, but he kept silent. He walked over to his chair and sat down.

"What can I do for you, my man?" Edward the 2nd asked. Terrance removed his glasses, and blew his breath on the lenses. He pulled out a linen cloth and wiped the lenses. He placed his glasses back on. "You like my bow tie? It's for cancer awareness month." Terrance said as he yanked on his bow tie. "Cancer what?" Edward the 2nd asked. "Cancer awareness! It's a big thing conjured up by the big wigs!" Terrance leans in closer to Edward the 2nd. "Between me and you, there's no cure. There will never be a cure. Not for breast cancer, lung cancer, pancreatic cancer. None of it!" Terrance whispered. "Bullshit!" Edward the 2nd shouted. "Foundations, medications, all types of treatments, have and will continue to make close friends of mine wealthy beyond your imagination." Terrance said. "If that shit is true, why did you buy the bow tie then?" Edward the 2nd asked. Terrance leaned back and crossed his legs. "Silly negro! I don't pay for anything!" Terrance chuckled. Edward the 2nd just shook his head. "There are a handful of physicians around the world who want to do the right thing, but they're on the endangered species' list, if you get my drift." Terrance chuckled. "I know you didn't really come here to brag about your power, man. What is it that you want?" Edward the 2nd sighed. "Oh, I just came to see how things are running so far. I took a stroll through the castle before coming to your office. I've noticed the south wing corridor, and it smells horrible! You need to patch up those cracks and holes in the wall! Christ! This is a castle! Not some project housing tenement your uncle used to live in!" Terrance said. Edward the 2nd was silent. Terrance could see fear in his eyes. Edward the 2nd gulped down the saliva in his mouth. "Are you ok? I hope you're taking care of things better than that wining, bitch, cowardly, poor excuse of a man, punk, useless piece of shit cousin of yours did!" Terrance shouted as saliva spewed from his lips. Edward the 2nd remained silent. His eyes were wide as saucers. Terrance just stared into the eyes of Edward the 2nd, not showing any emotion either way. All-of-a-sudden, Terrance bursts out laughing. "Don't pay me any mind! I just had to vent for a moment! I'm sure you would be a good boy and notify me about his whereabouts!" Terrance chuckled. Edward the 2nd showed a sigh of relief. "But seriously. Take care of that corridor, please." Terrance chuckled. Edward the 2nd shook his head laughing. "Man, you're all over the place! First your talking about cancer! Now, you're talking walls!" he said. Terrance beat his hands on the desk like a drum. "Let's get down to business!" he chuckled. "Yeah! One of my generals, Hakim. He's being muscled by the Italians. I've changed my mind and decided to put 10 agents at his disposal." Edward the 2nd said. "What do you mean by that?" Terrance asked. "I mean, use whatever force to send them spaghetti eating mother fuckers back to Sicily." Edward the 2nd said. Terrance thought for a moment while scratching his chin. "Mmmm! Think about that for a moment. If a force goes toe-to-toe with this mob family, the other crews around the country will most certainly retaliate. That would disrupt business, and we don't want that!" Terrance chuckled. Edward the 2nd pound his fist on the desk. "If they got Hakim all shook up; they're already disrupting business! Am I right?" Edward the 2nd shouted. "Take it easy. If a war breaks out, the last thing the public needs to see is a dead agent in the street. We need a less conspicuous approach." Terrance said. He pondered for a moment. Edward the 2nd sat impatiently tapping his fingers on the desk. "I guess I'll have to put the MK Ultra project into play." Terrance said to himself. "What the fuck is MK Ultra?" Edward the 2nd shouted. "Oh. Never mind. I'll have my assistance give you a call either today or tomorrow. You'll give him the information he needs to get the ball rolling." Terrance said.

"Thanks, man." Edward the 2nd said. "Is there anything else I can do for you?" Terrance asked. Edward the 2nd thought for a moment. "Nah. I gotta meet up with one of my generals tonight. Dumbass forgot to pick up his refill a few days ago. I need to see him face-to-face to straighten his ass out." Edward the 2nd said. Terrance started chuckling. "You're a boss now! You can easily send a message without being present! I'm sure you have an assistant since we've disposed of that piece of shit Kerouac fella! Right?" Terrance asked. "Ah, yeah!" Edward the 2nd reluctantly admitted. "Send a couple of agents with your assistant to the meeting place and work the fucker over a bit! Let those that might be with him know, you are serious! That's something I would do!" Terrance said. "He's a fucking country fuck." Edward the 2nd said. "Remember! Always keep a wall between you and your men!" Terrance said. "There you go talking walls again!" Edward the 2nd chuckled. "It's true! If you take that piece of advice, you can never go wrong!" Terrance chuckled. "I'll consider it." Edward the 2nd said. Terrance reached inside his suit jacket pocket and pulled out a device resembling a car remote. He pressed the button on the device. The 2 body armored agents enter the office. "Before I bid you farewell until next time, there's something I want you to do." Terrance chuckled. "What's that?" Edward the 2nd asked. Terrance stood up and leaned over the desk. He stuck his finger down his throat, causing himself to regurgitate on the desk. "What the fuck are you doing, man?" Edward the 2nd shouted as he jumped back in his chair. Terrance wipes his mouth. "I'm doing something for you, about this Hakim situation. Now, you have to do something for me." Terrance chuckled. "What the fuck are you talking about, man?" Edward the 2nd shouted. "You have 2 choices. You either slurp up the vomit! Every drop, or bend over the desk and let me fuck you in the ass!" Terrance chuckled. "Are you fucking sick?" Edward the 2nd shouted. The 2 agents pointed their weapons at Edward the 2nd. "I assure you, I'm neither sick nor kidding!" Terrance chuckled while undoing his trousers. Edward the 2nd shook his head in disbelief. "I can't believe yo ass is serious!" Edward the shouted. "I'm not leaving here until you perform one or the other!" Terrance chuckled. Edward the 2nd started trembling. He looked at the agents, then looked up at Terrance. "Now, you've caught a glimpse on what kind of entertainment I desire!" Terrance chuckled.

The MK Ultra project was a top-secret operation developed in the former Soviet Union during World War 2. Its original purpose was to delve into the minds of captured Nazi soldiers for interrogation. The prisoners were put into a drug induced state from chemicals extracted on what the American intelligence agency called, magic mushrooms. It wasn't until after the war, the American intelligence agency figured out that the younger the person was subjected to the procedure, the more effective. Young pregnant women who were from the dreads of society, urban and poor rural areas of America, would volunteer for the experiment. During their unwanted pregnancy, these women would be sedated in their third trimester at underground abortion clinics. They would be injected with a combination of natural and artificial chemicals. After giving birth, the young women would sign more documents, surrendering their parenting rights for a substantial amount of money. The new born babies would be taken to an underground facility located underneath the United States Capitol for further experiments. There, they would be subjected to more tests and monitored until the age of 5 years old. Those children who'd survive the process would then be moved to another underground facility for intense physical and psychological training. This now defunct facility was sold to the city of Chicago to construct a transit line to connect to the now Midway International Airport.

One of the personnel assigned to the Chicago operation was a young medical student who immigrated from Germany. Studying in physics and chemistry, the young man quickly rose through the ranks amongst his peers. Later, in his life, Alfred Zachmont became Chief of Research and Development of the National Agreement.

CHAPTER 21. THE DIRTY SOUTH JERSEY

It was around 9:00 pm, when Bex and his friend toby were on their way to Port Elizabeth just outside Newark, New Jersey. Bex had just purchased himself a 2001 Boeman pick-up truck. He had invested thousands of dollars to customize the truck with run-flat tires, bulletproof glass windows and ballistic stainless steel plates covering the chassis from bumper-to-bumper. After purchasing his truck, a month earlier, Bex had already put 200 miles on the odometer. Most of the mileage would come from his drive up to Port Elizabeth.

"What are you looking all nervous about?" Toby asked. "I ain't nervous about shit old man!" Bex said. "Boy, you're gripping that steering wheel like you on a roller coaster!" Toby said. The temperature outside the truck was 40 °F degrees. It was 80 °F inside the truck. Bex had to roll down the window a little, he was sweating profusely. Toby looked at the sweat dripping from his nose. "Not nervous, huh?" Toby chuckled. "Fuck you, man!" Bex said. "Don't worry boy. I got us covered." Toby said. Bex glanced over at Toby as he unveiled a revolver under his coat. Bex looked terrified. "Hey, man! You pull that shit out, we're dead! I want shit to run smooth! We just make the trade, and get the fuck back home!" Bex said. "Didn't Hakim say this Krayton kid was a punk?" Toby asked. "Yeah, but he's a punk with a lot of power! You should see that castle he lives in!" Bex said. "I saw it on the news. So, what?" Toby said. "So, what? Who the fuck builds a castle in Jersey? That shit just crazy!" Bex said.

Back at Lassenberry castle, Brandon knocked on the office door. There was no word for him to enter. He knocked some more. There was no answer. Brandon turned to see the 2 agents standing at parade rest not reacting. Brandon looked worried. He started banging on the door. "Come in!" Edward the 2nd shouted. Brandon looked back at the agents, shaking his head. He entered the office. "Where are you?" Brandon shouted. "I'm in here! In the bathroom!" Edward the 2nd cried. Brandon ran to the bathroom thinking Edward the 2nd was in peril. "You ok?" Brandon asked. Edward the 2nd was on his knees with his head over the toilet gagging and vomiting his brains out. "What the fuck are you looking at, man?" Edward the 2nd shouted. Brandon quickly put his head down. "Your instructions are on the couch to go make the transaction with Bex!" Edward the 2nd said as he was coughing and gagging. "You're not going?" Brandon asked as he looked down at the bathroom floor. "No! Take 4 agents with you! Make sure yo ass follow those instructions. Now, get the fuck out!" Edward the 2nd shouted as he was gagging. Brandon quickly left the bathroom. He went over to the couch. He saw the piece of notebook paper folded on the couch. He picked it up, frowning as he heard Edward the 2nd continue to puke his brains out. Brandon then looked over at the desk. He noticed dried streaks on the desk resembling oatmeal. He walked over to the desk. He then leaned over the desk to get a better look. He took a whiff. The scent of the dried substance made him gag. He looked at Edward the 2nd, still on his knees gagging. Brandon just shook his head. He left the office.

It was 10:12 pm when Bex and Toby arrived at the transaction spot out in Port Elizabeth. Brandon and his assigned agents had arrived a few minutes early. The 4 agents, who happened to be 3 Caucasians and 1 big burly African American were wearing heavy black leather trench coats. Brandon was wearing a black wool coat. Bex and Toby pulled up to the pier, a few yards from where a black Boeman SUV was parked. Brandon and the 4 agents exit the SUV. "Damn, those mother fuckers look mean!" Bex said to Toby. "Come on boy, and let's get this shit over with!" toby said. They both exit the truck. Bex grabbed the briefcase that was placed between him and Toby. He noticed Brandon holding a huge duffle bag, with the strap on his shoulder. The agents were standing close behind him. Bex walked up to Brandon, standing about a foot away from each other. Toby stood closely behind Bex. "We finally get to meet. I'm Brandon." He said as he and Bex shook hands. The agents slowly surrounded Bex and Toby. Bex began to get nervous. "This here is Toby. He's one of the dudes in my crew." Bex said. "You're the man with the briefcase. That's all I'm concerned about." Brandon said. One of the agents who was closest to Toby pulled out his pistol and pointed at Toby's ribs. "Hold on now! What the fuck y'all doing?" Toby asked. "Take it easy sir. This will all be over in a few minutes." Brandon said. "What's going on, man?" Bex shouted in a high-pitched voice. Brandon dropped the duffle bag. "Put the briefcase down." Brandon said. Bex slowly placed the briefcase on the ground. He put his hands up. Brandon scoffed. "Keep your hands at your side." Brandon said. "Man, just let me have my product and be out!" Bex said. Brandon pulled out the note book paper from his coat pocket. "Take it easy! This won't take long!" Brandon said. The 2 remaining Caucasian agents grabbed Bex by his collar and hands. Brandon looked at the paper. "Now listen. This is not my doing. This is coming from up top. I was given this note because the boss said you must learn to conduct business on time. The agent here is going to smack you real hard across the face 10 times so that you get the message that he's serious." Brandon said as he pointed to the black agent. "Ah, come on, man! You ain't gotta do this!" Bex cried. "This ain't how you conduct business, kid!" Toby shouted. "You can take the punishment for him, if you like, old man!" Brandon said. "Let me shut my mouth then." Toby said. "Yeah, you do that." Brandon said. The black agent took his left hand glove off. The other 2 agents held Bex firmly. "I'll keep count. Now brace yourself." Brandon said. The agent looked towards Brandon. "You can start." Brandon said. Bex shut his eyes tight while gritting his teeth. The agent brought his hand back, and then released a powerful amount of pressure on Bex's cheek with the palm of his hand. "That's one." Brandon said as saliva spewed from Bex's mouth. The smacks continued. "2…3…4…5…6…7…8!" Brandon shouted. After the eighth smack, Bex's knees buckled as blood trickled from his nose and mouth. "lift him up! You got 2 more coming!" Brandon said. The 2 agents had to hold Bex to his feet as his head dangled. "Please! No more! Please!" Bex said in a faint voice. The blood and snot had frozen to his face by this time. The black agent had to lift Bex's head up by the chin. "Continue." Brandon said. After the last 2 smacks, the agent's palm turned blood red. "You can take the duffle bag now." Brandon said to Toby. "This is some bullshit!" Toby said as he retrieved the duffle bag. "Bex was unconscious. The 2 agents had to drag him back to his vehicle. As Toby was making his way back to the truck, Brandon called him. "Hey, old man!" Brandon shouted. Toby turned towards him. "If it was up to me, it wouldn't have happened!" Brandon said. Toby just waved him off, and walked away. "Grab the briefcase, and let's get out of here." Brandon said to the agent.

A few days later, Edward the 2nd was in his master bedroom getting dressed for his blind date. He wore a white silk button up shirt, gray silk dress pants with dark gray leather winged tip shoes. There was a knock on the door. "Come in!" Edward the 2nd shouted. Brandon entered the room. "What's up?" Edward the 2nd asked. "Your limo. It's ready. The jet is all revved up, and ready to go." Brandon said. Brandon grabbed his boss's suit jacket from out of the closet.

"Nervous?" Brandon asked. Edward the 2nd turned towards Brandon and sneered at him. "Man, please! I ain't no god damn virgin!" he said to Brandon. Brandon just chuckled. "Did you call my family, and tell'em all to gather at my father's estate tomorrow night?" Edward the 2nd asked. "Already done." Brandon said. "All the envelopes filled?" Edward the 2nd asked. "Everything is done." Brandon said. Edward the 2nd grabbed his gray silk neck tie that was draped over the Victorian chair. It took him less than half a minute to put it on. Brandon assisted him with putting his jacket on. He turned towards Brandon. "How do I look?" he asked. "You look snazzy." Brandon replied. "Snazzy? You sound like an old white man!" Edward the 2nd chuckled. Brandon shook his head laughing. "So, what's the deal with Hakim?" Brandon asked. "It's all taken care of." Edward the 2nd said.

It was around 7:30pm when Edward the 2nd arrived in Hillside, a town 77 miles north of his home in Cherry hill. Just like Bex's truck, his chauffeur driven limo was custom built for his protection. Terrance Haggerty told him that the limo was well equipped the same as the vehicle used to protect the President of the United States. For extra protection, Edward the 2nd was escorted by 2 NA agents.

Moments later, the limo arrived in front of a huge colonial house located on Princeton Avenue. Edward the 2nd lowered the window to get a better look. "Not bad." He said. Here is your bouquet of roses, my lord." Said one of the agents. The other agent hopped out of the limo, and opened the door for his boss. Edward the 2nd exited the limo. "Wish me luck!" he said to the agent. "Good luck, my lord." The agent said. The agent stood by the limo as Edward the 2nd walked towards the property.

The house had beige vinyl siding trimmed in white. The shrubs were well trimmed. There wasn't a drop of snow on the premises. The support columns didn't have a scratch or a sign of chipped paint on them.

Edward the 2nd straightened his neck tie, then rang the doorbell. It had a soothing chiming sound to it. A few seconds passed. Edward the 2nd pressed the doorbell once more. Suddenly, the double doors slowly opened. The head of the Lassenberry organization's breath was taken away by the sight of the beautiful woman standing in the doorway.

Her name was Viola Carr. She stood about 5 and a half feet tall, with an hour glass figure. She had a smooth cocoa complexion. Her wavy jet black hair came down shoulders length. Edward the 2nd stared her down for a moment from head to toe. She wore a tight violet mini dress, with open toe pumps of the same color. Her legs were smooth and flawless. Her voluptuous breasts filled out the dress and then some. Her huge breasts were a sight to see, but it was her dreamy eyes that put Edward the 2nd in a hypnotic trance.

Good evening beautiful! I'm Kray-, I'm Edward of Lassenberry! It's good to finally meet you!" he said as he extended his hand in a friendly gesture. Viola responded by gently shaking his hand, while showing off an alluring smile. "I'm Viola Carr, as you already know! Pleased to finally meet you as well!" she chuckled. "Oh! These are for you! He said as he handed her the bouquet of roses. "Thank you so much!" she said after closing her eyes for a few seconds to take a whiff of the bouquet. "My goodness! Even your voice is beautiful!" he said in a dazed state. Viola giggled as their hands were still locked together. "Jesus! It's cold out here! Come inside so I can grab my coat!" Viola said. Edward the 2nd released her hand and followed her the house. Edward the 2nd quickly turned towards the agent standing outside the limo, giving him a thumb up before closing the door. The agent didn't respond. He just stood there at parade rest.

Inside the house, Viola opened the closet door next to the entrance and grabbed a long length mink coat off the coat rack. Edward the 2nd looked around from where he was standing at the house. He looked impressed on how spacious the house was kept. The house looked spotless from where he stood. The hardwood floors looked like they were just installed. The style of the living room was more Art Deco than anything.

"Let me help you with that, beautiful!" Edward the 2nd said when taking her coat as she donned it. "Thank you." She said. "What's that perfume you're wearing?" he asked. Viola looked nervous for a moment. "why? Is it too much?" she asked. "No! I love it! I would buy it by the case for you!" he said. "Oh, Jesus! A 2-ounce bottle costs a hundred dollars!" Viola said. "Ok then! Make it 2 cases!" he said. Viola started giggling. Edward the 2nd didn't chuckle or smile. "Oh, my god! Are you serious?" Viola shouted. "And to show you how serious I am, let's make it 4 cases." He said. "I can tell you're a wild one!" Viola said as she shook her head smiling. "You only live once." Edward the 2nd said. "Excuse me for a second. Hakeem! Hakeem! Come down stairs!" she screamed at the top of her lungs. At that moment, Edward the 2nd went from a smile to having a scowl on his face. "Hakim? What the hell he is doing here?" Edward the 2nd asked in his regular hood lingo. "What are you talking about?" Viola asked. Suddenly, a tall slim, dark skinned young man came running down the stairs. "Yeah ma, what?" he asked. "Don't what me! I want you to meet my friend!" Viola said. Edward the 2nd buried the scowl on his face to put on a forced smile. "What's up their young man?" Edward the 2nd asked. "Edward. This is my baby Hakeem. Hakeem. This Edward of Lassenberry. Both shook hands. Edward the 2nd felt the young man tightening his grip to express dominance. "You gotta strong grip kid!" Edward the 2nd chuckled. "What kind of name is Edward of Lassenberry?" Hakeem asked. "Mind your manners boy! Viola shouted. "It's cool. It's a long story kid." Edward the 2nd said.

Hakeem stood about a foot taller than Edward the 2nd. His hair was done up in neatly styled corn rolls coming down to his neck. He had a wide nose, his mother's eyes, and a little peach fuzz on his chin. That day, he wore a team jersey, baggie jeans, and tan hiking boots.

"Here! Take these flowers and put them in the vase in the dining room. The green one! Not the clear one!" she said. Hakeem scoffed at the bouquet of roses as he took them away from his mother. "I'll be back before mid-night. So, don't wait up for me." Viola said. "Don't worry young man. I'll have her back home in one piece!" Edward the 2nd said. "Whatever, man." Hakeem said. "Boy! Watch your mouth! I'm not going to tell you again!" Viola shouted. Hakeem stormed out of the living room, heading towards the dining room. "I'm sorry about that." Viola said. "Ah, that's ok! Anybody with an attractive, sexy mom like yourself would feel the same way!" Edward the 2nd chuckled. viola blushed. "Stop it!" she chuckled. "You ready to go?" Edward the 2nd asked. "Yes! I'm starving! Where are, we are going for dinner?" she asked. "I was thinking we do Italian tonight." Edward the 2nd said with a grin on his face. "Ooh, that's nice! Belleville has the best Italian restaurants in North Jersey! Matter of fact, better than the ones in dirty South Jersey!" Viola said. Edward the 2nd started cracking up. "The dirty South Jersey? Why you call it that?" he asked. "That's what the kids around here say now-a-days!" Viola explained. "Well, I have some place else in mind." Edward the 2nd said.

Once outside on the porch, Viola noticed the limo and the man dressed in black standing by the limo. "Wow! You're going all out tonight   ! You've rented a limo, and everything!" she said. Edward the 2nd looked towards viola. "It's not a rental." He said in a cool calm voice. "" What? Get out of here!" she shouted. "No! I'm serious!" Edward the 2nd chuckled. "What about the chauffeur, and the so-called body guard?" Viola asked. "24 hours, 7 days a week, employees." He said. Viola looked impressed. Edward the 2nd put out his arm. Viola wrapped her arm around his arm. They both carefully walked down the flight of stairs arm-in-arm as Edward the 2nd held on to the banister. The agent opened the door for them. 'The heat is blasting inside! You can take off the coat if you'd like!" Edward the 2nd suggested. She thought for a moment, and removed her mink. Viola entered the limo first. Edward the 2nd couldn't stop staring at her round firm ass. He had a look on his face like he had eaten a bowl of wasabi. Edward the 2nd then entered the limo, followed by the agent. The 2 agents sat across from the couple. They were silent and still, with their hands placed flat on their laps, and wearing their dark shades. "Don't they speak?" Viola whispered to Edward the 2nd. "I don't pay them to speak. In fact, I don't pay them at all." Edward the 2nd whispered. "Yeah right!" Viola whispered. "Ok! Don't believe me!" Edward the 2nd whispered. They both chuckled softly. Edward the 2nd grabbed the receiver to the limo phone. The chauffeur picked up the phone on his end. "All right. Take us to the spot." Edward the 2nd ordered. "Yes, my lord." The chauffeur said. Viola couldn't hear the chauffeur's words. She just smiled at her date. Edward the 2nd hung up the phone. The limo drove off.

30 minutes had passed. The limo was a couple of miles from its destination. The couple was engaging in small talk, until Viola changed the conversation. "Where in the world are

we going?" she asked. "You'll see." Edward the 2nd said. Kimberly said you were a nice guy! I hope she wasn't wrong!" Viola said with a nervous smirk. Edward the 2nd looked at Viola. "she said that, for real?" he asked. Viola just nodded her head.

Moments later, Viola noticed that the limo had made a turn down a road heading towards Teterboro Airport. "Why are we headed to Teterboro?" she asked. "You agreed to have Italian food for dinner! So, we're going where the best Italian food is served!" Edward the 2nd said. Viola's eyes had widened. "You're telling me, we're going to Italy?" she asked. Edward the 2nd looked at her and just smiled. "Oh, my God! You better have me back home before the holiday!" she shouted joyfully at the top of her lungs. Once arriving on the tarmac, the limo came to a halt just a few yards away from the private jet that's been used by the family since Eddie Lassenberry. One of the agents sitting across from Viola and Edward the 2nd hopped out and held the door open for them. The couple held hands while making their very short trek to the private jet. One of the NA agents followed close behind. Standing at the doorway of the jet, was a very attractive flight attendant. The sound of the turbines were 10 times quieter than that of a commercial airliner. Edward the 2nd assisted Viola up the stairs. "Welcome aboard Mr. Lassenberry!" the flight attendant said.

Once on board the aircraft, Viola was flabbergasted. "I've been flying first class for years, but this is ridiculous!" she said. The flight attendant smiled. I can give a quick tour of all the accommodations if you like." She said to Viola. "And you are?" Edward the 2nd asked the flight attendant. "Sorry. I'm Tiffany, sir. I will be making your flight as comfortable as I can until you reach your destination." She said as she shook his hand. Seconds later the captain emerged from the cockpit. "Mr. Lassenberry! Welcome aboard! It's an honor to meet you! I'm Tim Gabreski! I'm the captain of this fine piece of machinery!" the captain said with a big smile on his face. He and Edward the 2nd shook hands. "You're an hour early." The captain said. "Fuel is money!" Edward the 2nd chuckled. "We'll be landing at Milan-Malpensa Airport in approximately 8 hours and 30 minutes! Tiffany will make you and your beautiful companion as comfortable as possible during the flight! I'll announce over the PA system when we're ready for takeoff! Enjoy your flight!" captain Gabreski said. He then headed back towards the cockpit. Viola approached Edward the 2nd with a handful of strawberries in a napkin dipped in chocolate she spotted on the table of delectable treats. I know I'm going to spoil my appetite, but I just couldn't resist!" she chuckled.

It was about 2 hours and 20 minutes into the flight. Viola was gazing out the window at the specks of light coming from the ships in the Atlantic. She kicked off her high heels to get more comfortable. Edward the 2nd was in the reclining position next to her fast asleep, snoring like a lion. Tiffany, the flight attendant came over. "Can I get you a drink?" Tiffany asked. Viola noticed that her blouse was unbutton, revealing her lace bra. "Anything you desire. I would be glad to accommodate." The sexy blonde said. Viola looked nervous. "I'm fine for now! Thank you!" Viola stuttered. "Yes, you are!" Tiffany said before walking away. Viola started nudging Edward the 2nd. "Edward! Edward! Wake up!" she frantically whispered. Edward the 2nd jumped out of his slumber. "What? What is it?" he answered in an agitated manner. "Tiffany! The flight attendant! She was coming on to me!" Viola whispered. Edward the 2nd looked down the aisle. He watched for a moment as tiffany was mixing a concoction in the blender. He then turned to Viola. "Hey! Go for it!" he chuckled. Viola jumped back a little. She looked shocked. "What type of woman do you think I am?" she shouted. Edward the 2nd started laughing. "I'm joking! It was a joke! Damn!" he said. He looked at her huge breasts with a smile on his face. He then cleared his throat. "Look at you girl! You are sexy as hell! I'm surprised she didn't come at yo ass sooner!" he chuckled. "Trust me! I'm strictly dickly!" viola said. "Come on now! You don't find her attractive?" he asked. Viola scoffed at the question and turned towards the window. Edward the 2nd looked down the opposite end of the aisle. There, he saw the agent sitting in the same position since the flight began, with his arms on the arm rest, and his dark shades still on. "Goddamn! Are these motherfuckers' human?" he whispered to himself. "What?" Viola asked. "Oh, nothing sweetheart. Just enjoy the flight. I promise you, you're going to have the time of your life." Edward the 2nd said. He reclined his seat as he shut his eyes.

It was 1:30 am Central European Time when Edward the 2nd and party arrived at Milan-Malpensa Airport. Both Edward the 2nd and Viola were fast asleep. "Mr. Lassenberry. Mr. Lassenberry. Mr. Lassenberry. Wake up sir." Tiffany said as she slightly shoved his shoulder. Edward the 2nd made the sound of a pig snorting from his nose as he came out of his slumber. "What, what?" he shouted. "We've arrived sir! The captain will make his announcement momentarily!" she said in a joyful voice. Viola was still sleeping until Edward the 2nd gently tugged on her shoulder. "Beautiful. Beautiful! We're here!" he said. Viola let out a sweet moan as she shifted her head in his direction. Moments later, "This is your captain speaking. Hoped you've enjoyed your flight. Within a few minutes, the hatch to the aircraft will open. Then, you will be able to exit the aircraft safely. Thank you." Gabreski said over the PA system. Tiffany made her way to the cockpit. The NA agent approached his boss. "My lord. Once the hatch is opened, I will proceed to the car rental department. Do you have a preference of what type of vehicle you want, my lord?" the agent asked. "Something roomy!" Edward the 2nd said. "As you wish, my lord." The agent said. The agent went back to his seat. He took out his automatic pistol, placing it in the pouch on the headrest. Edward the 2nd watched, and stormed over to where the agent was. "What are you doing, man? Won't you need that to protect me?" Edward the 2nd shouted. "Forgive me my lord for not informing you sooner. National Agreement regulations forbid me the use of any weaponry within Italian borders. None-the-less, I am permitted to carry a syringe of a non-lethal toxin to incapacitate any threats to your well-being, my lord." The agent said. "Ok. But, just make sure you stay close." Edward the 2nd ordered. "As you wish, my lord." The agent said. Edward the 2nd walked back over to where his date was sitting. "Did that man just call you lord?" Viola asked. Edward the 2nd was hesitant to answer. "Ah, yeah! I sort of come from nobility." Edward the 2nd admitted. "What do you mean, sort of?" she asked. Edward th2nd sighed. "Ok! I am!" he admitted. "How could you be of nobility, and live in America?" Viola asked. Edward the 2nd just scratched his head. "Hell, if I know! Maybe one day, all that will change! Who knows?" he responded. Viola smiled. "I can't believe I'm on a date with royalty!" she said. "Just forget about that for now! Let's get out of here so I can give that real Italian dinner I promised." He said. "Let me run to the bathroom so I can freshen up." Viola said. "Forget about that! I got us a suite at the Bulgari hotel in Milan. I'll take you on a shopping spree in a few hours and then we can have that dinner. Ok?" Edward the 2nd insisted. Viola nodded her head. Edward the 2nd gently grabbed her hand as she stood up from her seat. Moments later, tiffany exits the cockpit. Edward the 2nd and Viola heard the turbines to the aircraft wind down. Captain Gabreski emerged from the cockpit minutes later. Tiffany opened the hatch. The NA agent exited the aircraft. "So, where are you crazy kids off to first?" the captain asked. "We're checking into the Bulgari first, to freshen up. Then I'm taking this beautiful lady here on a shopping spree." Edward the 2nd boasted. "The Brera district is the perfect place for that! You kids enjoy your stay!" Gabreski said as he and Edward the 2nd shook hands. Viola was leaning against a seat to put on her heels.

After minutes of back-n-forth small talk between Edward the 2nd, Viola and Tiffany, a black 2001 Stilo 5-door pulled up next to the jet. The agent exited the vehicle, opening the rear door for its passengers. "That's our que, I guess!" Viola said. "We'll be here! Fueled up, and ready to go, once you've returned!" Tiffany said with a smile. Unknown to Viola, Edward the 2nd tried his luck by brushing up against Tiffany's breasts before exiting the aircraft. There was no negative reaction from the sexy flight attendant. This put a big smile on his face.

It was around 3am on Thanksgiving Day, when Bex was at his home in Bridgeton, New Jersey. There was a short elderly dark skinned woman in the kitchen preparing food for the holiday dinner. Her name was Claudette Rouzier. She was of Haitian descent. She had prepared a combination of traditional American and Haitian cuisine for the holiday dinner. Diri ak Djon-djon and Tasso Ham were the main course for the Haitian dishes.

Down the hall, Bex was sitting in the living room on his leather recliner applying petroleum jelly to his wounds as he watched TV. The entire right side of his was still bruised from the beating received by the NA agent. He frowned from the pain as he gently smeared it underneath his eye and jaw. Moments later, Claudette had entered the room. "Excuse me Mr. Xavier. Both the ham and turkey are in the oven. I've made my famous soup Joumou." She said in a thick Haitian accent. He looked up at her with a painful frown on his face. "What the hell is Joumou?" he asked. She scoffed at his question. "You Yankees! Here in America they call it Pumpkin soup!" she said. Bex just nodded his head as he glared at the TV. "Is your son coming with his wife and new baby, like he said he was?" Bex asked. "Don't worry Mr. Xavier! He'll be here!" she chuckled. "It's important that he's does. I know it's the holiday, but I need all my people here tonight." Bex said. Claudette placed her hand on his shoulder. "Is there anything I can get you while I'm in the kitchen, like an ice pack?" she asked. "Thank you. Please." Bex said.

Claudette's son André was the biggest marijuana dealer in South Jersey. He'd just recently fell under the thumb of Bex's faction of the Lassenberry organization. After serving a few months in jail for assault with a deadly weapon, he was released having all his property and businesses seized and ordered by the judge to be deported back to Port-au-Prince, Haiti. Since he was very prosperous at distributing pot, Hakim and Bex bribed the judge with a duffle bag filled with cash to grant André and his mother permanent citizenship to the United States. Having to start over, André had to kick up 30 percent a month to Bex because it was his territory now. He also had to kick up 7 percent to Hakim for services rendered. After the demise of Buddy, and a few other cocaine and pots dealers in the region, André pulled in about a quarter of a million dollars' months after his release from prison.

It was around 1pm when guests started pouring in. Claudette, with Bex's assistance, had set up the food buffet style. 2 long folding tables, with the combined length of 20 feet were covered with a custom-made table cloth having Autumn leaf patterns. Bex's new home had a dining room big enough to hold the 2 buffet tables and another to hold a 20-foot solid oak table for the guests.

Toby, Jenny, Calvin, and Calvin's girlfriend Tamika were already at the house when André and his crew arrived. One of the crew members nick-named Frenchie, was from Camden, New Jersey. He had a reputation of being a hot head, as well as smoking as much pot to the people he sold it to. Even though he was of Haitian descent, people would assume he was Jamaican because of his long thick dread locks and his signature tie-dye shirts. Another crew member they called Peau Claire was a tall light skinned brother who ran pounds of marijuana back-n-forth though Ocean, Cape May, and Atlantic County to small time dealers. Despite not being of Haitian descent, he was an asset to André. Remy, another runner for André, was a 25-year-old brother whose parents came from Les Cayes had terrible social skills, but was quick with a gun. He ran pot in the remaining counties in Bex's territory. He didn't except excuses of customers coming up short with the cash. He would follow them home or wherever, until he received full payment for the product. One time he had sold a couple of pounds of pot to a group of college kids. They were a hundred dollars short. Remy held them hostage in one of the kid's dorm room until one of them came back and kicked up the money.

It was about an hour later when a man named Darnell Bradley walked in the house. Darnell used to be a runner for Buddy. When Buddy and the rest of the big-time dealers in South Jersey met their demise, Darnell was the first to run to Bex and Hakim offering his services. Not only was Darnell a runner, but he was a chemist. He knew how to cut the cocaine down so well; a pure kilo would quadruple in price at the street level. Hakim and Bex just started using him instead of using the Lassenberry safe house as a headquarters to cut the product. Darnell kept his method to himself. Not even Hakim nor Bex knew how he processed the product. He was their close guarded secret. Hakim knew if Butch and Mookie got wind of this golden goose, Darnell would probably be kidnapped by them and forced to process the product for their own self-interest. Darnell didn't even have a body guard watching his back. He was a loner in the lab, which took longer to process then if he had a team like the safe houses in North Jersey. Most of the customers in South Jersey were from poor urban and rural areas. The low quality of product made the high shorter to the point customers would come running back to the dealers even faster.

Moments later, Bex's top dealers had arrived. Kyle, Jason, and a guy known as white guy Gonzo. Rumor had it that Gonzo had sick methods of dealing with snitches. Most of these rumors were brought on by Gonzo himself to put fear in those he sold the product to. Kyle, Jason and Gonzo Were the faces of South Jersey. Far as the public knew, they ran the region in coke dealing. As far as Kyle, Jason and Gonzo knew, Bex was at the top of the Pyramid of power.

When Darnell came on board from runner to chemist, addicts gave the name Dirty South Jersey to the region because of its low quality of cocaine. This quality was as cheap as crack without the side effects. The ingredients Darnell used to cut the product was organic based, meaning it was less lethal unlike the chemicals used to make crack. Hakim still sold high quality product in Essex County. He just received 30 grand a week from South Jersey to keep the well-guarded secret.

Clint Rupert, who used to be Bex's mother old boyfriend arrived bearing a gift for Bex. Unknown to the crew, Bex used Clint as a courier to distribute their low-grade product beyond Bex's territory. Clint used his trucking business to sell the product as far as the mid-west. This was a big violation in the Lassenberry organization going back to the time Eddie Lassenberry took the oath with the National Agreement. The National Agreement were involved in the trafficking of Heroin for the most part. But, breaking the rules could start a chain reaction into the heroin, marijuana, and pill business. If Terrance Haggerty got wind of such an operation, Edward the 2nd would be the notified. It would be up to him to decide the fate of his South Jersey general.

Bex was in the game room with Toby and the crew. Clint entered the room greeting everyone. In his hand were 3 bottles of wine. "Happy Thanksgiving kid!" Clint chuckled as he handed Bex the bottles. Bex gave Clint a big hug. "So, when do we chow down?" Clint asked. "We got a couple of more people coming." Bex said. "Let me get one of them bottles Clint!" Toby said. "Man! You don't need no more to drink! You already staggering now!" Bex said. "Nigga! It's the holiday season! This is when you supposed to get fucked up!" Toby said. The guys in the crew started cracking up. Bex looked embarrassed. "What the hell happened to you?" Clint asked Bex as he gently touched the side of his bruised face. "Let's go into the other room, man." Bex said to Clint. "Who the hell are we waiting for? I'm starving!" Clint said. "Come on, old man." Bex said. Bex and Clint enter one of the many rooms in Bex's new home, which happened to belong to his former nemesis, Buddy.

When Clint and Bex were alone, Bex explained in detail what happened to him. "Jesus kid! When you're involved in this world, you gotta know everything moves fast! You can't be slacking off!" Clint said. "Yeah! Yeah! I got the message." Bex said. "I got a million big ones out in the truck for you!" Clint said. "That's what I'm talking about!" Bex said as he rubbed his hands together. "Them people out in God's country love that shit as much as meth!" Clint said. "The good thing about it, that it's all mine! All my shit! I can't believe just a year ago I was living in a shack doing odd jobs! Now, I'm a fucking millionaire!" Bex whispered. Clint put his hand on Bex's shoulder. "Enjoy the rewards son. But, be very careful." Clint said. Clint and Bex leave the room.

The house had a den. In the den, Jenny and her future daughter-in-law Tamika were smoking weed together from a bong. "I miss Peggy. She was like a sister to me. We used to have a lot of fun." Jenny said after taking a hit from the bong. Suddenly, there was a knock on the door. "You can come in!" Jenny shouted. In came Frenchie. "Se konsa, sa a se kote pati a reyèl k ap pase!" Frenchie said. "What you just say?" Tamika asked. "That's that Haiti creole girl! You need to know!" Frenchie chuckled. Frenchie then pulled out a fat joint and lit it. "What you ladies in here chatting about?" Frenchie asked. "Bex's mother. She was the coolest, down-to-earth white chick I've ever met." Jenny said. "I heard, man. That's fucked up about what happened to Annie too." Frenchie said. "I don't wanna talk about that!" Jenny said as she shut her eyes. "It's funny how life works out though! If it wasn't that, we all wouldn't be here together!" Tamika said. "Yes!" Frenchie said as he looked Tamika up-n-down. "Ooh! I gotta use the toilet!" Jenny said. Jenny gave Tamika the bong, then ran out of the room, leaving the 2 alone. Frenchie moved in closer to Tamika. "So, when is the wedding?" Frenchie asked. "June! I always wanted to be a June bride!" she said with a big smile on her face. "So, Calvin is the one? Huh?" Frenchie asked. Tamika nodded in a hesitant motion. "That's not a look of confidence, man." He said. "What about you? Where's Mrs. Frenchie?" she asked.

Back in the living room, Bex and Clint were talking about how Bex remodeled the place. "3o grand! Hakim hooked me up, man! He said I didn't have to pay him back!" Bex said. "How's he doing?" Clint asked. "He's still fucked up over losing a couple of his guys from his crew!" Bex said as he shook his head. The other guys came out of the game room laughing, making all sorts of ruckus. "When we're gonna eat, man?" André shouted. Suddenly there was a knock on the door. Bex rushed over to open the door. André ran past him. "I got it boss man!" he said. Once the door opened, Hakim came in with his arms spread eagle. In one hand, he had an open bottle of champagne. "Happy Thanksgiving mother fuckers!" Hakim shouted. "Speak of the devil!" Clint whispered. A few of the guys came running up to Hakim to greet him. Claudette came out of the kitchen to see what the commotion was all about. "Now, we can eat!" she said to herself with a smile on her face. Frenchie and Tamika come out of the den, into the living room as well. "The man is here!" Frenchie said to himself. "That must be the one and only Hakim, huh?" Tamika asked. "Yeah." Frenchie said as he rolled his eyes.

Standing behind Hakim was Chewie. He wore all black, with a long black leather coat and dark shades. Bex approached his brother, giving him a firm hug. Hakim gave his brother a kiss on the cheek. Hakim rubbed the petroleum jelly from his lips. "You ok, man?" Hakim asked. Bex just nodded his head in shame.

Out of respect, Bex's crew even Frenchie, were expected to greet Hakim when he entered the room. As shy as Remy was, he even approached hakim with a hand shake, and bowing his head as if Hakim was royalty.

"Everything good with you, brother?" Bex asked Hakim. "Where's the TV? Let me show you something!" Hakim said. Both Bex and Hakim walked through the crowd over to the other side of the room. "That's messed up what happened to Gunz and Mackie, man." Bex said. Hakim grabbed the remote from off the fire place mantle. He clicked on the TV. On the TV, breaking news flashed across the screen. *"This is Gloria Becker reporting live outside of Sangiero's Café in East Orange, where we've been reporting all day the gruesome slaying of reputed Sicilian mob boss Fernando Domenico. Police have taped off the crime scene hours ago. Authorities have said what's so bizarre about this crime was that the suspect happened to be a little boy, no older than 9 or 10 years old just walked into the café witnesses said, and pulled out an ice pick and started jabbing the alleged mob boss in the neck several times. When witnesses apprehended the child, it's reported that the unidentified child was in a trance of some sort. The reporter walked over to one of the by standers in the crowd, which happened to be a white male of Italian descent. "Sir. Could you tell me your thoughts that brought on this horrific crime?" Gloria Becker asked. "I…I don't know nothing! All I know is this is a nice quiet part of town! Everyone gets along! I…I just don't know how something so tragic could have happened!*

Especially on thanksgiving!" The man said shaking his head. The man was so distraught, he just walked away from the camera. *"I could only imagine how shaken up the people are on this Thanksgiving Day, in this quiet section of East Orange, New Jersey."* Gloria Becker said. Hakim clicked off the TV.

Hakim looked at his brother with a smile on his face. Bex looked confused. "What was that all about?" Bex asked. "That, my brother, is what happens when someone pisses me off!" Hakim chuckled. "Come everyone! Let's feast!" Claudette shouted. "Let's celebrate brother. Let's eat." Hakim whispered. He gave Bex another kiss on the cheek.

— CHAPTER 22. THE BREAD WINNER —

Returning to the Bulgari hotel after a night on the town and a late dinner, Viola decided to call her son to check in on him. "That's messed up ma! You're supposed to be here over at grandma's, instead of running around with that clown!" Hakeem shouted. Friends and family of Hakeem stopped what they were doing for a moment when being distracted by his shouting. "Listen, young man! I'm the parent! If I wanna go out on a date, whether it's Thanksgiving, Christmas, or Hanukah, I'm going to go out on a date! Now, you tell grandma and the family I said hi, and I'll be over her house in the morning! And don't forget to make me a plate! I love you!" Viola said. She hangs up. Edward the 2nd raised an eyebrow with a smirk on his face. Viola took a deep breath. She puts her hands on her hips. "That boy is my world, but he drives me crazy sometimes!" she said. Edward the 2nd walked over to the sound system and turned the dial, flipping through radio stations until he came upon some classical music. He turned up the volume, and then swaggered his way over to his sexy date. He then loosened his neck-tie. "I appreciate the outfits you bought me." Viola said. "What about the shoes?" Edward the 2nd asked. "Oh, I can't forget the 20 pairs of shoes!" she sighed. Edward the 2nd moved in closer to viola. "You know what I like best?" she said. "What's that?" Edward the 2nd asked as he gently grabbed her hands. "I have to say; the food was all that! That, what was it? Risotto alla Milanese, was delicious!" she said. Edward the 2nd gave her a gentle kiss on the neck. "Ok. You need to slow it down!" Viola said as she took a step back. "Come on, now! You're smelling all good! Looking all sexy! What you thought was gonna happen?" Edward the 2nd chuckled. "No! What do you think is gonna happen?" she said. Edward the 2nd moved in closer. He put his hands around her waist. "Didn't you have a good time out here, baby?" he asked. She grabbed his hands, putting them to his side. "Listen. I appreciate the shopping spree and the fine dining, even the trip itself, but you're moving too fast, now!" Viola said. Edward the 2nd went from smiling to having a serious look on his face. "I think you fail to realize who I am. I ain't no regular, simple brother from the streets." He said. "I thank you for the date, but we need to get back on that jet, like now!" viola said in a serious tone. He pulled her in closer to his body. He grabbed one of her breasts. She pushed him back. As she pushed Edward the 2nd back, he grabbed her dress, exposing her huge breasts. Viola covered her breasts with her hands, which didn't help much to hide them. "Shit woman! Damn you fine as hell!" he shouted as rubbed on his private parts. "Listen! I'm going into the bathroom to fix my dress! When I come out, that jet better be revved up and ready to go! I'm serious!" Viola shouted. She stormed out of the living room, straight to the bathroom. She locked the door. Edward the 2nd went over to the bathroom door, and started banging on it. "Come on! I was just playing!" he shouted. He continued to bang on the door. She didn't answer. "Oh, it's like that now?" he shouted. "This bitch ain't gotta clue who she's dealing with!" Edward the 2nd whispered to himself. "Alright! I'm calling the airport right now!" he shouted. Inside the bathroom, viola stood in front of a mirror with a gold-leaf frame. Her mascara began to run down her cheeks as she tried to stuff her breasts back into her dress. "Why did I come out here? Why did come out here? Shit!" she whispered to herself.

15 minutes had passed. Viola just flushed the toilet. She spent most of the time in there pacing in circles. She slowly unlocked the door. To her surprise, she came out of the bathroom to see Edward the 2nd sitting in the living, on the plush sofa, naked. He had his legs crossed, with a big smile on his face. "Have you lost your fucking mind?" Viola shouted. Before she could utter another word, her vision went blurry. She collapsed into the arms of the NA agent. "Take her ass into the bedroom!" Edward the 2nd said. "Yes, my lord." The agent said. The agent tossed the empty syringe on the glass coffee table. He threw viola over his shoulder, taking her to the bedroom.

Once in the bedroom, the agent gently laid Viola on the bed, face up. Edward the 2nd's eyes were wide as saucers. He started salivating. "What the fuck you waiting for? Get that fucking dress off her ass!" Edward the 2nd shouted as he started to masturbate. "Yes, my lord." The agent said. The agent slid the dress off her with ease. Edward the 2nd was prepping himself to take the unconscious victim. His face began twitching. When Edward the 2nd had his last encounter with Terrance Haggerty, not only did he force Edward the 2nd to slurp up his vomit off the desk, Haggerty reneged on his ultimatum to Edward the 2nd by bending him over the desk. One of the NA agents had held his face down on the desk. Terrance dropped his trousers down to his ankles. Chuckling like a mad man, Terrance loosened his victim's belt and unzipped his pants. He then yanked Edward the 2nd's pants down to around his ankles. Edward the 2nd began screaming and pleading with Terrance not to violate him. The more Edward the 2nd begged to be spared from a humiliating ordeal, the louder Terrance began chuckling.

Just the thought of Terrance's sexual assault made it almost impossible for Edward the 2nd to get an erection. "Get the fuck out!" Edward the 2nd shouted. "Yes, my lord." The agent said. The agent exited the bedroom, closing the door behind him. Edward the 2nd spread Viola's legs open by her ankles. He jumped on the bed, between her legs. He then ripped off her panties, throwing them on the floor. He continued to masturbate, stroking his flaccid penis next to her clitoris. Viola's body was near perfection. This did not help Edward the 2nd's erection at first. He had to use his imagination to ensure the sexual act. Visions of his cousin's wife entered his mind. Kimberly's dreadlocks were flowing freely as she laid her naked body next to Viola, caressing her huge breasts. The illusion of the 2 beautiful women tonguing each other caused Edward the 2nd to become fully erect.

He then rammed his penis inside of Viola's vagina. There was no making love here. Love had nothing to do with what he was doing. It was pure primal, without concern of consequence. He envisioned Kimberly egging him on to sexually conquer Viola's motionless body. "Come on! Come on!" he whispered to himself in a rage of lust. 5 minutes had passed when Edward the 2nd let out a loud horrific moan as he came to completion inside of Viola. Heavily breathing, he rested his head between her breasts for a moment. Once he raised his head, the vision of Kimberly had vanished. He then rolled over next to Viola, lying on his back. He sat up, then scooched over to the edge of the king size bed. The only sound in the bedroom was Viola's breathing. Edward the 2nd stood up to leave the bedroom. Standing outside the bedroom at parade rest was the NA agent. Edward the 2nd smiled at the agent. He put his hand on the agent's shoulder. "You're a robot! You know a lot of shit! What they call it when a man is beaten down by someone to feel like less of a man?" Edward the 2nd asked. "I guess you're referring to being emasculated, my lord." The agent said. Edward the 2nd smacked the agent on the shoulder. "What I just did in there, is what you do when you feel emasculated! See! I knew you were good for something other than carrying my bags!" Edward the 2nd chuckled. the agent didn't utter a response. "Listen. I'm going in the other room to lay down. Order room service at 5:30 am. Wake me up at 5:45. Make sure the jet is ready for take-off by 7:30." Edward the 2nd said. Very well, my lord." The agent said. "Oh! Make sure you lay out one of those outfits I bought her next to her on the bed." Edward the 2nd said. "Yes, my lord." The agent said.

It was 8:00 am, Central European time. Viola was slowly coming out of her slumber. She stretched her arms out wide as she yawned. It didn't take long for her to realize that she wasn't back at the hotel, but reclined back in one of the seats on the private jet. She went into a frenzy when she also realized that she had on a different outfit. She had on a tight sleeveless pink turtle neck sweater, a black skirt, that came down to her knees and a pair of black leather boots. She rubbed her body as her eyes teared up. She looked out the window of the jet. She saw Edward the 2nd shaking hands with a group of white men in suits who looked of some importants. Viola moved her seat upright. She got up and ran towards the hatch. Before she could get to the hatch, the NA agent stopped her. "Sorry ma'am. My orders were to keep you on the aircraft until we return to the United States." The agent said. "I wanna talk to that asshole out there! You better let me pass before I kick you in the balls!" Viola screamed. "It's fair to warn you ma'am, that I am highly trained in 5 forms of Martial Arts. Your actions would be futile." The agent said. Viola looked at the agent. She took a couple of steps back. "Please ma'am. Take a seat. Lord Lassenberry will be with you momentarily." the agent said. Viola, with fear in her eyes, slowly walked back to her seat as she kept her eye on the agent. Her purse was in the seat next to her. She searched through her purse and found her mobile phone. Unfortunately, her phone had no power. She then grabbed the aircraft's phone on the armrest. The phone's power was also down. In a fit of rage, she threw the phone across the aisle. The NA agent didn't flinch or react in any way. He just stood there at parade rest.

Moments later, Edward the 2nd boarded the aircraft. He had a big smile on his face. He walked to the back of the aircraft, towards Viola. "Damn! It's good to be me!" Edward the 2nd said as he rubbed his hands together. "Good morning beautiful!" Edward the 2nd said. Before he could blink, Edward the 2nd received a hard smack across the face, forcing him back into the seat across the aisle. His smile turned into a look of fury. The NA agent came running down the aisle. He grabbed Viola, restraining her from attacking Edward the 2nd. "Get your fucking hands off me!" Viola screamed. Edward the 2nd massaged the side of his face. "It's ok! It's ok! You can let her go!" Edward the 2nd chuckled. the agent released Viola and backed away. Viola started shaking. "What the hell did you do to me?" she cried as she fell back into her seat. Edward the 2nd took a deep breath. He sat down next to her, looking confident. "All you need to know, is that we had fun last night. That's our story when we get back to the states." Edward the 2nd said with a big smile. Viola began hyperventilating. "Why? Why me?" she cried. Edward the 2nd shook his head. "Kimberly told you I was a nice guy, and that's true! But, what she didn't tell you, is that I'm in a position that I can do anything I want. Anything! You see those men out there walking away from the jet? Well, one of those men is the president of this region of Italy. I don't know how he knew who I was, but he thanked me for being partially responsible for getting rid of a problem." Edward the 2nd chuckled.

Umberto Berlusconi was the man who headed the group walking away from the private jet. He was the president of Lombardy. It was one of the 20 regions in Italy. A region that Sicilian mob boss, Fernando Domenico wanted to control. Based on rumors spread by conspiracy theorists, Don Domenico's 10-year-old assassin was part of the MK Ultra program. The main stream media quickly denounced the conspiracy. Berlusconi and Domenico were third cousins, twice removed.

It was 8:35pm Eastern Standard time, when Edward the 2nd's private jet landed at Teterboro Airport. "Home sweet home." Edward the 2nd said to himself. Sitting on the other side of the aisle, balled up in the fetal position, viola just stared at Edward the 2nd with hate in her eyes. Edward the 2nd stood up. "Come on. Get your stuff. Let's go." He said to her. Viola slowly left her seat. Tiffany the flight attendant approached Viola with a smile on her face. "May I help you with your bags?" she asked. Viola put her face about 3 inches away from Tiffany's face. "Call the police! I think I was raped!" Viola whispered. Tiffany's facial expression didn't change one bit. She had a beautiful smile from ear-to-ear. "I hope you enjoyed Milan! It was nice meeting you!" Tiffany said. She didn't break her smile at all, as if it was programmed in her to do so. Viola looked terrified. She pushed Tiffany out of the way, heading towards the hatch. Tiffany did her job by grabbing the bags of clothes and shoes Edward the 2nd had purchased. After shaking hands with Captain Gabreski, Edward the 2nd exited the aircraft. Viola walked about 5 feet ahead of him and the agent. "Slow down, woman!" Edward the 2nd chuckled. Edward the 2nd was surprised to see Viola scurry across the tarmac, pass the limo. The weather was brisk that night. Viola folded her arms, trying her best to keep warm. "Hey! Where you going? You left your coat in the limo!" Edward the 2nd shouted. Edward the 2nd licked his lips as he watched Viola walk across the tarmac. "God damn! She is sexy as hell! Bring her ass back to the limo!" he said to the agent. "Yes, my lord." The agent said. With haste, the agent went to pursue Viola. Before Viola could get to the hangar, the agent swooped her off her feet, carrying her with one arm while pinning her wrists together to keep from attacking him. He took her back to the limo. The chauffeur, who happened to be another agent quickly opened the back-passenger door. Viola was gently tossed inside. Edward the 2nd entered on the opposite side of the vehicle. He closed his door. The agent hopped in and closed the door on Viola's side. The doors automatically locked. Viola sat as far away from Edward the 2nd as she could. Viola was shaking like a cornered animal, with tears trickling down her cheeks. Edward the 2nd leans back with his legs spread open, looking relaxed. "Here's the deal beautiful. You're gonna go back home with a smile on your face. If anyone asks how was your date, you're gonna say it was the best time of your life. Don't bother running to the police, because they can't help you. They won't help you. Don't go back and tell Kimberly, because she can't help you. Understand? Nod your head if you understand." Edward the 2nd said. Viola frantically nodded. "Just to make sure you keep your word; you'll be under surveillance until I say different. I'll be coming through from time-to-time to check on you. The next time I come over to your place, that son of yours will show me respect. To sum it all up, you're my woman now." Edward the 2nd said. At that moment, another vehicle pulled up next to the limo. It was a black Boeman SUV. An agent of African American descent hopped out of the vehicle. "My chauffeur will take you home. I'll see you, when I see you." Edward the 2nd said. He leaned over to give Viola a kiss. She flinched. He missed his shot to kiss her. He smiled. "You'll come around. Bye beautiful." He said. The agent hopped out of the limo. The chauffeur opened the door for his boss. "Make sure all her gifts are loaded up. Carry them in the house for her too." Edward the 2nd said to the chauffeur. "Yes, my lord." The chauffeur said. "Alright! Get me back to the castle!" Edward the 2nd shouted. Viola wiped the tears from her eyes as she watched Edward the 2nd hop in the back seat of the SUV. The chauffeur popped the trunk of the limo and loaded all the shopping bags with the help of tiffany.

A few hours later, the SUV pass through the gates of castle Lassenberry. Edward the 2nd hopped in the passenger side of a golf cart. "Take me to my office, man! Chop-chop!" he ordered. Another agent, who was Caucasian, hopped in the driver's seat. They drove over the mote, through the main entrance.

Minutes later, Edward the 2nd was dropped off in front of his office. Standing on either side of the door were 2 agents. One of them opened the door for him. He then entered the office. Edward the 2nd took off his suit jacket. He then loosened his neck tie. To his surprise, there was a plate of food on his desk with an empty wine glass and a bottle of cider next to it. "What the fuck?" he said to himself. Suddenly, there was a knock on the door. "Come in!" he shouted. Brandon entered the room with a smile on his face. "Happy late Thanksgiving!" Brandon shouted. Edward the 2nd looked at the plate of food. He noticed steam rising from the food. "I nuked it in the microwave! Didn't have time to do it the conventional way." Brandon said. Edward the 2nd looked at the food. He looked at his desk. He looked at the food again. Feeling nauseous, he covered his mouth. "Get that shit out of here! From now on, don't bring any food in here!" Edward the 2nd said. "What's wrong? You got mac-n-cheese, Collard greens, stuffing!" Brandon said. Before he could finish running down the list of what was on the plate, Edward the 2nd took the plate of food, and threw it across the room. "When I say get that shit out of here, I mean it, man!" he shouted. "You ok?" Brandon asked. "Never mind that shit! You arranged the meeting with me and my family?" Edward the 2nd asked. "Yeah, but a few of your cousins just blew me off." Brandon said. "Who? Who the fuck ain't coming?" Edward the 2nd shouted. "Tyson, Benny the 3rd, Joe-Joe and Malcolm said all they wanted was their envelopes." Brandon said. Edward the 2nd put his index finger in Brandon's face. "You call them back! Tell them they ain't receiving shit unless they come to the meeting!" he shouted. "I'll try to change their minds, but!" Brandon said. "But nothing! I run this organization now! I'm the bread winner up in this motherfucker! You go make that call again! Everybody, at my father's house tomorrow at noon! Send Lucy in here to clean up this shit on the floor! Now go!" Edward the 2nd shouted. "Long live the house of Lassenberry. Long live Edward the 2nd." Brandon mumbled before leaving the office.

Edward the 2nd stood there alone staring at his desk with the look of disgust on his face. He walked to the door. He opened it. "Listen! I want somebody in here to get rid of this desk by tomorrow and get me a brand new one! A bigger one!" He said. "Yes, my lord." One of the agents said.

The next morning, around 9:36 am Hakim stood over a tombstone shaped like a cross. It was windy and frigid that morning. Hakim had his arms folded to keep warm even though he wore a thick leather coat. The tombstone was located on the grounds of Eternal Life Cemetery in Newark, New Jersey. The tombstone had the portrait of a beautiful African American girl imbedded in it. In loving memory of Kenya Green. Jan 1966- June 1984, the words were inscribed. Hakim rubbed his hand across the top of the tombstone to remove the snow and frost. Standing about 50 feet away was Chewie. He was keeping a watchful eye out for Hakim's safety, at the same time giving him his privacy.

"It's been a long time. I know I should've stopped by sooner. But, I had to get my priorities straight." Hakim said as he stared at the tombstone. Hakim looked around the cemetery to see who was in listening range. There was young black couple off in the distance, where the man was consoling the woman. Hakim looked down at the tombstone. He took a deep breath. The cold air gushed from his mouth. "The real reason is…I was scared!" he said while wiping away his tears. "This might sound silly as shit, but I always thought we'd be married and all that, after high school. I thought about that shit since the fight in the cafeteria. When I let you keep my jewelry that day, I knew you was the one! I sure did. Shit! The world ain't safe no more. We got terrorists flying planes into buildings. I'm sure you probably know that. Know what? Between me and you, I want to get in the ground with you. God damn! I got all this money, and every nigga in Essex County kissing my ass. For some reason, I still feel like shit!" Hakim said. Suddenly, Hakim went from feeling sorrowful, to downright angry. "Check this shit out! I'm taking orders from this punk bitch half a man, all because he's a Lassenberry-n-shit!" Hakim said. He reached inside his coat pocket, and pulled out a blunt. The blunt looked like it was smoked prior to Hakim coming to the cemetery. Hakim lit it, and took a long drag from it. "I gotta go. But before I go! I just wanna say…I'm sorry." He said before taking another hit from the blunt. Hakim turned towards Chewie. "Yo! Go start the car up!" Hakim shouted. Hakim then turned to the tombstone. He gently rubbed his hand across the smooth surface. "I'll see you again." He said.

Elsewhere, at the estate of Jake Lassenberry sr., Most of the adults in the Lassenberry family had gathered in the entertainment room. In this room, Jake sr., had the same set up as his younger brother Mark sr., but minus the cigar bar. Janis Hernandez Lassenberry, Jake's second wife, who was dressed in a pink jumpsuit, and her long brown hair put into a ponytail, was walking around the room making sure the family members had enough to drink and had their fill of snacks. Maggie went over to her. "You sure you don't need any help? Where's Edwidge?" Maggie asked. "She's still visiting relatives in Haiti. But, believe me, I have it under control!" Janis said. "Where's that brother of mine?" Maggie asked. "He's out by the pool with Big L." Janis said. "Outside? It's freezing out there!" Maggie said.

Standing out in the cold pool side, was Jake sr. smoking a cigar, dressed in jeans and a thick sweater. His middle son, Big L was gulping down a beer. "Krayton? Krayton pop?" Big L said with a surprised look on his face. "That's what I said when I first heard!" Jake sr. said. "What you think happened to Mark?" Big L asked. "I don't know! Your aunt Tasha said his father went into the hospital this morning. It's his heart. Things don't look good, she said. I'm gonna stop by the hospital after this meeting with your brother." Jake sr. said.

At the estate, the family members were waiting for Edward the 2nd to arrive. His father, his 2 brothers Jake Jr. and Big L., his aunts Lula and Maggie, his cousins' BB, Donald, Mike Abbey, his uncle Danny Sr. and Terry showed up to represent her father Mark Sr. and her brother Corey, who was at the hospital tending to his father.

It was around 12:34 when a Boeman SUV pulled up to the estate. 3 NA agents get out of the vehicle. One of the agents opened the rear passenger door, allowing Brandon and Edward the 2nd to step out. Brandon wore a brown 2-piece suit and wool overcoat, while Edward the 2nd wore his uniform with red and green sashes. He had all 3 medals pinned on his chest earned by his uncle and cousin. At the last moment, under Brandon's orders, Stephen the clothing designer made Edward the 2nd a custom black leather trench coat similar in design to his uniform. Maggie ran to the back yard after hearing the SUV pull up. "He's here!" Maggie shouted. Jake Sr. and Big L leave the backyard and enter the house through the back door. The Lassenberry family stood in a semi-circle at the front entrance as Janis went to open the door. The first to step through the door was one of the NA agents. The Caucasian agent did a quick surveillance of the immediate area for security reasons before allowing Edward the 2nd to enter the house. "Wow.! These dudes are serious as hell!" Big L whispered to his father. The agent walked back to the front entrance. "All is clear!" he said to those outside. One agent strolled around the estate towards the rear of the house to stand guard. Another agent stood outside the front entrance, standing guard, while the agent that did surveillance inside stood behind Edward the 2nd and Brandon. Jake Sr. approached his son with a proud smile on his face. He put his hands on his son's shoulders. "Long live the House of Lassenberry. Long live Edward the 2nd." Jake Sr. said before giving his son a hug. "Good to see ya pop." Edward the 2nd said. Terry ran to Brandon, giving him a kiss on his lips. "Not now sweetie! I'm on the clock right now!" Brandon whispered to Terry. Terry nodded. "Sorry sweetie!" she whispered as she stepped back amongst her relatives. Brandon was carrying an attaché case. "What's up my people? Sorry for not showing up for the holiday, but certain changes needed to be taken care of first! The good news is, I have the envelopes with me! Brandon." Edward the 2nd said. Brandon reached inside the attaché case, pulling out a handful of thick envelopes. Each envelope had the names of the family members stamped on it. Edward the 2nd stepped toward his cousin Terry. He gave her a hug and a kiss on the cheek. "Hey cuz! I hope uncle Mark is feeling better." He said. Edward the 2nd leaned in closer to his cousin. "Your brother is safe. Just keep quiet about it for now." He whispered in Terry's ear. Terry nodded her head. "Hey, man! I thought we were close. Why didn't you come to me first about the change in command? What the hell is wrong with you?" Jake Jr. shouted. The NA agent stepped in between Edward the 2nd and his brother. "It's ok. My brother wouldn't dare lay a hand on me. Would you, brother?" Edward the 2nd said. The room was silent. "Would you, brother?" Edward the 2nd said again. Jake Jr. looked over towards his father. "Answer him, son!" Jake Sr. shouted. Jake Jr. put his head down. "You know i would never hurt you." Jake Jr. said. "Good! Now Brandon will call out your names, so you can get your envelopes!" Edward the 2nd said. "Ok. Larry! Lula! Donald!" Brandon shouted as each family member stepped forward to receive an envelope with 9 thousand dollars in cash. "Where is Tyson, Malcolm, Joe-joe and dear old cousin Benny? I thought I gave the order for them to be here!" Edward the 2nd shouted. Maggie approached her nephew. "Don't be too upset with them Krayton!" Maggie said. Edward the 2nd shook his head in disbelief. "What did you call me, auntie? He asked with rage in his voice. Maggie sighed. "I meant to say, Edward the 2nd!" she said. "That's better, auntie." Edward the 2nd said. "It's going to take some time for them to except that you're in charge of the family fortune now!" Maggie explained. "Ok! I want all y'all to listen up! Since my cousins don't respect my authority, I'm cutting their asses off for good! No Money! No protection! No nothing!" Edward the 2nd shouted. "You need to stop it! It's not that serious!" Maggie said. "Well, since you gave birth to those disrespectful motherfuckers, you'll be cut loose, just like them, auntie!" Edward the 2nd said as he snatched his aunt Maggie's envelope out of her hand. "Danny Sr. lunged at his nephew. The Agent and Brandon jumped in between them. "I don't care who you are now! Don't ever disrespect the elders in this family!" Danny Sr. shouted. "You can get cut off too, uncle Danny! Don't make me call off the search for Danny Jr. and Samara!" Edward the 2nd shouted. Danny Sr. backed off with a defeated look on his face. Janis came forward. "You're wrong! You're wrong for coming in my home with this attitude, and for disrespecting your aunt and uncle like that!" Janis said. Edward the 2nd scoffed at his stepmom. "Pop! I think You better handle your wife!" Edward the 2nd said. Jake Sr. looked furious. "I think, you better leave, son!" Jake Sr. said as his voice trembled. "Cool! All y'all remember this! I make shit happen now! And, I can make shit not happen!" Edward the 2nd shouted. He then turned to his cousin Terry. Tell your father, if he needs anything, I'll take care of it." Edward the 2nd said before kissing his little cousin on the cheek. "Let's get the fuck outta here!" Edward the 2nd said to the agent and Brandon. Brandon walked over to Terry. "Let's go!" Edward the 2nd shouted to Brandon. Terry and Brandon hugged each other. "I love you!" terry said. "I love you too! I'll see you this weekend!" Brandon whispered in her ear before giving her a long kiss on the lips. "I said, let's go, man!" Edward the 2nd shouted. Brandon looked at his boss with disappointment, then walked out the door. "Y'all can tell Benny and Joe-Joe don't expect any more envelopes either." Edward the 2nd said before walking out the door. The agent was the last in the group to walk out the door. Janis slammed the door shut. Jake Sr. and Lula went over to console their sister. "Please don't tell Tyson about what happened! He would lose his mind!" Maggie begged her family.

Tyson Richards was born on January 6th, 1964. He was 2 years older than his brother Malcom, and 7 years older than his cousin Edward the 2nd. Tyson was the perfect likeness to his grandfather, Benny Lassenberry. They both shared the same bulging eyes as many others in Benny's bloodline. Tyson had a dark complexion like his mother Maggie. He stood about 6 ft. 4 in., with a muscular build. His hair was always cut low and wavy.

Right after graduating college with a degree in business, Tyson took 8 envelopes he had saved and opened a hobby store called RICHARDS HOBBY SPOT located in Kearny, New jersey. His brother Malcom who wasn't as motivated, didn't graduate from college and blew his envelopes every week on gambling and fast women was put in charge of the store, which had a work force of 15 employees. His brother thought it would keep him out of trouble. Now, Tyson paid his brother 2 hundred dollars a week for tax reasons. Malcom didn't mind because he received 9 thousand a week from the family fortune.

Malcom stood about 6 ft., slim build and had a shaved head. He had more of a Richards than a Lassenberry likeness. Malcolm had no children and was considered as his brother's shadow to the rest of the family.

Later that evening around 7pm. Tyson was at his home in Hoboken, New Jersey having dinner with his wife Cindy and their 2 sons, Tyson Jr., and bobby. The million-dollar home was a gift from his mother after he'd graduated from college.

"Are you ready to go back to school, son?" Tyson asked his eldest son "Not really!" Tyson Jr. said with a mouth full of mashed potatoes. "What I told you about talking with your mouth full?" Tyson said. "I wanna go to school, daddy." Bobby said. "You're too young, boy. You'll have to wait until next year." Tyson chuckled. "I Have some good news!" Cindy said. "What's that?" Tyson asked. "I took that home pregnancy test this morning, and guest what? We… are…pregnant!" Cindy shouted. Tyson smiled from ear-to-ear. He jumped from his seat and ran over to the other side of the dinner table. He gave his wife a big hug. "Woo! I'm gonna be a daddy again!" he chuckled. Cindy cried tears of joy. "What's wrong mommy?" bobby asked. "You're going to have a little brother or sister! Isn't that great?" Cindy chuckled. bobby, who was just 4 years old, shook his head. "Nope!" he said. Tyson and Cindy cracked up laughing.

Suddenly, the doorbell rang. Cindy sighed. "Who's that coming over this time of night without calling first?" she said. "I have no idea. Be back in a sec." Tyson said. Tyson left the dining room, walked down the corridor to the front entrance. He opened the door. Standing there were 2 NA agents. One was Caucasian, the other African American. Tyson sighed. "Oh, it's you guys. You got my envelope?" Tyson asked. "Sorry to disturb you Mr. Richards, but I we are here to inform you from this moment on, you and your immediate family will be financially cut off from the family fortune, meaning you will no longer receive the amount of 9 thousand dollars every week. You're also no longer be under the protection of Lord Edward the 2nd. Enjoy the rest of your evening, Mr. Richards." The Caucasian agent said. The 2 agents simultaneously did an about face, leaving the premises. Tyson just stood there in shock for a moment.

Back in the dining room, Cindy was picking up food from the floor bobby had spilled. "You have to watch what you're doing, son!" she said. "Sorry mommy." Bobby said. Moments later, Tyson returned to the dining room. Cindy looked up and saw that her husband looked like he was in a trance. "What's wrong baby?" she asked. "I can't believe this!" Tyson said. "Can't believe what?" she asked "My cousin! That nigga just cut me off from the family fortune!" Tyson shouted. "Oooh! Daddy said the N word!" Tyson Jr. shouted. Bobby just covered his ears.

Back at castle Lassenberry, Edward the 2nd was sitting in his office, going over the books with Brandon about the dive bar and bed-n-breakfast businesses. "I think we should open up a dry-cleaning business! These mafia mother fuckers charging us a lot to clean our linen!" Edward the 2nd said. "Hey! Whatever you want! You're the boss, now!" Brandon said. Edward the 2nd leaned back in his chair, folding his arms. "I'm glad you said that! It didn't seem like it earlier today! When I tell, you let's go! I mean, let's go! Understand?" Edward the 2nd said in a high-pitched voice. "Understood." Brandon said. "Yo grandfather got a lot of faith in you! Don't make him look bad!" Edward the 2nd said. "Got it." Brandon said. Edward the 2nd looked at the clock on the wall. "Gotta wrap this shit up!" he said. "What'd you mean, wrap it up? You have 5 million dollars unaccounted for!" Brandon said. Edward the 2nd became agitated. He grabbed the pile of paper work, shuffling it all into a neat pile. "Here! Take all this stuff to your room! I want you to stay there until you figure all this shit out, and find where my 5 million went!" Edward the 2nd said. He hit the buzzer on the side of his desk. Moments later, an agent entered the office. "Yes, my lord. "Escort Mr. hart to his room! Make sure he stays there until I say fucking otherwise!" Edward the 2nd said. Brandon looked shocked. "What the hell? What am I? a prisoner, now?" Brandon shouted. "No, man! I just got some other shit I gotta deal with right now! I'll send for you in about a couple of hours! Now go!" Edward the 2nd said. Brandon took the paper work, neatly stuffing it into his briefcase. The agent held the door open for him. Brandon stood tall, straightening his neck tie. "Like I said. You're the boss." Brandon said as his voice cracked. "Yes, yes! I'm the boss! Now go!" Edward the 2nd said as he shooed Brandon away. "Long live the house of Lassenberry. Long live Edward the 2nd." Brandon said before leaving the office. "2 hours!" Edward the 2nd shouted before the agent closed the door.

About an hour later, Edward the 2nd was still in his office. He had removed the B.O.I from the safe. Going through the pages of the 4-inch-thick binder, he came upon a name familiar to the Lassenberry hierarchy. He jotted the name down on a sheet of paper with a pen he'd found in the desk drawer. Moments later, there was a knock on the door. Edward the 2nd quickly placed the B.O.I back in the safe, covering the safe with the painting. "Come in!" he shouted. One of the agents entered the office. "Kimberly Lassenberry is here to see you, my lord." The agent said. "Bring her ass in here, man!" Edward the 2nd said. "I heard that!" Kimberly shouted seconds before entering. Kimberly entered the office. "You wanted to see me?" she asked. "Yeah! Sit down." Edward the 2nd said. "How'd you feel about taking another trip out to that dumpsite?" he asked Kimberly. "Where?" she asked with a confused look on her face. "Lassenberia!" he whispered. "Oh! Ok." She said. "Here. Take this paper. It's got the name and address of the guy who can help you with the legal stuff written on it. Just tell him Lassenberry sent you." Edward the 2nd said. Kimberly read the name on the paper. "I heard this name before! Is he good? Will he help us?" she asked. "He better! He's on the payroll!" he said. Edward the 2nd took out another sheet of paper. He wrote down some more information on it. "When you get there, I'll wire this amount to you." He said as he held the paper up to Kimberly's face. "Goodness! That's a lot to wire!" she said. Edward the 2nd started writing more information on the paper. "You'll need to set up shop on the mainland to the…west! Yeah, the west. Since you're gonna be there for a few months, you should consider taking the little guy with you." He said. "A few months?" Kimberly shouted. "Take it easy Beautiful! At the most, 5 months! You can bring Lucy with you to take care of your son! I can hire a temp to clean up after me!" Edward the 2nd chuckled. "Here. Take a few minutes to Remember what's on the paper, because it's about to go up in flames." He whispered. Kimberly sat there looking over the notes repeatedly. After a few minutes of memorizing the notes. Kimberly gave Edward the 2nd the signal to burn them by nodding her head. Edward the 2nd then pulled out a cigarette lighter from the desk drawer. He made his way to the bathroom. Standing over the toilet, he lit the sheets of paper on fire. He was careful not to let the ashes land anywhere else, but in the toilet. The toilet was then flushed. He went back to his desk. Edward the 2nd looked at Kimberly's attire. "I hope you ain't traveling looking like yo ass going to a funeral!" he said. Kimberly sighed. "Don't worry! I'll dress for the occasion!" she said. "Good. You got 3 days to get going." He said. Edward the 2nd looked at the calendar that was on his desk. Kimberly sat there in silence for a moment with a smirk on her face. "So! Did you have fun?" she asked. Edward the 2nd looked at her with squinted eyes. "Have fun doing what?" he asked. "Viola! Viola Carr!" Kimberly shouted. "Oh, yeah! We had a shit load of fun!" Edward the 2nd chuckled. "That's good. She's really a good catch." Kimberly said. Edward the 2nd cleared his throat. You should uh, be getting on your way, beautiful." He said. "I guess that's my que." Kimberly said. She stood from her chair. "Long live the house of Lassenberry! Long live Edward the 2nd!" Kimberly shouted before leaving the office.

Edward the 2nd took off his red sash. He then unbuttoned his uniform top. He hit the buzzer on the side of the desk. An NA agent entered the office. "Yes, my lord. "Yeah! Once Mr. Hart returns from the north wing I don't want us to be disturbed for the rest of the evening." Edward the 2nd said. "Yes, my lord. The agent said before leaving the office.

—— CHAPTER 23. OH, NOT YOU! ——

Saturday, December 1st, 2001 was when Edward the 2nd received a surprise visit. He was in the gymnasium located in the West wing of castle Lassenberry. While running on one of the 12 treadmills, Brandon entered the gym wearing jeans, a jersey sweater, and sneakers. Once he saw Brandon coming towards him, he hit the stop button after a 20-minute run. "Damn, man! Can I get a chance alone to clear my mind? You're just as annoying as those fucking robots!" Edward the 2nd shouted. Brandon rolled his eyes. "You know I wouldn't be down here if it weren't important." Brandon said. "Pass me that towel!" Edward the 2nd said. Brandon grabbed the towel from off the weight bench. He tossed to his boss. Edward the 2nd wiped the sweat from his face. He then draped the towel around his neck. He took a seat on the weight bench. "Talk to me!" he said, breathing heavily. "Well, remember that situation you told me about what happened in Westside park a while back?" Brandon said. "The 3 niggas that got their heads chopped off, from Hakim's crew? Yeah!" Edward the 2nd said. "Ah, Well I found out through a copy of a police report I received, that the main suspect was some guy named Leroy Beckett." Brandon said. "Who the fuck is Leroy Beckett?" Edward the 2nd asked as he shrugged his shoulders. "Just so happens, Leroy Beckett is the husband of Fiona Beckett. Her sister's name is Alisha. Alisha Watson! Dubbs' wife!" Brandon said. "Oh shit!" Edward the 2nd said. "After I received the police report, I hired a private detective to follow him. Just yesterday, he was seen in the company of Robbie Davis! Robbie Davis is Dubbs' right hand man!" Brandon said. "I know him. They call him bulletproof." Edward the 2nd said. "What time is it?" he asked Brandon. Brandon looked at his watch. "It's 8:37." Brandon said. "You had breakfast yet?" Edward the 2nd asked. "No. not yet." Brandon said. "Ok, then. Let's go get some grub. Afterwards, I want you to make a call to the 5 generals. Have everyone meet at the Lodi office, in full uniform at midnight, tonight. By the way, tell them all to come alone. No body guards." Edward the 2nd said.

About an hour later, Edward the 2nd and Brandon were being served breakfast by one of the 2 male servants hired by Brandon. The one serving fresh fruit, omelets, bacon, and orange juice was the son of Brandon's business partner. Kevin was a 20-year-old Irish kid who was very interested in becoming a chef. His father, who was very successful, wanted his son to get some hands-on work under his belt. Kevin worked 4 hours a day or when summoned by Edward the 2nd to prepare and serve breakfast, and only breakfast. Edward the 2nd was chowing down on his breakfast. Kevin looked pleased that his boss was enjoying his food. "Mr. Lassenberry. Would you like to try my crepe suzette?" Kevin asked. Edward the 2nd looked up from his plate. He looked at Brandon as if he just witnessed a murder. It didn't take Brandon but a split second to catch on to his boss's facial expression. "Kevin! From now on, he's to be addressed as Lord Lassenberry. Got it?" Brandon said in a stern voice. "Understood Mr. Hart!" Kevin said. "Good. You can bring in that crepe suzette now." Brandon said. "Right away, sir!" Kevin said. Kevin left the dining room. "This kid can cook his ass off!" Edward the 2nd whispered. "He's looking to run his own restaurant someday." Brandon said. "Hey. Anything's fucking possible. Shit, look at my black ass." Edward the 2nd said with a mouth full of egg.

It was around noon, when Edward the 2nd was sitting in his office writing on a note pad. After writing, he ripped the sheet of paper from the pad. He then reached into his front pants pocket and pulled out a hundred-dollar bill. He placed the c-note on the sheet of paper. He rolled the c-note and paper together. He then placed it in his pocket. He left the office. "This is my me time, boys! I'll be back in a few hours!" he said to the 2 agents standing guard outside the office. "Yes, my lord!" they both shouted simultaneously. Edward the 2nd headed in the direction, towards the south wing. 5 minutes later, Edward the 2nd reached his destination. The destination, was the crack in the wall in the south wing corridor. He took out the rolled-up c-note and paper and quickly slipped it through the crack. He then headed back towards the west wing.

About an hour later, Edward the2nd arrived at the Whitman rest area just outside Mount Laurel Township dressed in a bulky overcoat, a plaid scarf to cover his mouth from the cold and wool cap. He donned a pair of shades to make himself unrecognizable to the public. He told the taxi driver to ride around for a long period before hitting the rest stop to make sure he wasn't being followed. About 10 minutes had passed, another taxi cab pulled up to the rest area. Getting out of the cab was Sir Marcus, who was also dressed incognito. His instructions were to catch a cab to one of Cherry Hill's 51 parks called Challenge Grove and grab the winter coat, fur hat and shades hidden in the public bathroom.

Once inside the rest area, Sir Marcus made his way to the back room where it said employees only on the door. He knocked 3 times, then knocked twice and then once more. It was the signal that Edward the 2nd needed to hear to allow anyone in. Hey Cousin!" Edward the 2nd said. "Good to see you cousin." Sir Marcus said. The men hugged each other. Edward the 2nd locked the door after Sir Marcus entered. "We gotta make this quick! The guy at the register said his shifts' about to end in 20 minutes! I ain't paying out another thousand bucks to keep his co-worker quiet!" Edward the 2nd whispered. Both cousins sat on folded chairs at a card table where the workers would have lunch. "So. What's the scoop?" Sir Marcus asked. "What's the scoop? Hah! I don't know who sounds white, you or Brandon." Edward the 2nd chuckled. "Come on. Stop it!" Sir Marcus scoffed. Edward the 2nd cleared his throat. "Well anyway. There's gonna be some big changes in the ranks." He said. "What are you talking about?" Sir Marcus asked. "Dubbs…He's the one responsible for the deaths of Hakim's people." Edward the 2nd said. "You sure?" Sir Marcus said. "One hundred percent, cuz!"

Edward the 2nd said. I did some investigating, and everything leads back to Dubbs!" Edward the 2nd said. Sir Marcus frowned at his cousin. "You, did the investigation?" he said. "That's right! Why you sound all cynical-n-shit?" Edward the 2nd shouted. Sir Marcus sighed. "Ok cousin. I believe you. Jesus!" he said. "I called a meeting with all the 5 generals out at the Lodi spot. And yeah, I read the rules from the Book of Information, that we all have to be in uniform and all that formal shit." Edward the 2nd said. "Glad to hear that cousin. We need to stick to the B.O.I to keep this thing going to maintain power." Sir Marcus said. "If Butch don't like my decision to get rid of Dubbs...Well, he might have to be dealt with too. Don't worry though. Hakim got my back. Especially what I did for him, getting that mafia fucker off his back." Edward the 2nd said. "What about Mookie and Bex?" Sir Marcus asked. "Mookie! I think Mookie just wanna get his product and make money. He'll more than likely agree with me just to keep his operation running smooth! Bex I heard, is still pissed off about me ruffing him up-n-shit! But, I ain't worried. He's just Hakim's puppet." Edward the 2nd explained. "Remember cousin! The B.O.I states that you must get permission from the other generals to take one of them out of the picture!" Sir Marcus whispered. "I know! I read the shit, ok?" Edward the 2nd said sounding agitated. "I'm glad you've took the time to tell me this cousin. I approve, and you have my permission to carry out your plan." Sir Marcus said. Edward the 2nd looked furious. He stood from his seat. "Permission? Nigga! I didn't call this meeting to get your permission! This shit is a done deal! It's gonna go down! I'm just keeping you informed out of respect, cause you the only nigga alive that walked in my shoes! End of story, nigga!" Edward the 2nd said. He stood there with his arms spread eagle, waiting for his cousin to respond. There was a moment of silence between the cousins. Sir Marcus sat there for a moment pondering while tapping his fingers on the table. Sir Marcus looked up at his cousin. "Ok, cousin. If you're keeping me informed, I can't complain too much." Sir Marcus said in a calm voice. "Thank you!" Edward the 2nd shouted as he put his arms down to his side. "Now, on another note. I sent yo wife back out to Lassenberia with that lawyer, Kent Mooney to investigate all that toxic dumping going on out there. He's gonna gather a team of lawyers and go to the U.N. and put a stop to that shit." Edward the 2nd said. "Kent Mooney?" Sir Marcus said. Sir Marcus looked at his cousin, breathing heavily through his nose. "No matter what you think or say, that's going down too." Edward the 2nd said. Sir Marcus put on a fake smile. "Is that it, cousin?" Sir Marcus asked. "Yeah. That's about it, for now. I'll keep you posted. You can go back inside the walls of the castle now." Edward the 2nd said. Sir Marcus stood up. He was about to leave the room. "Hey cuz! You forget something?" Edward the 2nd asked. Sir Marcus rolled his eyes. He stood at attention. "Long live the house of Lassenberry! Long live Edward the 2nd!" Sir Marcus shouted. Edward the 2nd smiled. "Now, you can go!" he said. The door was ajar as Sir Marcus turned towards his cousin. "Was this meeting really about showing me respect, or about you trying to prove something?" Sir Marcus asked before leaving. Edward the 2nd stood their looking furious.

It was around 4:30 pm when Edward the 2nd arrived in Hillside. He had gone home to castle Lassenberry earlier. He showered and shaved. He picked out a suit to wear from his huge wardrobe.

The limo turned on to Princeton avenue. Earlier, the snow on Viola's side of the street was removed. The snow was pushed on the opposite side of the street. The residents that lived on that side of the block were complaining about their cars being snowed in. Phone calls were made to City Hall. No one came to their aid. No police, sanitation department, no one. The limo parked in a dry area, right in front of Viola's house. Edward the 2nd had a big smile on his face when the NA agent opened the limo door for him. In his hand, Edward the 2nd carried a bouquet of roses and a brown shopping bag with the name of a prestigious clothing store stamped on it. "How do I look?" he asked the agent. "You look presentable, my lord." The agent said. Edward the 2nd trotted up the stairs of Viola's home in a gaily fashion. He rang the doorbell. He stood their whistling. He rang the doorbell once more. He looked to his left, and saw a shadowy figure behind the curtains. He waved at the figure. This person left the window. The front door opened. Standing at the door was Viola Carr. She wore a red bathrobe and matching slippers. Her hair was flowing down the side of her face. Edward the 2nd stepped in, handing her the bouquet of roses, and giving Viola a kiss on the cheek. "Hey beautiful!" He said. "Hey." She said in a soft faint voice. It looked obvious to Edward the 2nd that this woman wasn't too enthused to see him. Edward the 2nd looked up at the top of the flight of stairs. "Is the boy here?" he asked. Viola shook her head. "Where is he?" he asked. "I gave him some money to go shopping and to the movies with his friends!" Viola sighed. "Good!" he said as he handed her the brown shopping bag. "What's this?" Viola asked. "Girl, just look inside!" he said in an aggressive manner. Viola had placed the roses on the coffee table. She looked inside the bag. She pulled out a scantily clad outfit. It was a pink sheer cat suit. She also pulled out matching panties and a pair of shoe string stilettos. "What the hell you want me to do with this?" she shouted. "I want you to jump in the shower, spray on some perfume and head to the bedroom. Simple as that." Edward the 2nd said. "This is wrong! This is just wrong! I can't do this!" she said. Edward the 2nd gently grabbed her hand. "Listen beautiful. This is how it's going to be, until I say otherwise. Now, go do what I told you to do." He said in a soft quiet voice. Viola quickly pulled away from him. "I want you to get the fuck out of my house! Now!" she shouted as she pointed towards the door. Edward the 2nd took off his wool overcoat. He threw it on the sofa. "You wanna call the police? Here! Use my phone! Call'em! I bet you, ain't shit gonna happen! Better yet! Call that basketball player ex-husband of yours! Oh! I forgot, he's too busy with his new wife and child down in Florida! According to my sources, your son has a million-dollar trust fund set up by that clown! As soon as he turns 18, you'll be cut off! And don't let me start on that crooked father of yours! Having the Secretary of commerce involved in a child pornography scandal ain't cool!" he shouted. "What the hell are you talking about? Where did you get this information from?" Viola shouted. "Yo daddy, refused to play ball with some other big shots I know! And for that, he's going to be exposed! The only one that can save his ass from doing life in the penitentiary, is my black ass!" Edward the 2nd said. "I don't believe you!" she shouted. "Hey! I got possession of video tapes, surveillance photos, even aerial photos! Shit! I can have'em here within the snap of my fingers, just like I took you to Italy for dinner with the snap of my finger!" he chuckled. Viola looked at Edward the 2nd with hate in her blood shot eyes. She took a deep breath, then lifted the cat suit up to the light. She took off her bathrobe, letting it drop to the floor. "Come on. You wanna fuck? Let's fuck!" she said gritting her teeth. Edward the 2nd loosened his neck tie, simultaneously rubbing his private area. "Get yo sexy ass up them stairs!" he shouted with a grin on his face. As Viola climbed the stairs, she started switching her ass more. Edward the 2nd licked the palm of his hand, and smacked her on the ass. "We'll have to get right to it! Hakeem will be home in little while!" Viola said. "I know he's your son, but do me a favor, and don't say that name in front of me again!" Edward the 2nd said with a scowl on his face.

It was around 10 pm that evening, when Edward the 2nd was fast asleep in his king size bed he had purchased after ceasing control of castle Lassenberry. Suddenly, there came a knock on the bedroom door. Moments later, the knocking turned into banging. Edward the 2nd quickly sat up from his slumber. Come in! Come In! God damn!" He shouted as he rubbed his eyes. The door opened. Brandon entered the room. "What the fuck? I was sleeping good as hell, nigga!" Edward the 2nd shouted. "The 5 generals, my lord? You have to be in uniform for the ride to Lodi." Brandon said. Edward the 2nd scratched his head. He sat on the edge of the bed. "Have that butler lay out my uniform and run my bath water." Edward the 2nd said. "Your bath water?" Brandon asked. "Yeah, nigga! Can I soak in the tub for a change? Damn!" Edward the 2nd shouted.

It was 10:45 pm. Edward the 2nd, Brandon and 2 agents make their way down stairs to the main level of the west wing. Edward the 2nd was dressed in his Gestapo style uniform. He took upon wearing the 3 medals awarded to his uncle and cousin. He wore the red shoulder sash and the green waist sash. He wore a small replica of the family crest right underneath the red sash over the lower right side of his rib cage. As an added touch to show off his power, Edward the 2nd had gold uniform braids draped over each shoulder to distinguish himself from his generals. His jack boots were literally spit shined to near perfection by the butler who drew his bath water. This butler was called number 3. He was an elderly, frail Caucasian man that appeared outside the castle walls a couple of weeks earlier. His clothes were tattered. His fingernails were dirty. His shoes barely stayed on his feet due to the absence of shoe strings. Brandon went to the castle gates to meet the mysterious man, who was just standing there. He asked the man what was he doing standing out here. The man said that the head of this castle would take his estranged family to a better land someday. Going by his gut feeling, Brandon told Edward the 2nd that there was something too special about this old man for him to want to bring harm to Edward the 2nd. The old man never gave his name, which he said would be revealed in time. Brandon was given permission to bring him in and clean him up. Brandon was also told that if his instincts were wrong about this old man, they would both pay the consequences. He was given room and board in the west wing. Edward the 2nd wanted to keep him close as possible.

"We're going to be late, my lord! It's over an hour and a half drive to Lodi!" Brandon said. "I already know this shit!" Edward the 2nd shouted. "As you ordered, my lord, I've assigned a 15-agent detail to accompany you to the meeting." Brandon said. "Good!" Edward the 2nd said. Standing at the bottom of the long staircase was butler number 3. He was holding a black leather trench coat. When Edward the 2nd reached the bottom of the staircase, the old man helped him don his coat. "Thanks, old man! You know what? How would you like to come with me and see what I do for a living?" Edward the 2nd said. "I don't think that would be a good idea, my lord!" Brandon whispered in his ear. "Fuck that! Come old man! Follow me!"

Edward the 2nd said. The old man called number 3 nodded his head and followed Edward the 2nd to the golf cart. Edward the 2nd hopped in the golf cart. "Hold everything down until I come back!" Edward the 2nd shouted. Brandon just nodded his head. The NA agent drove off down the corridor, towards the main entrance.

It was 15 minutes after mid-night at the Lodi facility. As they were instructed, the 5 generals arrived on time, not a minute later. The meeting in Lodi was held in the basement as it was always since the days of Benny Lassenberry. This time there was a long marble table with 6 chairs. The seats were filled, except for the one at the head of the table. On the right side of the table sat Butch, Mookie and Dubbs, in that order. Hakim sat closest to the empty chair on the left side. Bex sat next to his brother.

Hakim looked restless, tapping his fingers on the desk. Butch sighed as he looked at his diamond wrist watch. Bex sat there in a daze. "What the hell is taking him so long?" Dubbs asked. "I remember when Benny used to call me and your father to a meeting. He hated when the old man was running late!" Butch said to Hakim. Hakim stopped tapping his fingers on the desk. He had the look of hate in his eyes. "That nigga never was, and never will be my father!" hakim said. Butch leaned in over the table. "No matter what happened to you in that prison or whatever happened to you until this point, you owe that man a lot!" Butch shouted. Hakim just scoffed at Butch. The room was silent. All eyes were on Butch to see if he'd react to Hakim's lack of respect. "Ok kid! Stay mad!" Butch said. Dubbs looked over at Bex. "Hey man! What happened to your face?" Dubbs asked. Bex just looked down at the table in shame. He didn't say a word. He just shook his head. "What? You can't speak now?" Dubbs chuckled. "Let it go, Dubbs." Hakim said in a calm voice. Dubbs turned his attention to what Mookie was doing. "Por favor dios en el cielo. Vamos todos a hacer de este lugar en una sola pieza." Mookie said, and kept repeating as he held rosary beads in his hands. "What the fuck, you're doing?" Dubbs shouted. Mookie slowly opened his eyes, and turned to Dubbs. "Praying that we all make it out of here in one piece, amigo!" Mookie said.

Moments later, an African American NA agent pushed open the double doors. He entered the room. "All that Are able to stand! stand!" the agent shouted. The 5 generals looked at each other. Butch, Dubbs, Hakim and Bex slowly stand at attention. Mookie was bound to his wheelchair. Moments later, 10 agents walked into the room 2 abreast. They surrounded the table, then stood at attention, with their backs a few inches from the wall. "I present to you, Lord of the House of Lassenberry, Edward the 2nd!" the agent shouted. Walking in first side-by-side, were 2 more agents. Behind them, Edward the 2nd entered the room. Following him, were 2 more agents. Finally, the old man called number 3 entered the room. The 2 agents closed and locked the double doors and stood guard there. "I'm tired of this shit!" Bex whispered to Hakim. "Just chill, man!?" he whispered to Bex.

Edward the 2nd stood at the head of the table. He slapped his hands together, loud. Bex winced. Edward the 2nd rubbed his hands together in a fast motion. "Sorry I'm late boys, but I was knee deep in some pussy earlier, and it drained the shit out of me!" Edward the 2nd chuckled. One of the agents pulled his seat out for him. Edward the 2nd took his seat. "Sit! Sit! Everybody sit!" he said. The 4 generals took their seats. "What's this all about kid?" Butch asked. "Butch. I know you're a O.G.-n-shit, but I'll be doing the talking until I say otherwise."

Edward the 2nd said. Butch looked around the room at the agents. "Ok! You got it!" butch chuckled. "Now! Where were we? Oh yes! A while back, 3 of my street bosses were found with their heads chopped off in Westside park. That's Hakim's area! Now, I know Hakim pissed about this shit, but I'm really fucking pissed! When people in this organization, no matter how low on the totem pole they are, get snuffed without my permission, somebody gotta pay! Now! I know who's responsible, but I want the motherfucker who had it done to man-up!" Edward the 2nd said. Mookie raised his hand. "What?" Edward the 2nd asked. "How did you conclude it was someone in here?" Mookie asked. "I just connected the dots, amigo!" Edward the 2nd chuckled. "You want somebody in here to admit to murder?" Dubbs asked. Edward the 2nd looked Dubbs square into his eyes. "Ah, yeah!" he said. "What are you gonna do, if one of us confess?" Bex asked. Edward the 2nd just laughed as he rubbed his hands together." I don't care how long it takes! We can be here until Christmas for all I care, but ain't nobody leaving this room until one of y'all fess up!" he said with a serious look on his face. Butch stood from his seat. "This is bullshit!" He shouted. "No! this is real! This is mother fucking real! We're all in this game, together! Somebody in here, violated the game! Now, sit down, old man. You're making me nervous." Edward the 2nd said in a calm voice. Looking at Edward the 2nd with hate in his eyes, Butch complied. "Good! This is how it's going down. I'm going into the next room. The agents will keep you fellas company until the culprit exposes himself. There will be no food or drinks served. So, if you guys don't wanna starve and die of thirst, somebody better come clean. "Man, you must be outta yo fucking mind!" Dubbs shouted. Edward the 2nd shrugged his shoulders. "Like I said. I'm going into the other room. When I come back into this room, I should only see 4 men sitting upright." He said. He gave his generals a half ass, lazy salute. Edward the 2nd then pulled out a fresh deck of playing cards from his uniform pants pocket. "Knock on the door when it's done." Edward the 2nd said to the agent standing behind Butch. "Yes, my lord." The agent said. Edward the 2nd smiled at the group then left the room, followed by 2 agents. Hakim looked around at his counterparts. "Well, I know my conscious is clear! I can sit here until the sun comes up!" Hakim said as he folded his hands on the table.

Only 2 hours had passed, when Edward the 2nd was cheering with a fist pump in the air when winning his third game of solitaire, after 19 games. He left his seat and tip-toed to the door. The 2 agents just stood there at parade rest. Edward the 2nd put his ear to the door. He heard someone snoring. He covered his mouth to keep from giggling. He then tip-toed back to his chair. "I guess somebody ain't worried." Edward the 2nd said to himself. The 2 agents looked at each other for a few seconds. They then return to looking forward.

Another 4 hours had passed. Edward the 2nd had taken off his uniform top. He had become bored from playing solitaire. Instead, he started to build a house out of the cards. Suddenly he jumped, causing the house of cards to tumble. The noise from the next room startled Edward the 2nd. He left his seat, heading to the door. The 2 agents went for their pistols underneath their black suit jackets. Edward the 2nd waved his hand at the agents, giving them the signal to stand down. The 2 agents went back to standing at parade rest. Once again, he put his ear to the door. He could hear chairs being toppled over. The sounds of bodies wrestling, as well as screams. This melee went on for about 5 minutes until there was silence. Just as Edward the 2nd ordered earlier, there came the knock on the door. He then rushed to the table and grabbed his uniform top. He quickly donned the top and the 2 sashes. Edward the 2nd stood in front of the 2 agents. "How do I look?" he said to one of the agents. "You look very presentable, my lord." The agent said. "Thanks!" Edward the 2nd said as he patted the agent on the shoulder. "Let's do this! Now, open The door!" he said. The agent who gave the compliment, went over, and opened the door for Edward the 2nd. Edward the 2nd turned around. "You! Stack those cards up in a neat pile!" he said to the other agent. "Yes, my lord." The agent said. Edward the 2nd passed through the doorway. He was in shock at what he saw. Hakim sat there with his head in his hands, sobbing. Edward the 2nd looked over and saw Butch and Dubbs just sitting there with the look of innocence. Bex, on the other hand, was leaned back in his chair, staring up at the ceiling. "What the fuck happened?" Edward the 2nd shouted. Hey! The kid confessed. What else is there to say?" Butch said. Edward the 2nd slowly walked passed Hakim. He made his way over to Bex's lifeless body. Bex's eyes were rolled back into his head. His skin was pale. His lips were dark from lack of oxygen. Edward the 2nd gently placed his hand on Bex's forehead. "Oh, not you!" he whispered as his eyes teared up. He then closed Bex's eyes shut. On the table was an empty syringe. "Well, did you get closure kid?" Butch asked. Edward the 2nd didn't say a word. He just stared Dubbs in his eyes. Dubbs eyes shifted in every direction, but not in the direction of Edward the 2nd. Butch stood from his chair. "What's done, is done! Dubbs! We should get going! There's money to make in them streets!" he said." Dubbs stood up as well. Mookie sat upright in his wheelchair. "Long live the house of Lassenberry! Long live Edward the 2nd! The 3 generals shouted simultaneously. The 2 agents at the exit allowed Mookie, Butch and Dubbs to leave. "Take old man number 3 back to the castle. I think he'd seen enough." Edward the 2nd ordered one of the agents. One general, still alive, didn't leave. Hakim just sat there in a daze. Edward the 2nd leaned over the table, dropping his head, looking disappointed. "I can't believe this shit! What the fuck just happened?" he said to himself. "He told me he was tired of all this! But, I didn't know it was this bad!" Hakim said. Hakim wiped the tears from his eyes. Edward the 2nd quickly turned his attention over to hakim. "What the hell?" Edward the 2nd said with a confused look. "When we had Thanksgiving at his place, he seemed fine and full of life! This is crazy!" Hakim said. Edward the 2nd stood tall. "You motherfucking right, this shit is crazy! The motherfucker who did your people in, just left the room!" Edward the 2nd said. Hakim looked up at Edward the 2nd in awe. He jumped from his seat, heading to the exit with great speed. "Stop him!" Edward the 2nd shouted. The agents at the exit obeyed their lord's cry. They stopped Hakim, tackling him to the floor. "Get the fuck off me!" Hakim shouted as he tussled with 2 of the agents. The agents pinned hakim to the floor. "I said get the fuck off me! I ain't fucking around with y'all!" hakim shouted. Edward the 2nd stood over Hakim. "Yo! Tell these motherfuckers to get off me!" hakim shouted. "Stop it, man. Bex made his choice. I hate to say it, but you can't put that on somebody else." Edward the 2nd explained. "Yo fuck you, man!" Hakim shouted as the side of his face was pinned to the floor. "You have to let that shit go. I asked for a body, and I got one. Don't push me into making it 2." Edward the 2nd said. Hakim used all his strength to get from off the floor as he growled like a wild animal. Edward the 2nd was getting nervous. "Quick! Put his ass to sleep!" Edward the 2nd shouted to one of the agents. The agent pulled out his syringe from his suit jacket as he had his knee on Hakim's back. The agent then injected the clear drug into the side of Hakim's neck. "No! No! No…No." were the last words Hakim said before passing out. "You 2! Get him back to the castle!" Edward the 2nd said to the 2 agents who had Hakim on the floor. They picked him up as another agent opened the door for them to pass. As soon as they left, Edward the 2nd walked over to where Bex's body was. He stood there in silence for a moment. He shook his head. "You fucked up, man." Edward the 2nd mumbled to himself. He then grabbed Bex's hand. He noticed rigor mortis had set in. Edward the 2nd took a deep breath. He removed the Lassenberry insignia ring from Bex's finger, placing it in his uniform pants pocket. Edward the 2nd shut his eyes, pinching the bridge of his nose to gather his thoughts. "What shall we do with the body, my lord?" one of the agents asked. "Let me think." Edward the 2nd said as he pounded his forehead with his fist. "It wouldn't be logical the leave the general here, my lord." The agent said. Edward the 2nd quickly turned to the agent. "What the fuck you think I should do, robot?" he shouted. "You have to make that decision, my lord." The agent said. Edward the 2nd looked at the agent, shaking his head. He then turned around looking at Bex's body. "Strip his clothes off! Take his body out into a ditch far away from here! Make it look like he was robbed!" Edward the 2nd said. The remaining agents split into groups of 3. One group stripped Bex's uniform off. Edward the 2nd checked all his pockets for personal items. He found his wallet, a set of keys and a wad of cash. "Here! Go out and burn this! I don't want any trace of this uniform to be found! Understand?" Edward the 2nd said to the agent. The other group of agents had already taken the body to the black van outside. The remaining agents secured the facility and escorted Edward the 2nd to the limo.

It was December 3rd when Hakim was becoming conscious. He found himself laid out on a king size bed in a strange room. Still groggy from being drugged, hakim rubbed his eyes to focus better. He sat up, noticing his uniform was still on, but his jack boots were off, placed near the dresser drawer. Hakim stumbled out bed, looking around the room, he noticed there were no windows. His source of light came from the ceiling. He went over and grabbed his jack boots. after putting them on, he slowly turned the metal door knob to leave the room. He opened the door the with caution. He became startled when seeing an agent standing at parade rest across the hall from the bedroom. "Where the fuck am I?" Hakim asked. The agent stood at attention. "You're at castle Lassenberry, General Bates." The agent said. "General Bates, huh?" hakim said. "Yes. We were ordered to address all generals appropriately. Sir." The agent said. Hakim looked down both ends of the corridor. "Where the hell is everybody?" he asked. "Lord Lassenberry should be in his office in the west wing, sir" the agent said. "West wing? What wing are we in?" hakim asked. "We're in the north wing, sir." The agent said. "Well, like they say in the movies, take me to your leader, nigga!" Hakim said. "Right-a-way, sir." the agent said. Hakim followed the agent down the corridor.

A few minutes had passed, when Hakim arrived outside the office of Edward the 2nd. One of the agents standing guard knocked on the door. "Come in!" the voice from inside the office shouted. The agent opened the door. Edward the 2nd was at his desk looking over some paper work. "General bates is here to see you, my lord." The agent said. Before Edward the 2nd could utter a word, Hakim pushed the agent to the side and entered the office. "Damn, nigga! You can get yo ass killed for that!" Edward the 2nd said. "Would you like me to stay, my lord?" the agent asked. "Nah. It's cool. You can go back to your post." Edward the 2nd said. The agent left the office, closing the door behind him. "Take a seat." Edward the 2nd said. "I'll stand, motherfucker!" hakim said. Edward the 2nd looked up at Hakim. "I know you ain't taking this shit out on, me!" Edward the 2nd shouted. "You're the one running the fucking show, nigga!" Hakim shouted. "It ain't my fault yo brother wanted to die!" Edward the 2nd shouted. Hakim balled up his fist. He looked infuriated, tightening his lips. Edward the 2nd recognized that look. "I'm telling you now! We ain't at BIG SHOTS! Here, you could end up like yo brother! Sit down. Now!" Edward the 2nd shouted. Hakim loosened his hand. He walked back into the couch and took a seat. He rested his elbows on his lap, covering his face. "Hey, man. I shouldn't have said that shit about Bex-n-shit." He said. Hakim peeked through his fingers to look at Edward the 2nd. "What'd you do with the body?" Hakim sighed. "I had no choice, but to dump his body on the side of the road." Edward the 2nd said with dread. Hakim jumped up. "You did what?" hakim screamed. "Listen, man! I talked to the other generals! I told them not to mention what happened! If our people on the streets found out, they'll think this thing is falling apart! I can't have that shit!" Edward the 2nd said. Hakim's eyes teared up. "You know you're full of shit, right?" Hakim chuckled as he wiped his tears away. "I'm curious as hell, Man! What the hell happened back there in Lodi?" Edward the 2nd asked. "You know what the fuck happened!" Hakim shouted. "No. I meant, what happened when I was in the other room? I heard a lot of noise-n-shit!" Edward the 2nd said. Hakim was silent for a moment. He looked Edward the 2nd in his eyes, with no expression on his face. He took a deep breath. "Like I told you before. He wanted out. I didn't know he was going to take the fall for killing my people. As soon as he admitted the shit, your goons grabbed him. I tried to stop it, but they held me down. I couldn't do shit but watch them pump this orange looking shit into his veins! He probably thought you would just kick him out! I don't know! Fuck! Fuck!" Hakim shouted as he buried his face in his hands. Edward the 2nd covered his sinister grin with his hand. He then cleared his throat. "I promise you. When his body is found by a passerby or the cops, he will get a grand funeral. You have my word." Edward the 2nd said. Hakim uncovered his face. His eyes were blood shot. "Are you gonna tell me who really killed my people?" He asked. "Let it go! What's done is done! You know all this shit is about business!" Edward the 2nd said. "This is about your business. The Lassenberry business. The rest of us are just along for the ride." Hakim said in a calm voice. Edward the 2nd leaned back in his chair, with his fingers interlocked and elbows on the armrest of his chair. "I'm sorry you feel that way, man. But, this is how it is. You came back into the picture wanting to be a part of it." Edward the 2nd said. Hakim quickly stood to his feet. "You forget who put yo black ass in that chair, nigga!" hakim shouted. Edward the 2nd leaned forward with his elbows on the desk, resting his chin on his interlocked fingers. "You want me to say thank you for the millionth time? Well thank you. Now, sit yo ass back down." He said with smirk on his face. Hakim reluctantly sat down. "If it makes you feel any better, I've decided to give you access to our cocaine connection. I'll connect you to the Gatano people too. They supply the weed and pills." Edward the 2nd said. "I never figured that out. Why don't they just sell the shit themselves? It ain't like it's coke or heroin!" Hakim said. "From the info, I have, they'd rather have us get our hands caught in the cookie jar. This shit was like this since pop-pop was running things." Edward the 2nd explained. "What about the heroin?" hakim asked. "What about it?" Edward the 2nd responded. "I can't do the transaction with the connection?" Hakim asked. Edward the 2nd frantically shook his head. No. No. No, sir! That's a whole different ball game! It's deeper than just selling drugs!" he said to Hakim. "When do I start?" Hakim asked. "After someone finds your brother's body, and not before. I want it to look like a sympathy promotion, not favoritism. That means, it's our little secret!" Edward the 2nd explained. Hakim staggered to his feet. "Are we done?" he asked. "What?" Edward the 2nd asked. "Are we done with this meeting? I got half a million coming to me today, and I need to be somewhere to collect it." Hakim said. Edward the 2nd stood to his feet. "Go on, and do the damn thing, man!" he said with a smile. The 2 men shook hands. Hakim stood at attention. "Long live the house of Lassenberry! Long live Edward the 2nd!" Hakim shouted. Hakim was about to leave. He turned to Edward the 2nd. "Who you're gonna get to take charge of my brother's territory?" Hakim asked. Edward the 2nd sat back in his chair. "I ain't decide yet." He said. Edward the 2nd hit the buzzer on the side of the desk. Seconds later, an agent entered the office. "Take general Bates to a place of his choosing." Edward the 2nd said. "Yes, my lord." The agent said. The agent followed Hakim out of the office. Edward the 2nd pulled open a desk drawer. He then took out Bex's ring. He held it up to the light. "Now, who's gonna wear you?" he said to himself.

CHAPTER 24. GREEN GOOP

After weeks of empty promises, Deputy Secretary of the United nations decided to take a trip out to the artificial island of Lassenberia to meet with Kent Mooney, his legal team, and Kimberly Lassenberry on December 20th. Deputy Secretary Jawara Soumah was reluctant about the endeavor until he received 12 million in Gambian Dalasi, which was the equivalent to $279,626.00 in U.S. dollars a week earlier.

It was 6:35 am, Central Africa Time when a military transport helicopter left the capital city of Mozambique called Maputo. 45 minutes had passed when the helicopter arrived at Lassenberia. The aircraft landed on a helipad 2o miles away from the dump site.

Weeks earlier, Kimberly hired construction contractors from Maputo to build a bungalow as headquarters for Kent Mooney and his team. Kimberly and Kent came out of the bungalow to greet the deputy secretary and his entourage as they landed 50 yards from the headquarters.

Kimberly had retired her black dress to something more comfortable for the 75° weather. She and the whole Mooney team wore khaki safari outfits. Her dreadlocks were tied back in a ponytail with a beige ribbon. Sandals were the choice of footwear for the group. Kimberly and Kent squinted as the rotors from the helicopter kicked up sand in their direction. As the rotors idled down, Kent, Kimberly and Kent's secretary made their way to the aircraft to greet the deputy secretary. It had to have been at least 20 people exiting the aircraft. Among those accompanying the deputy secretary was a tall muscular dark skinned young man, carrying a package under his arm. He happened to be the Prime Minister of Mozambique, Maxixe Guebuza.

Kent and the deputy secretary shook hands. "It's a pleasure to meet with you Mr. secretary!" Kent said. "The pleasures all mine, Mr. Mooney." The secretary said. "I would like you to meet the person who set up this meeting. This is Kimberly Lassenberry. The deputy secretary and Kimberly shook hands. Mr. Soumah didn't release her hand until he kissed the back of it. "It is also a pleasure to shake hands with a beautiful flower such as yourself!" he said with a creepy smile. Kimberly smiled, but kept shifting her eyes at the much younger, and more handsome prime minister of Mozambique standing next to him. "I would like to introduce to you good people, the Prime minister of the great nation of Mozambique! Maxixe Guebuza!"

the deputy secretary said. The prime minister shook hands with Mooney, then Kimberly. She blushed as the prime minister showed his perfect smile. "It's a good thing that we all speak English! Translators make conversations messy! Don't you agree?" the prime minister chuckled. Kimberly, still smiling, had a bewildered look on her face. "In some cases, yes!" Kimberly nervously chuckled as everyone else in the crowd followed suit with laughter. "If you and the prime minister would follow us inside, we could dine on some Yassa and Tapalapa bread, Mr. secretary!" Kent said. "Oh! I haven't had Tapalapa bread since I was a child! I am honored!" the deputy secretary said. "I apologize prime minister, but we weren't expecting your arrival! I would have prepared a dish from your homeland!" Kent said. "That's quite all right! All of mother Africa is my homeland!" Guebuza chuckled.

The prime minister, deputy secretary and their entourage followed Kimberly and Kent to the bungalow. They enter the place. The prime minister and the deputy secretary look at each other for a moment with scowls on their faces. Kimberly and a few others noticed their facial expressions. "You'll have to forgive me! We only had so much time to build the place!" Kimberly said. "But, we do have indoor toilets!" Kent said jokingly. The guests start laughing. "No, it's quite all right!" the prime minister said. "In that case, let's eat!" Kent shouted.

The food was set up in a buffet style display in aluminum pans. The utensils were plastic. The plates were foam. Kimberly was on a budget. Building a palace and eating from fine china wasn't her top priority. There was a long cafeteria table set up for the staff of the 2 groups. Kent's legal team and the staff of the deputy secretary sat together mingling, while there was a card table set up for the 4 main players. The prime minister and the deputy secretary served themselves just as Kimberly and Kent did. All 4 took their seats at the dining table. "Excuse me ladies and gentlemen, but I am a devout Catholic. I would like us to join hands in honor of our lord and savior." The prime minister said. Kimberly smiled at the prime minister as she took hold of his hand. Everyone at both tables joined hands.

"Eternal Father, I offer Thee the Sacred Heart of Jesus, with all its love, all it's sufferings and all its merits. To expiate all the sins, I have committed this day and during all my life. May we prosper this day and days come. In your name, amen." The prime minister said. "Amen!" everyone said simultaneously. The small group release each other's hands. "Oh! How rude of me!" the prime minister said. He grabbed the package that was on the floor next to his foot. He hands it over to Kimberly. "What's this?" she asked. "Open it. Please." The prime minister insisted. Kimberly giggling, tore apart the shiny gold wrapping paper like a child on Christmas day. She opened the box. Kimberly pulled out the contents. She held it up in the air, observing every angle of the object. "What is it?" Kent asked. "It's called a Shetani. I was about to buy one on my last trip to the mainland. This is beautiful!" she said. "Not as beautiful as you!" Guebuza said. "You are sweat!" Kimberly said. Kent rolled his eyes. The prime minister leaned into Kimberly. "I hope after this meal, I can fill my pockets just as the deputy secretary did! Maybe we could clean up that toxic mess faster than expected!" he whispered with an evil grin. Kimberly stopped smiling when she realized the seriousness of the prime minister's comment.

After the meal, Kimberly, Kent, the deputy secretary and the prime minister trek their way through the sands of Lassenberia in a convoy of 4 jeeps. Kimberly rented the jeeps a day earlier from the city of Toliara in Madagascar, which were brought over by ferry. Within that 20 miles' drive, the personal in the convoy could smell the fumes of the toxic waste as they drew near. "Kimberly, Kent and the deputy secretary covered their mouths and noses with handkerchiefs. Prime minister Guebuza held his head in shame for a moment as he saw the wall of steel drums appearing over the dunes.

Within 3 miles of the dump site, the convoy had to come to a halt. The fumes were so strong, covering ones' mouth and nose could not help. There were those in the convoy gagging and tearing up. "It's gotten worse since the last time I was here!" Kimberly shouted. "Everyone! Turn back!" prime minister Guebuza shouted. The meal the prime minister had eaten earlier didn't have a chance to digest. He regurgitated right in the front seat. This led to a chain reaction of vomiting from the others riding with him. Including Kimberly. The convoy made a U-turn from once they came.

Back at the bungalow, secretary Soumah kicked over a chair. "How in the hell could this have happened? This is all your doing!" he shouted at the prime minister with a thick accent. Prime Minister Guebuza rushed toward the much older and frail looking secretary. "Do not point the finger at me, Mr. secretary! As you can see, this was happening long before my administration came into power!" the prime minister shouted. Kimberly got in between them. "I'm the one who should be pissed! This island belongs to my husband's family!" she shouted. "I understand your frustration Ms. Kimberly, but this is a legal matter between men!" the prime minister said. "What kind of man sends his wife to tend to his business?" Secretary Soumah shouted. "First of all, it's Mrs., not Ms.! I don't care who you are, Mr. secretary! You say one more word about my husband, I'll kick you in your Gambian nuts!" Kimberly shouted. "Hey! Hey! Hey!" Kent shouted as he pulled Kimberly away from threatening the deputy secretary. "He's a foreign diplomat!" Kent whispered to Kimberly. "So!" Kimberly whispered. "So? You can't threaten a foreign diplomat! Not to his face, anyway!" Kent whispered. Kimberly pushed Kent out of the way. "Vocês dois são nada mais do que egoístas gananciosos, lápis empurrando covardes!" Kimberly shouted. "What the hell did she just say?" secretary Soumah asked. Kimberly turned to the secretary. "Ask the prime minister. He speaks Portuguese. At least he should, coming from Mozambique." She said before stepping outside. The room was silent for a moment as she walked outside. "Ela é muito bonita demais para estar com raiva!" Prime Minister Guebuza said to himself.

The next morning, Kimberly had awakened in her small room. She stared at the clock on the wall. It was 9am. She sat up from her army cot. She ran her fingers through her dreadlocks. She stood, and walked over to her gym bag on the floor. She pulled out her tooth brush, a tube of toothpaste, a shower cap, a bar of soap and a wash cloth that was inside a plastic baggie. The last thing she grabbed was her towel. She left her room, wearing a tank top and Bermuda shorts. Sitting at the table, eating breakfast, were Kent and his 4-person legal team. "Good morning, boss lady!" Kent shouted. Kimberly gave him an odd look. "Someone has a lot of vigor this morning." She said as she walked by. "Good morning Mrs. Lassenberry." The team said simultaneously. "Stop it! You all sound like elementary school kids!" she chuckled. "Come sit with us, and have a good old fashion American breakfast!" Kent said. Kimberly looked over the table to see what the team was eating. "Powdered eggs, greasy bacon!" Can't wait to dig in!" she said with sarcasm. "You paid for this stuff!" Kent said with a mouth full of food. "Sue me! We're on a budget!" she yelled as she left the bungalow.

About 50 yards away from the Bungalow, stood a 500-gallon water tower supported by 4 10-foot metal stilts. There was a long pipe connected to a shower head. Kimberly stepped into the enclosed shower stall. After she donned her shower cap, she removed her clothing and pulled a chain connected to the shower head.

Kimberly only stayed in the shower for a couple of minutes, to conserve water. That was the rule for the group. She rapped the towel around her, covering her breasts, on down to her knees. She made her way back to the bungalow after removing her shower cap.

Inside the bungalow, Kimberly passed by Paul, who was one of Kent's paralegals. It was Paul's turn to clear the table.

Paul was a 20 something year old white guy from Hope Township, New Jersey. He's been Kent's assistant ever since the Lassenberia project began. He was the tall slender preppy type. As he was putting the foam plates in the trash bag, Paul couldn't help himself for staring, as Kimberly walked by him wearing nothing but her towel. She turned her head and noticed Paul staring.

As Kimberly passed by Kent's room, she noticed him packing his bag. "What, on earth are you doing?" Kimberly asked. Kent stopped stuffing his clothes inside his duffel bag. "I radioed into the mainland. Me and my people are catching the first barge off this island!" Kent said. Kimberly walked into his room. "You realize we have more ground to explore!" she said. Kent stood a few inches away from Kimberly. "Kimberly! The prime minister and deputy secretary already signed the documents! My job is done here!" Kent said. "Your job is done when I say it's done!" Kimberly said as she kept poking Kent in the chest. "Fuck sakes! I'm no geologist!" Kent shouted. "No, but Tom is!" she shouted.

Tom Shaffer was a middle aged white guy, who not only had an environmental law degree, but a master's degree in geology. He worked for New World Construction about a decade ago, before resigning for morality differences with CEO Charles Scott.

Scott wanted to turn the former Alcatraz Federal Penitentiary into a housing project exclusively for low income families in the Los Angeles area. Tom was hired to inspect the foundation of the island, and found deadly bacteria in the crevices of the rock formation beneath the prison. Once Mr. Scott calculated how cost effective it would be to decontaminate the rock formation, he ignored Tom's warning and continued with his plans to construct the housing project. Unlike constructing Castle Lassenberry, Mr. Scott didn't have the financial backing from the National Agreement. The purpose of Castle Lassenberry was to keep Eddie Lassenberry pleased and the Lassenberry bloodline under the thumb of the National Agreement. The top echelon of the National Agreement didn't see any gain in the Alcatraz project. Just before construction could begin at Alcatraz Island, an anonymous call was made to the Environmental Protection Agency. New World construction abandoned the project shortly after.

After Kimberly and Kent had their heated discussion, she went to her room to get dressed. Moments later, Kimberly went into the kitchen. She grabbed a few pieces of bacon. She squeezed the excess grease from the pieces of bacon by rapping it in a paper towel. Paul was sitting at the small table reading a lawbook, brushing up on his legal skills. "Where's Tom?" Kimberly asked. "He should be with the others loading up the jeeps for our extraction." Paul said. "Could you tell him I want to see him?" Kimberly asked. "I'm reading!" Paul said. "May I remind you, you're still on the clock." She said. Paul sighed as he slammed the book on the table. He got up and stormed out the door.

Minutes later, Tom showed up at the bungalow. Kimberly noticed he looked agitated. "What's up?" he asked. "I Hate to put this on you, but we're going to have to stay behind. 2 days at the most." Kimberly said. "Oh, come on, Kimberly! I have a wife and kids to go home to!" he shouted. "Do you realize how big this island is? Do you realize how much of this island is uncharted? I don't want to leave until this mass of sand is thoroughly inspected! Understand?" Kimberly shouted. "Je…sus!" tom sighed.

A couple of hours had passed. Kent's team, minus Kimberly, and tom, had boarded the barge in route to the shores of Madagascar. 3 of the 4 jeeps were loaded on the barge. Kimberly waved goodbye to the legal team as the barge drifted off, while Tom just stood there with his arms folded. "Do we have enough gas in the jeep?" Kimberly asked tom as she continued to wave goodbye to the legal team.

Back in New Jersey, Edward the 2nd and Sir Marcus meet in the back room of the Whitman rest area once again. Sir Marcus removed his sun glasses. "So, what news you have for me, this time?" he asked. "Yo cuz. I was thinking, man." Edward the 2nd said. Sir Marcus leaned back in his chair. "Oh! You're thinking now!" he said with sarcasm. "Yo, man! Fuck you!" Edward the 2nd chuckled. Sir Marcus laughed as well. "Seriously cousin. What's on your mind?" he asked. "This Dubbs thing. It's fucking with me." Edward the 2nd said. "Did you handle that?" Sir Marcus asked. Edward the 2nd looked down in shame, tapping his fingers on the table. "Is he dead? Is he alive? What?" Sir Marcus shouted. "That fucking Bex, man." Edward the 2nd whispered to himself. "What are you talking about?" Sir Marcus asked. "Bex. Bex to took the wrap!" Edward the 2nd sighed. "Bex took the wrap for what?" Sir Marcus asked. Edward the 2nd shook his head. "I put the generals in a room. I gave Dubbs a chance to confess. He didn't. Bex wanted out of the game. So, he took the wrap, and confessed to the murders. I looked Dubbs straight in the eye. That nigga had guilt all over his face! Then I fucked up and told Hakim, what's done is done." Edward the 2nd explained. Sir Marcus looked around the room. There were 2 vending machines in the room. One was for snacks. The other, for soft drinks. "If you got something to say, cuz, just say it!" Edward the 2nd shouted. "You have a dollar?" Sir Marcus asked. "A what?" Edward the 2nd asked. "Do…you…have…a… dollar?" Sir Marcus asked again. Edward the 2nd looked confused, but he reached into his pocket anyway. He pulled out a wad of cash. He flipped through the wad until he came upon the only dollar bill in the stack. "Here!" he shouted. Sir Marcus took the dollar. He went over to the vending machine. He inserted the dollar into the soft drink machine. Edward the 2nd rolled his eyes. "I'm talking some serious shit here! And, yo ass thirsty!" Edward the 2nd said. Sir Marcus pressed his selection. The can fell through the slot. Sir Marcus removed his glove. He popped open the can and took a gulp. "Send Dubbs a private message." He said. "What kind of private message?" Edward the 2nd asked. "Whoever he gave the order to, send his head to Dubbs." Sir Marcus said. "What if he tells Butch? Then we gotta deal with the both of them-n-shit!" Edward the 2nd said. Sir Marcus took another gulp. "Trust me. He won't tell. All he'll do, is realize you're not stupid, and you knew it was him after all. Damn, I miss the taste of root beer!" he said. Edward the 2nd stood from his chair. He was in awe of his cousin. "Damn! No wonder uncle Eddie picked you!" he said. Sir Marcus shrugged his shoulders, then took another gulp of root beer.

"What's the word on my wife?" Sir Marcus asked. "Oh yeah, Kimberly! She sent me a coded message. She said she got those dignitary fuckers to clean up the Lassenberia dumpsite." Edward the 2nd said. "She said fuckers?" "Nah. That was me." Edward the 2nd said. Sir Marcus just chuckled.

"How's business?" Sir Marcus asked. Edward the 2nd flopped back into his chair, and sighed. "Well. I gotta find somebody to take over Bex's territory." He said. Sir Marcus took another gulp of root beer. "Simple. Give the job to Hakim to decide. But, don't tell the other generals!" Sir Marcus said. "Hakim? Why should I give him that responsibility?" Edward the 2nd asked. "Come on, cousin! You really think Bex, was running South Jersey? He's a bumpkin! Or, he was!" Sir Marcus said. Edward the 2nd looked up at his cousin gulp the last of the can of root beer. "You sure I won't regret that shit? You sure we, won't regret that shit?" he said. Sir Marcus quickly sat in the chair. He reached over and put his hand on his cousin's forearm. "Hakim! Hakim is the light at the end of the tunnel!" Sir Marcus whispered. "End of the tunnel, huh?" Edward the 2nd said. "Make it clear to him. If he screws up on his choice, you'll be replacing 2 generals. Trust me on this one too, cousin. Edward the 2nd nodded. "Is there anything else?" Sir Marcus asked. Edward the 2nd shook his head. "I'll send more supplies to you tonight." Edward the 2nd said in a soft voice. "I guess this meeting is adjourned then." Sir Marcus said. He stood at attention. "No, wait cuz!" Edward the 2nd said. He slowly stood from his seat. He stood at attention. "Long live the house of Lassenberry! Long Live… Sir Marcus!" Edward the 2nd said. "Thank you, cousin." Sir Marcus said. "This ones' on me. Yo ass earned it." Edward the 2nd said. They give each other a hug. "Until next time cuz." Edward the 2nd said. "Just keep me posted." Sir Marcus said.

The next day on the island of Lassenberia, Kimberly and Tom started their trek early in the morning. Tom drove the jeep towards the southern part of the island. Even though she had on her seat belt, Kimberly held on for dear life as the jeep sped over the uneven sandy terrain. "So, where exactly are we going?" Tom shouted over the noise of the jeep's engine. "For now, we're just driving straight! Or, until I see something out of the ordinary!" Kimberly shouted. Tom looked over and saw that Kimberly didn't look too well. "Is the ride getting to you?" He shouted. "Is it that obvious?" Kimberly shouted as she clutched her stomach. A couple of minutes had passed. It was that last bump on the rough terrain that Kimberly finally said enough is enough. "Stop the jeep!" She shouted. Tom nodded his head. He made a quick stop just before coming over a small dune. Kimberly unbuckled her seat belt and jumped out of the jeep. She covered her mouth as she ran towards the dune. On the other side of the dune she crouched over, puking her brains out. On the other side of the dune Tom hopped out of the jeep. He took off the linen scarf wrapped around his neck. He then took off his straw fedora and wiped his brow. He looked towards the west and saw the scenery of Madagascar off into the distance. He looked up staring at the clear blue sky.

Moment s had passed. Tom looked at his watch. Kimberly hadn't returned. "Kimberly! Are you all right?" he shouted. There was no answer. "Kimberly! Kimberly!" He shouted. Tom hopped back into the jeep. He started the engine. He hit the accelerator, but could not gain traction over the dune. The more he hit the gas, the more the jeep kept sliding in every direction. To add insult to injury. The jeep started to overheat. Tom screamed obscenities as steam came from under the hood. He cut off the engine. He frowned from the fumes of anti-freeze. As he opened the hood to unveil the engine, a gush of steam hit him in the face. Not having the patience to let the engine cool down, Tom grabbed the radiator cap bare handed. "Shit!" he screamed as he grabbed his singed hand. As it started to blister, he wrapped his scarf around his injured hand. In a fit of rage, he kicked the tire. "I'm a fucking geologist! I'm a fucking lawyer! Not some fucking mechanic!" he screamed as he jumped up and down in a tantrum. He looked up at the sky. "I should be home with my family! Fuck! Fuck!" he shouted. At the top of the dune, Kimberly appeared. "Tom! Tom!" she shouted. "What?" he shouted. "Are you ok?" she asked. He turned towards Kimberly. "No, I'm not ok! I burned my fucking hand!" he shouted. She rolled her eyes. "Can you wiggle your fingers?" she shouted. Tom looked agitated. "Yes! I can fucking wiggle my fingers!" he shouted. "Well, shake it off! I need you to see something!" she shouted. Kimberly disappeared over the other side of the dune. "Fuck!" Tom shouted as he kicked the sand. He climbed to the top of the dune. He lost his footing and rolled down the rest of the way. He looked up as he spat out sand, and saw Kimberly standing over him. She reached out and helped him up. "I've should've stayed at the bungalow!" he shouted. "You're here because your smart! And I need you!" Kimberly said after picking up his fedora. Tom clutched his hand over his injured hand. "It hurts like a son-of-a-bitch!" he said in agony. "Is there a medical kit in the jeep?" Kimberly asked. "No! it's back at the bungalow! All I have is my chemistry test kit!" he said. "Come on! I need you to see something!" Kimberly said. Tom shook his head. He followed Kimberly over 50 yards away from the dune. They came upon a wet patch in the sand. It was about 2 feet in diameter. "What is that?" Tom asked. Kimberly sighed. "That's why you're here, so you can tell me!" she said. "That's odd! We're far away from the shore. No foul weather for days. Did you touch it?" Tom asked. "No! I didn't even dip my toe in it!" Kimberly said. "Let's head back to the jeep. I need you to give me a hand carrying my chemistry kit back here." Tom said.

Minutes later, Kimberly and Tom arrive back at the wet spot in the sand. Both each had a handle on carrying Tom's chemistry kit. "Since the jeep is on the fritz, we'll conduct our little experiment here." Tom said. Kimberly assisted Tom in emptying the contents of his test kit. Tom handed Kimberly a pair of safety goggles, and a pair of rubber gloves. Kimberly and Tom donned their goggles. A set of beakers, funnels, droppers, and a thermometer were placed about a yard away from the site. As he applied pressure on to his injured hand, Tom gave Kimberly instructions on how to take samples of the moist sand. With a plastic scoop, Kimberly carefully scooped off a thin layer of moist sand, placing each layer into separate beakers. As Kimberly scooped up the 10th and final layer, she noticed a strange substance seeping to the surface. "Do you see what I'm seeing?" she asked tom. "Whatever it is, don't touch it! We can take the last 3 sand samples back with us!" Tom said. "Kimberly! Take the flask out of the kit, then carefully fill it with whatever that is." Tom said. Kimberly scowled as she collected a sample of the strange substance. "Wow! What do you call this green goop?" Kimberly asked. Kimberly held the flask in the air before putting the cap on. This slimy green goop gave off a florescent green hue when held up to the sun. "Careful Kimberly! you already have some on your glove!" Tom shouted. "Take it easy Tom." Kimberly chuckled. Kimberly could hear tom mumble under his breath out of frustration. "Let's just get this back to the bungalow! I can get a better analyst under the microscope!" Tom said. Kimberly smacked the cap on the flask, placing it in the kit box. She then placed the beakers filled with the sand samples in the kit box as well. Kimberly in a playful mood, spooked Tom with her stained glove by pretending she was going to touch him.. "Jesus! We don't know how toxic this stuff is!" Tom shouted. Kimberly laughed herself silly. "Whatever it is, it can't be the same as the filth at the dump site!" she chuckled. Before they picked up the chemistry kit box, Kimberly's attitude went from being jovial, to professional. She grabbed Tom by the arm. "No one is to know about this! Not even Kent or your wife, or else!" she said. Tom looked at Kimberly for a moment. "That sounds like a threat!" he said. "I could never be more in earnest, tom!" Kimberly said. "You forget young lady. I'm a lawyer." Tom said with a smirk on his face. Kimberly stood face-to-face with Tom. "You forget. I'm a Lassenberry." She said. Kimberly could see Tom's throat move as he gulped down saliva. Sweat began to trickle down his cheek. "Now, we can go back!" she chuckled.

It was Christmas day back in the United States, when hakim received the dreadful visit he was expecting since his last meeting with Edward the 2nd. The visitor, or visitors were 2 detectives from the Garfield, New Jersey police department. Hakim was sitting in his Manhattan penthouse, once owned by Edward the 2nd, when he received a call from the concierge. "Mr. bates. There's a detective Murray and detective Midland down here in the lobby. They would like to have a word with you. Should I send them up, sir?" the man said. Hakim sighed as his eyes teared up. "Ok frank…send them up." Hakim said.

Hakim was wearing silk pajamas, a silk bathrobe and cashmere bedroom slippers. Outside the double doors of Hakim's penthouse stood his alternate bodyguard, Bilal Forte. Forte was the nephew of Rufus Forte, a.k.a Chewie. Since the deaths of Mookie and 2 Gunz, Hakim needed another inner circle of thugs and killers to protect his interests.

Bilal was a 21-year-old husky guy, who had admired his uncle's reputation since he was a child. He was a dark-skinned guy with a muscular build, standing about 6 feet 2 inches. He even had his hair dreaded like his uncle. His job was to guard hakim at his residence. He was given a pay of 3 grand every time he was on duty.

Moments later, the 2 detectives step out of the elevator. They turned down the carpeted corridor. They see Bilal standing at the entrance of the penthouse. Both detectives dwarf Bilal, but they weren't intimidated by his appearance. Detective Murray, who stood about 5 feet, 8 was a rough looking Irish American. "We're here to see Hakim Bates, kid!" Murray said as he showed his badge. "Hold on!" Bilal said in a deep voice. Bilal knocked on the door, still facing the detectives. "Yeah!" Hakim shouted. "Five-o wanna see you, boss!" Bilal shouted. Seconds later, Hakim opened the door with an friendly expression on his face. "Officers! Can I help you with anything?" Hakim asked. "Yes. I'm detective Murray, and this is detective Midland of the Garfield, New Jersey Police Department." He said as the officers flashed their badges.

"Nice shiny New Jersey badges! Good for you!" Hakim said sarcastically. "May we come in? we have some horrible news, as well as a few questions." Murray said. Hakim looked at Bilal, then at the officers. "No, you may not." Hakim chuckled. "Your brother, or half-brother, Biron Eric Xavier was found in a ditch in my town!" Murray said. "Is he dead?" Hakim asked. The 2 detectives looked at each other for a split second. "Sorry to say, he is." Murray said. Hakim looked up at the corridor ceiling for a moment. He sucked his teeth as if food was caught in between them. "How did he die?" Hakim asked. "They're still doing an autopsy. But there were no signs of physical harm to his body. He didn't have any ID on him at the time. Or clothes for that matter. We suggest he was a victim of a robbery." Murray said.

Before detective Murray could continue his conversation with Hakim, 2 Caucasian men stepped out of the elevator dressed in black suits and dark shades. One of them came face-to-face with detective Murray. "Can I help you?" Murray asked. Hakim stood there with a smile. Both men with the dark shades pulled out badges. "We're here with the DEA elite task force." One of the men said. "DEA elite, what? Never heard of you guys!" Murray said. The other man pulled out a card. This was no ordinary business card. It was metallic with an indigo hue. With the words of the agency engraved on it. "You realize the young man standing here is an alleged drug lord. His brother's body was found in our jurisdiction!" Murray shouted. "That's why we're here detective. We're taking over this investigation now. If you would like to resolve the matter, we suggest you take it up with your chief, Andrew Raymond I believe it is?." The man said. Murray took another look at the business card. He looked at Hakim, then the 2 men in dark shades. "Detective Midland!... Let's get the fuck out of here!" Murray said. As the 2 detectives walked down the corridor towards the elevators, Murray turned around, and stared at Hakim. "Mr. Bates! Don't let me catch you in Garfield doing something you shouldn't be doing!" he shouted. Hakim smiled. "Don't worry! It's not my Jurisdiction, anyway!" Hakim shouted. Hakim, Bilal and the 2 men in dark shades watched as the 2 detectives entered the elevator. "Wow!" hakim said with a sigh of relief. "How did you guys know the cops would show up here, at this particular moment?" Hakim asked. One of the men pulled out a syringe from inside his jacket pocket. Before anyone could react to his movement, he plunged it in the side of Bilal's neck. Within seconds, Bilal dropped to the floor like dead weight. "What the fuck you just do, nigga?" hakim shouted. Don't worry General bates. He will awaken within a few hours. To answer your question, we were assigned to you by Lord Lassenberry after the meeting in Lodi. "Good day general". The man said as he and his counterpart turn in the opposite direction towards the elevator.

Back on the island of Lassenberia, Kimberly impatiently paced the room in the bungalow with her arms folded as Tom conducted more tests on the green goop they've discovered a few days earlier. They were low on supplies and food, but Kimberly wanted an official conclusion to this strange phenomenon they've stumbled upon. The generator that supplied the power to the bungalow was on its last leg of fuel.

Kimberly had rented a centrifuge from one of the universities in Madagascar a day earlier. Tom had run test after test, but to no avail, he couldn't find a purpose for the green goop. Kimberly was a vigilant soldier, while Tom was drained and at the same time terrified if there weren't any results.

Tom had stared into the microscope numerous times. He rubbed his eyes to focus. He wiped the sweat from his brow. Even though his hand was properly treated, he could still feel the discomfort from the burn.

"Why don't we just pack it up, and go home! It's probably more toxic waste!" Tom desperately shouted. Kimberly stopped pacing. "Come on, tom! You're talking out of despair! You know as well as I do that puddle has nothing to do with toxic dump on the other side of the island! You're smarter than that! We're not leaving until I get results! Now get me, results!" she shouted. In his usual fit of rage, tom turned around to give Kimberly a piece of his mind. Suddenly, he clumsily knocked over one of the beakers filled with the green goop. His quick reflexes allowed him to catch the beaker before it fell to the floor. Without thinking, he caught it with his injured hand. Some of the green goop spilled over on to his hand. Tom was terrified. "Look what you've made me do, now!" he shouted. Kimberly rushed to his aid. "Quick! Let's get you to the water tower and flush your hand!" she shouted. "You bitch! I could be dead by the time I walk out there!" tom cried. Kimberly rolled her eyes and shook her head in disbelief. "Let's take off the bandage and Gauze to see if it soaked through!" Kimberly shouted. "Jesus! I should've been home with my family!" tom cried as he unwound the bandage. Tom was shaking. He turned his head away. He didn't want to see his hand morph into something horrific. As Kimberly removed the gauze, she noticed something miraculous. "Tom! Look!" she shouted. "No! I can't! The pain is gone! Did my hand fall off?" tom cried. Kimberly carefully examined his hand. "Tell me! I can take it!" tom cried aloud. "Just look, and stop acting like a big baby!" Kimberly said. Tom slowly turned. He looked down at his hand. Not only was the pain gone, so were the blisters. His hand looked like it was never burned. "What the hell?" he whispered. He wiggled his fingers. He started laughing hysterically. He wrapped his arms around Kimberly as he jumped up and down. Kimberly pulled away from him. She looked around the room. She noticed a big nail head sticking out of the wall. She ran over to it. "Kimberly! what are you doing?" tom asked. Kimberly shut her eyes, and took a deep breath. She quickly slammed her hand against the wall, allowing the nail to pierce her hand. She let out a scream as she saw the head of the nail impale her hand. She pulled her hand away, causing the gash to expand. Her hand was dripping with blood. She ran over and poured some of the green goop over the wound. Within seconds, she felt no pain and her wound magically closed right before her eyes. Kimberly cried tears of joy. She went over and hugged tom. They both jumped for joy.

About a half hour later, Kimberly and tom were sitting at the long table celebrating their great discovery with a bottle of scotch tom had brought at the beginning of their arrival. They didn't use cups. Both drank straight from the bottle, passing it back-n-forth. Kimberly was tipsy, as well as tom. "I can't wait to get this…this green goop back to the mainland! Do you realize we've discovered the fountain of healing? We're going to be rich beyond our wildest dreams!" tom shouted. Kimberly staggered from her chair. She raised the bottle in the air. Long Live the House of Lassenberry!" she chuckled "What the hell does that mean?" tom asked. Before he could get an answer, 2 African men with machine guns stepped into the room. "Yes! What the hell does that mean?" one of them asked.

The 2 dark skinned men were dressed in tattered military garb. They looked like they haven't eaten in days, maybe weeks, they were so thin. Their weapons were the AK-47. It looked like they could barely keep aim, due to their lack of nutrition.

Tom was wide eyed and petrified. Kimberly was terrified as she slowly lowered the bottle of scotch. She immediately sobered up as her heart was racing. "What…what do you want?" she asked. "Everything you have to offer, beautiful one!" one of the men said. "We…we have nothing!" she said. "It looked like you were celebrating! You must have something!" the man said with a thick accent. As Kimberly placed the bottle on the table, she stealthy grabbed the pair of surgical scissors used to cut tom's bandages. The African man moved in closer, as the other stood by the doorway wobbling at the knees. "Your friend looks weak! We have barely enough food, but you can take it!" Kimberly said. "We'll take it, and whatever else you possess!" the man said. As the man approached Kimberly, aiming the weapon at her, Tom snapped out of his frightened state. He flew into action. He jumped from his seat, grabbing the barrel of the weapon. He over powered the frail man. The weapon was pointed towards the ceiling as tom struggled for possession. The man had enough strength to pull the trigger. Tom pointed the weapon in the direction of the other man standing in the doorway. He was cut in half by the barrage of bullets. But before he fell, his weapon went off, hitting tom in the chest and face. Kimberly quickly lunged at the man that was struggling with tom, putting a gash across his neck with the surgical scissors. At the end of the melee, 3 bodies lay on the floor. 2 dead, and one critically injured. Kimberly cried hysterically as she kneeled over tom's lifeless body. She looked around and noticed that all but one of the beakers of green goop wasn't damaged during the chaos. She quickly ran over and grabbed the beaker. In an act of desperation, she poured it over tom's face and chest, covering his wounds. The man with gash in his neck, was struggling for air as blood was spewing from his mouth. Less than a minute had passed. Tom's body did not reanimate from his wounds. Kimberly realized it was too late for tom. She looked over at the African man struggling for air. She took a deep breath, wiping away her tears. She walked over to the man, standing over him with what remained of the beaker of green goop. She was angry, but focused. "Do you want to live?" she shouted to the man. The man couldn't speak. All he could do is nod his head. "If I let you live, do you swear your life to me?" she shouted. "I…Iska…Leh…In…Aad!" the man struggled to say before his eyes rolled back into his head. Kimberly kneeled over him and poured the remaining green goop over his gash. Within seconds, the man started to catch his breath as his wound closed. The man sat up by himself, coughing. "Thank you! Thank you!" he said. "You're Somalian, aren't you?" Kimberly asked. The man nodded frantically. "I'm a little rusty with Somali. What does I iska leh in aad mean?" she asked. He turned to Kimberly. "It means…I… belong…to…you!" he would pant to Kimberly. Kimberly stood up. She picked up the AK-47 from the floor. She went over and grabbed the other weapon next to the dead body in the doorway. Kimberly walked passed the African, who remained seated on the floor. She took a seat as she placed one of the weapons on the table, while the other was propped across her lap. "What's your name?" Kimberly asked. Still in shock about what had occurred, the African man took a moment to catch his breath. "My…name…is… Ali Mogadishu Mohamed!" he said as he gasped for air. Kimberly stared at the ceiling, then focused her eyes on the African man. "Well Mr. Mohamed, despite what just took place, today is your lucky day." Kimberly said.

— CHAPTER 25. NORTH VS. SOUTH —

It was December 28th when the biggest event in Bridgeton, New Jersey was taking place. Hakim had arranged the funeral services for his brother Bex, costing close to a half million dollars. Hakim was dressed in his jack boots and uniform underneath a long leather trench coat. The trench coat was buttoned up to his neck. He wore a green sash around his waist and a red shoulder sash.

Inside the funeral hall, Clint, and Toby both wore black suits. They were sitting in the first row on either side of Hakim. The hall was packed with people in the narcotics game from all over South Jersey. Even Philly mob boss Mr. Nice came to pay his respects. Those who were absent from the services were the remaining 3 generals, Butch, Dubbs and Mookie and their people. A meeting was held prior to the event by the 3 generals not to attend because of exposure by the press. This was the justification to Hakim. He took it as a slap in the face when explaining his feelings about it to Chewie. On the other side of the isle sat the top guys in Bex's crew. André, Frenchie, Peau Claire, Remy, Darnell Bradley, Kyle, Jason, and white guy Gonzo, all were dressed in black suits. Toby looked over at the crew, then leaned in to Hakim. "I know Calvin's hands are cleaner than a motherfucker in all this! You think one of them other boys had something to do with this shit?" Toby whispered in Hakim's ear. Hakim frowned from the stench of Toby's breath. "Old man! You gotta stop drinking, fore real!" he whispered. "I was just asking, man!" Toby whispered. "Man! Don't ask me nothing right now! You know what? Go over there and sit with them niggas! Go!" Hakim whispered in a stern voice. Toby looked at hakim with disappointment. "Nigga! Don't let me embarrass you up in here!" hakim whispered. Toby just shook his head and stood from his seat. Jenny looked confused. She grabbed Toby by the arm. "Where the hell you are going?" she asked. Toby yanked his arm away. "Leave me the hell alone, woman!" he shouted. Toby had drawn attention to himself after making the outburst. Toby went over and sat at the end of the isle next to André. Jenny moved over towards Hakim. "What's wrong with that fool?" she whispered. "Nothing! He's just being Toby." Hakim said. Calvin tapped jenny on the arm. "What's up with Toby, ma?" he asked. "Mind yo business, boy!" she whispered.

Clint had leaned over to Hakim. "He was a good kid. This should've never happened. If you need help on getting back at the bastards who did this…" Clint whispered. "Don't worry. I'll handle it." Hakim whispered as he stared at the casket.

After the eulogies, Tamika stood before the crowd, if front of a microphone. She began singing her heart out to a familiar tribute song. This was part where people started breaking down in tears. Hakim tried his best to hold back his, but when that first trickle came from his eyes, he excused himself. He walked at a fast pace, heading towards the lobby. All eyes were on him as he left the room. Moments later, Clint left his seat, and followed him.

Hakim went out to the lobby to bum a cigarette from one of the ushers. "You ok, kid?" Clint asked. Hakim started pacing back-n-forth as he blew out cigarette smoke. "I swear to god! I hate funeral's, man! Especially when bitches start singing!" hakim said as he continued to pace. "He was your brother! It's ok to let it out!" Clint said. Hakim took a drag from his cigarette. "Since when you started smoking?" Clint asked. "Never mind that, old man! I need you to do something for me!" Hakim said. Hakim took one of memorial funeral cards from the stack next to a vase. He pulled out an ink pen from inside his trench coat and wrote on the card. He then gave the card to Clint. "Tell the crew to meet me at this place after all this shit is over. Tell them, if they don't wanna piss me the fuck off, they better be there!" Hakim said. "Got it. Are you coming back inside?" Clint asked. Hakim took another drag from his cigarette. He blew out the smoke. "After that bitch stops singing!" he chuckled. Clint patted him on the back, then went back inside.

Hakim made sure his brother had the best send off. He had a team of white Clydesdales pull a white carriage, which the body would be carried. He used Lassenberry influence to have the funeral procession start from Bridgeton, 13 miles to Vineland. A caravan of 3 white limos and 30 vehicles followed the carriage with no interruptions with the help of police escorts.

The people in the limos consisted of Bex's crew and close friends. The 30 vehicles were the people Bex had helped financially through their hardships. Bex didn't hesitate to put envelopes filled with cash in the mailboxes of those in need.

When the funeral procession reached its destination an hour later, Bex's body was finally laid to rest next to his mother Peggy and Annie. White roses thrown by the mourners, practically covered the casket as it was lowered into the earth. After what was all said and done by the pastor, everyone headed back to their vehicles. The last white rose to be thrown on the casket belonged to Hakim. There were 2 men standing a few yards behind Hakim as he said his final words. One of the guys was Chewie, the other was a new bodyguard named Martin(Clip)Johnson, whom Eddie Lassenberry's former body guard Darnell(clip) Washington got his nick name.

Clip was an old-school gangster, going back to the days of Eddie Lassenberry. He was in his late 50's at the time when reuniting with Hakim. He was one of a handful of killers involved in the purge back in the 80's allowing Eddie Lassenberry to take control of the drug trade in north jersey. After Eddie Lassenberry took control, Clip and his cohorts were paid to go into hiding. Clip was short in stature, with a pudgy build. He was bald, sporting a gray beard. Due to his light skin and facial features, some said he could pass for an Arab or middle easterner. He returned to the fold due to splurging his hush money on women and traveling the world.

Hakim recognized him as one of the body guards that followed him on his way to school for a time, by the orders of Eddie Lassenberry.

"Don't worry brother. I got shit under control. You can rest now." Hakim whispered as he tossed the white rose on the casket. He turned to Chewie and Clip. "Let's go and tell these south jersey niggas what time it is." Hakim said. The 2 body guards followed Hakim back to the limo.

It was around 4pm when Hakim and his 2 body guards arrived at a disclosed place back in Bridgeton. When Chewie opened the door for him, Hakim was overwhelmed to see his brother's crew gathered together in the room. Instead of jumping for joy, he walked in the room with a slow swagger, covering up his pride with a smirk.

"Glad to see all y'all showed up!" hakim said. Kyle was seated, but when Hakim entered the room, he stood to his feet. "First, I'd like to say thank you on behalf of my brother, may he rest in peace! I hope you all enjoyed the food at the after wake! Now! I know what all of you are thinking! Who's gonna run shit now that Bex ain't with us anymore! It's simple! That person would be me!" Hakim said. At that moment, Frenchie took a step forward. "With all due respect, Hakim! That shit should be decided amongst us!" he said. Clip was always on point, but became more vigilant as he stealthy reached for his pistol. Hakim stepped to Frenchie, standing about a foot away from him. Frenchie towered over Hakim. Hakim showed that Frenchie's verbal prowess did not faze him. "Listen nigga! Y'all ain't gotta clue how this pyramid we in works! I dropped bodies when y'all was playing with action figures! So, the best thing to do, is to do what I tell ya!" hakim said with thunder in his voice. Frenchie smiled, as he slowly applauded. "That was cute! Did you rehearse that on your way here?" Frenchie said. There was little chuckling from the peanut gallery. Hakim cleared his throat. He looked Frenchie in the eye, not blinking one bit. "Listen. You're going to turn all y'all territories over to me. Because without me, y'all lives won't be worth shit. It was me who made the deal with Mr. Nice. without me, he will break that deal, turning all y'all into slaves, basically." Hakim said in calm soft manner. Frenchie lost his composure. He took a step back from hakim, expressing himself with flinging hand gestures. "Nigga! You ain't nothing but a foreigner just visiting! We can make our own deal! So, take yo ass back to north jersey, Pitre!" Frenchie shouted. Hakim turned to Chewie. "What the hell is a pitre?" hakim chuckled. Chewie just shrugged his shoulders out of ignorance. "I just called you a clown, nigga!" Frenchie shouted with saliva spewing from his mouth. Hakim dropped his head, staring at the floor for a moment. He looked at Frenchie. Chewie and clip had drawn their weapons by this point. Some of the south jersey crew looked nervous. "After New Year's Eve, I'm dropping off a hundred pounds of weed. I'm dropping off 4 cases of Oxy, which you will sell at 20 bucks a tablet. I'm dropping off 50 kilos of pure heroin. I'm dropping off 50 kilos of pure cocaine. Y'all can chop it up however y'all see fit. Here's kicker, now listen carefully. If y'all don't have my money by the end of the month, so y'all can get y'all refill, everyone you love and cherish will disappear." Hakim said with a big grin on his face. Frenchie was about to physically reach for Hakim's throat until gonzo stepped in between them. "Yo motherfucker! You wanna go to war? North vs. South? Je vais te tuer, salope!" Frenchie shouted as gonzo held him back. "Whatever, Haitian harry!" hakim said as he turned and walked away. "I'll call you guys to let you know where the drop will be!" hakim said as he and his body guards left the room. Frenchie still infuriated, smacked Gonzo's hand out of the way. "Take it easy friend!" gonzo said. Fuck that shit! I ain't Buddy, or Bex! I'm Frenchie! The one and only!" Frenchie said as he stuck out his chest. "Frenchie! I hear you! But you have to calm down!" gonzo said. "I am calm, white boy!" Frenchie shouted. "André. Could you talk some sense into him?" gonzo said. André was leaned up against the wall with his arms folded. "Go ahead and talk some sense into me, fearless leader!" Frenchie shouted. André took a deep breath. He approached Frenchie and put his hand on his shoulder. "Tu as raison. Mais vous ne pouez pas perde votre cool tout le temps." André explained. Frenchie calmed himself. "So, what the hell we should do then?" he asked André. "Nous lui faisons penser qu'il est incharge pour l'instant. Mais, Clint, Toby et Calvin doivent partir. Nous n'avons pas besoin d'espions." André said. "Let me and Remy handle that shit! I gotta sharp ass machete just dying to meet them!" Frenchie said. "Rappelles toi! Les corps doivent disparaître! Cette merde ne puet pas être remontée à nous!" André said. Frenchie smiled from ear-to-ear. "Yo Remy! Let's go! We got shit to do!" Frenchie chuckled.

Elsewhere, in a supermarket located in West orange, New Jersey, 2 men of Italian descent huddle over by the produce section. These 2 men were the Loa brothers. The big burly one was jimmy, who towered over his older brother Tony. "How long we have to wait?" jimmy asked as he took a whiff of the fresh parsley. "Jesus jimmy! People have to eat that!" tony said. "You want me to buy? I'll buy it! Stop breaking my balls!" Jimmy said. Just put it back!" Tony said. Moments later, another man of Italian descent wearing a wool overcoat joined the 2. "Hey Paul. how's it going?" Tony said. He and Paul shook hands and kiss each other on the cheek. "Paul." Jimmy said as he and Paul just shook hands.

Paul Rita was a capo in the Gatano crime family. Since the death of his mentor Mario Felini, Paul moved up through the ranks. "What you got for me?" Paul asked. Tony looked around first. "This whole thing is fucking bizarre as shit!" tony whispered. "Paul looked agitated. "I didn't ask you that!" Paul whispered. "Finding out who was behind a 10-year-old whacking a boss is gonna take more time, Paul!" Tony whispered. "Listen you fucking deficiente! I brought you in this thing of ours! You got your button, but one thing you ain't got, is too much time left! Get your hands on that ice pick if you have to!" Paul whispered. "What's that gonna solve?" tony whispered. Multiple finger prints, dummy!" Paul whispered. "I don't see why we're running around for these zips!" Jimmy whispered. Paul came face-to-face with Jimmy. "I'm gonna pretend you didn't say that!" Paul whispered. Paul looked around as a precaution. "The game has changed boys! They run the family now! It makes me fucking sick, but that's the way things are.! Now get back out there, and get that ice pick!" Paul whispered. "Not for nothing, Paul! When I'm gonna get made?" Jimmy whispered. "If you don't wanna end up like the Don, I suggest you shut the fuck up!" Paul whispered. Paul then picked up a floral of broccoli. He took off the rubber band that held it together. "Now! What you 2 got for me?" Paul whispered. Tony looked at his brother, shaking his head. The 2 brothers reached in their pockets, each pulling out a wad of cash. They hand it over to Paul. Paul took the cash. He rapped the band around the bundle of cash, and stuffs it in his own pocket. "Now, get back to work." Paul said. Paul walked away, exiting the super market. "You still have that guy in the evidence room in your back pocket?" Tony asked. "Ah, yeah!" Jimmy said. "Well, let's go pay him a visit." Tony said. Jimmy picked up an apple, taking a bite out of it as the 2 brothers walked towards the exit.

Back at Lassenberia, Kimberly stood over the site where the green goop was discovered. Earlier, she had covered the site with wooden planks left behind by the construction crew who had built the bungalow. She then covered the planks with a mound of sand. All this was done after she tied up Mohamed back at the bungalow. Now, she and Mohamed were waiting by the shore for the ferry to take them back to Mozambique.

Her alibi for Tom's death, there was only one Somali pirate. Mohamed was buried alive on the other side of the island breathing through a tube sticking out of the sand when the authorities arrived.

Awaiting by the shore for the next transport, Mohamed and Kimberly were chomping on some snacks. She noticed that Mohamed was jittery. She tapped him on the elbow. "Relax! Everything will be fine!" she said with a smile. "You don't understand! I am a wanted man!" he said nervously. "My people have the resources to help you with a new identity." She said. Suddenly, Kimberly and Mohamed see their ride to the mainland.

It was New Year's Eve, just a couple of hours away from the year 2002. Just like last year, the Lassenberry family, along with the Jenkins family had gathered in the ballroom of the north wing of castle Lassenberry to bring in the new year. There were fewer members of the Lassenberry family in attendance do to financial disputes and illness. The entire Richards family, including the matriarch Maggie had turned down the invite from Edward the 2nd. Mark sr. was at his estate being cared for by a live-in nurse.

Edward the 2nd was proud to show off his new girlfriend, Viola Carr to the family. Viola was dressed in a sexy green backless Minnie dress. Her voluptuous breasts were practically pouring out of the top. She stood a little taller than her boyfriend due to her high heels. It was at Edward the 2nd's request that she dressed so provocative. Viola stood at a distance with her son with a drink in her hand away from the crowd, also upon Edward the 2nd's request. His insecurities over girlfriends was well known amongst his brothers and male cousins.

There were at least 10 NA agents in the hall scattered about, making sure the guests stayed within the north wing. Edward the second didn't want anyone wandering off, especially towards the south wing. Edward the 2nd was feeling buzzed from his fifth drink of cognac. His behavior was somewhat belligerent as he stood in a huddle with his brother Big L, cousins BB, Joe-Joe, and Donald, who also had drinks in their hands. "Y'all should've seen hakim yo! That nigga looked like he had shit his pants when I told his ass I run Essex County, and not him! I said, get yo ass back on those streets and get me my money! Just like in the movie!" Edward the 2nd chuckled loud. "One of my boys who works for the city of Newark said he and his goons bum rushed a rap video because they didn't get his blessing!" BB said. "If he did that shit, it was because I told him to!" Edward the 2nd chuckled as he spilled some of his drink on Joe-Joe's shoes. "Come on cuz! I paid 2 thousand for these kicks!" Joe-Joe shouted. "Man! I can buy you the whole store where you got them shits from!" Edward the 2nd shouted. "You gonna buy me the store?" Joe-Joe asked with excitement. "Hell no, nigga! That's why I give y'all an envelope every week!" Edward the 2nd chuckled. Donald couldn't help glancing over at Viola, even though his girlfriend was at the party. "Your woman doesn't look happy, man!" Donald said. Edward the 2nd looked pissed at his cousin. "You don't look at her! You don't talk to her! Understand?" Edward the 2nd said. "I was just saying, cuz!" Donald said. "Listen! You saw what happened to Malcolm and Tyson? Well, the same thing can happen to anybody if they fuck with me!" Edward the 2nd said. Edward the 2nd's outburst made his cousins feel uncomfortable. There was a moment of silence amongst the cousins until something astonishing caught Edward the 2nd's eyes. Kimberly stepped into the ballroom wearing a long sleek black dress with a split on the side. The dress was held up by spaghetti shoulder straps, with a V cut neck line. Her dread locks were pulled back in a ponytail by a sparkly gold scrunchie.

Most of the crowd turned their heads towards this beautiful woman standing in the doorway. Kimberly's best friend Carmen spotted her at the doorway. They both screamed at the top of their lungs with joy. Carmen ran to Kimberly in her high heels as fast as she could. They hugged each other tight, rocking side-to-side. "I missed you so much, sister!" Carmen screamed. "I missed you too, my sister!" Kimberly screamed. Carmen released her and held her hands. "Girl! We got so much to catch up on!" Carmen shouted. "Girlfriend! You don't know the half!" Kimberly shouted. Suddenly, Kimberly received a tap on the shoulder. She turned around to see it was her sister-in-law Terry. They both screamed at the top of their lungs. "Hey, sis!" Terry shouted. "I missed you sis!" Kimberly screamed hysterically. "Where have you been?" Terry asked. "Uh! It's a long story!" Kimberly said. Standing next to Terry was a tall light skinned brother with curly hair. "Kimberly! I would like you to meet my fiancé Brandon!" Terry said. Even though Kimberly spotted Brandon roaming the halls of castle Lassenberry, she refrained from telling him what she knew. "Welcome to the family!" she said. Brandon was a gentleman. He put out his hand in a friendly gesture. "Please to meet you!" Brandon said. "Get out of here with that handshaking nonsense, please! Come and give me a hug!" Kimberly shouted. she pulled Brandon in towards her. "Nice catch!" Kimberly told Terry. Brandon put his arm around Terry's waist. "Could you excuse us for a moment sweetie?" Terry asked Brandon. "Of course, baby!" Brandon said. He gave Terry a peck kiss on the lips. Brandon strolled over to another group at the party. Terry placed her hands on her hips. "Now, tell me! Where the hell is my brother?" she asked. Kimberly noticed an agent standing nearby. She grabbed Terry by the forearm. She took Terry over to another side of the ballroom that was more secluded. "Do yourself a favor! Do us a favor! Please don't mention your brother in this place! I know he's all right, but there's something odd about this whole thing!" Kimberly whispered. I need to tell him that my fathers' not doing so well!" Terry cried. "I need to go see him!" Kimberly said as she hugged Terry.

On the opposite side of the ballroom, stood Benny the 3^{rd,} his wife Bridget and his sister Sarah. All 3 of them each had a plate of food in their hands. "Look at him over there acting a fool!" Benny the 3rd said. Sarah sucked her teeth. "Krayton just having a good time! Leave him alone!" she said. "Don't call him that to his face! You probably won't see another envelope!" Benny the 3rd chuckled. Sarah just shook her head. "Look at him, sis! He supposed to be the head of the family! This is the guy running New Jersey?" Benny chuckled. "Honey! You have to admit, your uncle Eddie was into more than getting drunk, from what you told me." Bridget said. "True! But, Uncle Eddie was feared, and respected! A room would go dead silent when he walked into it!" Benny the 3rd shouted. "So, you think you should be in charge?" Sarah asked. Benny the 3rd shrugged his shoulders. "I don't see why not! After all, I am the oldest grandchild!" Benny the 3rd shouted.

Back at Edward the 2nd's huddle, he started stumbling and slurring his words. He put his arm around his cousin Donald. "You don't know how serious this shit is, cuz!" Edward the 2nd cried. "What're you talking about?" Donald asked. "I'm serious cuz! This shit ain't no game! I can't stand vomit, cuz! Help me out!" Edward the 2nd cried. At this moment, he started sobbing like a baby. "I ain't no faggot! I don't like dick!" he sobbed. His cousins were finding his incoherency hilarious. Joe-Joe grabbed him by the waist to keep him from falling to the floor. One of the agents standing close by looked concerned. "I'm a grown ass man!" Edward the 2nd sobbed. He then looked in the direction where Kimberly was standing. His eyes lit up. "Kimberly! Kimberly! beautiful!" he shouted. "Chill, cuz!" Joe-Joe chuckled. Edward the 2nd pulled away from his cousin. He then stumbled through the crowd in her direction, bumping into people, knocking drinks and plates of food out of people's hands. His older brother Big L followed him as a precautionary. The agent that was standing near them, followed close behind. "Kimberly! beautiful! I love you! help me!" Edward the 2nd shouted. Kimberly smiled with embarrassment. Edward the 2nd lunged at Kimberly, knocking her off balance. "Take it easy, man! You're out of control!" Big L said. 2 more agents break through the crowd to get to their boss. Edward the 2nd pushed his burly older brother back. "Man, don't be grabbing me! I'm the fucking Lord of Lassenberry!" Edward the 2nd shouted. the agents get between Big L and his inebriated brother. "I don't care who y'all are! That's my brother!" Big L shouted with his fists balled up. An agent reached for his pistol. "Mr. Lassenberry. You don't want to make any aggressive moves. You will lose." The agent said to Big L. Brandon saw what was going on, and decided to pacify the situation. He ran over and told the agent to stand down. Since Brandon was the official care taker of the castle, the agent returned his weapon back into its holster. Edward the 2nd had put his arms around Kimberly, pleading with her to kiss him. She frowned from the smell of his breath. "You need to go to bed and get some sleep!" Kimberly said as she tried to push him away. "I love you Kimberly! help me! I ain't no faggot!" Edward the 2nd sobbed. Kimberly looked Brandon in his eyes. "I know who you are! Do your job!" Kimberly whispered to him in a stern voice. Brandon grabbed Edward the 2nd by the shoulders. "Come on, boss! Let's get you to bed!" Brandon said. 2 of the agents came to Brandon's aid. They picked Edward the 2nd off his feet. They carry him out of the ballroom. "I don't wanna eat vomit! I don't wanna eat that shit!" he screamed as they carried him out. Sitting over in the corner next to the snack table, was old man Sleeves Hart with his walking cane in hand. "Another Lassenberry about to lose it." He said to himself. Kimberly stood there fixing her dress. She turned her head and saw Viola standing a few feet away with tears in her eyes. "Why didn't you warn me?" viola cried before storming out of the ballroom. The DJ that was hired for the night had stopped the music. Kimberly decided to take control of the party. She stood in the middle of the dance floor. "Everybody! He just had one too many! So, let's get back to having fun, and bring in the New Year right! DJ! Put that damn that music back on!" Kimberly playfully shouted. "And, who are you Beautiful?" the DJ playfully shouted on the microphone. "If you must no, I'm the mistress of the castle!

Now turn the music back on!" Kimberly shouted. "Alright! All right!" the DJ shouted on the mic. He kicked the music back on, playing a very popular club song. Kimberly put everyone back in a fun mood by taking off her high heels, pulling her dress up to her knees. She started jumping, and dancing with sex appeal and feeling no shame about it. This apparently lured some the other women to come on the dance floor, which caused the guys to follow. Soon, the dance floor was packed.

The next day. The 1st of January 2002, Edward the 2nd was coming out of his comatose state. He slowly rose from his bed with a throbbing headache. He took a few moments to gather his thoughts rubbing the back of his head. Suddenly, there was a knock on the door. "Come in!" he shouted as his face frowned from the headache. One of his agents entered the room. "My, lord. Kimberly Lassenberry wishes to come in." the agent said. "Shit! Edward the 2nd said to himself. "My, lord? Do you wish her to enter?" the agent asked. "Ok! Let her ass in!" he said. Kimberly entered the bed room with a glass of water. She was still in her party dress. "You better let me in!" she jokingly said. Edward the 2nd noticed that he was in his underwear. He quickly covered his body from the waist down. "Oh! All-of-a-sudden, you're shy?" she chuckled. "You can leave us, now!" Kimberly said to the agent. The agent looked over at his boss, Edward the 2nd. "You heard her! Get the fuck out!" he shouted. "Yes, my lord." The agent said before leaving the bedroom. Kimberly sat on the side of the bed close the Edward the 2nd. In her other hand was a couple of pills. "Here. This should help." She said. Edward the second was so embarrassed, he could barely look her in the face. "Go on! Take it!... My lord!" she chuckled. "Trying to be funny, now?" he said. He held out his hand. She placed the pills in his hand. "I hope you ain't trying to poison me!" he said. "Shut up and swallow the damn pills!" she sighed. Edward the 2nd popped the pills in his mouth. Kimberly handed him the glass of water. He gulped down most of the water due to dehydration. "Thanks." He said as he handed her the glass. Kimberly placed the glass on the night stand. She looked at Edward the 2nd for a moment in his eyes without blinking. Edward the 2nd looked intimidated, glancing away from her stare. "What?" he shouted out of suspense. "We have to talk." She said in a calm voice. "Well talk!" he shouted. Kimberly leaned in closer to him. So, close, that Edward the 2nd could feel her soft lips on his ear. "Really…We need to talk." She seductively whispered in his ear. Edward the 2nd turned his head slightly, staring at her full lips. "Damn woman! You are fine as hell!" he whispered. "Damn man. You need to gargle some mouthwash." She whispered with a sexy smile.

It was the 3rd of January of 2002. The weather forecast for north jersey was particularly mild on that day. Instead of sheets of ice on the ground, there were puddles of water forming from the mounds of snow.

In the back room of Hakim's place of business BIG SHOTS, another one of Hakim's henchmen stood guard by the door wielding a high-tech machine gun. His name was Aaron Poole. Chewie had recruited and vouched for him around the same time he recruited his nephew Bilal. Aaron was also in his early 20's like Bilal. He was part of the Springfield avenue crew in Irvington, New Jersey. Aaron had a reputation of beating deadbeat drug addicts. Sometimes he would beat the men and women to a pulp for his own sick entertainment. Chewie got wind of his actions and informed Hakim. Hakim didn't want hot heads attracting attention on the streets. Hakim was going to send Clip to make Aaron disappear, but Chewie intervened, convincing Hakim that the young thug would be an asset to the inner circle.

Aaron was a short chubby brown skinned kid, who always donned a baseball cap. Guys on the streets knew Aaron was about to wreak havoc on someone when he turned his ball cap backwards and pulled out a pair of workout gloves from his back pocket. Just like Butch, Aaron was known for knocking out his victims with one punch, most of the time. This earned him the nick name, South Paw Poole.

Hakim sat at the table with a pen and pad calculating how much cash should be coming at the end of the month. He could hear the muffled sounds of patrons on the other side of the door. Suddenly there was a knock on the door. "Who is it?" Aaron shouted. "Chewie!" he shouted. Aaron cracked the door open, peaking out. Chewie look frustrated. He pushed the door open. "When I say it's me, it's me, nigga!" Chewie shouted. "My fault!" Aaron said. "What's up?" Hakim asked. Chewie took a seat across from Hakim. "You won't believe this shit!" Chewie said. Hakim interrupted Chewie with a hand gesture. He looked over at Aaron. "Yo! Put your shit down on the couch and stand guard on the other side of the door." Hakim said. Aaron looked puzzled. "What if someone tries to bum rush in here?" Aaron asked. Hakim sighed. "By the time, you get a beat down, or get shot, I'll have my hands on your machine gun. Now, get the fuck out!" he shouted. Aaron walked out of the room with his tail between his legs look. "Speak." Hakim said. "I got a guy on the inside of Bex's crew. He said it took him days to get away to contact me." Chewie said. "Whatever happen to using the fucking phone?" Hakim asked. "I've been in this game a long time. I like seeing my contacts in person." Chewie said. "Fair enough." Hakim said. "He said that the dirty south crew is seeking their independence, and made the decision to go after Clint, Toby and Calvin to keep you out of the know." Chewie said. Hakim dropped the pen on the table. "Get the fuck outta here! These rootie poot, Haitian motherfuckers make me sick, man!" Hakim shouted. "What you wanna do?" Chewie asked. Hakim scratched his head, and thought for a moment. "OK! Take out André and Frenchie! Especially Frenchie! The rest of them should get the message and fall in line! Now go!" Hakim said. "I'm on it." Chewie said. Chewie had left the room. Hakim was puzzled why Aaron didn't come back in the room. He stood up and walked over to the door. He opened the door. "Man, get yo ass back in here!" Hakim shouted.

Elsewhere, at a diner in Red Bank, New Jersey. Clint was sitting at a booth alone, eating a T-bone steak, roasted potatoes, and large root beer for lunch. The only patrons in the diner were himself a family of 5, a skinny black kid wearing a tattered imitation leather coat sitting at the counter eating a cheeseburger and fries, and an elderly couple.

Unknown to Clint, he was under surveillance the day after Bex was laid to rest. Moments later, the waitress approached Clint, offering him a refill on the root beer. Clint turned the refill down, claiming to be bloated. A few minutes had passed when Clint stuffed the last roasted potato in his mouth. He leaned back rubbing his stomach until he starts to flatulate. All eyes turned in his direction. The kids belonging to the party of 5 start laughing. "When nature calls, you better answer!" he chuckled along with the kids. He pulled out his wallet, laying 60 dollars on the table. "Sweetie! Never mind the check! Just keep the change! I have to run to the little boy's room!" he said to the waitress. Clint slid out of the booth, on his way to the rest room. The kid sitting at the counter pulled out his mobile phone. He dialed a number. "He's in the bathroom now!" he whispered on the phone. "Excuse me! Can I get a chocolate shake?" he asked the waitress. "Why sure you can!" she said. As the waitress turned her back to make the shake, Frenchie entered the diner wearing a long coat and a back pack draped over his shoulder. With great haste, he headed toward the men's rest room. The waitress put the metallic cup filled with ice cream, milk, and flavoring in the mixer to make the kid's milk shake. The noise from the mixer muffled the noise that was going on in the rest room. Moments later, Frenchie had left the rest room with a much bulkier back pack. He walked pass the kid at the counter, heading towards the exit. The waitress turned around only to see the back of his head. Outside the diner, Frenchie took off the back pack and jumped into the passenger side of a blue Boeman sedan. Remy was the driver. "You should've saw the face on that Blanc when I came in there!" Frenchie chuckled. "Was it quick" Remy asked. "Did You know your eyes can still blink when your head is removed from your body?" Frenchie chuckled. "Hey! Don't let that shit leak blood in my ride!" Remy shouted. "Easy, man! I lined the back pack with a plastic bag! Now, let's get the fuck out of here and pay a visit to that drunk Toby!" Frenchie said.

Later that evening, André was watching TV at his luxury condominium in Maurice, River Township, New jersey. Using the remote, he kept channel surfing unsatisfied of what was on the tube. Moments later he heard keys jingling at the door. In came his wife with shopping bags in both hands. She was wearing a full mink coat André had recently purchased for her. "Bonjour ma douce. La poubelle a besoin de sortir. Où est le bébé?" she said. "Hey, my love. I just put the baby to sleep. The trash goes out tonight, right?" he asked. "Oui!" she said. André had put down the remote, and headed towards the kitchen. He pulled the overflowed trash bag from the waste can. He headed towards the door to take it out to the dumpster. "Dépêchez-vous, alors je peux vous montrer les chaussures que j'ai achtées!" she said. "Baby! Don't you have a thousand pair of shoes, already?" he sighed. His wife just smiled as he walked out the door. It was a breezy 40° that night. All André wore to take the trash out was a t-shirt, sweat pants and flip flops. The entrance to the condominium was well lit, but the area where the dumpster was pitch black. A gate surrounded the dumpster. The shrieking noise of the gate opening frightened a racoon away from the dumpster, which in turn startled André. He quickly tossed the trash bag in the dumpster and shut the gate. As he turned to head back to the condominium, he saw a flash of light. André had fell to the ground. He had fell victim to someone holding a semi-automatic pistol with a silencer. That someone was Clip. He let off 2 more shots in the back of André's head. After André's body stopped twitching, Clip walked off calmly into the night towards a parked car.

Moments later, about 21 miles away in Bridgeton. Toby and Jenny were packing the remainder of Calvin's belongings, who had just purchased a home a few miles away in Millville, New Jersey. "It's about time that boy got his own place!" Toby said. "Well, he wants to start a family with Tamika! Now that he's got the money, he can do right by her!" Jenny said. "Damn! Did he have to wait until he turned 35?" Toby asked. "Oh, man! Shut your mouth!" Jenny said. Suddenly, there was a knock on at the door. "Who the hell is that at this hour?" Jenny asked. Toby went to answer the door. "Who is it?" he asked. "It's Chewie!" he shouted. toby peaked through the curtains. "What the hell that fool want?" Jenny asked. Chewie kept banging on the door. "Come on Toby! Let me in, man! It's important!" Chewie shouted as he banged on the door. Toby was hesitant at first. He went to the door. "Don't open that door, fool!" Jenny shouted. "Maybe Hakim sent him!" Toby said as he turned the door knob. Chewie came in out of breath. "Good! Y'all ok! I need y'all to pack up and come with me!" Chewie said. "Why? What happened?" Toby asked. "They got Clint today!" Chewie said. "What hell you talking about? Who's they?" Toby asked. "Unbelievably, your crew wants to kill you and your family!" Chewie said. Jenny began to panic. "Why? Why they wanna do that?" She asked. "I got somebody on the inside that gave me a heads up! Clint's dead, and y'all next! Where's Calvin?" Chewie asked. "He ain't here!" Toby shouted. Pack a suitcase really quick, and come with me!" Chewie said. "Hold on! Slow sown! Now, start from the beginning!" Toby shouted. "Toby! We ain't got time for this shit! We gotta go, now!" Chewie shouted.

The front door was wide open. The cold air was rushing in. Chewie had glanced over at Jenny. When he looked back at Toby, he noticed red laser dot on his forehead. Chewie quickly turned to see where the source of the light was coming from. Suddenly, Toby's head was pierced by a projectile, which blew a big hole in the back of his head causing blood to splatter on Jenny's face. Jenny screamed at the top of her lungs. Chewie quickly pulled out his pistol and commenced to firing at random spots outside. There was a car sitting in the middle of the street with the engine running. Chewie hit the rear passenger window, causing it to shatter. The car took off down the street. Chewie ran out into the middle of the street and fired more shots, missing his target. He ran back in the house. He saw Jenny crying like crazy, kneeling over Toby's body. "Where's Calvin? I gotta get to Calvin before they do!" Chewie said. "Get out!" Get the Fuck Out!" Jenny screamed. Chewie looked around. He closed his eyes for a moment. He opened his eyes. "Go. Be with your husband." Chewie whispered. He pointed his pistol at Jenny's head. He squeezed the trigger. Chewie ran towards his car as Jenny laid there lifeless next to her husband.

It was around 2 in the morning, when Frenchie and Remy were parked out in an open field in Salem County, New Jersey. The only source of light came from the full moon. They sat in the car with the engine and head lights off. "Man! That shit was crazy!" Remy said. "Refroidissement! Refroidissement! Asseyonsnous ici et laissons-moi réfléchir." Frenchie said. Remy started feeling over his own body. "What the hell you are doing?" Frenchie asked. "Checking to see if I got shot, man!" Remy said. "Nigga! That was 4 hours ago, when that shit went down!" Je jure devant Dieu que tu es stupide!" Frenchie shouted. "I'm shocked to see that nigga Chewie was there. You think he was on to us?" Remy asked. "If he wasn't, he is now! Ain't no turning back!" Frenchie said. Moments later, Frenchie felt his mobile phone vibrating in his front pocket. "Pour l'amour de dieu, qui est-ce?" he said. "It's probably Hakim!" Remy said. "Shut up, man! Hello?" Frenchie said. "André est mort! Ils l'ont tué! Ils l'ont tué!" shouted the female voice on the other end. "Oh shit!" Frenchie shouted. "What? What happened?" Remy asked. "Calmez-vous Michelle! Juste calmer l'enfer vers le bas!" Frenchie shouted. "What happened?" Remy shouted. "André dead, man! They got him!" Frenchie shouted. "Remy covered his face and started balling like a baby.

A few hours later, the sun was coming up over the horizon. Frenchie and Remy were fast asleep in the car that was riddled with bullets. What kept them alive from the bitter cold was that Frenchie thought to turn on the heat before dozing off. It wasn't as warm in the car as it should've been since one of the windows was missing because of gun fire. Suddenly, Frenchie jumped out of his slumber when a Blue jay entered the vehicle and flew passed his face, landing on the dash board. "What the hell?" Frenchie shouted in fear. The bird took off when Frenchie shouted. Frenchie just chuckled at the situation. He rubbed his hands together for warmth. He put his hands over the heater vents. He tapped Remy on the shoulder. "Wake yo ass up!" He shouted. Remy didn't respond. Frenchie shook him. Remy didn't respond. "Wake up!" Frenchie shouted. "Oh shit! Don't tell me you froze to death, my Nigga! Damn!" Frenchie said. "He didn't Frenchie." A male voice said next to him. It was a tall Caucasian New Jersey state Trooper standing outside Frenchie's door. Frenchie jumped. He was terrified as he quickly turned in his seat towards the officer. "You've picked the wrong vehicle to steal. This vehicle has a navigation tracking device, young man. Frenchie was breathing heavily out of fear. He was speechless. The State Trooper was saying all of this with a big smile on his face. "How…How?" Frenchie stuttered. "If you would've checked the other side of your friend's face, you would've noticed a hole in his temple. Frenchie finally gathered his thoughts. "If you gonna arrest me, arrest me!" Frenchie shouted. the officer chuckled. "Arrest you? Hakim didn't Pay me to arrest you!" the State Trooper said. "Oh merde!" Frenchie shouted with fear in his eyes. The State Trooper pulled out a pistol from the back of his utility belt. It wasn't his standard issued police weapon. This weapon had a silencer attached to it. Before Frenchie could utter another word, he caught a bullet between the eyes. Frenchie slumped over the steering wheel with his eyes open. The Trooper walked off into the brush where his patrol car was parked on the other side.

Back at Hakim's pent house in Manhattan, hakim, Bilal, and Clip were lounging next to a roaring fire place playing cards. Hakim's mobile phone vibrated. Hakim answered it. "What?" he said. "The Haitian is gone." The voice said on the other end. Hakim clicked off his phone. He had a big smile on his face. "Well, boys! The dirty south part of Jersey belongs to us!" Hakim chuckled.

— CHAPTER 26. THE NEGOTIATOR —

Later that day, Kimberly, and Edward the 2nd took a stroll together through the courtyard of castle Lassenberry. They were locked arm-and-arm with big smiles on their faces as the NA agents standing at various posts watched them.

Kimberly was dressed in her usual long black mourning dress underneath a long wool coat, while Edward the 2nd was in jeans, sneakers, and a button up shirt. He wore a goose down jacket and gloves.

"So, you're telling me this green shit, this green goop as you call it, heals people?" Edward the 2nd whispered. "I'm telling you, I saved a man from dying!" Kimberly said. "Where is this lucky bastard at, now?" Edward the 2nd asked. "His name is Ali Mohamed and I made him my assistant while we were on the Island! He's still on the Island, waiting for me to come back!" she whispered. "Is he Muslim?" Edward the 2nd asked with concern. Kimberly rolled her eyes. "Don't tell me you're one of those people who believe it was Muslim terrorists who knocked down those towers!" she said. "Hell, fucking yes!" Edward the 2nd shouted. Kimberly placed her hand over Edward the 2nd's mouth. "Keep your voice down, and keep smiling! These agents are watching us like hawks!" she whispered. Edward the 2nd removed her hand from his mouth. "I Need your resources to give him a new identity!" Kimberly whispered. "A new identity? What the fuck? You just said the Muslims didn't blow up the towers, but this guy needs a new identity!" he whispered. "He's not a terrorist, but he is…a pirate!" Kimberly said as she shrugged her shoulders with a shameful look on her face. Edward the 2nd sighed for a moment. "Ok! Ok! So, what else about this green shit?" he asked. "It seems like it's seeping through the sand on the southern part of the Island forming a puddle about 2 to 3 feet in diameter! I've searched around, and couldn't find any other signs of seepage! I think we discovered a gold mine!" Kimberly said in a giddy manner. "Fuck! I wish I could come out there and look, but this Terrance guy is up my ass! Metaphorically speaking of course!" Edward the 2nd said with a look of guilt. "I have connections with some big shots from the U.N., but you're the one who should stand before them and stake your claim on this phenomenon! After all, the Island does belong to you, or does it?" she said. Edward the 2nd went silent for a moment. He looked Kimberly in her eyes. "I hate to say this again beautiful, but your husband, my cousin, had a nervous breakdown-n-shit. He signed all powers of the family business over to me. So, the Island is mine." He confessed. "But, he's still alive, like you said. Right?" Kimberly asked with a nervous look on her face. Edward the 2nd nodded his head. Kimberly smiled. Like you said! I need to get to the U.N. officials without Terrance and his people knowing!" he whispered. "Screw them! Let's just go, and handle our business!" Kimberly whispered. Edward the 2nd sighed. "It's not that simple! These people are responsible for all the shit this family has! I hate to say it, but they own us! If they find out I have a way to get free from them, they'll kill all of us! That's why I made sure your husband stayed well hidden!" Edward the 2nd admitted. Kimberly expressed a sorrowful look on her face. "You sold out your family for power?" she asked. Edward the 2nd and Kimberly's stroll came to a halt. "No! It wasn't me! Uncle Eddie, did that shit! I just gotta follow suit to keep them from killing us-n-shit!" he whispered. They continued walking. Kimberly had her head down, until she came up with an idea. "I got it! Get your lawyers to draw up some paper work, and sign everything back over to Mark! Then he could leave to negotiate with the U.N. big shots!" she whispered. Edward the 2nd shook his head. "That won't work, beautiful. When the paper work gets filed into the computer system, Terrance and his people will find out we lied about his existence! These people have their hands in everything!" he whispered. There was a moment of silence amongst them. "What about my son?" Kimberly asked. Edward the 2nd scratched his head for a moment to think. "He is a Lassenberry male. But, I think his comprehension skills might fall flat, since he's a fucking baby!" Edward the 2nd shouted. Kimberly shushed him as she looked around at the agents standing guard. "Come on! I'll be there with him, of course!" Kimberly whispered. Edward the 2nd gazed at the castle walls for a moment. "Hellooo!" Kimberly said. "All right! But, I'm putting my name in the fine print! After this green goop becomes the miracle cure all, I'll need to resume power! Deal?" Edward the 2nd said as he extended his hand in a friendly gesture. He and Kimberly shook on it. Kimberly jumped around in a gleeful manner. "This is going to make us the most powerful family in the country once we manufactured it into pill form!" Kimberly whispered. "Fuck that! If what you said is true, we're going to be the most powerful family in the fucking world!" Edward the 2nd said with bravado. "How soon can we make the move?" Kimberly asked. "As soon as I get Brandon to get into contact with Kent Mooney, we're in business!" he said. Kimberly gave Edward the 2nd a big hug. "Oh, yes! My dick is rock hard, now!" he said in a sultry voice. Kimberly quickly shoved him away. "God! I'm married to your cousin, and your dating my friend! Remember?" she said with disgust.

Suddenly, one of the NA agents approached them. "My, lord. General Bates is here to see you." the agent said. "Now?" Edward the 2nd asked. "Shall we allow him to pass through the gates?" the agent asked. Edward the 2nd rolled his eyes. "Ok! Bring him to my office." He said. "Yes, my lord." The agent said before walking away. Kimberly shook her head. "I can't believe you have everyone calling you Lord! "she said. "Not everyone. They don't say it to my face, but the rest of the family thinks I'm a joke." he said. "Awe, poor multi- millionaire baby!" she said as she pinched his cheek. Edward the 2nd pushed her hand out of the way. "You watch! I'm taking this family to the next level! Then they all gonna be kissing my ass!" he said. Kimberly expressed a sexy smirk. She and Edward the 2nd part ways without saying a word to each other.

Moments later as Kimberly was driving towards the gate to leave, she sees a black Boeman

Sedan coming in the opposite direction. As both cars were parallel to each other, they come to a complete halt. Kimberly noticed the man in the driver's seat. At the same time, Hakim noticed the woman in the driver's seat. He gets out of the car. He leaned over to get a better look at her. "Don't I know you from somewhere?" he asked. Kimberly smiled. Hakim smiled back. He snapped his fingers. "The liquor store in Bridgton, right?" he asked. "I don't remember. Sorry." She said. "Yeah! Me and my people were stranded and I asked you for a ride. You said no!" Hakim said. Kimberly squinted her eyes to focus on Hakim's face. "Wait a minute!" Kimberly rolled her eyes. "That, was you?" she shouted. Kimberly stepped out of her vehicle. "What are you doing here?" she asked. "I was about to ask you the same thing!" Hakim said. Hakim wrapped his arms around Kimberly, giving her a firm hug. Kimberly looked shocked and was hesitant to reciprocate. She gave in and gave Hakim a lite pat on the back. He then released her. "I have to say, you still look gorgeous!" he said. Kimberly started blushing. "Thanks for the compliment, but what was your name, again?" she said. "Oh! My fault! My is name is hakim!" he said as he reached out for her hand. Kimberly reached out and shook his hand. "I'm Kimberly." she said. Hakim squinted as he looked at her for a moment. "Kimberly what?" he asked. "Kimberly... Jenkins." She said. "You wouldn't be related to a Jabbo Jenkins, would you?" he asked. "He's my father." She said. Hakim slowly walked in a small circle as he shook his head in disbelief. He had a big smile on his face. "I tell ya! This is really a small damn world! You look just like him!" he chuckled. "Everyone tells me that." Kimberly said as she folded her arms. "My condolences go out to you and your family. He was a great man. "Let's keep it real. He was a gangster." She said with a smile. "Yeah, but he was great at being one!" Hakim said in a wining voice. They both starting laughing. Kimberly cleared her throat. "So! What is it that you do, that brings you to castle Lassenberry, General Bates?" she asked with an inquiring look on her face. Hakim chuckled. "Oh, shit! You must have overheard one of the agents!" he said. "Yep!" she said in a cute voice. "I tell you what! You give me your phone number, and I'll explain to you who I am and what I do over a candle lit dinner!" he said with a big grin. Kimberly looked up at the castle walls for a moment with a big smile on her face. She stared into Hakim's eyes. "Even though you're very handsome, I'll have to decline on the giving you my number and going on a dinner date, for now! I smell a conflict of interest, here!" she chuckled softly. Hakim rubbed his chin, pondering her words. "Ok! Cool! Well it was nice meeting you, anyway!" he said with a smile. Kimberly licked her lips in a sensual manner. "I didn't say I didn't want, your number!" she said with a smile. Hakim raised an eyebrow. "Ok." Hakim said in a calm collective voice. After he gave Kimberly his phone number, she just waved goodbye to him, jumped into her car and drove off the castle grounds. Hakim just stood there in awe as she drove out of sight. An agent approached hakim from behind. "General Bates. Lord Lassenberry is very busy, and requests that you come to his office immediately." The agent said. Hakim quickly turned to the agent. "I'm coming motherfucker! Goddamn!" he shouted. he and the agent jump into one of the golf carts and entered castle Lassenberry.

Minutes later, the golf cart pulled up outside Edward the 2nd's office. "State your business here?" the agent standing guard by the door said. "General bates was ordered to report to Lord Lassenberry's office." The agent in the golf cart explained. The agent standing guard knocked on the door. "Come in!" Edward the 2nd shouted. "General bates is here to see you, my Lord." The agent said. "Bring his ass in here!" he said. "Yes, my Lord." The agent said. At that time, Edward the 2nd had just hung up the phone.

Hakim entered the office. "What's up? Close the door and have a seat!" Edward the 2nd said. Instead of sitting in the chair across from Edward the 2nd, Hakim flopped down on the couch. Edward the 2nd paused for a moment, but didn't comment. "Just got off the phone with the governor. He's a greedy fat motherfucker!" Edward the 2nd chuckled. "What's up with him?" Hakim asked. "The routine shit. He makes a drug bust. The cops put all the product and cash on a table to show the media. He looks like the hero, and at the end of the day, they bring the product and cash back to me. I told him they could bust one of Mookie's safe houses." Oh! You sure he'll put it back?" Hakim asked. "We got so much dirt on that white man, from a distance he looks like a nigga!" Edward the 2nd said. Hakim started snickering. "Check this! This motherfucker asked me if he could keep 60 grand from the confiscated cash, so he can pay off his kid's tuition! I said, fuck it! Take it! I'll get his ass back!" Edward the 2nd chuckled. "Thinking like a true business man, now!" Hakim said. "You're damn skippy!" Edward the 2nd said.

"I didn't know you knew Kimberly!" Hakim said. Instantly, Edward the 2nd's facial structure changed. He looked like a man who was facing death. "What?" he asked in a stern voice. "Kimberly! I ran into her on the way in here! Me and her go waaaay back! Damn! She still looks fine as hell! Too bad I didn't get to tap that ass, yet!" Hakim said with an evil grin. Hakim could read Edward the 2nd's emotions without him saying a word. Edward the 2nd was infuriated, but held his composure. He cleared his throat. "So! What brings you here unannounced?" he asked Hakim. "Oh, yeah! I came to tell you I got South Jersey now!" Hakim said. "I thought you were gonna pick a new general! You sure you can handle all that extra property?" Edward the 2nd asked. Hakim leaned forward. "Your uncle once asked me if I can do what he did, when I was kid. I told him yeah. I'm sure somewhere in the fiery pits of hell, he's watching me do it." Hakim said with confidence. "What about the other 3 generals?" Edward the 2nd asked. "What about them?" hakim asked. "You gonna tell them?" Edward the 2nd asked. Hakim frowned. "They'll find out, when they find out! Fuck them! I know one thing! If we ain't holding a meeting, that nigga Dubbs better stay clear of me!" hakim said with fury in his voice. "I know you've been in the game a long time! I know you brought me into the game! But, don't go breaking my fucking rules! Don't touch him! That's a warning!" Edward the 2nd said as his voice trembled. Hakim put on a fake grin. He slapped his hands, rubbing them together. He stood from his seat. "Ok, boss man! Whatever you say! I'm a busy man now! I gotta check the layout on my expanding territory! After paying off everybody, what's that, an extra 10 million a year in my pocket? Damn I'm good!" Hakim boasted. "Don't get too cocky, man. You got a lot more people to keep happy now." Edward the 2nd said. Hakim folded his arms as he walked closer to Edward the 2nd's desk. "You know what? I think I'm gonna get reacquainted with Kimberly. I'm sure I can make, her happy." He said. Edward the 2nd's bulging eye started twitching. "You ok, man?" Hakim asked. "Go! Handle your business!" Edward the 2nd said. Hakim stood at attention. "Long live the house of Lassenberry! Long live Edward the 2nd!" Hakim shouted, trying not to laugh. Before hakim exited the office, he turned to Edward the 2nd. "I forgot! You said I can do business directly with our cocaine connection!" he said. Edward the 2nd sighed. He then took out a pen and pad from his desk. He jotted down the information Hakim would need. He handed the piece of paper to Hakim. "Here! This is the connection's phone number, his name, and the code you're gonna need to do the transactions! Remember it, and burn that paper! Don't fuck this up for me! That's another warning!" Edward the 2nd said. Hakim looked at the paper. "1970h? what's that?" Hakim asked. "That's your new code name! it's all been arranged! They're just waiting for you to make the call! Now, get the fuck out!" Edward the 2nd shouted. "When were you gonna tell my ass?" Hakim asked. Edward the 2nd stood from his seat. "I said, get the fuck out!" he screamed. Hakim walked out of the office, slamming the door behind him. Edward the 2nd returned to his seat. He began fidgeting. He stood up. He began pacing the room.

10 minutes had passed. Edward the 2nd continued to walk around his office in a restless state. "That nigga thinks he can get Kimberly? I'll fix that shit!" he said to himself. He went back to his desk and grabbed the pen and pad. Once again, he jotted down something on a piece of paper. He then rolled the notepaper as tight as he could. He placed it in his front pocket. As usual, there was an agent standing outside the office when Edward the 2nd came out. "I need 15 minutes of me time!" Edward the 2nd said. "Yes, my lord." The agent said. Edward the 2nd went for a walk, heading towards the south wing.

Once Edward the 2nd reached the south wing corridor, he was shocked to see the cracks in the wall had been sealed up. He felt the spackling with his fingertips. The work was fresh. He frantically looked around to see if there were any other cracks in the wall to shove his note through. He finally felt relieved, when at the middle of the corridor, near the floor, was a small hole in the wall. He kneeled, and kissed the note. "Please find this!" he whispered to himself. The hole was so small, Edward the 2nd had to twist the note through like a screw. He stood up. He looked down at both ends of the corridor. In a fit of rage, he trotted back towards the west wing.

Once he returned to the west wing, Edward the 2nd stood toe-to-toe with the agent standing guard outside of his office. "Who was the last person to enter the south wing? I thought I told everyone not to go down there!" he shouted. the agent stood at attention. "While you were outside strolling the castle grounds with Mrs. Lassenberry, Mr. Haggerty sent a message to have the cracks in the wall sealed, my Lord." The agent said. "Listen to me very carefully, robot! If I am lord of this castle, my orders will be fucking obeyed! Understand?" Edward the 2nd said in a low but harsh voice. "Yes, my Lord." The agent said. Edward the 2nd rushed back into his office, slamming the door behind him.

Inside his office, Edward the 2nd stood behind his desk, staring at the red phone. This was the phone used to call top level characters in The National Agreement, and the Colombian Cartel. Edward the 2nd touched the phone, then released it. He touched the phone again, then released it, again. He repeated this motion a few more times before gathering enough nerve to a make a call. He picked up the phone and punched in a code on the key pad. Moments later, someone responded on the other end. "Enter your DOC number and press the # key to continue this call, please" the female voice said. Edward the 2nd entered 666-654-10-01-00#. "Please say your code name, please." the voice said. "God damn!" Edward the 2nd sighed.

"That is the incorrect code name. Please say your code name, please." The voice repeated. "No! I meant to say Goldfinch 3!" Edward the 2nd shouted. "Thank you. please hold." The voice said. Suddenly elevator music was played on the phone. "What the fuck?" Edward the 2nd said to himself in a high-pitched voice. "Krayton, my man!" said the male voice. "Terrance! I prefer you call me, Edward the 2nd!" he said. "I'm just joshing you, silly! What I can I do you for?" Terrance chuckled. "I'm calling to say…I'm calling to…!" Edward the 2nd stuttered. "Don't dither! It makes you sound weak!" Terrance said in a serious manner. Edward the 2nd took a deep breath, then exhaled. "I want you to stop interfering in my fucking personal life!" Edward the 2nd shouted. "Bravo! You finally grew a pair of balls!" Terrance chuckled. "Fuck you, man!" Edward the 2nd shouted. "Since you've brought up fucking, I'll be glad to stay clear of your private life, but we'll have to rekindle our last encounter for old times' sake!" Terrance chuckled. "No! You ain't doing that shit to me no more!" Edward the 2nd shouted. "Awe! Is that any way to treat the guy who's letting run your own life?" Terrance chuckled. "I'm telling you, man! Don't fuck with me!" Edward the 2nd shouted. "Here's the deal, Edward the 2nd! The only way I'm leaving you alone, is if you let me dip my vanilla stick in your chocolate!" Terrance shouted. "Man! You're a sick evil motherfucker!" Edward the 2nd shouted. "You think I'm evil, wait until you see the master!" Terrance chuckled. "The who?" Edward the 2nd shouted. "Oh, I'm jumping the gun here! Never mind!" Terrance chuckled. "I don't want you setting one foot in this castle! I want you to leave my agents alone!" Edward the 2nd said. "Your castle? Your agents? You are cute! Have it your way, but I'll be at the castle this weekend for the last time! Wear that sexy uniform of yours!" Terrance chuckled before hanging up. Edward the 2nd slammed the receiver down.

Moments later, there was a knock on the door. "Fuck! Come in!" Edward the 2nd screamed. The door opened. An agent of African American descent entered. "What do you want?" Edward the 2nd asked. "My lord. Your cousin Tyson Richards is at the gate. He wishes to speak with you." the agent said. "I'm busy! Tell him to go away!" Edward the 2nd said. "Yes, my lord." The agent said before leaving the office.

Outside at the main entrance of the gate, Tyson Richards, along with his brother Malcolm were waiting in the car for their cousin's response to see them. "I don't think he's gonna let us pass through the gates." Malcolm said. "I've been trying to call that nigga for days! He even ignored mom's calls! If he knows what's good for his ass, he better let us through!" Tyson said.

Minutes later, 3 agents arrive at the gate, to join the other 4 agents already standing guard. The African American agent passed through the gates. He walked up to the car where the 2 Richards brothers were sitting in. Tyson was sitting in the driver's seat. "Mr. Richards. I regret to inform you that Lord Lassenberry will not be seeing you. now, would you kindly vacate the premises, sir?" the agent said. "Told you!" Malcolm said. Tyson looked infuriated. "Tell that cousin of mine, if he's a man, he'll meet me one-on-one at my house tomorrow at noon!" Tyson said. "I'll be sure to tell him, sir." The agent said. Tyson put the car in reverse. The tires screeched as the car quickly backed away from the gates. Missing the agent by inches.

It was January 4th, around 9 am when Tyson Richards was at his home alone, sitting in his den going over his tax forms. He sent the wife and kids out shopping. Suddenly, he heard his door bell ring. On his desk was a semi-automatic pistol. He grabbed it, checking the clip to see if was loaded. His weapon was locked and loaded. He placed it in the holster on his hip. He went to the door. He saw the silhouette of a man through the glass door. He opened the door to see Brandon hart standing there wearing a black wool overcoat. He was alone. In his hand was a briefcase. He took off his leather glove. "How's it going? I'm Brandon. Brandon Hart." He said as he put out his hand in a friendly gesture. Tyson reluctantly shook his hand. "Happy New Year!" Brandon said. "Same to you." Tyson said with an untrusting look on his face. "Come on in." Tyson said. Brandon entered. Tyson closed the door. Brandon followed Tyson down the corridor to his private study. "Have a seat, man." Tyson said. Brandon placed his briefcase on the side of the meridian chair before taking a seat. "You want something to drink?" Tyson asked. "Nah! I'm good." Brandon said. Tyson sat across from him in his favorite chair. Brandon briefly looked around the room. "Nice set up you have here!" Brandon said. "The encyclopedias belonged to my grandfather." Tyson said. "He was a great man!" Brandon said. "Damn right! Can't say the same about my cousin, though!" Tyson said. Brandon crossed his legs. "That's what I'm here to talk about. What's the problem about excepting your cousin as financier and head of the family business?" Brandon asked. What family business? He's the only family member in that business! Why can't someone like me or my brother be a part of that business? Why, because our last name ain't Lassenberry?" Tyson asked. Brandon chuckled for a moment. "Oh! That's fucking funny?" Tyson asked. "No, not at all! It's just strange that someone receiving 9 thousand dollars a week of tax free cash wanting to get involved in the narcotics trade!" Brandon said. "I'm not receiving shit, right now! Not my brother, nor my mother! Listen to me, man! I'm an educated business man! But, I have my ears in the streets! Having someone who hasn't one drop of Lassenberry blood in his veins run the most profitable territory in north Jersey! Someone who has a rap sheet for murder! Come on, man! That's a slap in the face to every man in my family!" Tyson said. "So, that's what this is all about? Hakim not being a Lassenberry?" Brandon asked. Tyson leaned forward. "Don't get me wrong! Butch is a legend! He earned his spot! That Vasquez kid! He's in a wheelchair for the rest of his life, because of his loyalty, and keeping my family wealthy! No disrespect to the dead, but from what I've heard, that Bex guy is in a better place because he wasn't built for the life! Dubbs! I'll throw him a bone because Butch vouched for him! But that other guy! He comes out of jail, and becomes a multimillionaire overnight! Overnight! I know guys on the police force down in south Jersey! Now, they're saying that he's the one running the drug game down there!" Tyson explained. Brandon ran his fingers through his curly hair. "So, you're telling me you want to run that part of south Jersey?" Brandon asked. "Yes! Not just that part of south Jersey, but his territory too!" Tyson shouted. Brandon sat there for a moment tapping his fingers on the arm rest. "All I can do, is go back to your cousin and tell him your request." Brandon said. He reached over and grabbed the briefcase from off the floor. "In this briefcase, is your 9 grand and the difference owed to you for time passed. There's a timer on it. It will open in about a half hour. Your cousin didn't want anyone, including me, dipping their hands into your money! You understand!" Brandon chuckled. "Wow! You work for my cousin, and he doesn't trust you? That's a new one!" Tyson said. "Hey! It's all business. You need to know, none of it's personal! At least that's the way I see it!" Brandon said. Brandon looked at his wrist watch. "Well, I have a lot of things on my plate. So, I'll be going now." He said. Both men stood. They shook hands. "I promise that I'll tell your cousin your concerns." Brandon said. "I appreciate it, man. I thought you was gonna be a hard ass when we talked over the phone this morning!" Tyson chuckled. "I'm the peacemaker! I think Lord Lassenberry will be pleased to hear someone in the family wants to step up and help him run things!" Brandon said. "Lord Lassenberry, huh?" Tyson said with cynicism. Tyson walked his guest to the front door. "Catch you later!" Brandon said as he walked off the porch. Tyson closed the door. There was a limo waiting for Brandon.

15 minutes had passed as Brandon was sitting in the limo, on the phone talking to his boss. "Hurry up back to the castle!" Edward the 2nd ordered. "We can only go so fast through traffic!" Brandon said. "Just get here!" Edward the shouted.

A couple of hours had passed when Brandon arrived at castle Lassenberry. It took him another 8 minutes to pass through the gates, to Edward the 2nd's office. Once he arrived at the doors of the office, he could hear objects falling and bumping around. Edward the 2nd could hear someone knocking on the door. "Come in motherfuckers!" he slurred. The agent guarding the door opened and witnessed what Brandon was seeing. Brandon came into the office to see Edward the 2nd's pants down by his ankles, with his face buried in the couch, and an empty bottle of champagne in his hand. "Come on, motherfucker, and get it over with!" he said. Brandon went over and took the bottle from his hand. He placed it on the desk. Brandon then went over and pulled Edward the 2nd from the couch, pulling his pants up around his waist. "What…what the fuck, man? What happened to my bottle?" Edward the 2nd said with slurred words. He then looked at the man who came to his aid. "Brandon? Brandon! My friend! Turn on the TV! You gotta see this shit!" Edward the 2nd said. Brandon carefully leaned his boss up against the desk. "Hurry up, motherfucker, and turn on the TV!" Edward the 2nd shouted as he wobbled back-n-forth. Brandon did what his boss had ordered and grabbed the remote that was on the floor. He clicked on the remote. Coincidently, the TV was tuned to the NJ news channel. "*fire fighters are battling the blazing fire which occurred just a couple of hours ago, in this affluent neighborhood in Hoboken. Witnesses say the explosion from the home of Tyson Richardson, grandson of alleged drug czar Benny Lassenberry shattered windows in neighboring homes a few blocks away.*" The reporter said. Brandon had heard and saw enough. He quickly shut off the TV that was mounted on the wall. The remote fell from his hand. His hands gripped his hair as he fell to his knees. "What the hell did you do?" Brandon shouted as he looked up to Edward the 2nd. "No, nigga! What you did!" Edward the 2nd said as he leaned on the desk to keep his balance. Brandon, still holding his hair in his hands, fell to the floor on his back and let out a manly scream. "Noooo!" he shouted. "Welcome to my world, motherfucker! You can thank me later!" Edward the 2nd said as he could barely keep his eyes open.

Elsewhere at the south wing side of the castle. Inside the walls, there was a space of about 4 feet which separated the plaster walls from the stone walls identical to the stone walls displaying the castle's extravagance to the world. A man stood between these walls holding a military issued flashlight. He shined the flashlight on a piece of note paper. "*You will be with your wife and son soon, cousin. I promise.*" The note read. The man, who happened to be Sir Marcus felt relieved as a tear trickled down his cheek.

Around this time off the Florida Keys, Kimberly was spending time with her one-and-a-half-year-old son, mark the 3rd on the Jenkins family island, which was ¼ the size of Lassenberia. She repeatedly rolled a beach ball towards her son as he kicked it. "Good boy!" she cheered as he kicked the beach ball in her direction for the first time.

Coming out of the Jenkins family mansion was Kimberly's older sister Jenna and her daughter Corina. Jenna and her daughter were dressed in matching outfits. Kimberly turned to see them coming towards her. "Don't you two look cute!" Kimberly said. "We're going to the mainland in a few to do the whole mother daughter thing!" Jenna said with a big smile.

Jenna Marie Jenkins was born 5 years before her only sister. Her husband, Sheldon Bartholomew was a half German Jew, and African American novelist, philanthropist, and a wild life preserver. Unlike Kimberly, who wore dreadlocks, Jenna kept her hair long and wavy coming down to the mid of her back. Instead of attending college overseas like her sister, Jenna attended and graduated from one of the most prestigious universities in Massachusetts with honors. At a very young age, her father told her and her sister to be multilingual. Kimberly spoke fluently in several African languages, whereas Jenna spoke fluently in mandarin, Cantonese Russian, French, and Spanish.

Kimberly carefully swooped up her son, lifting him into the air. Baby mark started giggling as his mother was slowly spinning in circles. "That's my little man!" she harmoniously shouted. Hey sis!" Jenna shouted as she and her daughter approached Kimberly. Jenna walked up to her sister and gently tugged on one of her locks. The 2 sisters hugged. "Sorry I missed you when landed last night!" Jenna said. Kimberly held her son with one arm, resting on her hip. "This new project is draining me! But, I'm sure eventually it's going to benefit us!" Kimberly said. "So, what's the word on Mark? Is he, all right?" Jenna asked. Kimberly sighed. "I was told he's ok, but just us being apart makes me sick!" Kimberly said as her voice started to crack. Jenna carefully took the baby from her sister's arms. "Corina. Take mark over to the swings, but don't push him too high or too fast." Jenna said. Mama! Ya dostatochno star, chtoby znat', kak tolkat' rebenka na kachelyakh!" Corina said. Kimberly looked impressed. "Wow! Was that Russian she was speaking?" Kimberly asked her sister as Corina walked away. Jenna had a proud look on her face. "Yes! It didn't take long for her to learn it either!" Jenna said. "At 12 years, old! That's great! Daddy would be so proud!" Kimberly said. Jenna folded her arms. "We barely knew him, Kimmie!" Jenna said. "But the times he was around, they were great!" Kimberly said. "Enough about that. You, young lady, need to start dating." Jenna said. "News flash! I'm still married!" Kimberly said as she waved her fingers on her left hand. You're still young and beautiful! You need to enjoy your life! Besides, you don't know if he's ok! You're just going by hearsay!" Jenna said. Kimberly eyes started to tear up. Jenna put her hand on her sister's shoulder. "Remember! You're Jabbo's daughter! No crying!" Jenna chuckled. Kimberly gave her sister a hug. She released Jenna. "The help prepared brunch. Go get some food in your stomach, girl, and stop all this emotional nonsense!" Jenna said. A burst of laughter came from Kimberly as she wiped away her tears. Jenna gently put her hand on her sister's cheek then walked away towards the swing set. Kimberly looked out into the ocean. She then reached in her pocket and pulled out her cell phone. She clicked it on and scrolled through her contact list. She stood there gazing at the name, Hakim.

It was Sunday January 6th, when Terrance Haggerty's limo passed through the gates of castle Lassenberry. Edward the 2nd, dressed in his uniform as Terrance ordered, was in his office nervously pacing back-n-forth. Minutes had passed when Terrance burst into the office without knocking, with his arms wide open. "Honey, I'm home!" he shouted. Edward the 2nd stopped pacing. He began breathing heavy through his nose. He did not blink one time as he stared Terrance in his eyes. "Hey friend! Since this is my last visit, I suggest we get things started, and fuck the foreplay!" Terrance chuckled. Edward the 2nd didn't utter a word. He just stood there with fury in his eyes. "Oh, come on! Having a piss pore attitude about this won't change the inevitable!" Terrance chuckled. Edward the 2nd walked over to his desk. He slowly unbuttoned his uniform pants as Terrance rubbed his hands together with a gleeful look on his face. Edward the 2nd's pants dropped to his ankles. He then bent over the desk as his eyes started to tear up. Terrance followed suit by unzipping his pants, letting them drop to his ankles as well. "This is going to be a good day! Yes-n-deed!" Terrance said as he approached Edward the 2nd from behind. Before Terrance could penetrate Edward the 2nd's backside, there was a knock on the door. "What the fuck?" Terrance shouted as he stomped his foot on the floor. The door opened. An agent in full body armor, toting a sub-machine gun had entered the office. "Mr. Haggerty. I've just received an urgent transmission from the council. Your presence is required. In Florida, sir." The agent said. Terrance jumped up and down, throwing a tantrum like a child. "Fuck! Fuck!" he shouted as saliva spewed from his mouth. Terrance gripped the back of Edward the 2nd's head with one hand. "This will just have to do!" he whispered. With his other hand, he made a fist and rammed it quickly up Edward the 2nd's rectum. Edward the 2nd screamed like a banshee as Terrance twist and turned his fist up inside his victim until only his wrist was visible. "Ahh, Yes! Yes! You like that?" Terrance chuckled. Edward the 2nd had the face of a man in excruciating pain. Moments later, Terrance yanked his hand out of Edward the 2nd. His hand was stained with blood and fecal matter. "Lucky for you, I'm a man of my word!" Terrance chuckled. Edward the 2nd knees buckled, causing him to fall to the floor. Terrance whipped out a handkerchief from his suit jacket. "You won't be able to sit for week! Trust me! You're not my first, pal!" Terrance said as he wiped his hand clean. He then tossed the soiled handkerchief on Edward the 2nd's head. "Get rid of that for me, will ya?" Terrance chuckled. Edward the 2nd looked up at Terrance. "Now, get… the fuck…out of my castle!" he cried. "I'll be glad to! By-the-way! Be more like your uncle, and embrace what I just did to you." Terrance said before leaving the office. Edward the 2nd just stayed on his knees crying like a child.

It was January 28th, around 2 in the afternoon when Kimberly was preparing to board a flight to Mozambique. Edward the 2nd had wired more funds to the country to hire a construction crew from Mozambique to build more bungalows on Lassenberia. Edward the 2nd had stretched his budget doing so, but knew it would pay off 10 times over.

Kimberly didn't take this trip alone. She took her pride-n-joy, mark the 3rd with her. She had already received the documents proving that her son had inherited the family island, and that she was his negotiator. She was to rendezvous not only with Kent Mooney, but with the UN deputy secretary Jawara Soumah, prime ministers of Mozambique, Tanzania, and Madagascar. These men of political power thought they were being invited to Lassenberia to invest in the island to become a tourist attraction, but they were really invited for a demonstration of the green goop's healing factor. The only people who knew the real reason for their visit were Edward the 2nd and Kimberly. Edward the 2nd's plan was to market this green goop to these countries to be recognized as a sovereign nation.

Before Kimberly and her son boarded the plane, she pulled out her cell phone and scrolled through her contacts. She came upon Hakim's name. Kimberly hesitated to tap the call button at first. "Here goes nothing!" she said to herself. She hit the call button. The phone rang 4 times. Suddenly, there was an answer. "Who the fuck is this?" Hakim shouted. Kimberly was shocked as she pulled the phone from her ear and stared at the phone with a scowl on her face. She put the phone back to her ear. "Hellooo! Is that any way to answer a phone?" Kimberly said. "When I don't know who, the fuck is calling me! You damn right!" Hakim shouted. "It's Kimberly." she said in a sweat voice. In a split second, Hakim changed the tone of his voice. "Oh! Hey lovely! How's it going?" he said in a more pleasurable tone. "That's better!" Kimberly said. "Hey. When you're a big shot, you make a lot of enemies. Even bitches…I mean women, want to put a bullet in your head. Know what I'm saying?" Hakim chuckled. "I heard the stories about my father! Yes, I do know what you're saying!" Kimberly chuckled. "So, you finally called to tell me your head over heels in love with me?" Hakim said in a cool voice. "Whoa! slow it down a couple hundred notches! I called to tell you that I'm going out of town for a couple of weeks. I wanted to know if we could get together for a cup of coffee when I get back?" Kimberly asked. She could hear Hakim suck his teeth in disbelief. "A cup of coffee? Right!" Hakim said with cynicism. "Yes! Coffee, and coffee only! You seem like a cool guy." Kimberly said. There was a moment of silence. "Jesus! Don't think too hard about!" she said. Kimberly could hear Hakim sigh. "Ok, Kimberly. We'll do the coffee thing. You said a couple of weeks, right?" Hakim asked. "Yes! And don't try calling me back! I'll call you!" she said. "So, what if I decide to call you? you're not gonna pick up?" Hakim chuckled. "I'm changing my number as soon as I hang up!" Kimberly said. "Whatever beautiful." Hakim chuckled. Kimberly was holding little mark in her arm. He started getting restless, reaching for the phone. What's that in the back ground? A baby?" Hakim asked. "It's my son." Kimberly said. "Wow! Who was the lucky nigga that knocked yo ass up?" Hakim asked. "See you when I get back. Bye!" Kimberly said in a playful voice before clicking her phone off.

Hakim was sitting in the back room of his night club. He just stared at the phone with a puzzled look on his face. Moments later, Chewie had walked in. "What's up boss man?" Chewie said. He noticed the look on Hakim's face. What's wrong?" he asked Hakim. "Just got a call from this chick named Kimberly." hakim said. "What? She sounds suspect or something? Want me to run a back-ground check on her?" Chewie asked. Hakim thought for a moment. "Nah! She's Jabbo's daughter." Hakim said. "Street legend Jabbo? Damn!" Clip said with a surprised look. "I'm sure he left her a shit load of cash. So, I know she ain't out to get me for mine." Hakim said. "Hey! These dirty south niggas and white boys out there earning like a motherfucker! No back talk! No coming up short! We got them motherfuckers shook!" Chewie chuckled. "That's how you do it!" Hakim said. "Oh, yeah! What we do when the Italians make a comeback?" Chewie asked. Hakim started laughing. "We ain't gotta worry about them for a while! They're still trying find out how a ten-year-old kid killed their boss! They're gonna investigate that shit from here to eternity! It's all about image with those people." Hakim said. "Speaking of white boys. I took care of my inside man. He's sleeping with his forefathers." Chewie mentioned. "Who? White guy Gonzo?" hakim asked. "I don't trust a guy who would rat his own crew out, ya know?" Chewie said. "Fuck'em." Was Hakim's response.

It was January 30th when Kimberly was about to demonstrate the power of the green goop. Kimberly was dressed in a seductive white summer dress and sandals.

In the bungalow, there was a huge round table in the middle of the room. There were 10 chairs surrounding the table. The design of the chairs was fit for royalty.

Kimberly was given carte blanche on Edward the 2nd's dime. She had hired 3 butlers from a luxury hotel in Madagascar. The food being served was at the highest quality fit for a king. Caviar, Bluefin tuna, truffles, Madagascan pochard, and a Bawean warty pig. For dessert, vanilla bean cupcakes sprinkled with edible gold was to be served.

Kimberly stood amongst the men holding a small vial of green goop. Before the men could dig into these fine delectable dishes, Kimberly tapped the glass to make a toast. "Gentlemen! I would like to thank you all for taking the time out of your busy schedules to make the biggest investment of a life time! I would like to thank UN Deputy Secretary Jawara Soumah, Prime Minister of Mozambique Maxixe Guebuza, Prime Minister of Tanzania Tunduru Othman, Prime Minister of Madagascar Saka…how do say your last name again?" Kimberly asked. "It is Solonandrasanaty, beautiful!" the prime minister chuckled. "Ok! Whatever he said!" Kimberly said. The men around the table laughed. "Kent! Once again, I would like to thank you for your participation!" Kimberly said. Kent blew her a kiss. "Thanks to all of your assistants for joining us, as well! You all may think that you're here to invest into making this island a tourist attraction!" Kimberly said. The African leaders, even Kent stared at each other with confusion. "What is this meeting about, Kimberly?" Kent asked. "I will be glad to tell you, my dear, if you would allow me!" Kimberly said in a sweet voice, followed by a gorgeous smile. Kimberly held the vial of green goop up high. "This gentleman, what I have in my hand is the future! What I have here, is the end to the pharmaceutical industry as we know it! This is what I jokingly called green goop! But, from this day, it will be called GLC!" Kimberly said. "What does that mean?" Prime Minister Guebuza asked. "Simple! Green Life Cure." Kimberly said. Standing a few feet behind Kimberly dressed in black military garb and black combat boots was the man whose life she spared.

Ali Mogadishu Mohamed was born and raised in the poverty-stricken city of Mogadishu. He was the last of 12 siblings. With a clan of nieces and nephews, Ali became the soul provider for the remaining family members, which led him to piracy.

"Why is that man behind you wielding a machine gun?" the prime Minister of Tanzania asked. Kimberly turned her head towards Ali. She then turned towards the men seated. "Oh, Ali? He's here to make sure we all walk away healthy, wealthy, and safe!" Kimberly said. "Why will we not, walk away safely, my dear?" Secretary Soumah asked. "What I possess in my hand is more precious than gold or diamonds! Like I said, it will put an end to an industry that was responsible for the deaths of millions of disenfranchised people around the globe! After I've shown you all a demonstration, the reptilian part of your brain might get the best of you fine gentlemen!" Kimberly explained.

Attached to the hip of Kimberly's bodyguard was his secondary weapon. Ali not only armed with a machine gun, but a Billao.

The Billao sword was a popular weapon used during the Dervish resistance at the beginning of the 20th century. Ali's grandfather used this weapon as he fought on the side of the resistance. This weapon of Somalian origin was passed down to Ali from his father.

"Kent. Would you be so kind to assist me?" Kimberly asked as she unhooked the double-edged sword from Ali's belt. Kent looked nervous. "Would you excuse us gentlemen?" Kimberly asked 2 of the prime Ministers. Solonandrasanaty of Madagascar, and Othman of Tanzania quickly move their chairs apart from each other, making way for Kent to stand between them. "Now, I need you to place your hand on the table, my dear!" Kimberly said. Kent gave Kimberly a smirk. "Come on, Kent! We're about to perform a miracle!" Kimberly chuckled. The room was dead silent. All eyes were on Kent. "You gotta be kidding me!" Kent said. Kimberly sighed. "I promise! This won't hurt one bit!" She said. Kent's hand started shaking. Kimberly realized he needed a little push. She grabbed his wrist, placing the palm of his hand on the table. Kent turned away, shutting his eyes tight as he could. Kimberly raised the sword. "Take a deep breath." She whispered to Kent. Suddenly, Kent let out a scream. His eyes opened so wide, his iris was surrounded by his sclera. Kimberly had put a gash so deep into Kent's forearm, his radius and ulna were exposed. Kimberly tossed the sword on the table. Kent fell to the floor, cradling his forearm screaming like a baby. Kimberly quickly unscrewed the cap off the vial of goop. "Hold on!" Kimberly shouted as Kent's blood spewed on to her dress. The Prime Minister that was sitting nearby, could smell that Kent lost control of his bowels. Kimberly kneeled and poured the GLC over his traumatic injury. "Hold still!" Kimberly shouted over Kent's screaming.

Within seconds, Prime Minister Othman moved in closer and witnessed something miraculous. Kimberly, whose hands were soaked in blood held Kent's arm as the GLC mended his bones, arteries, and muscle tissue. Kent began to quiet down and take control of his breathing. Kimberly smiled from ear-to-ear. All the political powers in the room stood to their feet. Kimberly stood to her feet. She reached out her hand to Kent, grabbing the hand of his healed arm. He stood to his feet, shocked that he could wave his arm. Everyone in the room had gathered around Kent, touching, and poking at his arm. Kimberly stepped away from the crowd with a proud look on her face. Deputy Secretary Soumah turned to Kimberly. "Do you have more of this, GLC?" he asked. Kimberly smiled. "Enough to last a thousand life times." She said. "Where is it, my dear!" the deputy secretary said as he rubbed his hands together. "I'm glad you asked Mr. secretary! Gentlemen! Gentlemen! Would you take your seats, please?" Kimberly shouted. Kent stepped outside and headed to the water tower to wash off the dry blood. "Soon as Mr. Mooney returns, we can do business!" Kimberly said. Prime Minister Solonandrasanaty summoned one of his assistants. The assistant leaned over. "Izany dia hahatonga ny GLC be ny fahavalony. Mety tsy mainsty mitandrina ny Iavitra." The Prime Minister whispered in his assistant's ear. "Tena Tomopoko." The assistant whispered.

Moments later, Kent returned from cleaning himself up. "Pull out the paper work."

Kimberly whispered to Kent. Kent went over and fetched his briefcase. "Gentlemen! I've drawn up a few, well more than a few international contracts to bind us to this new business venture!" Kent said as he passed out copies of the legal forms to political leaders.

Each of the prime ministers received a stack of forms as thick as an inch. "In front of you gentlemen, as you may be familiar with, are sales, distribution, agency, supply, franchise, sales representative, strategic alliance services, and my favorite, the gag order!" Kent chuckled. "Yes, gentleman! For us to commence with this business venture, we must stay away from the press, local and abroad! Gentlemen! Excluding the UN deputy secretary, once you've signed these forms, as it is written in the Montevideo Act of 1933, you must recognize this land as a sovereign nation! Mr. secretary, we'll discuss more about this after the signing, ok?" Kimberly said. "Does anyone need a pen?" Kent asked.

CHAPTER 27. NUMBER 3

It was Tuesday February 14th, when Edward the 2nd was staggering down the corridor of the west wing around 2 in the morning. In his hand was an empty bottle of scotch. He was wearing a bathrobe and nothing underneath. He was mumbling to himself until he bumped into his butler called number 3. "Hey, number 3! What's happening!" Edward the 2nd shouted. "Is everything ok, my lord?" number 3 asked. Edward the 2nd placed his hand on number 3's shoulder to get his balance. "This being head of a big drug organization, ain't all it's cracked up to be!" he said. Number 3 looked up-n-down the corridor to see if anyone was around. "Come with me, my lord. Let's go take a walk outside." Number 3 said as he grabbed the empty bottle. "No! it's cold outside!" Edward the 2nd whined. "The cold air will do you some good. Let's go!" number 3 insisted. Number 3 had picked up some weight since his arrival, so it was possible for him to put Edward the 2nd's arm over his shoulder.

Once outside the walls of castle Lassenberry, number 3 aided Edward the 2nd by keeping him upright and mobile. 2 agents riding in a golf cart, followed close behind. "Will lord Lassenberry be ok?" asked one of the agents. "He's fine! He just needs some fresh air, is all!" number 3 shouted. "Take me back inside! please! It's cold!" Edward the 2nd continued to whimper. "I am Colonel Braxton. Remember the name, Colonel Braxton." Number 3 whispered in his ear. "Huh?" Edward the 2nd said. "Just remember the name, Colonel Braxton. The next time we speak, it will be far away from the castle, alone." He whispered. "I hate that Hakim, that mother fucker! I'll fix'em!" Edward the 2nd slurred before passing out. Number 3 stopped. He then properly placed Edward the 2nd in the back of the golf cart. "Take us back inside, please!" number 3 said. The agent driving, did just that.

Later that day, around 12 in the afternoon, Kimberly's plane had just landed at Fort Lauderdale-Key West. Accompanying her and baby Mark was her servant Ali. He was dressed very dapper in a gray 2-piece suit, white button-up shirt, and sandals. His hair was trimmed into a short afro. "Do I look presentable, Miss Kimberly?" he asked in a thick accent. "Kimberly smiled. You look smashing!" she said. Ali was in awe of all the technology around him at the airport. "America, it's so rich!" he said. "You ain't seen nothing yet! Come on! Let's get to baggage claim!" Kimberly said.

Once they made it to baggage claim, Kimberly pulled out her cell phone. "Aad qaban lahaa ilmaha? I leedahay in la sameeyo wicitaan oo taleefan ah." Kimberly said. Ali looked impressed. "Your Somali is improving, miss Kimberly." Ali said. "I'm a fast learner." She said. Ali gently took baby mark from his mother's arms. Kimberly then scrolled her contact list. She hit the name, Hakim. The phone rang 3 times. "Who this?" Hakim shouted. "Calm down! It's me, Kimberly." she said. "Oh! Sweet thang!" he said with joy in his voice. "I've just arrived in Fort Lauderdale. I'm on my way to my family's compound." She said. "What's the address? I'll catch a plane out there!" Hakim said. "You can't catch a plane out there. Only by boat. It's on a private island." She said. "God damn! Y'all gotta island? How big is it?" Hakim asked. "It's about the size of… Augusta, Georgia. "What can I say? My father was a good provider." Kimberly said. "You can say you'll be out here, ASAP!" Hakim Said. "Just let me rest up, and I'll be in Newark around 9 tonight." Kimberly said. "Make sure you wear something sexy when we get that coffee, wink, wink!" Hakim chuckled. "Sweetie. I can wear coveralls and still be sexy." She said in a seductive voice. "Oh, damn! Make sure it has easy access." Hakim said. "You haven't earned that, yet!" she chuckled. "Earned what?" he asked. "Gotta go! See you tonight! Smooches!" she chuckled before clicking off the phone. Hakim slammed the phone down on his glass coffee table as he rubbed his genitals.

Hakim was at home when Kimberly made the call. He ran out into the corridor of his penthouse where Bilal was standing guard. "Yo, Bilal! Get in here and pack me a suitcase! I need an Enough to wear for 2 days! No! fuck that! Make it enough for 4 days!" Hakim ordered. "You got it." Bilal said. Bilal went inside the penthouse. Hakim followed him back inside. He went to grab his cell phone and noticed he had caused a small crack in the glass coffee table. "Shit! Oh well. I'll just get another one." He said to himself. He then scrolled his phone, hitting Chewie's name with speed dial. The phone rang 4 times. "Yeah boss! Everything good?" Chewie asked with concern. "Yeah, yeah! Shut the fuck up, and listen! Book me a flight to Fort Lauderdale! I wanna be out there by 4pm!" Hakim said. "Today?" Chewie asked. "Yeah today, nigga!" Hakim shouted. "First class?" Chewie asked. "Always, my nigga! You know that! I'm going out there to meet Kimberly! she's supposed to come here, but I wanna surprise her!" Hakim said. "Oh, come on, boss man! You're a playa! You know better than to go off chasing tail! She said she's coming there! Let her come there!" Chewie said. Hakim thought for a moment, until what Chewie was saying had sunk into his head. "You know, you're right, my nigga!" Hakim said. "Of course, I am! Just go take a cold shower and wait for her!" Chewie said. Man! I fucked a lot of bitches, but this bitch is a 10 plus, for real!" Hakim said. "Take it easy, boss man. Peace!" Chewie said before clicking off his phone.

Bilal was in Hakim's bedroom looking through his wardrobe to find what to pack. "Bilal! Get yo ass out here!" Hakim shouted at the top of his lungs. Bilal came running out with his pistol in hand. "What the fuck you're doing? Put that shit away, man! Cancel packing my shit, and get back out in the hall and do your job!" Hakim ordered. Bilal put his pistol back in its holster and went back out into the hall.

Back at the airport, Kimberly, with her son in her arms and Ali, made their way to the exit where there were a group of chauffeurs waiting, holding up signs for their passengers. Edward the 2nd had cautioned Kimberly some time ago to only use her maiden name while she was heading project Lassenberia. So, when she and Ali came to the exit of the Airport, there was a chauffeur holding up a sign for K. Jenkins. "Come on Ali! There's our ride to the port!" Kimberly said.

When Kimberly and Ali arrived at the port, there was a 100-foot yacht waiting for them. The Jenkins family clearly owned this vessel. The name Jabbo was painted on the stern. "Jabbo? What is a Jabbo, miss Kimberly?" Ali asked. Kimberly couldn't help but chuckle. "Jabbo is not a what. He was my father. He's sort of responsible for the great future we're about to encounter." She said.

The captain of the yacht was an old friend of the family named Rusty(salt)Holness a Jamaican born fisherman and scuba diver, who worked for the Jenkins family since the day Jabbo purchased the island. Salt's gray dreadlocks, which came down the middle of his back, inspired Kimberly to do the same with her hair before she went off to college.

Hey, Salt! How's things lately?" Kimberly asked as he helped her board the vessel. "Oh, young lady! These bones ain't what they use to be!" he said as he took baby mark from Ali. "This is my new assistant, Ali! He'll be coming with us!" she said. Ali and Salt shook hands. "Pleased to meet you, mon! You're working for a good person." Salt said. Ali looked at Kimberly. "I know! I owe her my life!" Ali said. Ali brought the luggage aboard as Salt prepared to get the vessel underway.

Inside the skin of the yacht, Kimberly was giving Ali a quick tour of all the luxuries the vessel provided. Kimberly showed Ali wear the bathroom was so he could freshen up. "My goodness! There are 2 toilets right next to each other, miss Kimberly!" Ali said. "The one on the right is called a bidet!" she chuckled. "What is it used for, miss Kimberly?" He asked. "Ah, don't worry about using it for the time being! Let me show you to your quarters where you can get some rest. It's a 3-hour ride to the island." She said. "I can't thank you enough miss Kimberly for what you've done for my family!" Ali said. "If there's a Lassenberia, your relatives will always have a place to call home!" Kimberly said as she patted him on the shoulder. "Thank you! Thank you so much, miss Kimberly!" Ali said after kissing the back of her hand.

A few hours later, the yacht had docked at Jenkins island. Kimberly had awakened Ali from a deep slumber and ordered him to help Salt moor the yacht to the dock. Kimberly was the first to disembark the ship with her son in her arms. As Ali was giving Salt a hand, he couldn't help but notice how snug Kimberly's jean shorts fit on her. Just like castle Lassenberry, the island's main source of travel were custom built golf carts. The family also had a team of horses that grazed on a manmade pasture about a half a mile away from the mansion.

"Hurry up, Ali! I want to give you a tour of the island!" Kimberly shouted. "Coming right away, miss Kimberly!" Ali shouted. "Do you have it from here, Mr. Salt?" Ali asked. "It's just Salt. Now, get going and enjoy your stay." Salt said. "Yes sir!" Ali said with a big smile. Ali ran across the gangway, heading towards the golf cart that Kimberly and baby mark were in. "Oh no! I forgot the luggage!" he shouted. "Forget about that! I want you to meet my family! Come on!" Kimberly said. Ali hopped in the passenger's seat, while baby Mark was strapped into the back seat.

The ride to the family estate was a smooth one, since 12-foot-wide roads were built a couple of years earlier. There were 3 main roads leading from one end of the island to another. Ali was in awe of what he saw so far. The palm trees reminded him of home in Somalia. There were life size sculptures of African art spread out hundreds of yards apart. Ali couldn't believe what had just flown by the golf cart in the opposite direction. That's impossible!" he said. "What's impossible?" Kimberly asked. I just saw 2 grey hornbills fly towards us! They're native to my land! How could this be?" he asked. "My sister is an ornithologist in her spare time." She said. "What is this orno-?" Ali tried to pronounce. "An ornithologist! Someone who studies birds! She imported dozens of birds from around the globe! Only those that can survive in this climate, of course!" Kimberly explained. "Oh, I see." Ali said. "Too bad my sons' in the back seat! I love flooring the gas pedal on these golf carts!" Kimberly chuckled.

About a half hour later, Kimberly reached her destination. Ali was amazed at how huge the family estate was. "Who else lives here? This place is too much for just you and your son!" he said. "No silly! There's my sister, her husband and their 3 kids! We also have a few hired hands living here to care for the livestock!" Kimberly said. Ali noticed the smaller homes that were a few yards away from the mansion. "Who lives there?" he asked. "I suppose you do now! That's 1 of the 2 guest houses. I called my sister a few days ago, and told her you would take up residence there, while the help would move into the other guest house, over there. They weren't too crazy about the idea, but they don't have to pay for room and board." Kimberly said. Ali gave Kimberly a suspicious look. "Well, how much are you paying these people?" he asked. "Ah! You catch on quick!" Kimberly said with a smile. Before Kimberly could utter another word, her sister and 2 of her children emerged from the mansion.

Jenna's other daughter, Jamila was10 years old and the perfect likeness to her mother combined with the vigor of her auntie. Jenna and Jamila waved to Kimberly. Kimberly responded by waving back. Jenna had a puzzled look on her face when Ali appeared to be waving with a big silly grin on his face. "Hey little sis!" Jenna yelled in a harmonious tone as they approached each other with hugs and kisses. Jenna gently grabbed baby mark from her sister's arm's. "How's my handsome little nephew?" Jenna said to the baby as she cradled him in her arms. "Where's Sheldon and Oliver?" Kimberly asked. "Oliver is on the other side of the island jet skiing with his friends, again! Sheldon. He's in the house. And, who is this stranger with you?" Jenna asked. "This is Ali! The guy I called you about who'd be working for me on some overseas business!" Kimberly said as she gently stroked his arm. "So, you're the one invading my guest house!" Jenna said. "Ali. This is my big sister, Jenna, and these are her daughters Corina and Jamila." Kimberly said. "What precious looking young ladies!" Ali said. Ali gently grabbed Jenna's hand, kissing the back of it. "It is a pleasure!" Ali said as he smiled from ear-to-ear. "Go ahead sis! You've picked a charmer! You've made a lot of people upset by kicking them out of their quarters, jamming them all up in the other guest house!" Jenna said. Ali went from smiling, to being embarrassed. Jenna burst out laughing. "I'm just teasing you, silly! Tell'em Kimmie! He needs to loosen up if he's going be around us!" Jenna said. "I tried to tell him!" Kimberly chuckled. "The master of the house hold. Is he home? I would like to meet him as well. Out of respect." Ali said. Jenna put her hands on her hips. "Master? There is no master on this land, sweetie! I've kept, my maiden name!"

Jenna said in a sassy tone as she waved her finger in Ali's face. Ali just smiled. "Gotcha!" he said. Jenna and Kimberly burst out laughing. "This guy is cool, Kimmie!" Jenna said. "I hope he's not too cool! He's my body guard as well! Oh! I almost forgot! My mind was stuck on giving him a tour of the island! You need to go to your quarters now, Ali. Everything you'll need, should be there." Kimberly said. "Right away, miss Kimberly! It was a pleasure, miss Jenna!" Ali said. Ali trotted all the way to the guest house, which was about a 50-yards away. "Mommy! Aren't you going to show auntie Kimmie the surprise?" Jamila shouted. Corina stomped her foot out of anger. "Be quiet, Jamila!" Corina shouted. "Don't talk to your sister like that!" Jenna shouted. "What surprise?" Kimberly asked. "Go on in the house! It's there!" Jenna said. "Sheldon's' not in there, ready to pull a practical joke, is he?" Kimberly said with suspicion. "Girl, that man is not thinking about playing any jokes! Now, go on in there!" Jenna said. Kimberly walked with haste on her way to the mansion. "This better not be a joke!" she turned around and shouted. a few seconds had passed, when Kimberly entered the house. Suddenly, Jenna and her daughters heard Kimberly scream at the top of her lungs. All 3 of them started to giggle.

Inside Ali's new living space, he became ecstatic at the layout. He headed towards the master bedroom. There, on the king size bed, were 2 briefcases. He slowly walked over to the bed with caution. He then unhooked the latches on one of the briefcases. He flipped open the top. He jumped back a little. A smile came upon his face. There were 5 items incased in foam. He picked up one of the items, which happened to be an automatic pistol. Another item he picked up was an 8-inch silencer. He placed both items back in their slots, next to 2 boxes of 10mm hollow point bullets. He then picked up an 8-inch high carbon steel double edge hunting knife, with sheath. With the look of joy, he quickly latched it on to his belt. He went over to the other briefcase, and unhooked the latches, and to his surprise there was a AK-107 assault rifle imbedded in foam, along with 4 30-round detachable box magazines, 4 60-round casket magazines and a detachable grenade launcher, with 4 explosive grenade cartridges, 4 smoke cartridges and 1 flare cartridge. "Miss Kimberly, you've out done yourself!" Ali said to himself. Also on the bed, was a clear plastic bag containing false documents and passports.

Back at the Jenkins mansion, Kimberly had fell to her knees crying tears of joy. "Come on, my love! Get up from the floor!" the masculine voice said. Kimberly slowly stood up sobbing like crazy. She then jumped into the arms, wrapping her legs around the waist of her best friend, her lover, the father of her child. She started smothering him with kisses, wetting up his chin, cheeks, and nose. "I love you so much" he said as they were slobbering each other's face. "No! I love you so much!" Kimberly cried. "No! I love you so much!" he said. "No! I love you so much!" she cried. This went on until Sheldon had seen enough. "I'm going to leave you 2 alone, so you straighten out your problems!" Sheldon chuckled as he left the kitchen. Suddenly, Kimberly started unbuttoning his shirt. The love of her life lifted her tank top over her head, throwing it on the marble floor. Kimberly then snatched his shirt right off his shoulders. His shirt, fell to the floor. He then ripped off her bra, exposing her size C breasts. He grabbed them, plucking her nipples with his teeth. As both were breathing heavy, Kimberly dropped to her knees once more. This time to un due his zipper. She yanked out his dark member, placing into her mouth as if she hadn't eaten weeks. He started to moan with pleasure. Kimberly then yanked his pants down to his ankles, clawing at his legs and buttocks like a wild animal. He then fell to his knees, putting his hands in her shorts. He then laid her on her back, wrestling to get her shorts off. She helped, of course. He then ripped her panties off, flinging them into the air, which they landed in the sink. He then placed his erect penis inside of her, causing her to let out a gasp of air.

Outside the mansion, Kimberly screams of pleasure could be heard from outside. "Are they fighting?" Jamila asked her mother. "No baby! They're in love!" Jenna said. "It sounds like he's beating the crap out of her!" Jamila said. "Just mind your business young lady, and don't go in there until they come out!" Jenna shouted.

An hour had passed. Kimberly and the love of her life were still on the kitchen floor stark naked. He was on his back, staring up at the kitchen ceiling, twirling his fingers through one of her locks while Kimberly straddled him, with her head was on his chest. Beads of sweat were all over them.

"How did you find me?" Kimberly asked in a soft drowsy voice. "My crazy cousin decided to smuggle me off the mainland like drugs" he chuckled. "By-the-way. Long live the house of Lassenberry. Long live Sir Marcus." Kimberly chuckled. "Oh, wow! I forgot about that for a moment!" Sir Marcus said as he rubbed his eye. Kimberly looked up at Sir Marcus. "You forgot that you're head of a drug empire?" she asked. Sir Marcus looked at his wife. "Am I?" he asked.

Later that evening around 9:30, Hakim was pacing back-n-forth in his penthouse waiting for Kimberly to call. He was dressed in a burgundy 2-piece silk suit, burgundy gator wing tip shoes, a white silk button up shirt, diamond cuff links, his Lassenberry pinky ring, and a diamond incrusted wrist watch. Every minute that passed, he kept looking at that watch.

It was now 10:37 pm, and no call from Kimberly. Hakim looked at his watch for the hundredth time. "No, this bitch didn't! I got stood up! I can't believe I got stood the fuck up!" he said to himself. He walked around the penthouse with his hands on his hips, dazed and confused. Hakim snapped back to reality by smashing that glass coffee table with his foot. He then let out a big manly yell. Bilal, now, was on the toilet reading a comic book. He heard the noise, pulled up his pants and came running out of the bathroom with his pistol in hand. "What happened, boss?" Bilal asked. Hakim balled up both of his fists in a fit of rage. "I swear to god, Bilal. If you don't put that fucking gun away, I'm gonna choke you to death, and then throw you outta the fucking window. No joke." Hakim said in a calm but stern voice. Bilal had put the gun back in his holster. He headed out back into the corridor with his head down. "Wait a minute!" Hakim shouted. Bilal turned towards him. "Did you flush that fucking toilet?" hakim asked. Bilal marched back to the bathroom with a shameful look on his face. "I can't believe this shit! First this bitch run game on me, then this grown ass, chimpanzee looking motherfucker, don't even know how to use the fucking toilet!" Hakim said to himself.

It was around 7 in the morning when Sir Marcus came out of his slumber. He realized that he was still on the kitchen floor, and that his wife was lying on top of him, fast asleep. "Baby. Baby!" he said as he shook her arm. Kimberly started moaning as she was coming out of her sleep. She lifts her head up, rubbing her fingers through her locks. "Damn woman, you're beautiful." Sir Marcus said. "You're just saying that because you didn't have any in while, and you probably want some more right now." Kimberly said as she yawned. "You've read my mind!" Sir Marcus said. Moments later, someone started knocking on the wall. "You guys decent? I gotta let the cooks in to feed my kids!" Sheldon shouted. "Guess you'll have to take a raincheck, my love!" Kimberly said as she lightly slapped her husband on the chest. Kimberly sat up looking around as she was putting on her bra. "Where on earth are my panties?" she asked.

About an hour later in a rest room off exit 10 on the Garden State Parkway, Edward the 2nd had paid the gas station attendant a 1000 dollars to make sure he and his butler number 3 wouldn't be disturbed. Edward the 2nd leaned up against the sink, with arms folded, while number 3 leaned against the bathroom stall. "I don't usually make secret meanings with the help. But, for some reason, my gut feeling told me I needed to speak with you in private." Edward the 2nd said. Number 3 folded his arms as well. "Lord Lassenberry, do you know what the power of suggestion means?" number 3 asked. "What?" Edward the 2nd asked. "The power of suggestion. Let me be frank, sir. The reason you called this meeting with me is not by chance, but through the power of suggestion. You've spent a large amount of time in pain, psychological and otherwise, since I've took up residence at castle Lassenberry. I thought it was time for you to know the truth on how this country has been under siege from within for decades." Number 3 said. Edward the 2nd shook his head in a confused state. "Why is the name colonel Braxton popping up in my head? Who are you, old man?" Edward the 2nd asked. Number 3 stood at attention. "Colonel Theodore Alan Braxton, former United States Army intelligence officer! I've served 2 tours in Vietnam, served as translator in Burma, the Republic of Cyprus, Saudi Arabia, South Korea, Brazil and Afghanistan U.S. embassies." He said. Edward the 2nd shook his head in disbelief. "Wait a minute. How the fuck you get from being an intelligence officer, to being a homeless man?" Edward the 2nd asked. Colonel Braxton looked down at the bathroom floor, sighing. He then looked Edward the 2nd in his eyes. "Back in 1985 I was assigned to operation National Agreement as a translator. The NA's, main objective was to control all the narcotics trafficking throughout the country. At first, it was perfect, so it seemed. Homicides were down 60 percent. But things took a turn for the worse for me when I witnessed the first gathering. Men, women, and even children were subject to the vilest acts of carnage by men who are in high society. The reason I sought you out was your family, along with a couple of other organizations run your operation through the bloodline only, which I consider honorable. I went to these other organizations to help me bring this demonic entity to an end, but they were blinded by the power and social status that was bestowed upon them. I even approached your uncle to warn him before they put their claws in him, but he didn't heed my words. My crusade was made public to the upper echelon of the NA." number 3 said. "So, what happened? Surly you're not fucking dead!" Edward the 2nd said. "My punishment was to abandon my wife and 4 sons. My whole identity was wiped clean. I couldn't even get a job mopping floors! Bank loans to start my own business were impossible to obtain. It's damn near impossible to catch a flight or a ship to go overseas and start over." Number 3 said. "So, what do you want me to do? Smuggle you out of the country?" Edward the 2nd asked. "No Lord Lassenberry! I can't leave the borders of this country! Before releasing me to roam the country as a vagrant, they've implanted an RFID chip within my pancreas." Number 3 said. "What the hell is a RFID chip?" Edward the 2nd asked. "It stands for Radio Frequency Identification. If I were to go as much as 50 feet into the air, and for some strange reason fly off U.S. soil, the chip will activate a signal, causing me to go into convulsions and die." Number 3 said. "How do you know this RFID shit really works?" Edward the 2nd asked. "I was in the room when the chip was designed!" number 3 said. "I can set you up with a good doctor to remove the chip, if that's what you want!" Edward the 2nd suggested. "You don't understand! There are no good doctors! The pharmaceutical companies control our medical institutions! The NA controls the pharmaceutical companies! They are not in the business of saving lives, Lord Lassenberry. Their only function is to poke and prod at the population through their health insurance until the person dies! The disenfranchised, the ones without health insurance, are nothing more than the lowest level of human Ginny pigs." Number 3 said. "So, what are you telling me?" Edward the 2nd asked. Number 3 sighed. "There is, and there will never be a cure for cancer, HIV, diabetes, heart disease! It's about the people consuming their prescription medicine!" number 3 said. Edward the 2nd thought for a moment. "Terrance did say there was no cure for cancer." He said. "And he's right! These charities and fund raisers are a fluke! Those save the children commercials, are an elaborate scheme to drain the public's pockets!" number 3 explained. "So, what can I do for you?" Edward the 2nd asked. "It's not what you can do for me, Lord Lassenberry. It's what you can do for my family. I've taught my boys some survival skills. They share the same ideology as I do, but I don't think they will survive when they go to the public and become vocal. I want you to use all your power to protect my family!" number 3 said. Edward the 2nd cleared his throat. "Where is your family from?" he asked. "Salt Lake City! Born and bred!" number 3 said proudly. Edward the 2nd walked towards number 3, putting his hands on his shoulders. "You're a good man. I can see that. I can protect your family, but I can't bring them to castle Lassenberry!" Edward the 2nd said. "Basically, you're telling me there's no hope for them?" number 3 asked. "I think there is, if you wanna call Lassenberia hope." Edward the 2nd said. "What the hell is Lassenberia?" number 3 asked. Edward the 2nd just smiled.

— CHAPTER 28. GET THAT CROWN —

Back at the Jenkins island, Sir Marcus and his beautiful wife strolled the island together hand-n-hand, with Ali following close behind. Sir Marcus turned towards Ali. "So, Ali, how do you like the other side of the world?" he asked. "It is amazing! I was wondering sir. How should I address you? surly a courageous woman such as Miss Kimberly would be married to a phenomenal man!" Ali said. Sir Marcus looked at Kimberly and smiled. He looked at Ali. "I wouldn't use the word phenomenal! I'm just a man trying to rebuild!" Sir Marcus said. "Your cousin demanded that the agents at the castle call him Lord Lassenberry. I think you deserve the same honor." Kimberly said. "Lord Lassenberry?" Sir Marcus said. He took a deep breath. He looked at Ali. "Well, it official then, Ali! You can address me as Lord Lassenberry from now on!" Sir Marcus Said. "So, it shall be!" Ali said. The couple continued their stroll.

"I'm sorry that my cousin got you mixed up in all of this." Sir Marcus said. "My love! I am not complaining! You, need to figure out a way to see your father and your cousin!" Kimberly said. "My father? Which cousin?" Sir Marcus asked with concern. "Your father's health is failing! He doesn't have much time with us!" Kimberly said. Sir Marcus sighed. "I can't show my face! Not now! If Terrance finds out I'm still alive, he'll come after the whole family thinking Krayton lied!" Sir Marcus said. "You have to do something! It's your father!" Kimberly said. "I know! I know! Just give me a moment to think, baby!" Sir Marcus said as he closed his eyes, pinching the bridge of his nose. "Tyson's home was almost demolished in an explosion a few weeks ago, Cindy and the kids are fine! They weren't home at the time!" Kimberly said. "Sheldon mentioned it to me when I arrived, but he didn't go into details! What about Tyson?" Sir Marcus asked. He was lucky! He lost hearing in one ear! But, besides that, just minor burns on the left side of his body!" Kimberly said. "Why the hell didn't Krayton tell me or send me a message about that? Damn!" Sir Marcus said. "I hate to say it, but maybe he had something to do with it." Kimberly said as she shrugged her shoulders. "Krayton? He doesn't have it in him to do something that sick!" Sir Marcus said. "I'm just saying, my love!" Kimberly said. Sir Marcus looked around, gazing at the scenery with his hands on his hips." My father! I have to do something!" Sir Marcus whispered to himself. "GLC! I'm so stupid!

Why didn't I think of this sooner?" Kimberly shouted. sir Marcus looked puzzled. "What the hell is GLC?" he asked. "It's our ticket to freedom from that Terrance guy! Your fathers' bed ridden, but we can fly him over to Lassenberia by tomorrow!" Kimberly said. "What's in Lassenberia that can help him?" Sir Marcus asked. "Like I said! GLC! Follow me! I'll explain it on the way to the mansion!" Kimberly said. Kimberly was so excited, she trotted all the way back to the mansion, which was a mile away, followed closely by her husband and Ali.

It was February 20th on a Monday in the East Bench neighborhood of Salt Lake City, Utah. It was a windy 42° F as a crowd of people were gathered around a young Caucasian man standing at a podium. He was tall, thin with blonde hair. He looked about in his late 20's. The Wasatch Range could clearly be seen in the distance behind him. The crowd of a hundred or so were shivering, but stayed to listen to the young man's speech.

The man's name was Gabe Braxton. He was the youngest son of colonel Braxton. Gabe graduated from one of the most prestigious universities in Salt Lake City with a degree in political science. He taught history at one of the private schools located in Salt Lake City as well. He resigned shortly after his father being exiled. Like his father and 3 brothers, he was trained to survive in the most dangerous and most desolate places around the globe such as the Siberian taiga, the Amazon Rain forest, Northern Forest Complex, Myanmar, and the Star Mountains of Papua New Guinea. Under the training of his father, he became a highly skilled marksman. His weapon of choice when hunting Mule deer was the takedown bow. Just like the other citizens of Utah it was legal for Gabe to carry around an unconcealed firearm. Gabe nor his brothers carried a firearm on them like the rest of the citizens of Utah. Their reasons were more severe. The Braxton brothers were aware of the National Agreement's existence, but didn't know the inner workings of this secret order. The only information they had about the NA came from their father, who was long since banished. Terrance's rule over New Jersey, just like the other 26 NA directors throughout the country was unknown to the Braxton brothers.

"I know what I've been telling you good people for the last hour sounds like something out of a sci-fi movie, but this is real! This is the world we live in now! This is the world we've been living in for decades!" Gabe shouted through the bullhorn. The crowd's reaction was mixed. Some laughed it off, some nodded, pumping their fists in the air, while others just walked away and went on about their business. But there was one person in the crowd that Gabe noticed. This man was of African American descent. The total population of East Bench was 100 percent Caucasian. Gabe had a worried look on his face as he noticed that this man just stood there motionless looking him straight into his eyes with his arms folded. "I would like to thank you fellow East Benchers for your time! God willing, I will be here again tomorrow! Have a blessed day!" Gabe concluded. Suddenly the crowd slowly departed in all directions. Everyone but the African American stranger. For a few seconds, Gabe stood his ground staring down the man that was staring at him. The man smiled as he slowly walked toward Gabe. Gabe slowly put his hand on his sidearm. The man stood about 5 feet away. He raised his hands in a surrendering gesture. "Can I help you?" Gabe asked. "No, Mr. Braxton. But, I'm here to help you." the man said. Gabe, still having his hand on his holster, stepped from behind the podium. He towered over the man. "Just to let you know, I'm quick on the draw!" Gabe said. "Yes Mr. Braxton. Your father informed us of your skills." The man said. "You didn't answer my question, Mr.!" Gabe said. The man extended his arm in a friendly gesture. "Hi! I'm Brandon Hart! I'm an ally of your fathers'!" he said. Gabe looked around, still with hand on his sidearm. "Is that so, Mr. Hart?" Gabe said. "Yes, it's so!" Brandon said.

Brandon was wearing a long, black wool trench coat, black leather gloves, and plaid scarf draped over his shoulders. Red blotches formed on his cheeks due to the cold weather. Gabe had a keen eye. He noticed Brandon's teeth chatter as he smiled. "It's obvious you're not from around here." Gabe said. "You can say that!" Brandon said. "I come in peace, Mr. Braxton! I come with good news! News of salvation!" Brandon said. "Only my lord and savior Jesus Christ, can do that!" Gabe said. Brandon smirked. "Yes, that may be true, but for the time being, me and my people should suffice!" Brandon chuckled. "Who are your people?" Gabe asked. Realizing he wasn't going to receive a hand shake from Gabe, Brandon lowered his arm. "Could we discuss this in a more closed in, warmer place? I'm freezing my balls off!" Brandon said. "How did you get here? Who's with you?" Gabe asked. "My rental is parked over there." Brandon said as he pointed towards a gray Boeman sedan. "I came alone. Trust me." he said. "Ok, Mr. Hart, follow me." Gabe said. "Will do!" Brandon said with a chipper attitude. Gabe turned and picked up the podium, and walked towards a pick-up truck.

After Gabe secured the podium on the back of his pick-up, he jumped into his vehicle. He grabbed the microphone attached to his CB radio. "Brother 4, to brother 1. Brother 4 to brother 1. Come in." Gabe said. There were a few seconds of static. *"Brother1 to brother 4. Coming in loud-n-clear."* The voice said. "Gotta a possible threat. I'm having him follow me to Delta spot." Gabe said. *"Is he alone?"* the voice asked. "From what I see. Yes." Gabe said. *"Doesn't matter. We'll be ready and waiting. Over."* The voice said. "Copy that. Over." Gabe said. Gabe drove off. He looked in his rear-view mirror. He watched as the Boeman sedan followed him.

It was about an hour later when Brandon had followed Gabe to the Traverse Mountains of Utah. Gabe led him off the paved road onto a bumpy terrain. Brandon held the steering wheel tight with 2 hands as he tried to keep control of his vehicle. Moments later, Gabe's pick-up came to a halt. Brandon stopped about a few yards behind. Brandon noticed a metal fence blocking their path. Brandon stepped out of his vehicle. He noticed behind the metal fence, the path led to a cavern inside the mountain. Gabe stepped out his vehicle. "Mr. Hart! Follow me, please!" Gabe shouted. "What is this place?" Brandon shouted as he gazed upon his surroundings. Gabe just smiled. He gestured Brandon to follow him. "I don't like this! I don't like this!" Brandon whispered to himself. Gabe approached the fence. He pulled out a remote from his coat pocket. He pressed the button on the remote causing the fence to automatically slide open. "We walk from here, Mr. Hart!" He shouted. as Gabe walked pass the fence, Brandon followed with caution. The only sounds Brandon could hear was the whistling wind and the gravel beneath his feet. The sounds were soon drowned out by his heart rapidly beating.

Gabe led Brandon down a narrow path. About a hundred yards into the cavern, the men came upon a metal door. On the door was a keypad lock. "Would you mind?" Gabe asked Brandon before punching in the code. Brandon sighed as he turned his back towards Gabe. Gabe punched in a 6-digit code. He turned the handle, opening the door. "You first, Mr. Hart." Gabe said as he opened the door even wider. Brandon slowly walked through the doorway. Gabe shut the door. There was total darkness until Gabe turned on the lights, unveiling a trail of light fixtures lining the rocky walls. The further the 2 men walked down the corridor, Brandon noticed the sound of his rapid heartbeat was soon drowned out by the sound of generators. Gabe came upon another metal door. This time, all he needed was a master key to unlock the door, which he had dangling around his neck. As soon as he opened the door, he insisted that Brandon walk through first. When Brandon entered the room, he was ambushed and thrown to the floor by a group of men wearing military garb. "What the hell?" Brandon shouted while the barrel of a M-16 machine gun was pointed at his face. "What in the name of God brought you here, Mister?" the man with the M-16 shouted. Brandon laid on his back trying to catch his breath. "If I were you Mr. Hart, I'd answer the man!" Gabe said. "Ok! Ok! Just don't shoot!" Brandon pleaded. The man with the M-16 slowly lowered his weapon, while the other 3 men kept theirs on Brandon. Can I get up, first?" Brandon asked. "You're fine just where you are, for now!" the man with the M-16 said. "I'm Brandon hart! Assistant to Lord Lassenberry of New Jersey! I was ordered to come here and give asylum to you and your family!" Brandon said. There was a moment of silence as the men looked at each other. Suddenly, the man with the M-16 burst out laughing. "Lord Lassenberry? Asylum?" the man chuckled. "He said salvation before we arrived, brother!" Gabe said. "First, Mr. Hart, there is only one Lord. And his name is Jesus Christ! And only he can bring salvation!" the man with M-16 said. "Let me guess! You people are Mormons, right?" Brandon asked. "Aren't you the smart one!" one of the men sarcastically shouted.

Elsewhere, on the island of Lassenberia, a ferry had recently docked at the new pier that was constructed by a Mozambique marine contractor. The passengers on the ferry besides the captain and his first mate, were Kimberly, her sister-in-law Terry, her mother-in-law Tanya, Ali, and her father-in-law Mark Senior, who was bound to a wheelchair.

Sir Marcus's brother Corey stayed behind back in the states to keep watch over his father's estate. Kimberly's son was back on the Jenkins's island being cared for by her sister.

"This is amazing! How come this was never mentioned to the family before?" Terry asked. "From what I was told, your uncle didn't have the funding to finish the project." Kimberly said. "That was my brother! If he couldn't do it right, he wouldn't mention it, or do it at all!" Mark senior said.

Not only was mark senior bound to a wheelchair, he also depended on an oxygen tank to support his breathing. He had lost a considerable amount of weight due to a failing digestive system.

"Sorry I couldn't get you here sooner, dad! But this had to be quiet as kept!" Kimberly said. "Don't be silly, young lady! This is better than being stuck in that damn hospital! If I'm going to spend my last days on this earth somewhere, I'd rather be here, on my family's land! By-the -way! Why the hell you bring me here in the first place?" Mark senior asked. Kimberly displayed a big beautiful smile. "Dad! Trust me! Your life is about to change!" Kimberly said.

From the time, Kimberly, had struck a deal with 3 prime ministers, the infrastructure of Lassenberia started growing at a rapid rate. Bungalows were being replaced by town houses, roads were being constructed, dendrologists and botanists were hired to install a variety of botanical life from parts of south Africa and Madagascar. Only the northern part of

Lassenberia was ordered to be built into a metropolis. The southern part of the island where the GLC was discovered was to remain desolate.

"I can't believe it, Miss Kimberly! less than a month, and so much progress has taken place!" Ali said. "When you have the power of god at your fingertips, you'll be surprise on fast people can move!" Kimberly boasted. Ali just chuckled. "The power of god? What are you two yapping about?" Mark senior asked. "In a few moments, you'll see, dad!" Kimberly said.

Kimberly and the group walked across 20-foot-long wooden boards to get to her temporary headquarters. Inside her headquarters looked like a typical office with a long conference desk and chairs, a map of Lassenberia pinned to the wall and a tall iron safe. Kimberly went to the safe and where she punched in the numbers on the keypad. She was so excited, she punched in the wrong code. "Just give me a second!" she said. Seconds later, she gained access to the safe. Inside the safe were 4 8 ounce beakers. Inside the beakers were samples of the GLC. Kimberly took one of the beakers and quickly closed the 200-hundred-pound door to the safe, automatically resetting the code. "I know it looks strange dad, but you need to ingest this!" Kimberly said. Mark senior looked frightened. Terry and her mother had scowls on their faces. "What in the world are you giving my father?" Terry shouted. "Yes! What is that?" Tanya asked. "This? This is the reason those construction workers outside are building us a new nation so fast! This is the reason we will become the most powerful family in the world!" Kimberly said as she held the beaker in the air. Kimberly handed Mark senior the beaker. He was so weak, he had to hold the beaker with 2 hands. "What are you doing, young lady?" mark senior asked as Kimberly carefully pulled the breathing tubes from his nostrils. Mark senior began gasping for air. The beaker slipped from his hands, then shattered on the floor. Tanya quickly tried to insert the breathing tubes back into her husband's nostrils as Kimberly punched in the code to reopen the safe. "Oh, my god, daddy! Kimberly! why did you do that?" terry screamed. "Everyone, stay calm! Please!" Ali said. Kimberly took out another beaker. She ran over to her father-in-law. She squeezed his jaws together, forcing his mouth to stay open. She poured half the contents into his mouth. Mark senior began spewing some of the GLC as he coughed. Kimberly took a step back, smiling. Moments later, Mark senior stopped coughing. His breathing came under control. He looked up at his wife. There was a big smile on his face. Mark senior slowly grabbed the arm rests on the wheelchair. Terry and her mother were in shock as Mark senior slowly pushed himself up, standing on his own. Ali smiled. Kimberly started crying tears of joy. "Welcome to your new life, dad!" she cried. Mark senior stared crying. His wife Tanya couldn't believe her eyes. She fell to her knees, with her hands waving in the air. "Praise the lord!" she screamed.

Later that evening, Kimberly and terry sat outside on the steps of her office. It was a clear night sky. There was a cool desert breeze blowing in their direction. The construction crew had stopped work an hour ago, taking the ferry back to their homeland. The only sounds of machinery were the sound of the generators maintaining power to her office. Inside Kimberly's office, Mark senior and his wife Tanya were dancing cheek-to-cheek to Kimberly's smooth jazz CD.

"I can't believe it! It still feels like a dream!" Terry said. "Want me to pinch you?" Kimberly chuckled. "Noooo!" Terry chuckled. moments later, Ali came from around the side of the office. "Everything is secure, Miss Kimberly, as ordered." Ali said. "Thank you, Ali. As soon as they finish painting your new home, your family can start bringing their belongings over." Kimberly said. Ali smiled. "Thank you, Miss Kimberly!" he said. "You can leave us now, Ali." Kimberly said. "Thank you for having the construction crew build me a hammock. Now, I can sleep peacefully under the stars! Raaxaysan inta kale ee fiidkii, Mudanayaal." Ali said as he bowed his head before walking away. "You do the same, Ali." Kimberly said. "Good night!" Terry said. Terry looked puzzled as Ali walked away. "What did he say?" Terry whispered. "I think he said to enjoy our evening! I'm still working on my Somali!" Kimberly chuckled. "You never told us! Where did you find that stuff?" Terry asked. "The GLC? I'll say this. When the rightful owner of this island arrives, you'll know what you need to know." Kimberly said. "Who's the rightful owner? Krayton?" Terry asked. Kimberly looked at Terry, and just smiled.

A couple of days later, 2 elderly Caucasian men were standing in a dimly lit corridor talking. One of the men was Dr. Zachmont, one of the top men working for the NA. the man he was holding a conversation with was the new United States secretary of Defense, Carter Gates.

Both men were dressed in black tuxedos. Dr. Zachmont wore his National Agreement insignia, which was a gold pentagram with a red jewel set in the middle of it on his lapel, while Secretary Gates wore the U.S. flag on his. "I can't thank you enough sir for pulling strings for me!" Gates said. "Believe me. It wasn't easy. Most of the senate don't seem to be team players. But, now we have you, with your hands on the trigger, Mr. Secretary! So, fuck them!" Zachmont chuckled. "And I won't hesitate to pull it, with the master's permission, of course!" Gates said. "Good boy. Oh! I almost forgot!" Zachmont said. He reached inside his tuxedo jacket and pulled out a gold envelope. He hands it to the secretary. "What's this?" Gates asked. "It's an invite. You read what's on the card inside. Remember it. Burn it!" Zachmont said. Gates stuffed the invitation inside of his jacket. "I'm famished! What's on the menu?" Zachmont asked. "I believe it's, duck. Roasted duck." Gates said. Zachmont looked down at both ends of the corridor. "How the hell do we get out of this fucking maze. he asked. "Follow me, sir!" Gates said.

Zachmont followed Gates down the narrow corridor, making a left down another corridor. They came upon a freight elevator. They stepped inside. Gates pushed the button. The doors closed, going up. 200 feet later, the elevator came to a stop. The doors opened. Both men step out. "Want to go get us a couple of young bitches after this shindig is over with?" Zachmont asked. "It's hard to ditch the wife nowadays!" Gates said. Dr. Zachmont frowned at Gates. "Grow a pair, why don't ya! You're the secretary of Defense, for Christ's sake!" Zachmont said. Moments later, a black man in a dark blue suit approach the 2 men. "Mr. Secretary. The president is waiting for your arrival, sir." The man said. "Dr. Zachmont! I would like you to meet Jerry! He's rumored to be the best damn secret service agent in Washington!" Gates said. "Pleased to meet you, Jerry." Zachmont said. "Now Jerry. Would you be so kind, and show us to our seats?" Gates asked. "Follow me, Mr. secretary." Jerry said. The men didn't have to travel far. They were a few yards from the dining hall in the east wing of the White House.

It was the 15th of march, on a Wednesday morning when Kimberly was standing on the pier at Lassenberia. She watched from a distance as the marine construction crew was working on another dock. Her flower print dress was flapping in the breeze. In her hand was a ham radio. She received a signal from one of the 2 seaplanes coming in low off in the distance. About a couple of hundred yards behind her was Terry walking in her direction. The first seaplane made a perfect landing in the water. It drifted smoothly closer to the pier, stopping parallel to the dock. Kimberly watched as a man exited the seaplane. He jumped on to the dock, then grabbed a mooring line to secure the plane to the pier. One-by-one, a group of men exited the seaplane. Terry approached Kimberly from behind. "Who are those guys?" Terry asked. "We'll soon find out, sis." Kimberly said. "I don't understand, Kimberly! why'd you let my parents leave the island and told me to stay? This place is beautiful-n-all, but I want to get back to the states to see Brandon." Terry said. "When I sent a message to your cousin that you and your parents were here, he sent a message back saying that you should stay behind for some reason." Kimberly said. "Why? I serve no purpose here in building this place!" Terry said. Kimberly ignored Terry's last words and smiled as she recognized the face of the last man exiting the seaplane. She tapped Terry on the arm. "I think your purpose just arrived. Look!" Kimberly said. Terry looked towards the seaplane. She screamed for joy, jumping up and down like a little kid. She made a dash down the pier, towards the seaplane. The last man to exit the seaplane was her fiancé Brandon.

The men that exited the seaplane were the four Braxton brothers. Terry ran passed them, bumping into Gabe to get to Brandon. The Braxton brother smiled as terry jumped into the arms of the man she loved. Brandon firmly held the love of his life in his arms as she wrapped her legs around him. They kiss each other in a wild passionate manner. "Get a room!" one of the Braxton brothers chuckled.

Brandon and Terry released each other. "I've missed you so much!" Brandon said. Terry put on a façade of anger. She slapped Brandon across the chest. "Where have you been? I was worried about you!" she shouted. "I was on a mission, baby! These good men here, agreed to help your cousin's dream come to fruition! I'll explain later! Where's Kimberly?" he asked. Terry didn't say anything. She just pointed towards the end of the pier. Brandon squinted as he saw Kimberly off in the distance, waving her hand in the air. "Come on, guys! Let's meet the woman incharge!" Brandon said. The Braxton brothers followed Brandon and Terry as they walked down the pier hand-n-hand.

Kimberly met the group halfway. "Kimberly." Brandon said. "Brandon!" Kimberly said with a raised eyebrow and a smirk. "Kimberly! I would like you to meet the Braxton brothers! This is Tim!" Brandon said. "Please to meet you." Tim said as he and Kimberly shook hands.

Tim, or Timothy Braxton was the eldest of the 4 brothers. He looked rugged with a long scruffy beard and had a pudgy build. Standing 6 feet, 5 inches tall, he looked like an over the hill outlaw biker, but like his brothers, he was a true man of god.

"This is Simon!" Brandon said. "Aren't you pretty!" Simon said to Kimberly as they shook hands. "Kimberly blushed, even though she's been hearing this most of her life.

Simon was the second eldest of the brothers. He stood as tall as Gabe, and slim. He was bald, having a long gray beard and handle bar mustache. He sported a crucifix earing in his left ear. Kimberly noticed the huge hunting knife strapped to his leg.

"This is Matthew!" Brandon said. Mathew nodded his head as he shook Kimberly's hand. "What's the matter? Cat got your tongue?" Kimberly chuckled. Mathew looked at Brandon. "He's a mute!" Brandon said nervously. "Oh! I'm sorry!" Kimberly said. Mathew just smiled, putting his hands up, gesturing that it wasn't a big deal.

Mathew wasn't as tall as his brothers, but looked just as intimidating. Both of his arms were covered in tattoos displaying passages from the bible, and a crucifix on each forearm. Kimberly noticed that he had animal bite marks on the side of his face. "Did you piss off your dog?" she asked. "It was a cougar, ma'am." Gabe said. "Wow!" Kimberly said. "Oh, yeah! This is Gabe!" Brandon said. Kimberly quickly looked Gabe up-n-down. "Hello, Gabriel!" Kimberly said as she gazed into his eyes. Gabe shook her hand. Theirs hands slowly slid away from each other. Kimberly blushed as she folded her arms. Gabe couldn't take his eyes off her. Simon noticed the attraction between the two. "Excuse me! Aren't we here to discuss business?" Simon asked. "Yes, we are! If you gentlemen would follow me." Kimberly said. Everyone followed Kimberly off the pier. "So, this is the Garden of Eden!" Tim said as he took his first step on the sand.

Moments later, the second seaplane had pulled up next to the pier. At this moment, Ali and his 6 of nephews' approach Kimberly. Kimberly stopped. "Is everything all right, Miss Kimberly?" he said. Kimberly turned to Brandon. "What's in the other plane?" she asked. "Luggage! Ah, Supplies!" Brandon said. "Good! Ali. Take your people and unload the plane. I'll be in my office when you're done." Kimberly said. Ali turned to his family. You heard her! Aynu tago!" Ali shouted. Ali looked Simon up-n-down as he walked pass. "Follow me." Kimberly said.

Minutes later, Kimberly and the group hop in 2 jeeps to take them to her office. Kimberly drove the first jeep, while Terry followed behind in the other. It was a bumpy ride on the sandy terrain, since the roads were still under construction.

"That was interesting!" Tim chuckled as Kimberly stopped the jeep in front of her headquarters. Well, gentlemen, we're here!" Kimberly said before turning off the ignition. "Follow me, please." She said. The group of men followed Kimberly inside her office. She stopped Terry from entering the office. "What's wrong? Why can't I be in on this?" Terry asked. Kimberly sighed. "As of now, I'm the care taker of this island. There's some things you don't need to know right now. If things go bad here, go to Ali and his family. They'll protect you. you'll be incharge until he, arrives." Kimberly whispered before closing the door in Terry's face. "Who's he?" terry shouted.

Please, take a seat, gentlemen! As you can see, we have a huge selection of good eats and spirits on the other table for you!" Kimberly said. "Sorry little lady, but we believe alcohol is the devil's cool-aide." Tim said. "Very well, then!" Kimberly said. The men stood until Kimberly took her seat. Tim sat at one end of the conference table, while Kimberly sat the other end, with Brandon sitting to her right. Serving the food were 2 of Ali's teenage nieces.

After the 2 girls passed out plates of food, they stood off to the side. "Hawa. Fatima. Thank you for your service. You can leave us, now." Kimberly said. The 2 young ladies leave the office, heading back to their brand-new town house.

"Before we begin, Mrs. Lassenberry…" Tim said. "Kimberly! Just call me, Kimberly."

She said. "If you insist. I would like to lead us in prayer." Tim said. Tim grabbed his brother Simon's hand with his left hand, and grabbed his brother Mathew's hand with his right. Kimberly grabbed Brandon's hand with her left hand, and reluctantly grabbed Gabe's hand with her right hand. "Let's bow our heads." Tim said. Everyone bowed their heads, as they closed their eyes. "Dear God in Heaven. Please guide us, and give us the wisdom to proceed in our future endeavors, and give us the strength to take on the great evil that will soon cross our paths. Please bless this new land, and give the proprietors of this land, the courage to stand strong against this evil." Tim said. Kimberly opened her eyes for a quick second, looking in Gabe's direction. "In the name of our lord and savior Jesus Christ. Amen." Tim said. "Amen!" everyone else said. Kimberly and the men raise their heads and released their grips from each other. Kimberly and Gabe's grip lasted a few seconds longer.

"Now, can we get down to business?" Kimberly said as she rubbed her hands together. "I guess I'll start! We understand that you Braxton brothers are on a, shall we say, a crusade, against this entity called the National Agreement!" Brandon said. Brandon was interrupted when Simon raised his hand. "If you know anything about history, Mr. Hart. The crusades that were fought ages ago, weren't about righteousness. The crusades were about gaining power. The crusades were about controlling the masses. The crusades were about forcing one's God on another human being! I don't think that way! My brothers don't think that way! So, I take offense to being called a crusader!" Simon said. "Sounds fair!" Brandon said. "I would like to know, what you can contribute, if there's blood to be shed, Mr. Braxton?" Kimberly asked. "I can answer that, young lady." Tim said. "Be my guest!" Kimberly said. "We're here to do God's work! And if it comes to taking someone's life for the benefit of good people, so be it!" Tim said. "I hear you when you say you're here to do God's work. But, if you're going to work with us, you'll have to understand, that this operation will be ran and overseen by the head of our Family, Lord Lassenberry." Kimberly said. The Braxton brothers look around the table at each other. "Fair enough!" Tim chuckled. "Brandon explained to us Lord Lassenberry's situation. How can he run this island? How can he run this operation, thousands of miles away from a castle in New Jersey?" Simon asked. "We're working on that! But," Brandon said before being interrupted by Kimberly. "The work is actually done! Lord Lassenberry will be with us sooner than you think." Kimberly said. Brandon had a look of confusion after what Kimberly had said, but kept silent. "We've noticed construction going on outside from various construction crews. It must cost a pretty penny. A giant penny, to have something like that! Do you mind telling us how all of this is being funded?" Tim asked. Kimberly glanced over at Brandon. "I can tell you this. None of this is being funded with blood money. We're, shall we say, using a very big, green credit card!" Kimberly chuckled. "Is this credit card, tangible?" Tim asked with a smirk on his face. There was a moment of silence. "So, you want me to show you this credit card? That's what you're saying?" Kimberly asked. "That would be nice! Especially, if we're all on the same team." Tim chuckled. Kimberly shook her head. "No! you'll just have to put your faith in what I'm telling you!" Kimberly said. Tim leaned back in his chair. His brothers looked at him for guidance. Brandon glanced over at Kimberly. "I guess you're the captain of this, then! Or, shall I say the coming of Lord Lassenberry is!" Tim said jokingly. Kimberly's face was unimpressionable. She stood from her chair. Tim stood from his chair. "You don't have to get up!" Kimberly said. "Oh! I was just coming over to shake on our agreement!" Tim said. "I looked at the table. The girls forgot to bring over the salt-n-pepper shakers. I was just going to fetch them." Kimberly said. "Uh, ok! We can still shake on it!" Tim said. "What is it today? Wednesday? I'll have my team of lawyers come to the island with the proper documents for you gentlemen to sign by Saturday, to solidify our agreement. With all due respect, Tim, I believe the pen is mightier than the sword, also mightier than a hand shake." Kimberly said. Kimberly walked away from the table to retrieve the salt-n-pepper shakers. "If I didn't know any better, I'd swear she was Lord Lassenberry." Tim whispered to one of his brothers. Moments later, Kimberly returned with the seasonings. She placed them on the table. "Ok gentleman! Let's dig in!" she shouted.

An hour later, Tim was seated at the table massaging his beer gut. The abundance of food that was served was practically demolished. "Belly full?" Kimberly asked Tim. "That was some meal!" he said. "I have to admit, this was a meal fit for kings!" Gabe said. Kimberly stood from her seat. "Speaking of kings, when Lord Lassenberry makes his arrival, I'm sure he'll give you all the information you will need to help build our new nation! Yes!" Kimberly shouted with joy.

The Braxton brothers also stood from their seats. "If it's ok with our hostess, we would like to take time tour this fascinating place!" Simon said. At that moment, Ali entered the room. "What a coincidence! Ali is here just in time to give you fine gentlemen that tour! Ali! Would you do me the honor?" Kimberly said. "Of course, Miss Kimberly!" Ali said with a big smile on his face. "Oh! It almost slipped my mind! I would like to say, that the southern part of the island is off limits for the time being, for environmental reasons! But, I'm sure this side of the island will be most impressive to you!" Kimberly said. "This way, gentlemen!" Ali said. 3 of the Braxton brothers followed Ali out the door, as the youngest brother Gabe, gave Kimberly a kiss on the cheek. "You, are a bad boy!" Kimberly giggled. Brandon with a worried look on his face, stood from his seat. Everyone, but Brandon and Kimberly had left the room. Brandon walked over to Kimberly. "I'm curious! When you talk about Lord Lassenberry, who are you preferring to?" he asked. For a split second, Kimberly looked up at the ceiling fan. She looked at Brandon. "You know in your heart who's really running this show!" she said as her eyes teared up. Brandon folded his arms. No, I don't! tell me! But, before you answer, just know, Edward the 2nd wears the crown! You do know this!" Brandon said. Kimberly had a smirk on her face, until her facial expression transformed to something that looked dead serious. "Sir Marcus! Sir Marcus will get that crown back! Trust me! He…will…get…that…crown!" she said standing inches away from Brandon's face. Brandon looked down at the floor.

CHAPTER 29. VIOLA CARR

A couple of months had passed since the Braxton brothers had visited the island of Lassenberia. It was a warm Tuesday afternoon when Edward the second was being chauffeured in a Boeman Sedan to Hillside, New Jersey. He was singing along to a rap song on the radio. There were 2 NA agents sitting on both sides of Edward the 2nd. He turned to one of the agents. "I was never really into this rap shit until now! Ya feel me?" he said. Edward the 2nd said. "You'll have to elaborate, my lord." The agent said. Edward the 2nd frowned. "Never mind!" he said.

The chauffer made a left turn on to Princeton avenue. The vehicle parked. "I swear! I'm forming a new inner circle! Y'all some boring mother fuckers! Let me the fuck out!" Edward the 2nd shouted. "Yes, my Lord." One of the agents said. The agent hopped out of the vehicle. He held the door open for Edward the 2nd. Edward the 2nd exits the vehicle. He went to the door of his girlfriend Viola Carr. He rang the doorbell. Moments later, the door opened. Standing in the doorway was her son Hakeem. "What's up, young man? Your mother home?" Edward the 2nd asked. Hakeem looked out into the street. He saw 2 agents standing outside the vehicle. "Don't lie to me and tell me she's not home, and she is!" Edward the 2nd said. Hakeem didn't say a word. He just opened the door even wider to let Edward the 2nd pass. "Thank, you!" Edward the 2nd said in a jovial manner.

Once inside, Edward the 2nd took off his jacket. "Here! Hold this!" he said to Hakeem. Hakeem took the jacket, tossing it on the head rest of the couch. "Honey! I'm home!" Edward the 2nd shouted with his arms spread. Moments later, Viola came down the stairs with the look of disappointment on her face. In her hand was a pregnancy test strip. "There's my sexy flower! You ready to go out?" Edward the 2nd asked. Viola approached him, handing him the test strip. "What's this shit?" he asked. "Hakeem! Leave us alone for minute!" Viola said. "Ma! I'm not leaving you here with this clown!" Hakeem said. Edward the 2nd turned to Hakeem. "Boy! You better listen to yo mama!" he said. Hakeem was about to come at Edward the 2nd, with his chest out. "Hakeem! Go outside! Now!" Viola shouted as she pointed towards the door. Hakeem stopped in his tracks. He stomped his foot on the floor. "Fuck this!" he shouted. "Watch your mouth!" Viola shouted as her son went outside, slamming the door behind him. Edward the 2nd started to giggle. "Do you know what the hell is in your hand?" Viola asked. "Ah, it's one of those pregnancy things, right?" he asked. "Yes! It is! Jesus!" she shouted. Edward the 2nd dropped the test strip on the floor. His bugged eyes were wide open. He had a smile from ear-to-ear. He wrapped his arms around viola's waist, lifting her in the air. "Oh shit! I'm gonna be daddy!" he shouted. "Put me down! Now!" she shouted. Edward the 2nd put her down. "What's wrong baby?" he asked. Viola turned and walked away from him. "I'm getting rid of it!" she said with her back turned towards him. "What the fuck you are talking about?" he asked. Viola turned around, facing him. She took a deep breath. "I don't want your baby!" she said as her eyes teared up. "What the fuck you mean, you don't want my baby? Do you know who the fuck I am?" Edward the 2nd shouted. "I know exactly who the fuck you are! That's why I want to get rid of it!" she shouted. "That's bullshit! If you wanted to get rid of it, you would've done it already!" he said. "How can I do anything when you have your goons following me around 24/7?" viola shouted. "You're my woman! I need to protect you!" he said. "I'm not your woman! I'm your hostage! At least that's the way I've been feeling since I got involved with your ugly ass!" viola shouted. "Oh! I'm ugly, now? Bitch! I run this whole fucking state! I can fuck any woman I want! I can kill, l anybody I want! I'm a fucking god! So, don't tell me you ain't keeping my mother fucking baby!" he shouted. viola put her hands together in a praying position. "Don't you get it! I don't love you! please! Please! Just let me go!" she cried. Edward the 2nd had fury in his eyes. His lips had tightened shut as he breathed heavily through his nose. Suddenly, an evil smile appeared on his face. "Check this out. Either you have my baby, and have 2 kids, or, or! You have no kids." He said in a calm voice. "What are you going to do? Hurt my son, now?" she shouted. Edward the 2nd approached her, putting his hands gently on her shoulders. "Listen baby. I don't want to be the bad guy here. But, like I just said, I'm a god. Now, how far along are you?" he asked. Viola didn't answer. She just had her arms folded, staring at the floor as the tears dripped from her cheeks. "I'm gonna ask you again. How far along are you?" he asked in a stern voice. "I don't' know! I haven't seen my gynecologist yet." She said. "I tell you what. You move in with me at the castle, and I'll see to it that you have the best care givers money can buy. Viola pushed his hands off her shoulders. "I…don't …want you! I don't want this baby!" she shouted. Edward the 2nd started chuckling. "Silly woman! You have no idea who you're dealing with." He chuckled. "Oh, my god!" Viola shouted as she massaged her temples. Edward the 2nd slapped his hands together. "fine! You stay here then! But I'm leaving a detail of guards here to watch yo ass until this baby is born! If I find out if you've tried to hurt my baby by hurting yourself, that pretty face of yours, won't stay pretty for long! Then, nobody will want yo ass! Not even me! You know what? Now I'm pissed off! I don't even wanna go anywhere with you right now! Now open the fucking door, so I can leave!" Edward the 2nd shouted. Viola was furious. She stormed to the door, and opened it. Edward the 2nd grabbed his jacket. "If you see a group of men standing around outside in a little bit, they work for me. I'll have a couple of nurses stop by later to check on you." he said. Edward the 2nd leaned in to Viola to give her a kiss. She turned her head away. Fine! Be that way!" he chuckled. "Just leave! Please!" she shouted. "You ok. Ma?" Hakeem asked. Edward the 2nd stood face-to-face with Hakeem. "Listen son. Just to give you a tiny idea of who I am. I'm gonna get a couple of real street niggas to come over here and beat the shit out of you, for disrespecting me. The police, your guidance counselor, not even yo bitch ass father, can save you from that." Edward the 2nd said with a smile on his face. Hakeem started trembling. Edward the 2nd looked down and saw a small puddle at Hakeem's feet. "Look at this shit! Nigga done pissed on himself!" he chuckled. "Hakeem! Come inside! Now!" Viola shouted. "Go inside son, and let mommy change your diaper." Edward the 2nd said. Hakeem stood petrified. Viola had to grab her son by the arm to bring him inside. "Oh! Buy him one of those mouth pieces the boxers use, so he doesn't get his teeth knocked the fuck out." Edward the 2nd said. Viola slammed the door shut. Edward the 2nd started laughing as he walked off the porch. "My Lord. We've just received a message from castle Lassenberry that your aunt Maggie, and your cousin Tyson are at the gate." The agent said. "Shit! Tell'em to come back tomorrow morning, around 9!" Edward the 2nd said. "Yes, my lord." The agent said. Edward the 2nd hopped into the vehicle. "Take me around the streets! I wanna see how these niggas doing out here!" Edward the 2nd said. "Yes. My lord." The chauffeur said. The vehicle pulled off.

Edward the 2nd and his agents drove around for hours through the streets of Hillside, Newark, Irvington, Bloomfield, Jersey City, Warren Township, Newton, Cape may, and 50 other areas that were under his rule, until finally, around 6pm, reaching castle Lassenberry. Edward the 2nd noticed a black limo parked on the castle grounds. "Whose limo is this?" he asked the agents standing guard at the gate. None of the agents gave an answer. "I just asked you robots a question!" Edward the 2nd shouted. "You'll find your answer inside, my lord." One agents said. Once the golf cart carrying Edward the 2nd stopped in front of his office, he noticed that the door to his office was ajar. "What the fuck?" Edward the 2nd said to one of the agents standing guard. "Come on in, Mr. Lassenberry!" a voice from within his office shouted. "Who's in there?" he whispered to the agent said. "It's not for me to say, My lord." The agent said. "Mr. Lassenberry! Come on in! I won't bite!" the voice said. Edward the 2nd peeked inside the office. There, he saw an overweight Caucasian man sitting at his desk. Edward the 2nd slowly walked in. "Hey friend! How's tricks?" the man said. "Who the fuck you're supposed to be, man? And how the fuck you get into my office?" Edward the 2nd shouted. "I'm sorry, Mr. Lassenberry! I just wanted to look cool sitting at your desk! You must admit! I did look kind of cool when you first came in, didn't I? come on! Admit it!" the man said with grin on his face. "If you don't get out of my chair, and get out of my house within the next 5 seconds, I'm gonna have my men here put a bunch of bullet holes in ya!" Edward the 2nd said. The man started laughing. "Mr. Lassenberry! Look around! Your agents won't do a damn thing you say, unless I tell them to!" the man chuckled as he stood up. He held out his hand. "I'm Doug Reed! I'm the new assistant director of new Jersey, replacing Mr. Haggerty!" Doug said. Edward the 2nd ignored the man's friendly gesture. "What happened to Terrance?" Edward the 2nd asked. "Mr. Haggerty was promoted! That's all you need to know!" Doug said. "So, you're the one on my ass, now?" Edward the 2nd asked. "It's funny you mention ass, Mr. Lassenberry! Mr. Haggerty has a reputation of indulging in bizarre sexual activities! I assure you, you won't have to worry about being violated anymore! Just do your job, being the top guy in Jersey, and we'll get along fine! Ok?" Doug said. "So, I can run things without you sticking your nose in my affairs?" Edward the 2nd asked. "Pretty much!" Doug said. Edward the 2nd rubbed his hands together. "Ok! Now that we know each other, you can get the fuck out now!" he said with a grin. "I guess that's my cue to leave!" Doug said. Before Doug left, he reached inside of his jacket pocket. "I almost forgot!" he said as he handed Edward the 2nd a gold envelope. "What's this?" "You are one of the honorees to the next gathering! It's your turn to pay the piper, Mr. Lassenberry!" Doug said. "What the hell you mean it's my turn to pay the piper?" Edward the 2nd asked. Doug walked over to Edward the 2nd, looking him straight in the eye. "Blood, Mr. Lassenberry. It's your turn to pay in blood." Doug said. "You want me to kill myself?" Edward the 2nd shouted as he scratched the side of his head. Doug sighed. "Like your uncle before you, he knew that one of his relatives had to feed this gestalt phenomenon of ours. Unlike that piece of shit, punk, yellow bellied, faggot cousin of yours that went into hiding, we believe that you will stand and deliver like a man and bring us that blood relative! All the information is in that envelope. Once you open it, read it, then burn it! There's no turning back after that, my friend! Just one more thing. If you can't decide on which relative to offer us, we'll make the decision for you." Doug said before patting Edward the 2nd on the shoulder and exiting the office.

Back at Lassenberia, Brandon was sent back for second time to check on Kimberly's day-to-day operations. This time, he brought along his fiancé Terry. Brandon noticed that there were 12 more town houses built, making it a total of 30, an urban park half the size of Central park was in development, a bank, a courthouse a police station, and a fire house were completed but not operational. 2 cell towers were in operation, 1 paved 4 lane road was completed starting from the southern pier, passing through the new town named after Kimberly called Kim Town. Only 3 square miles of the island was habitable. The residence so far consisted of Ali and his entire family, the Braxton brothers, along with their wives and children became permanent citizens as well.

It was around noon when Kimberly and Brandon were having a meeting in her office. "It looks like thing are coming together. Good!" Brandon said. Kimberly looked agitated. "I know you're doing your job, but this is my baby! Don't forget that!" Kimberly said. "With all due respect, I know you did all the heavy lifting, but this is still a team effort!" Brandon said. "Team? This feels more like a me effort!" Kimberly shouted. "That's why I'm here! We have a police station and a courthouse with no judicial system put in place! If this is going to be a nation, we need to have laws! Some form of constitution! By-the way! How are we funding all of this infrastructure?" Brandon asked. Kimberly smiled. "That's classified." She said. "Classified? I'm Lord Lassenberry's advisor!" Brandon shouted. "And I'm building him a nation! What's your point?" Kimberly said. At that moment, Kimberly's laptop had an incoming cryptic message. "You'll have to excuse me! I have to take this message!" Kimberly said. Brandon waved his hand at Kimberly, leaving her office in frustration.

Standing outside of Kimberly's office, Brandon gazed upon the construction work going on all around him. Moments later, Terry, driving one of the island jeeps, stopped right in front of her fiancé. "Hi baby!" Terry shouted. she felt a gesture of indifference from Brandon. "Baby! What's the matter?" she asked. Brandon shook his head. "I feel like I'm out of the loop around here!" he said. Terry looked around for a few seconds. She turned to Brandon. "To be honest with you, I feel the same way!" she said. "How so?" Brandon said with cynicism. "I just came from the southern part of the island! It's closed off by a tall electrified fence from end-to-end! On top of that, 6 of Ali's nephews are spread out standing guard with machine guns!" she said. "Did you tell them who you were?" Brandon asked. "Yes! But they didn't care! They told me they only take orders from Miss Kimberly!" Terry said with sass in her voice. Brandon scoffed. Before Terry could say another word, Kimberly came out of her office. "Good! You're both here!" Kimberly said. "What is it, now?" Brandon asked. "I've received word that there's trouble back home!" Kimberly said. "What kind of trouble?" Terry asked. "Terry, please! What kind of trouble?" Brandon asked. "First, don't ever interrupt her again! Not if I'm standing around!" Kimberly said. Brandon sighed. "For god sakes, Kimberly! What kind of trouble is happening back home?" he asked. "The kind of trouble to the point, where you and Terry can't go back to the states!" Kimberly said. "Why Not!" Terry said with concern. "I can't go in to details, but it's not safe for you to go back!" Kimberly said. "What about my parents? What about the rest of the family?" Terry asked. "Don't worry! We're arranging a way to get them all here, safely!" Kimberly said. Terry stepped out of the jeep. She ran over to Brandon, wrapping her arms around him. "I'm scared!" she cried. Kimberly rolled her eyes. "I'll have Ali set you 2 up in one of the town houses for the time being!" Kimberly said before going back into her office.

The next day back at castle Lassenberry, Edward the 2nd was sitting in his office waiting for the arrival of his cousin Tyson Richards. It was May 20th. It was a breezy Saturday afternoon. There was a knock on the office door. "Come in!" Edward the 2nd shouted as he was reading the B.O.I. "Shit!" he said as he shoved the binder in one of the drawers of his desk. An agent of Asian descent entered the office. "Your cousin Tyson Richards just arrived, my Lord." The agent said. "Is he alone?" Edward the 2nd asked. "Yes, my lord." The agent said. "Bring him here." Edward the 2nd said. "Yes, my lord." The agent said. "Don't forget to check his ass for weapons! I also want you to double up on the security when he comes in here! Now go!" Edward the 2nd said. "Yes, my lord." The agent said before leaving the office. Edward the 2nd sat at his desk nervously, twiddling his thumbs. He opened the top right hand drawer to his desk. In that drawer, he always kept a revolver locked and loaded. Like his cousin before him. Because of the doubt in his mind, checked to see if it was fully loaded. "A man's gotta do, what a man's gotta do." He said to himself. He put the revolver back.

Moments later, there was a knock on the door. "Hold on!" Edward the 2nd shouted as he put the B.O.I back into the safe. "Come in!" he shouted as he rushed back to his desk. The door opened. 2 agents entered the office, followed by Tyson Richards, then 2 more agents. Edward the 2nd noticed that his cousin looked frail and fearful. He also noticed Tyson's left arm was bandaged up, and that the left side of his face was badly bruised. "What's up cuz?" Edward the 2nd said. Tyson had his head down. "Nothing much." Tyson said in a meek voice. "You look like shit, man!" Edward the 2nd said. Tyson responded with a nervous smirk. "I see you didn't bring your mommy with you this time." Edward the 2nd said. "I told her I can handle this on my own." Tyson mumbled. "Handle what? What did you come here to handle, cuz?" Edward the 2nd asked. Tyson sighed. "I want to apologize for talking shit in the past." He mumbled. "What? What's that? I can't hear you!" Edward the 2nd said. Tyson stared his cousin in the face. "I'm sorry!" he cried aloud. "Sorry? Sorry for what?" Edward the 2nd asked with a grin on his face. "I just wanted to say! I want to say…you run the family business!" he cried. Edward the 2nd stood from his chair. He walked over to his cousin, giving him a hug, being careful not to touch the injured side of his body. "It's ok! It's ok! That was fucked up what happened to you, cuz! My men are too passionate! Loyal to a fault! Sometimes they get carried away! I made sure this shit won't happen again!" Edward the 2nd said. "Thank you." Tyson mumbled. "What about you, cuz?" Edward the 2nd asked. "What?" Tyson asked. "How loyal are you?" Edward the 2nd asked. Tyson looked around at the agents standing close by. He took a deep breath. He looked at his cousin. "Long live the house of Lassenberry... Long live...Edward the 2nd." He mumbled. "Not good enough, cuz! Edward the 2nd shouted as he walked back to his seat. "What else can I say?" Tyson shouted in desperation. "It's not just what you can say, but what you should do when in the presence of a god!" Edward the 2nd shouted as he leaned back in his chair. Reluctantly, Tyson struggled as he fell to his knees. "Long live the house of Lassenberry. Long live...Edward the 2nd." He mumbled. Edward the 2nd had a smile from-ear-to-ear. "Cool! Help him up!" Edward the 2nd ordered the agents. "Now, you and your side of the family can get your envelopes!" Edward the 2nd said. "What about back pay?" Tyson asked. "Back pay? Nigga! You should be grateful that you're still alive!" Edward the 2nd shouted.

Elsewhere, at the home of Viola Carr in Hillside, Viola was in her bedroom, sitting at the edge of her bed sobbing. She went to the window. Outside her window, she saw 2 of Edward the 2nd's hired goons standing in the driveway. She slowly went to the bedroom door. She opened it, sticking her head out. There, sat another goon sitting at the top of the staircase reading a book. The hired goon quickly looked up, staring her in the face. Viola slammed the door shut. Viola massaged her belly. She looked over on her dresser. She stared at her nail file just lying there. She went over and grabbed it off the dresser. She then sat back down on the bed. she put the sharp end of the file to her belly. She then raised the file above her head. Her arm came down with speed. The sharp end stopped less than an inch away from her belly. She dropped the file. She covered her face, sobbing uncontrollably. Moments later, the goon guarding the staircase bursts in. "What the fuck?" the burly black man shouted as he noticed the nail file on the floor. "Bitch! You trying to get me killed." He shouted as he went over and picked up the file off the floor. "You know if you injure yourself, we all get our domes blasted.?" he shouted. "Don't try that shit again!" he said as he squeezed Viola's jaw, slamming her head back on the bed.

Later that evening, Tyson was in the Kitchen of his mother's home. Maggie let him and his family stay at her home in Vineland, New Jersey, one of many located throughout jersey. He slowly unwrapped the bandage that was on his injured arm, unveiling a small tape recorder. "I got your ass now, cousin!" he whispered to himself. At that moment, his wife Cindy entered the kitchen. "Changing your bandage?" she asked Tyson. "I need to! But, this right here in my hand, is all I need to bring that piece of shit cousin of mine down!" Tyson said as he held up the tape recorder. "What's on it?" Cindy asked. "I have him confessing that he put the hit on me, in so many words! I'm taking this to the Hoboken police first thing in the morning!" he said. "Good! Jesus! Our kids could've been home at the time!" she said.

The next day around 8 in the morning, Tyson was in the bathroom standing in front of mirror brushing his teeth. He paused for a moment. He caressed the disfigured side of his face. In a fit of rage, he slammed the toothbrush down into the sink.

A half hour later he gave his wife a long kiss on the lips. He kissed his sons on their foreheads before leaving the house. He cautiously walked around his car, checking for anything out of the ordinary. "Is everything ok?" Cindy shouted as she stood in the doorway. "I'm good! I won't be long! I love you!" he shouted. "I love you too!" she shouted as she waved goodbye. Tyson jumped in his car. He took off, heading towards the Garden State Parkway.

A couple of hours later, Tyson parked across the street from the Hoboken police department. He entered the facility, heading towards the receptionist's desk. The female officer was on her cell phone, speaking Spanish. "Excuse me. Excuse me!" Tyson shouted through the Plexiglas window. "¡Espera a Carmen!" the officer said to the person on the other end of her phone. "I need to speak to someone in homicide, or the terrorist task force division." Tyson said. "What is your name, sir?" she asked. Tyson Richards." He said. "Hold on a second, sir." She said. "¡Déjame llamarte, Carmen!" the officer said. "¿Dijo que se llamaba Tyson Richards?" Carmen asked. "¡Si, lo hizo! ¿Por qué?" the officer asked. "Pregúntale si está relacionado con la familia de Lassenberry." Carmen said. "Are you related to the Lassenberry family?" the officer asked. Tyson became frustrated. "Could you connect me to someone that can help me? Please!" Tyson shouted. "There's no need to shout, sir!" the officer said. Tyson took a deep breath through his nostrils. Yes! I'm related to the Lassenberry family!" Tyson said with restraint. "El dijo que sí." The officer said. "What does your name tag say? What is it, Ocampos?" Tyson asked. "Yes! It's Ocampos!" officer Ocampos said. "Well, officer Ocampos, since you know who my family is, could you kindly get off the phone and tend to a tax payer's needs?" Tyson said. Officer Ocampos looked at Tyson for a second as if he'd committed a felony. "Déjame salir de este teléfono Carmen!" officer Ocampos said. "Ok Barbara Hablaremos más tarde. Adios!" Carmen said before hanging up. "Now Mr. Richards, if you could take a seat, I'll find someone here that can help you." officer Ocampos said. "Thank you!" Tyson shouted before walking away. Tyson found a seat. He sat there watching police officers and administrative types walking back-n-forth.

10 minutes had passed when a Caucasian man in a suit approached Tyson. He looked like he was in his late 50's. "Hello Mr. Richards. I'm lieutenant Brown, Homicide division." He said as he and Tyson shook hands. Tyson stood up. "How's it going lieutenant? I've some important information to give you about the guy who runs a criminal organization!" Tyson said. "Ok. Follow me to my office, please." Brown said.

Moments later, Tyson was sitting at lieutenant Brown's desk. Brown pulled out a pen and pad from his desk. He jotted down all of Tyson's personal information. Tyson pulled out the tape recorder, sliding it across the desk towards Brown. "What's this?" Brown asked. "This is evidence that a relative of mine tried to have me killed!" Tyson said. "Have you killed?" Brown asked. "Yes! Remember that house that exploded back in January? We'll, if you check your records, that was my house!" Tyson said. Brown turned to his desk top computer. He typed in Tyson's information. "Here it is! Wow!" Brown said. "I told you so!" Tyson said. Brown scrolled down as he was skimming through the information. "This is what we'll do Mr. Richards. I'll take the tape recorder, and if I get enough to convict, what's his name?" brown said. "It's Krayton! Krayton Lassenberry! He goes by the Name Edward the 2nd!" Tyson said. "Edward the 2nd?" Brown chuckled. "Sounds ridiculous, don't it?" Tyson said. Brown just shrugged his shoulders. "He's my cousin, but he's gotta be brought to justice!" Tyson said. "Where does this Krayton reside?" Brown asked. "You can't miss it! It's the only castle in Cherry Hill!" Tyson said. "Oh! That Lassenberry! Every precinct from here to Cape May says this guy is untouchable! But now, because of you, and this tape recorder, we can finally bring this guy to his knees!" Brown said. "Glad to hear that, lieutenant!" Tyson said. "Are you staying nearby?" Brown asked. "Actually, I drove all the way from Vineland!" Tyson said. "Can you stay at the hotel nearby until tomorrow? I need to get in touch with the Cherry Hill task force and get a warrant to get this guy!" Brown said. "Sure! No problem! I'll do what I have to do!" Tyson said. "Well, I'll come pick you up in the morning from the hotel to be on the safe side! You're valuable to this case at this point! In fact, I'll follow you to the hotel from here! So, let's go!" Brown said.

About 3 blocks away, Tyson pulled up in front of the Hoboken inn, followed by lieutenant brown. Brown stepped out of his unmarked car. He went over to Tyson's car. "Go check yourself in, and then come out and give me the room number!" Brown said. "Got it!" Tyson said with a grin on his face. Tyson went inside the hotel to check in. Brown pulled out a pack of cigarettes. He took out one and lit it. After a few drags off his cigarette, he threw it on the ground when he saw Tyson come out. "It's room 328." Tyson said. "Great! I'll send someone to check on you until I come pick you up in the morning." Brown said. "Sounds great!" Tyson said. "So, Mr. Richards! Ready to rid the state of New Jersey of this scum bag?" Brown asked. "Damn right!" Tyson said. Brown patted him on the shoulder. "Go get some rest! There's a lot of paper work you need to fill out in the morning!" Brown said as he shook Tyson's hand. "Ok! See you in the morning, sir!" Tyson said. "Good day Mr. Richards!" brown said before walking back to his car.

A couple of hours had passed. Tyson was in his hotel room, sitting at the edge of his bed looking at a menu for some take out. He just ended a conversation with his wife about his situation. Suddenly, there was a knock on the door. Tyson looked at the door. "Who is it?" he shouted. "It's detective Martin of the Hoboken police!" the man shouted through the door. Tyson showed a sigh of relief. He went to the door, opening it. "Mr. Richards! Pleased to meet you!" detective Martin said as he shook Tyson's hand. "Come on in, detective! Come right in!" Tyson said.

Detective Martin looked between 20 to 25 years old. He was a clean cut, physically fit Caucasian guy, looking like he just left the police academy.

"Are we comfortable, Mr. Richards? Have everything you need?" Martin asked. "I was just about to order something to eat! You want me to order you something too?" Tyson asked. "No thanks! Just ate." Martin said. "I've got some bottled water in the Minnie frig!" Tyson said. "Sure! I'll take one, please!" Martin said as he closed the door. Tyson turned towards the Minnie frig. He grabbed a bottle of water. He turned around to face detective Martin. To his surprise, there was a pistol with a silencer attached at the end pointed at his face. Tyson froze. He dropped the bottle of water. "What? What? What's going on?" he shouted in fear. "This is a message from Mark Vasquez. You should've went to the Feds. They're not on Edward the 2nd's payroll, you fucking rat piece of shit." Martin said before squeezing the trigger. Tyson received a bullet to the forehead. He fell to the floor on his back. Martin walked over towards him and put 2 more bullets into his chest. Tyson lay there with his eyes wide open. Martin put the weapon back in its holster. He took out a handkerchief from his suit jacket. He wiped off the door knob, then exited the room. Moments later, Martin exited the hotel. He looked across the street. He saw lieutenant Brown sitting in his car. Martin just nodded at Brown. Brown nodded back, then drove off.

The next day around 10 in the morning, Cindy, Tyson's mother Maggie, Danny Sr., Malcom, Jake sr., Big L, Joe-Joe, and Maggie's sister Lula all gathered at the city morgue in Hoboken. "You sure you can handle this, young lady?" Jake sr. whispered to Cindy. Cindy didn't say a word. She just nodded her head repeatedly as she covered her mouth. "Everyone! Would you follow me, please?" the mortician said. Once everyone arrived at the cold chamber, the mortician unveiled the body of Tyson Richards. The site of her nephew's body made Lula turn away. Cindy almost collapsed until Jake sr. wrapped his arms around her. He took her out of the room. Big L wiped the tears from his eyes. "You know your brother is responsible for this!" Danny sr. said to Big L. Big L turned to his uncle. "All due respect, uncle Danny, if you say one more word about my brother, I'm gonna knock you on your ass!" Big L said. Joe-Joe stood in front of his uncle anticipating his cousin's threats. "Come on! Do something!" Danny sr. shouted at his nephew. Big L came charging at his uncle like a rhino. It took all of Joe-joe's strength to hold his burly cousin back from hurting his uncle. "Stop it! Just stop it!" Maggie shouted. "You heard her, man! Just calm down!" Joe-joe said. "Fuck that! He just accused my brother on some bullshit!" Big L shouted before storming out of the room. "That Krayton is more dangerous than Eddie was Maggie! You know that!" Danny sr. said. "Just shut up, Danny! Please!" Lula shouted. "I'll tell you all something else! I don't think he's running the show like everybody thinks he is!" Danny sr. said.

Moments later, Lieutenant Brown entered the room. He stood before Tyson's body, shaking his head with disgust on his face. "Mrs. Richards. I'm lieutenant Brown. We've spoke over the phone earlier. I've just consoled his wife a moment ago, and my heart goes out to you all! We've done everything in our power to keep something like this from happening!" Brown said to Maggie. "What are you and the rest of law enforcement in Jersey going to do before another family member ends up dead or missing?" Joe-joe asked. "I don't know about you all, but I'm moving my family out to Lassenberia!" Danny sr. said. "Lassenberia?" Brown asked. "It's an island ran by my niece!" Maggie said. Brown stood there pondering as he nodded his head repeatedly. "Would you excuse us, lieutenant? I would like to have a talk with my family, alone." Lula said. "Of course, young lady!" Brown said. He reached into his jacket pocket. "Here's my card. If you have any information that could help us in this investigation, please don't hesitate to call. By the way, I'm a big fan of your movies." Brown said to Lula. Brown put his hand on Maggie's back. "I promise, we'll get those responsible." Brown said. Maggie nodded her head. "You fine people take care of yourselves, and call me if you need anything." Brown said before leaving.

"How do we know if we can trust this guy?" Lula asked. What? He's the police! Why not?" Danny sr. asked. "He didn't know about Lassenberia!" Lula said. "Neither did we, until a short time ago! What's your point!" Danny sr. asked. "I can't put my finger on it, but there's something not right with that guy! Actors know actors, and he's a terrible one!" Lula said. Maggie took a deep breath and exhaled as she stared down at her son's body. "We have to pack our things and get to Lassenberia! All of us!" Maggie said. "The whole family?" Malcom asked. "Everyone!" Maggie shouted. "Even the grandkids, still in school?" Malcom asked. Maggie turned to her son. "Malcolm, Please! Just do what I tell you to do! That goes for everyone! Despite my nephew's claim, I'm still head of this family! Kimberly said she can have a jumbo jet ready for us at Teterboro in a few days! We'll have to leave everything behind, taking only what we can carry!" Maggie said. "What about all our property, our careers, our friends?" Lula asked. "We'll just have to leave all of that behind, and trust that Kimberly knows what's she's doing!" Maggie said. "What about Krayton? What if his Father, Jake Jr. And Big L don't want to leave him behind?" Lula asked. Maggie just smiled at her little sister. "My nephew can keep his castle, his envelopes, and if his father and brothers want what he wants, well, they can stay behind! I'm taking the rest of us to the promise land! If there's such a place!" Maggie said.

Later that evening, Edward the 2nd was standing in the corridor of the south wing. He stood there staring at the cracks that he used to pass notes through to his cousin. "Damn! Why did I let you leave? I can't do this shit by myself!" he whispered to himself. Edward the 2nd paused for a moment. He looked around. The corridor was dead silent. He hopped in the golf cart. Minutes later, he ended up in the crossroads of the east wing. He hopped out of the golf cart. He was slowly in spinning circle. It was dead silent. Not even a peep out of the agent standing guard in the east wing corridor. He hopped in the golf cart again. Minutes later, he made a stop outside the castle walls, a hundred yards from the main gate. He hopped out the golf cart. All he could hear were the sound of crickets. All he could see were 4 agents posted at the main entrance, and 5 agents walking the castle grounds with machine guns. He looked up at the night sky, staring at the stars. He then turned slowly around in a circle. "I'm alone! Oh shit! I'm alone!" he said to himself as he turned. Edward the 2nd started laughing hysterically. "I'm fucking alone! He shouted as tears came down his cheeks. The agents nearby caught wind of his outcry, and came running. "My lord. Is everything all, right?" one agent asked as they surrounded Edward the 2nd. "I'm alone! I'm alone!" Edward the 2nd chuckled. One of the agents tried to grab his arm. "Get away from me! Get fuck away from me! Y'all ain't real! None of y'all real!" he shouted. "My lord. Calm down. You're suffering from anxiety. You need to go back inside, my lord." One agent said. Out of nowhere, colonel Braxton appeared. "Come on, son! It's me! Let's get you back inside!" the colonel said as he grabbed Edward the 2nd's shoulders. "Get these robots the fuck away from me!" Edward the 2nd shouted. "Ok, son! Let's go! Help me get him in the cart!" Braxton said. 2 of the agents pick Edward the 2nd off his feet. Once in the cart, Braxton takes off, driving over the moat, back inside the castle. "Robots or not! You can't show weakness in front of the troops! Not here! Not in Lassenberia!" Braxton said. Edward the 2nd was coming out of his mode of insanity. "Lassenberia. Lassenberia. I gotta get to Lassenberia." Edward the 2nd whispered to himself. "That's it, son! Think about that, and everything will work out the way it's supposed to!" Braxton said.

The next day, in the village of Saltaire, located on Fire island, Terrance Haggerty was having a little get together with a few friends in a town house. The windows were blacked out, about 50 agents surrounded the town house, as well as a blockade of luxury vehicles surrounding the entire property.

Inside, there were a group of men dancing to loud party music. The men were either dressed in Mardi Gras style apparel, or G-strings. Outside, a Boeman SUV had just pulled up to the barricade. 2 Latino men get out of the SUV. One of the men head to the back and pulled out a wheelchair. The other man opened the rear passenger door. ¿Listo, jefe?" the man asked. "Simplemente no bang mi cabeza, ok?" the handicapped man said. The handicapped man was gently pulled out of the vehicle, then placed into the wheelchair. The man was wheeled towards one of the NA agents. "This is a private gathering. State your business." The agent said. "I am general Mark Vasquez Jr. of the Lassenberry organization, here to see Terrance Haggerty!" Mark said. "Wait here, sir." The agent said. The agent gave another agent the signal to fetch Terrance Haggerty.

Moments later, Terrance comes out of the house, wearing a purple bathrobe, a purple G-string, and purple high heel shoes. He had a wide smile on his face, and a Martini in his hand. "Mark Mookie Vasquez! My favorite cripple! How the hell are you?" Terrance shouted. the NA agents had cleared a path for Terrance to walk through. "We need to talk!" Mookie said. "You know damn well to go through the proper chain of command! Edward the 2nd is your boss!" Terrance chuckled. "I'm not so sure of that!" Mookie said. "Oooh! Do I smell dissention in the ranks?" Terrance chuckled. "Listen! It cost me a half million to get information to find your ass! Only a couple of people in Washington DC know of your existence! ¡Dios mío! It's like you're a ghost, or something!" Mookie said. "Yes! Call me the ghost in heels!" Terrance chuckled as he was spinning slowly around. "This is serious, ¡Tú, loco!" Mookie said. Terrance sighed. "Very well! Let's go to the garage, you, crazy cripple!" Terrance chuckled. Mookie gave his assistant the signal to push him in his wheelchair, and to follow Terrance to the garage connected to the town house.

Once in the garage, Terrance pulled out a wicker chair. He sat in it with his legs crossed. "Puede dejarnos ahora." Mookie said to his assistant. The assistant left the 2 men alone. "Now, that you have my undivided attention, make this good." Terrance said. "What the fuck is Lassenberia?" Mookie asked. Terrance shrugged his shoulders. "I have no idea what you're talking about!" Terrance said. "The island of Lassenberia? You mean to tell me you have no clue on what's going on?" Mookie asked. Terrance started to laugh hysterically. "Silly cripple! There's no such place!" he chuckled. "Bullshit! My guy on the inside of the Hoboken police department said that the Lassenberry family is making a move to this place!" Mookie said. Terrance tilted his head to the side. "You're kidding! Right?" Terrance said. "I wish I was!" Mookie said. Terrance went from having a jovial mentality, to looking serious. "Ok, cripple! You can leave now!" Terrance said. "Ain't you gonna do something? I'm tired of being out of this Family's loop! I just recently found out Hakim took over Bex's territory!" Mookie shouted. "¡Rueda tu culo fuera de aquí antes de que te echen!" Terrance shouted. "You don't scare me!" Mookie said. Terrance smiled. He then jumped from his chair, running over to Mookie. He turned Mookie's wheelchair around. "What the hell, man?" Mookie shouted as he held on tight to the arm rests. Without hesitation, Terrance, with all his might, sent Mookie crashing through the door. Mookie's wheelchair tipped over, causing him to go flying to the ground. His assistant pulled out his pistol. 10 NA agents pulled out theirs. "¡Sácame de aquí! ¡Rápido!" Mookie screamed. Mookie's assistant dropped his pistol, and went over to turn the wheelchair upright, then placed Mookie in the chair. The assistant scurried Mookie to the SUV. The driver got out of the SUV, and assisted in holding the door open for Mookie to be placed in carefully. The driver and the assistant jumped back into the SUV, and sped off.

"Get doctor Zachmont on the commlink! Tell him I'm going to pay him a visit first thing in the morning!" Terrance said to one of the agents. "Right away, sir." The agent said. "But, for the time being! I'm going to indulge some man ass!" Terrance said as he marched back to the town house.

A couple of days later at Teterboro airport, the entire Lassenberry family, Minus Edward the 2nd, were getting ready to board a jumbo jet provided by Kimberly, who wired funds to the airport's accounting office. At the same time, on the other side of the world, a ferry boat was pulling up to the pier in Lassenberia. The ferry boat captain blew the ship's whistle. Out of nowhere, Kimberly, Ali, and Brandon came running to the pier. "Why in the hell are we coming out here to meet that ferry?" Brandon asked. "The future of this place is being dragged by that ferry, that's why!" Kimberly said as the ferry came closer to the pier.

At the stern of the ferry was a mooring line tied to a bit. At the other end of that line was something being dragged, but submerged. Once the ferry came close enough to the pier, the captain hit the throttle, making a U-turn away from the pier. The first mate scurried to the stern with a machete in his hand. "Quick, Ali! Grab one of those hooks!" Kimberly shouted. "What are you doing?" Brandon shouted. "Grab one of those hooks, and help!" Kimberly shouted as she grabbed another 8-foot-long metal hooks. Before the first mate could cut the mooring line, Kimberly and Ali twirled their hooks around the part of the mooring line that was close to the water. "We need your help, Brandon!" Kimberly shouted. "What you want me to do?" Brandon asked. "When we pull the line, try and hook what's under the water!" She shouted. Brandon stuck his hook into the water, fishing around until he hooked on to something. Something quite heavy. "I don't know what I have, but i got it!" he shouted. "Ali! Help him pull it in!" Kimberly shouted as she leaned over the edge of the pier to get a closer look of the object as it emerged. At that moment, the first mate severed the mooring line from his end. The ferry took off, back into deep waters. "Assholes!" Kimberly said to herself. "Jesus! Whatever this is, it's heavy as shit!" Brandon shouted. "Just shut up and help Ali pull!" Kimberly shouted. "I know it's not lady like, but could you give us a hand?" Brandon shouted as he pulled in the object with all his might. Within moments, Gabe came out of nowhere, giving Brandon and Ali a hand. "Let's heave-ho, guys!" Gave shouted. "That's it! That's it! I see it! I see it!" Kimberly shouted. "What is it?" Brandon asked. What Kimberly saw was a 55-gallon plastic blue drum surfacing. It took the 3 men all their strength to pull it out of the water, and on to the pier. "Hurry! Stand it upright!" Kimberly shouted. What's in it?" Brandon kept asking. "Gabe! Go over there, and grab a couple of crowbars!" Kimberly shouted. "Got it!" he said. Gabe grabbed the crowbars, and tossed one to Kimberly. "Let's get this lid off!" she said. From opposite ends, they quickly put wedges between the seal and lid as they went around the drum until they completely broke the seal off the lid. Kimberly tossed the lid to the side. Brandon looked inside of the drum. "Holy shit!" he shouted. Kimberly looked inside. She had a big smile on her face. "Hurry! Pull him out!" she shouted. "How in the hell?" Brandon shouted.

Inside the drum was the future of Lassenberia. Inside the drum, was the presumed unconscious body of Sir Marcus, about 10 oxygen canisters, and 2 center blocks. Gabe reached in the drum, and put his finger tips to Sir Marcus's neck. "It's faint, but I got a pulse!" he said. The guys had no problem pulling Sir Marcus out of the drum. He'd lost a considerable amount of weight so he could fit inside the drum comfortably. It was more weight loss compared to the time he was inside the walls of castle Lassenberry. Gabe and Ali frowned from the smell of feces and urine coming from inside the drum. They carried him off the pier, into the jeep nearby. "My love!" Kimberly cried in a meek tone. They carefully placed him in the back of the jeep. Gabe jumped into the driver's seat. Kimberly jumped into the passenger's seat, as Ali sat in the back with Sir Marcus.

"Good thing you hired that medical team from Mozambique, otherwise there's no chance for him." Gabe said. Kimberly just nodded her head. Back at the pier, Brandon looked out on to the ocean, with his hands on his hips. "I can't wait to see how all of this is going to play out!" he said to himself.

Back at Teterboro Airport, all the remaining Lassenberry family members were on board, ready to head to Lassenberia. Maggie stood in the middle of the isle. "I know this is a big change for us, but I believe we were destined to make this exodus, if you will, to a new land where we can flourish as a family again!" Maggie said. "Trust me when I tell you all! This move will change our lives for the better! Just look at, me!" Mark senior said with a grin on his face. His wife Tanya wrapped her arms around him. "Hell Yeah! Long live the house of Lassenberry!" Big L. shouted. "Long live the house of Lassenberry!" all the family members shouted simultaneously. Danny sr. didn't cheer. He just stared out the window with a worried look on his face. "What's wrong pop?" Donald asked. "This just don't feel right!" he said. Corey was sitting in the seat in front of his cousin and uncle, when he overheard his uncle's words of dread. He turned around to face them. "Come on uncle! If that green stuff fixed my pop's illness, imagine how we can heal the world! This is a new beginning! With all due respect, chill, unk!" Corey said. Maggie trotted to the cockpit. She tapped on the door. The door opened. It was the co-pilot who stuck his head out. "Get this baby rolling, and take us to the promise land!" Maggie shouted with joy. "Just a few more minutes, ma'am! The mechanic is still out there making a few final checks before we take off." The co-pilot said. "Great!" Maggie said.

"What are we going to do about the bodies of the family members that passed away?" Sarah, Benny Jr's daughter asked. "Don't worry young lady. We've already taken care of that. Your grandmother's body, along with everyone else's will be shipped to Lassenberia within a week." Jake sr. said. Moments later, the mechanic walked in plain sight of the pilots, giving them a thumb up. "Say bill! You ever see that tech guy before?" the pilot asked his co-pilot. "No. can't say that I have!" bill said. "Must be new. Well, anyway, let's get the ok from control tower, and prepare for takeoff."" The pilot said.

Once the pilot was cleared for takeoff, the aircraft started its trek down the runway. "All right ladies and gentlemen. You've been given your safety instructions, and shown all the exits in case of an emergency landing. The weather forecast calls for clear skies. Our arrival to south Africa in 12 hours." The pilot said over the PA system.

The next day at castle Lassenberry around 2 in the afternoon, Edward the 2nd had just awakened from a night of binge drinking. He was stark naked, but wearing one sock. He rolled over, falling face down on to the floor. Moments later, his bedroom door was kicked in. "What the fuck?" he shouted with slurred words. 2 agents picked him off the floor. Edward the 2nd was being dragged out of his bedroom, down the corridor, down the spiral, stone staircase. "I order you to put me the fuck down!" Edward the 2nd screamed. The 2 agents bring Edward the 2nd to the doors of his office where 2 more agents were standing. They use his head as a battering ram to open the doors to his office. Once the doors were open, Edward the 2nd was tossed on the office floor. He struggled to his knees. As he looked up, he saw Doug Reed, and Terrance Haggerty standing over him. "What's… going…on, man?" Edward the 2nd cried. "Lassenberia! Lassenberia! When were, you going to fucking tell me about, Lassenberia?" Terrance shouted as he put his foot on Edward the 2nd's hand. Edward the 2nd expressed excruciating pain on his face from the pressure of Terrance's foot on his hand. "I didn't think it was important!" Edward the 2nd cried. "You didn't think it wasn't important? You fucking black son-of-a-bitch! I own you, prick! Every fiber of your body, belongs to me!" Terrance shouted. "What should we do with this, this…Ahh! I wanna kill him right here, right now!" Doug shouted. "Pick 'em up!" Terrance said. 2 of the agents stood Edward the 2nd on his feet. Terrance started to gently stroke the side of Edward the 2nd's face. "Listen. We're not going to kill you, really! We need a guy like you on the frontline! There are still people in power that believe in humanity, the human spirit, and all that other bullshit! You're the distraction! Remember that!" Terrance said. "Show him, Mr. Haggerty! Show him how the real world works, please!" Doug said. "Turn on the TV, Mr. Reed!" Terrance chuckled as he pointed to the remote. Doug grabbed the remote, and clicked on the TV. Doug turned to the news. "Take a close look, Lord Lassenberry! Look at what happens when you keep secrets!" Terrance chuckled. Edward the 2nd slowly turned to face what was on the TV. "Turn up the volume, Mr. Reed! Turn it all the way up!" Terrance chuckled.

"Continuing our breaking news, search-n-rescue teams are still trying to salvage what's left of the plane crash that carried members of the alleged notorious Lassenberry family, off the Dominican Republican shores. At this point in time, there seems to be no sign of survivors." The reporter said. Doug turned off the TV. Edward the 2nd dropped to his knees. Terrance laughed as he witnessed excrement discharge from Edward the 2nd's body. "Please, tell me I'm dreaming!" Edward the 2nd cried. "Please, tell me I'm dreaming!" Terrance said in a high pitch, taunting voice. "I'm gonna kill you, white boy!" Edward the 2nd screamed. Terrance and Doug started laughing. "Please, Lord Lassenberry! if you wanted to, you would've done it a long time ago! Besides, they didn't respect your authority anyway! Did they?" Terrance chuckled. Edward the 2nd's head dropped. "Did they?" Terrance asked once more. Edward the 2nd then realized that Terrance was telling the truth. Edward the 2nd nodded as he wiped the tears from his eyes. "Very well! Now, that you're acting like a man, just say the word, and I'll make a phone call to some people I know, and get rid of all the press and camera men standing outside the gate." Terrance chuckled. Edward the 2nd stood tall. "Get me a robe out of the bathroom!" he ordered one of the agents. The agent looked over at Terrance for confirmation. "You heard the man! Get the fucking robe!" Terrance shouted. "Yes, Mr.

Haggerty." The agent said. The agent ran to the office bathroom, and retrieved the robe. Edward the 2nd donned the robe. "Now, get that fucking media away from my home!" Edward the 2nd said in a deep, teeth grinding tone. Terrance clapped his hands together. "Good!" Terrance chuckled as he rubbed Edward the 2nd's shoulders. "With all due respect, Mr. Haggerty, I can take it from here." Doug said. "With that said, I'll be on my way!" Terrance chuckled. "Me and Lord Lassenberry have a lot to discuss." Doug said. "Great! But before I go!" Terrance said. He snapped his fingers in the air. "Now you have control over your agents again." Terrance chuckled. "Don't forget about those media mother fuckers!" Edward the 2nd shouted as Terrance left the office.

"You can leave me and Mr. Reed alone, now!" Edward the 2nd said to the 4 agents. "Yes, Lord Lassenberry." the agents said simultaneously. The agents leave the office. "Good! Now that we're alone, let's talk about that girlfriend of yours, what's her name?" Doug said. "Viola. Her name is Viola Carr." Edward the 2nd said. "Viola! Pretty name. I hope she's as pretty as her name!" Doug said. "Man, she's fine as hell!" Edward the 2nd said with a big smile on his face. "Good! At least your kids will have a chance in the looks department!" Doug chuckled. Edward the 2nd looked pissed, but didn't react. "Come on! I'm just busting your chops!" Doug chuckled. Edward the 2nd snapped out of his anger. "It's funny you mentioned kids. She's pregnant." Edward the 2nd confessed. At that moment, Doug's eyes lit up. He started salivating. "How far along is she?" Doug asked. Edward the 2nd looked confused. "The nurse said she's in her first trimester! Why?" Edward the 2nd asked. "Oh, never mind! It's too early." Doug said in a creepy tone. "Too early, for what?" Edward the 2nd asked. "I gotta go. Just keep her healthy. That's your future she's carrying in her belly." Doug said before leaving the office. Edward the 2nd became worried. He ran out into the corridor. "Too…early…for…what?" Edward the 2nd screamed at the top of his lungs as Doug was being driven off in a golf cart.

CHAPTER 30. THE B.O.I

A day later, back at Lassenberia, around 1pm, UTC+03:00 time construction crews continue to build Kim Town. About 5 miles north of Kim Town, Kimberly led a small ceremony in honor of a new territory being established.

Kimberly changed from wearing a sun dress to wearing army fatigues, combat boots, and a camouflage doo rag, holding her dreadlocks in place. In her hands was a long flag pole. At the top of the pole was a flag with the symbol representing the new town.

Surrounding Kimberly were the citizens of Lassenberia. Ali and his 12 teenage nephews also wore army fatigues, with each of them armed with sub-machine guns. They stood at the outer layer of the crowd. The crowd consisted Brandon, the rest of Ali's family, the 3 African prime ministers and all their assistance in their entourages, and the wives and children of the Braxton brothers, the Secretary, and Deputy Secretary of the United Nations, with their entourage, and Kimberly's sister Jenna and her family. Jenna held Kimberly's son in her arms as the ceremony proceeded. Terry stayed back at the new medical facility with her brother Sir Marcus, who was in a coma due to poor health brought on by his unorthodox journey to Lassenberia.

"On this day! May 28th, 2002, in the name of our leader, Lord Lassenberry! I hereby name this territory the borough of Braxton!" Kimberly shouted as she drove the sharp end of the pole into the sand. Everyone applauded. Tim, the eldest brother stepped up to represent the Braxton family. Tim looked up at the flag waving in the breeze with tears in his eyes. The flag was white with the Christian crucifix, and a shotgun overlapping it. It later became the Braxton coat-of-arms. A couple of kids from Ali's family helped pack in the sand around the base of the flag pole so it could stand upright. Standing behind Kimberly was Ali's niece Fatima, holding a ceremonial Somali short sword on a red velvet pillow. "Now, to make this official, at least official enough until the true Lord of Lassenberia rise from his coma!" Kimberly shouted. The crowd went silent. "Tim Braxton! Kneel!" Kimberly ordered. Tim looked around the crowd with a smirk on his face, until he realized she was serious. He kneeled in front of Kimberly, which was a struggle due to his weight. Kimberly took the sword from off the velvet pillow. "In the name of the Lord of Lassenberry, I hereby name you, Timothy Braxton the first Duke of Braxton!" she shouted as she tapped his shoulder with the tip of the sword. "You may stand!"

Kimberly shouted as she placed the sword back on the pillow. It took Tim's brother Simon to help him off the ground. "Congratulations, big guy!" Kimberly said as she gave Tim a hug. Tim gave Kimberly a kiss on the cheek. "Thank you, little lady!" He said.

Back at the medical facility where Sir Marcus laid in a coma, Doctor Nyusi Magumbwe from Mozambique was monitoring Sir Marcus's vital signs as he lay in a bed on life support. Terry sat at his bedside massaging his hand. "Wake up big brother, please! Mom and dad are on their way! You need to be awake to see them!" Terry whispered in her brother's ear.

Back at the Braxton ceremony, everyone was in a festive mood, eating a cultural mixture of culinary dishes. The music was also mixture of cultures. It was Kimberly who made the choice to have this mixture. She made it mandatory to lay down this custom in Lassenberia's infancy.

Kimberly was in a conversation with Ali when Tim approached them with a plate of food in his hand. "I have to tell you, this cambuulo is delicious!" Tim said. "Have you tried the Muufo?" Ali asked. "Muufo?" Tim asked. "Yes! It's like what you call cornbread back in the United states." Ali said. Kimberly spotted secretary general Ban Chin standing in the crowd speaking with deputy secretary Soumah. "Could you guys excuse me for a moment? I want to speak with the U.N. secretary." Kimberly said. "Yes, Miss Kimberly!" Ali said. Tim respectfully bowed his head. Kimberly made her way through a crowd of people. "Mr. Secretary! Mr. Secretary!" Kimberly shouted. secretary Chin turned to see who was calling him. "Ah! Mrs. Lassenberry!" He shouted. Kimberly stood before the 2 U.N. officials. "I have to say, that was a very impressive ceremony you've orchestrated." Chin said. "Thank you!" Kimberly said. "I was just telling Mr. Chin that this island has the potential to become a superpower one day!" deputy secretary Soumah said. "Well, we're just looking to help move the medical and pharmaceutical business around the world in the right direction." Kimberly said. "I don't mean to alarm you, Mrs. Lassenberry, but with what you and your family possess, you will have no other choice to be, especially against rouge nations!" Soumah said. "Are you saying, Mr. secretary, that we need to raise an army?" Kimberly asked. "What I'm saying is, what you have, is more precious than gold, oil, and diamonds combined." Soumah said. "On that note. When are you people going to go before the U.N. council and make the announcement of Lassenberia becoming a sovereign nation?" Kimberly asked. Secretary Chin cleared his voice. "First, you must draw up a constitution of laws and bring them before the council to see if it meets humanitarian standards." Mr. Chin explained. Kimberly pondered his words for a moment. "We can do that!" she said in a chipper voice.

Back in the United States, Hakim was being driven by his bodyguard Bilal back to his penthouse in Manhattan. "That's fucked up!" Bilal said. "What's fucked up?" Hakim asked. "The whole family, is just gone, man!" Bilal said. "Nigga! It was just a matter of time! I can't put my finger on it, but I guarantee you it was that faggot ass white boy Terrance behind it!" Hakim said. "Who the hell is Terrance?" Bilal asked. "Never mind! Goddamn! I might as well be talking to this cup holder!" Hakim said in frustration.

Suddenly, hakim felt his cell phone vibrating in his pants pocket. He pulled it out. He looked at the screen to verify who it was. He recognized the coded name. "What's up, boss man? My heart goes out to you, man! That shit was fucked up!" Hakim said. "Don't fuck with me, man!" Edward the 2nd said. "Come on, man! I mean that shit!" Hakim said. "Listen! I need you to come out to Hillside!" Edward the 2ⁿᵈ said. "What's in Hillside?" Hakim asked. "Me, nigga!" Edward the 2ⁿᵈ shouted. "Take it easy, boss man." Hakim said. "Just bring yo ass to 516 Princeton ave." Edward the 2ⁿᵈ said. "That's Mookie's territory! If somethings about go down, call him!" Hakim shouted. "Yo, Hak! I'm not asking you! I'm telling you!" Edward the 2ⁿᵈ said before hanging up. "Fuck! Turn this shit around!" Hakim shouted. "We're going to Hillside?" Bilal asked. "Yeah, nigga! 516 Princeton avenue!" hakim said. Bilal maneuvered his way through traffic to jump back on the George Washington bridge.

About a half hour later, Bilal pulled up to 516 Princeton avenue. He and hakim noticed the 2 NA agents standing outside the limo. "I guess he's here." Bilal said. "You strapped?" Hakim asked. "Got it right here!" Bilal said as he showed his pistol to Hakim. "Now, you might be able to use it!" Hakim said. "That's what I'm talking about!" Bilal shouted. "Stay here, and keep the engine running." Hakim said in a relaxed voice. Hakim stepped out of the vehicle, fastening the button on his silk gray suit jacket. He walked passed the agents with a cool strut. The agents watched as he walked up the stairs and rang the doorbell. Hakim pressed the doorbell once more. The door opened. It was Viola's son Hakeem. "Goddamn, kid! What happened to your face?" Hakim asked. Edward the 2ⁿᵈ had kept his promise to Viola's son Hakeem. The young man came to the door, with a puffy black eye, a swollen upper lip, and a cast on his right arm. "I guess you're here to see that clown looking bitch ass nigga!" Hakeem said. "Hold on, kid! He is a funny looking nigga, but show some respect, ok?" Hakim said. Hakeem didn't say a word. He just opened the door to allow Hakim come in. "Ma! Ma! What's your name, man?" Hakeem asked. "It's general Bates." Hakim said. "Ma! It's a general Bates down here!" Hakeem shouted. Hakeem could hear mumbling coming from upstairs. "Tell him to come up!" Viola shouted. "You heard her." Hakeem said. Hakim took a quick glance around the living room before heading up stairs. "Yo! Where you at, man?" Hakim shouted as he came to the top of the stairs. "In here!" Edward the 2ⁿᵈ shouted. "Where the fuck is here?" Hakim shouted. "Second door on your left!" Viola shouted. Hakim followed Viola's directions. He tapped on the door before entering. "Come in!" Viola said. Hakim opened the door. "Come on in, negro!" Edward the 2ⁿᵈ said. Hakim scoffed when he saw Edward the 2ⁿᵈ in bed, wearing nothing but his boxers. Viola was sitting on the edge of the bed with his bare feet on her lap, massaging his toes. Hakim's nostrils flared up. "Smell like corn chips in here, man!" hakim said. Viola giggled a little. "What you are laughing at, huh?" Edward the 2ⁿᵈ said to her as he lightly kicked her on the side of her head. "Why you call me, man?" Hakim asked. Edward the 2ⁿᵈ grabbed a piece of paper off the end table. "Here. Take this." Edward the 2ⁿᵈ said. Hakim walked over to retrieve the paper. As he was approaching Edward the 2ⁿᵈ, he noticed Viola giving him a seductive look. Hakim gave her a quick wink, which put a smile on her face. Edward the 2ⁿᵈ kicked her on the side of her head again. "Why the fuck you looking at him, bitch?" he shouted. Hakim took the paper, shaking his head. "Read it quick, and give it back!" Edward the 2ⁿᵈ said. Hakim skimmed over what was written on the paper. He crumbled the paper and threw it back at Edward the 2ⁿᵈ. "Don't mess this up Hakim!" Edward the 2ⁿᵈ said. "I got it, man!" Hakim said. Hakim was about to leave the bedroom. "You forgot something!" Edward the 2ⁿᵈ said. "What?' hakim asked. Before leaving my presence, nigga, what you supposed to do?" Edward the 2ⁿᵈ shouted. "In front of her?" hakim asked. "Yes, nigga! In front of her!" he shouted as he sat up from the bed. hakim sighed. He stood at attention. "Long live the house of Lassenberry! long live Edward the 2nd!" Hakim shouted. "Now, you can go!" Edward the 2nd said with a smirk on his face. Hakim stormed out of the bedroom. Edward the 2nd smacked Viola up side her head. She turned towards him with fury in her eyes. "If I ever catch you smiling at another mother fucker again, that big mouth son of yours gonna find himself getting another beat down! Now finish rubbing my feet!" he said to viola as he rested his head on the pillow.

About an hour later, Hakim came upon the place where he was instructed in the note to show up. It was in Lodi, New Jersey, behind the facility owned by the Lassenberry family. In the back was a dumpster. Hakim cautiously walked back behind the dumpster. The site of a raccoon startled him, causing him to pull out his pistol. He shot at the nocturnal creature, missing it, causing it to run off. "They ain't supposed to be out this time of day!" he said to himself. He looked down on the ground and saw a shopping bag. He Looked inside the contents. It was something sealed in a priority mail package. Hakim read the mailing address. "Kimberly Lassenberry P.O. box 567, 25 de Setembro Avenue, Maputo, Mozambique?" Hakim said to himself. "No fucking way! It can't be her! Don't tell me she married this mother fucker!" he said to himself. Hakim ripped open the package. The contents were unveiled. "What the fuck? He said to himself. What Hakim had in his hand was decades of information about the Lassenberry Organization. What he had in his hand was, the B.O.I "Oh shit!" Hakim said as he flipped through the pages. Coincidently, he came upon a page pertaining his life just before being incarcerated for 15 years. It explained how Jabbo arranged a meeting for Eddie Lassenberry to make a deal with a judge and the warden at F.C.I, in Fairton, New Jersey.

"He knew you was going to look through it! He knew it!" a voice said. Hakim quickly turned around to find his right-hand man pointing a pistol at him. "Chewie? What the fuck you are doing?" Hakim asked. "You shouldn't have opened it, man! He told me if you opened it, Essex County was mine!" Chewie said as his voice started to crack. "Listen to me Chewie! That nigga doesn't care about neither one of us! You see how he reacted to his whole family getting killed!" Hakim said. Chewie wiped away his tears. "He said you had the code to the Colombian connection! Give it to me, and I'll let you walk!" Chewie said. Hakim rolled his eyes. "Bullshit! I'm a dead man either way! If he wanted you to be incharge, don't you think he would've given you the code himself? Man, you might as well shoot me, and turn the gun on yourself!" Hakim said. Chewie's hand started to tremble. "I'm telling you, Hak! Give me the code, and hand over the book! I promise to make it quick!" Chewie said. Hakim held the book under his arm tight. He held his other hand up in a surrendering gesture. "Man, you helped raise me! Now, you wanna kill me! For what? a punk ass ugly mother fucker, living in a castle, In the middle of New Jersey? How sick is that shit? We're street niggas! The Lassenberry people want to live some fantasy like them mother fuckers in Europe, or some shit! Man, if we put our heads together, we can take this shit from them!" Hakim explained. Chewie thought about it for a moment. He slowly lowered his weapon. "See! Now you're thinking! Now, think about it in the afterlife, you weak motherfucker!" hakim said as he drew his weapon, and pulled the trigger. Chewie's body fell to the ground, face down. Hakim quickly put the B.O.I back into the shopping bag, putting it under his arm as he made his way back to his vehicle. Bilal was sitting in the driver's seat. "I heard gun shots, boss! What happened?" Bilal asked. Hakim looked down both ends of the road for witnesses. "This is when you should've had your gun out! You're as dumb as your uncle!" Hakim said as he pulled out his weapon, pointing it at Bilal's face. He then pulled the trigger. Bilal's head ended leaning out the window. His brain matter splattered on the ground and the car door. Hakim tossed the shopping bag in the passenger's seat. He ran around the other side of the car, pulling Bilal's body out of the car. He then jumped in the driver's seat. The back tires were spinning and screeching as he floored the gas pedal. He unintentionally ran over Bilal's head, busting it like a cantaloupe before taking off down the road. Hakim used his arm to wipe the blood off the door as he was driving. He pulled out his cell phone. He hit the speed dial. He heard the phone ring. After the 4 rings, someone picked up. "Hello?" the voice said. "Yo Butch! It's me!" Hakim shouted. "What you want, nigga?" Butch asked. "I know you ain't gonna believe this shit, but Edward the 2nd just put a contract on all of us, man!" Hakim said. "What? Get the fuck outta here!" Butch shouted. "I'm telling you, man! He put a contract on all of us! Me, you, Mookie, and Dubbs! I got the info in this book that goes all the way back decades, about the Lassenberry Family! He wants to kill all of us, and replace us with them robots, I mean those agents in black suits!" Hakim said. Butch sighed. "Look, man! You gotta show me this book before I can believe this shit!" Butch said. "Where are you? I'll be there with a quickness!" Hakim said. "All right. You better not be lying, kid! You're talking about war!" Butch said. "It is what it is, old man! I got the proof right here, next to me!" Hakim said. "I own a Boeman dealership out in Chatham Township, not too far from the train station. Meet me out there in a couple of hours." Butch said. "Copy that!" Hakim said before hanging up. "Damn! I gotta get me an ink pen!" Hakim said to himself.

Back in Lassenberia, the ceremony for the Braxton regime was winding down. It was a clear night sky. Kimberly stood at a distance from the crowd, brooding over her next move. "Ali!" she shouted. Ali came running over to his mistress. "Yes! What is it, Ms. Kimberly?" he asked. I need you to follow me!" She ordered. Ali followed her to a jeep. They both hop in and drive off, heading south. "Where are we going Ms. Kimberly?" Ali asked. Kimberly didn't say a word. She pressed on the gas pedal even harder. Ali hung on for dear life as the ride became bumpier.

Finally, they pull up in front of Kimberly's office. Standing guard at the door was one of Ali's nephews, armed with a sub-machine gun. Kimberly and Ali hopped out of the jeep. She rushed into her office, gently pushing Ali's nephew to the side. "Maxaa ka khaldan, adeer? Ma I samayn wax qalad ah?" his nephew asked. Kimberly took a few steps backwards. "It's ok Kwame. You did nothing wrong. Somali is a hard language to learn, but I'm getting the hang of it." Kimberly said with a smile before reentering her office. Kimberly made her way to her personal safe. She punched in the code to open the safe. She pulled out one of the 2 remaining beakers of GLC. "What are you doing, Ms. Kimberly?" Ali asked. Kimberly held the beaker up to the light. "It's time to cut the bullshit. This island needs a leader. This up-n- coming nation, needs a king. Let's go!" Kimberly said before closing the safe back.

THE END?